'A great read, moves along at a fair old pace and is often very funny . . . A highly entertaining and accurate description of the lows – and highs – of loving a child with Asperger syndrome' *National Autism Society Magazine*

Acclaim for *Nip 'n' Tuck*:

'Classic Lette – comic farce laced with wry observation and enough puns to fill a 36D implant' *Eve*

Acclaim for *Altar Ego*:

'Lette is the queen of the wisecrack, the Mae West de nos jours . . . Hugely funny' *Women's Journal*

Acclaim for *Mad Cows*:

'*Mad Cows* should be renamed Wet Your Knickers With Laughter . . . read it, love it and be prepared to change your undies!' *Company*

Acclaim for *Foetal Attraction*:

'I adored Kathy Lette's novel. It is utterly outrageous, irreverent and screamingly funny' Jilly Cooper

Acclaim for *Puberty Blues*:

'I don't recall reading *Puberty Blues* as much as devouring it. I was fascinated. The honesty of the story made it hysterical and terrifying at the same time' Kylie Minogue

'*Puberty Blues* is a profoundly moral story' Germaine Greer

By Kathy Lette

Love is Blind
The Boy Who Fell to Earth
Men: A User's Guide
To Love, Honour and Betray (Till Divorce Us Do Part)
How to Kill Your Husband (and Other Handy
Household Hints)
Dead Sexy
Nip 'n' Tuck
Hit and Ms
Puberty Blues (co-author)
Altar Ego
Foetal Attraction
Girls' Night Out
Mad Cows
The Llama Parlour

The Boy Who Fell to Earth

Kathy Lette

BLACK SWAN

TRANSWORLD PUBLISHERS
61–63 Uxbridge Road, London W5 5SA
A Random House Group Company
www.transworldbooks.co.uk

**THE BOY WHO FELL TO EARTH
A BLACK SWAN BOOK: 9780552776820**

First published in Great Britain
in 2012 by Bantam Press
an imprint of Transworld Publishers
Black Swan edition published 2013

Addresses for Random House Group Ltd companies outside
the UK can be found at: www.randomhouse.co.uk
The Random House Group Ltd Reg. No. 954009

The Random House Group Limited supports The Forest Stewardship
Council® (FSC®), the leading international forest-certification
organisation. Our books carrying the FSC label are printed on
FSC®-certified paper. FSC is the only forest-certification scheme
supported by the leading environmental organisations, including
Greenpeace. Our paper procurement policy can be found at
www.randomhouse.co.uk/environment

Typeset in 11/14pt Palatino by Falcon Oast Graphic Art Ltd.
Printed and bound by CPI Group (UK) Ltd, Croydon, CR0 4YY.

2 4 6 8 10 9 7 5 3 1

For my darling children

Contents

Prologue   11

Part One: Merlin

Chapter 1.   I've Just Given Birth to a Baby but
I Don't Think It's Mine   17

Chapter 2.   Planet Merlin   28

Chapter 3.   UFO – Unidentified Fleeing Object   49

Chapter 4.   Asparagus Syndrome   57

Chapter 5.   My Family and Other Aliens   77

Chapter 6.   The Coven   91

Chapter 7.   Relationship Roulette   109

Part Two: Archie

Chapter 8.   There Came a Tall, Dark
Stranger . . .   157

Chapter 9.   You Say Tomato   169

Chapter 10.   A Walk in the Park   180

Chapter 11.   Train of Thought   198

Chapter 12.   Nothing Risquéd, Nothing
Gained   211

Chapter 13.   Dr Love is in the Building   234

Part Three: Jeremy

Chapter 14.   The Born-again Human Being   243
Chapter 15.   Daddy Dearest   254
Chapter 16.   Paying Lip Service to Love   263
Chapter 17.   The Ham in the Man Sandwich   278
Chapter 18.   A Rip in the Designer Genes   293
Chapter 19.   Dr Love Has Left the Building   301

Part Four: Merlin and Me

Chapter 20.   Sexual Politics   323
Chapter 21.   BitchesRUs   330
Chapter 22.   Smuggery, Buggery and
              Skulduggery   337
Chapter 23.   Life, Liberty and the Pursuit of
              Happy Hour   343
Chapter 24.   Testicle Carpaccio on the Disorient
              Express   358
Chapter 25.   The Idiot and the Savant   374
Chapter 26.   Merlin and Me   381

Acknowledgements   397

Prologue

The car hits my sixteen-year-old son at 35 miles per hour. His body jack-knifes skywards then falls with a sickening thud on to its bonnet before bouncing down to the bitumen. The last words I've said to him just two minutes earlier are 'You've ruined my life. I wish I'd never had you. Why can't you be normal?!'

I'd tried to claw back these words as we faced each other in the kitchen but they rained down upon my child like blows. He'd stood, silent as a monument for a moment – then he was gone in a wild blur of limbs.

As I heard the door slam, I sat there aghast, helpless, horrified. I then gave chase, calling his name. I could see the pale denim of his legs scissoring towards the busy road. I heard the low rumble of a car cresting the hill. I spasmed with fear and then the world crumpled.

The windscreen winced at the impact, then shattered. The smashing glass tinkles like waves on shingle. The wheels throw up dirt and noisy gravel as the driver brakes in a belch of petrol. The earth moves slowly up towards my son's golden head. He collapses, like a crushed cigarette packet. I freeze in the tourniqueted silence. The pedestrians are so still they're like a concert audience hushed in anticipation ... Then terror detonates inside me. Each ragged breath feels as though I'm inhaling fire. I hear a primal, bloodcurdling scream and realize it's my own.

I fall to my knees beside him. A thickening, lacquered pool of blood is forming on the road. And then the air is cleaved by my wailing. The world darkens and everything goes black.

I'm in the ambulance now. How much time has elapsed? I replay the impact, over and over. The smell of burning rubber. The full-throated roar of the crash. The terror exploding on to the screen of my eyelids. I feel again the shriek in my blood. The earth and sky merging, imploding, then finally coalescing into fact: my son has been hit by a car. My eyes start to burn and my body trembles. Grief shakes me between its jaws like a lion shakes a half-dead gazelle.

Intensive care. The doctor's voice seems to shout, as if from far away: 'Your son's in a coma.'

And then I'm vomiting in the toilet, dousing my face with water over the sink and shaking myself dry like a wet animal.

So the vigil begins. I watch over my darling. His skin is the colour of a cold roast. I strain my eyes until they sting but see no movement. I stroke a bruise which is erupting with the speed of a Polaroid on his soft cheek. Where is Superman when I need him, to reverse the earth's rotation so that I can go back in time and not utter those hateful words to my dear, dear boy? Where is Stephen Hawking's wormhole in space, his gateways linking different parts of the universe so I can quantum-leap backwards and bite my tongue? I whisper into Merlin's ear about how much I love him. Knowing how uncomfortable he is with emotion, I jokingly promise to eat my own foot so I won't put it in my mouth ever again. All the time my tears splosh on to the sheet, and a great stalactite of snot hangs from my nose.

'Is there anyone you want to call?' a nurse asks, under the glare of naked electricity. 'His father?' she suggests, tentatively.

'His father?' After Merlin's diagnosis, Jeremy retreated into work. I used to joke that it was a wonder British Airways hadn't embroidered his monogram on a business-class seat as he was in the sky more than he was on the ground. The smell of antiseptic cuts pungently through the air. Outside, the night is seeping away, dwindling into dawn. Below the hospital window, I see the cars parked diagonally, like sardines nosing up to a tin can – cars belonging to workers who will soon be going home to happy lives and unhurt children.

The nurse places her hand on my arm and guides

me down into a chair. She sits beside me. Still holding my arm and stroking my skin, she repeats in a gentle voice, 'Is there anyone you'd like me to call, pet?'

'This is all my fault.' Raw with weeping, racked with guilt, my voice is seesawing with emotion.

'I'm sure that's not true. Why don't you tell me all about it, love. But first, there must be somebody you'd like me to call?'

'No. There's only ever been Merlin and me.'

She takes my hand. 'Tell me,' she says.

Part One: Merlin

1

I've Just Given Birth to a Baby but I Don't Think It's Mine

Like many English teachers, I dreamt of being an author. All through my pregnancy I made cracks to Jeremy, my husband, about naming my firstborn 'Pulitzer' – 'just so I can say I have one'. But I was sure about one thing. I wanted our son to have a name which would make him stand out in a crowd, something out of the ordinary to mark him as different . . . Well, not in my wildest imaginings could I have known how different my son would turn out to be.

My wunderkind started speaking early, then, at eight months, just stopped. No more cat, sat, hat, duck, truck . . . Just a perplexing, deafening silence. By the time he was one year old, his behaviour was repetitive, his moods fractious, his sleep erratic, his only comfort being plugged into my raw breast. I was worried I'd be breastfeeding him until he went to university.

Until I began to wonder if he ever would . . .

As Merlin was my first child, I wasn't sure if his behaviour was abnormal and made tentative enquiries to relatives. Since my father's fatal aneurism while in bed with a Polish masseuse (and part-time druid priestess), my mother had been mending her broken heart by spending his life insurance on a never-ending globetrot. Unable to reach her in the Guatemalan rainforest or halfway up Mount Kilimanjaro, I turned to my in-laws for advice.

Jeremy's family enjoyed a wealthy lifestyle on the land, just outside Cheltenham – and before you start picturing the kind of family that has a wealthy lifestyle outside Cheltenham, let me assure you that you're absolutely spot on. When I tried to broach the subject, my father-in-law's eyebrows took the moral high ground. Jeremy's father had achieved his life's ambition of becoming a Tory MP, for Wiltshire North. He had a broad, severe forehead like Beethoven but was completely tone deaf to life's lyricism. It's quite a Newton-defying feat, really, to rise by gravity. But that's what he'd done. The very earnest Derek Beaufort was the coldest, smoothest man I'd ever met. He was remote, chilly, self-absorbed; I'd often glimpse him on news programmes working hard at turning up the corners of his mouth into what could be mistaken for a smile. He didn't even attempt to simulate friendliness now.

'The only thing wrong with Merlin is his mother,' he proclaimed.

I waited for my husband or my mother-in-law to leap to my defence. Jeremy squeezed my hand under the heavy mahogany heirloom dining table but kept wearing his expression of bolted-on politeness. Mrs Beaufort's (think Barbara Cartland but with more make-up) smile thinned out between twin brackets of condemnation. She had always let me know that her son had married beneath himself. 'Which is true, as I'm only five foot three,' I'd joshed to Jeremy at our engagement party. 'Just think, darling, you can use me as a decoration on our wedding cake.'

Merlin was two when the doctor made his diagnosis. Jeremy and I were sitting side by side in the paediatric wing of the London University College Hospital. 'Lucy, Jeremy, do sit down.' The paediatrician's voice was light and falsely cheery – which was when I knew something was seriously wrong. The word 'autism' slid into me like the sharp, cold edge of a knife. Blood pulsed into my head.

'Autism is a lifelong developmental disability which affects how a person relates to other people. It's a disorder of neural development chiefly characterized by an inability to communicate effectively, plus inappropriate or obsessive behaviour . . .' The paediatrician, kind but robust, his white hair floating above him like a cumulus cloud, kept talking, but all I heard were exclamations of protest. Rebuttals clattered through my cranium.

'Merlin is not autistic,' I told the doctor emphatically. 'He's loving. He's bright. He's my perfect, beautiful, adored baby boy.'

For the rest of the consultation, I felt I was buckling with pressure, as if I were trying to close a submarine hatch against the weight of the ocean. I glanced through the glass panel at my son in the waiting-room playpen. His tangled blond curls, ruby-red mouth and aquamarine eyes were so familiar. But this doctor was reducing him to a label. Suddenly Merlin was little more than an envelope with no address.

An ache of love squeezed up from my bone marrow and coagulated around my heart. Dust motes danced in the heavy air. The walls, a bilious yellow, looked how I felt.

'He will have developmental delays,' the doctor added parenthetically. This was a diagnosis which pulled you into the riptide and dragged you down into the dark.

'You can't be sure it's autism,' I rallied. 'I mean, there could be some mistake. You don't know Merlin. He's more than that.' My darling son had become a plant in a gloomy room and it was my job to pull him into the light. 'Isn't he, Jeremy?'

I swivelled towards my husband, who sat, rigid, in the orange bucket chair next to me, gripping the armrests as though trying to squeeze blood from them.

Jeremy's profile was so chiselled it belonged on a coin. He looked dignified but suffering, like a thoroughbred coming in last in a hacking event.

Falling in love with Jeremy Beaufort, I had scraped the top of the barrel. When I first saw him – tall, dark, turquoise-eyed and tousle-haired – if I'd been a dog I would have sat on my hindquarters and hung my tongue out. The first thing he told me when we met on the red-eye from New York – the flight had been a gift from my sister, an airline stewardess, for my twenty-second birthday – was that he loved my laugh. A few weeks later he was telling me on a daily basis how much he loved my 'succulent quim'.

But it wasn't just his 'Quite frankly, my dear', Rhett Butler good looks that attracted me. The man had a towering intellect to match. The real reason I fell for Jeremy Beaufort was because he'd graduated from the College of Really Erudite Personages. Besides his MBA, fluent Latin and French, and reputation as the Scrabble ninja, he just knew so much. Wagner's birth-place, the origins of the Westminster system, that the Lampyris *noctiluca* and the Phosphaenus *hemipterus*, though commonly known as glowworms, are in fact beetles, that the Bunker Hill Monument is in Massachusetts . . . Hell, he could even spell Massachusetts.

'Is that an unabridged dictionary in your pocket or are you just pleased to see me?' I teased him on our first date.

My main claims to fame (apart from a Mastermind knowledge of Jane Austen's unfinished novel, *Sanditon*, T. S. Eliot's pornographic limericks and all the anal-sex references in the novels of Norman Mailer) were knowing how to gatecrash a backstage party at a rock gig, put a condom on a banana using my mouth, and sing all the words to 'American Pie'. Jeremy, on the other hand, only had Big Talk and no small. While my financial analyst boyfriend found it endearingly funny that the only bank I knew about was the sperm bank, I found it hilariously charming that when I mentioned the Marx brothers, he thought I was referring to Karl and his comrade Lenin.

Jeremy was so good-looking you wouldn't even consider him as date material unless you worked full-time as a swimwear model. I was a lowly English teacher with a moth-eaten one-piece Speedo and literary aspirations. So, why did I get to play Lizzie Bennet to his dashing Darcy? To be honest, I think it was mainly because my name wasn't Candida or Chlamydia; he'd come across too many upper-class females curiously named after a genital infection. These women not only owned horses but looked like them. They could probably count with one foot. If you asked for their hand in marriage, they'd answer 'Yeah' or 'Neigh!' After years of dating and mating with such mannequins, he told me that he found my spontaneity, mischief, irreverence, sexual appetites and loathing of field sports liberating. And then there was my family.

Jeremy, an only child, rattled around in an aloof-looking country mansion, while our Southwark garden flat was crammed with books and musical instruments and paintings waiting to be hung and delicious kitchen smells and too much furniture – a home which was comfortable with its lot in life. As were we. And Jeremy loved it.

Whereas meals at the Beaufort mansion were sober, 'Pass the mustard', 'Drop of sherry with that?' semi-silent affairs, dinner at my house was a riot of heady hilarity, with Dad arabesquing about the place in a tatty silk robe quoting from *The Tempest*, mother denouncing the Booker Prize shortlist whilst shouting out clues from the cryptic crossword and my sister and I teasing each other mercilessly. Not to forget the various blow-ins. No Sunday lunch was complete without a bevy of poets, writers, painters and actors, all regaling us with richly honed anecdotes. To Jeremy, my family was as exotic as a tribe from the deepest, darkest jungles of Borneo. I wasn't sure whether he wanted to join in or simply live among us taking anthropological notes and photographs. In his world of strained whispers, my family was a joyful shriek.

While the Beauforts were meat and three veg, Yorkshire pudding people, the only thing my family didn't eat were our words. Garlic, hummus, Turkish delight, artichokes, truffles, tabbouleh . . . Jeremy devoured it all, along with Miles Davis, Charlie Mingus and other jazz musicians, and foreign films, and performances by banned theatrical groups fleeing from dictatorships like that in Belarus, whom my father was always bringing home to crash on the over-crowded couch.

And, to be honest, an allergy to my father's excesses is partly why I fell in love with Jeremy. Jeremy was all the things my feckless father wasn't. Employed, trustworthy, stable, capable, hard-working, as dependable as his expensive Swiss watch. Nor was he the type to come home with a nipple piercing or purple pubic hair, as my pater had been known to do. Whereas my dissolute dad ran up debts like others ran marathons, Jeremy was as reliable as the mathematical formulas he pored over at his investment bank. The man put two and two together to make a living.

My father, a character actor from the Isle of Dogs, had a lemon-squeezer-diamond-geezer accent. My mother, an alabaster-skinned, willowy woman from Taunton, Somerset, boasts a sing-song accent, as though everything she says has been curled by tongs. Her lilt makes other accents, including my own South London twang, sound flat to my ear. Except for my beloved's. His voice has more timbre than Ikea. Just one word in that dark-chocolate baritone of his could calm all chaos.

But not now ... Now, in the doctor's consultation room, he sat mute as sadness flowed down his face from brow to chin.

'Lucy, it's clear something is wrong with the boy.

Face facts,' Jeremy finally said, all staccato stoicism. 'Our son is mentally handicapped.'

I felt the sting of tears in my sinuses. 'He's not!'

'Pull yourself together, Lucy.' With his emotions now held in check, my husband's voice was as clipped and precise as that of a wing commander from a Second World War film.

We drove home from the hospital in numbed silence. Jeremy dropped us off and careened straight back to his City office, leaving me alone with Merlin and Merlin's Diagnosis.

Our tall, anorexic Georgian house in Lambeth, which we'd bought cheaply as a 'renovator's delight' – sales spiel for 'completely dilapidated' – leans tipsily into the square. It's just like all the other houses in the street, identical in style, paintwork, latticing, flower boxes – except for the little boy inside. My son was sitting on the floor rolling a plastic bottle back and forth, rocking slightly, oblivious to the world. I scooped him up and crushed him to me, a hot smudge against my neck. And then I began the agony of self-doubt.

Was it something I ate whilst pregnant? Soft cheese? Sushi? Or wait! Was it something I *didn't* eat? Organic tofu, perhaps? Or maybe I ate too much? I hadn't just been eating for two, I had been eating for Pavarotti and his extended family . . . Was it the glass of wine I shouldn't have drunk in the final trimester? Was it that one martini at my sister's wedding-anniversary party?

Was it something I *should* have drunk – like puréed beetroot? Was it the hair dye I'd used to brighten up my bouffant when pregnancy made it lanky and dull? But, oh my God! Wait. Maybe it wasn't me at all? Did a teenage babysitter drop him on his head? Did the nursery heater leak carbon monoxide? Did we fly with him too early on that holiday to Spain and burst his Eustachian tubes, leading to a seizure and brain damage?

No. It must have been the negativity I'd exuded while carrying him. Merlin wasn't planned. He'd come along two years into our marriage. Even though we were excited at the prospect of parenthood, I had slightly resented the unexpected intrusion into our extended honeymoon. The only time in my life I wanted to be a year older was when I was pregnant. It's putting it mildly to say that I didn't embrace the moment. In fact, I shunned it. I didn't feng shui my aura in yogalates classes chanting to whale music like Gwyneth Paltrow and Organic Co. Instead, I moaned and complained and railed against the dying of the waist. Especially as I'd recently spent a whole week's wages on lacy lingerie to celebrate our anniversary. I said to anyone who would listen that 'Pregnant women don't need doctors, they need exorcists.' Birth seemed Sigourney Weaveresque to me. 'Get this alien out of my abdomen!' . . . Could too many caustically black-humoured jokes have affected his genes?

But stop. What if it was the difficult birth? Why do

they call it a delivery? Letters, you deliver. Pizzas. Good news. This was more like Deliver*ance*. Forceps, suction, the episiotomy ... Was it telling the doctor that I now knew why so many women die in child-birth – because it's less painful than going on living?

Or perhaps it was the flippant remarks I made in the delivery room to my mother as we peered at the scrunched-up little blue ball I'd just brought into the world? 'I've just given birth to a baby, but I don't think it's mine.'

On and on I fretted. I would stop worrying occasion-ally to change a nappy – usually the baby's. But for days after The Diagnosis, a San Andreas of fault lines ran through my psyche, coupled with an overwhelm-ingly protective lioness-type love, waiting, watchful, my claws curled inside me. I kissed my baby boy's soft, downy head all over. He coiled into the circle of my arms. I held him close and cooed. I looked into his beautiful blue eyes and refused to believe that they led inwards to nothingness. The doctor had reduced him to a black and white term – 'autism'. But the prism of my love bathed him in bright and captivating colours.

I had to save him. It was Merlin and me against the world.

2
Planet Merlin

I'm a great believer in ignoring things until they go away. When Facebook and Twitter came along, I turned a blind, technical eye. Just like I ignored the 'Protein Only' diet, doing the Macarena, those weird Masai running shoes, bubble skirts and Esperanto. If you wait long enough, these fads fade. But the same logic just wouldn't apply to Merlin's diagnosis. It was not something he was going to grow out of.

There was no choice but to begin the disorientating journey through the labyrinth of social workers, speech and occupational therapists, top paediatric psychologists ... For the next year I trekked here, there and everywhere, in the endless search for experts. They ranged from National Health doctors locked away in sooty Victorian mausoleums flannelled with dust, linoleum floors overlaid with reeking antiseptic, to the private clinics of Harley Street with their low, plexiglass coffee tables laden with copies of *Country Life*. I hate to think how many specialists' kids I've now put through law school. (When visiting a private doctor, be sure to note carefully where you leave your car, because you will probably have to sell it to pay off their astronomical bills.)

My son had so many tests, he must have thought he was being drafted into the elite moon mission astronaut programme. I had to hold him as he was measured, weighed, blinded with torches, probed, prodded, pinched, stethoscoped and syringed, despite the fact that his body would twist into a spasm of despair as he wept inconsolably.

And, oh, the constant battle to keep my gaze neutral and unperturbed though I was dying inside as various labels were hurled his way – dyspraxia, dyslexia, dysphasia, aphasia, attention deficit disorder, sensory defensiveness, Fragile X, chromosomal abnormalities ... Apparently autism was only the tip of Merlin's diagnostic iceberg. How it made me burn with love for my strange little son.

Meeting after meeting, in government buildings full of grimacing cracks, social workers told me that being the mother of a child with autism would be a challenge but an exciting one ... This is as accurate as the captain of the *Titanic* telling his passengers that they were in for a diverting little dip in the briny. Mothering a child on the autism spectrum is as easy as skewering banana custard to a mid-air boomerang.

Denial was my first response, hence the years of alternative medical rounds. I tried everything from cranial massage to karma maintenance and other areas of scientific expertise based on medical ideology that's been rigorously and methodically proven by Goldie Hawn and other well-known academics.

Anger came next, mostly towards the farcically solemn, flat-shoed educational psychologists with their expressionless expressions. The way to recognize an expert is by the clipboard. A parent needs United Nations headphones to decode what these clipboard-wielders are saying. 'What a fascinating child' decodes as 'He's retarded.' 'A true original' means 'I've never met a child quite so retarded.' 'Your son is differently interesting' translates as 'Your life is screwed for ever. You might as well put yourself up for adoption immediately.'

I found myself snapping at all clipboard-wielding, euphemistic people. 'So, let's stop beating around a dead horse and cut right to the conversational mustard, shall we? Will my son ever lead a normal life?'

'What do you define as "normal"?' asked a social worker with ferrety alertness. As her eye twitched and she chewed on her half-gnawed nails, I got the feeling there might be a very fine line between social worker and sociopath.

While I ricocheted from psychologists to

bio-feedback practitioners and other nouveau-voodoo nut-jobs until my own inner child wanted to throw up, Jeremy retreated into work. When Merlin was born, Jeremy had been so besotted. He'd spend all day planting kisses on our baby's soft, plump belly, warm as freshly baked bread, before wriggling and giggling him in and out of his little pyjamas. Jeremy, an only child, had happily professed he wanted three, four – no, five – more children. He took every second day off, left for work late and came home early, his face alight with joy.

But not any more. Now he left for the office pre-dawn, getting home at ten or eleven. Saturdays he indulged himself with a little sleep-in till, say, 6 a.m. His only son was damaged goods. Humiliated, he implored me not to tell anybody. My instinct was to blurt it out, to scream it from rooftops, a howl of indignation and terror. But, under Jeremy's strict instructions, when people asked about Merlin, I produced a mechanical smile and placed a platitude or two on my lips. Which brought on stage three – a bad case of the 'Why me?'s

I'd been teaching English at the local state school for a year. I now downgraded to part-time but didn't give up altogether, reasoning that it might prove therapeutic. After all, monosyllabic teens whine 'Why me?' constantly, so perhaps no one would notice my own self-absorption. When my sister, in whom I'd confided, asked me why I didn't quit work completely as I was clearly going gaga, I glibly replied that London mothers had to be able to afford to buy their kids the latest iPhone or their offspring would put themselves on the 'at risk' register. But in truth, now that Jeremy had abandoned me emotionally, single-parenting every night and weekend had quickly made me realize that the only good thing about being a domestic goddess is that you can't commit suicide by putting your head in the oven as there's bound to be a casserole in there already. If I gave up work it wouldn't be long before I'd be licking the cake beaters . . . while they were still whirring.

Still, I felt so guilty about the relief I experienced when I dropped my son off at the childminder in the mornings . . . (What kind of heartless mother was I?) . . . only to feel even more guilty when I picked him up in the afternoons. After all, I was obviously on parental 'L' plates. Surely he'd be better off with professionals? Worry became my Mastermind specialist subject. Even though four hours a day teaching a group of truculent teens better armed than your average Colombian drugs cartel was a lot like hosting a hurricane, I found it a respite from mothering Merlin.

Day's end, though, seeing my pupils spurt out of the school gates like toothpaste from a tube, only reminded me that my own son would never know those normal, exhilarating pleasures. Merlin was like a rubber glove turned inside out. Everything I took for granted – smiling, laughing, loving – all as natural as breathing, were alien to him. My son was exiled on to a planet beyond my understanding, beyond logic. Looking up at me, his eyes as bare and round as light bulbs, I knew he was not in the same space-time continuum as the rest of us. The kid was all currents and impulses. Merlin's moods were so erratic it was as though he were responding to some invisible conductor's baton. I'd often find him smiling at something secret, as if being tickled from the inside with a feather ... only for this to be followed by a sudden darkening of his mood, as the poison of anxiety branched through his little being.

I was also going through childminders like tissues. Even though I only left him with carers who assured me that they were trained in 'special needs', a frazzled Tracey or Leanne or Kylie would invariably hand my son over as though he were some rare feral creature recently netted in the Amazon and still adjusting to captivity. Merlin would go rigid with horror when I tried to wrestle him into his car seat, flapping his arms and legs like a trapped bird which was panicking and frantic and crashing into walls. My son's muteness meant that all I could do was peer into the disturbed, empty reaches of his eyes while pleading with him to be calm. 'Earth to Merlin, come in. Are you reading me? Over. Ground Control to Major Mum.'

I then drove home, white-knuckled with stress. Eventually Merlin's crying would subside into a brooding, sullen, twitching silence. Unless I deviated from the usual route, that is. Then he would thunk his head against the car seat, screaming with terror. Once home, he would shudder with exhaustion, clinging to me desperately as he sobbed into my chest. My heart quivered with pity and I would have to blink away tears. And then I would look into his eyes and realize that they weren't empty but brimming with fear. It seemed there was a place in him which I could not reach, where he dwelt in solitude. Beneath the surface of his daily existence was a life he lived as if underwater.

My son was like something that had appeared in a magician's hat. I had no idea where he'd come from and he was unlike anybody I'd ever met. Merlin seemed to broadcast signals all day but nobody was on the same wavelength. He would raise his face up to the heavens, as though listening intently to cosmic harmonies beyond the constraints of my earthbound senses. Merlin and I could look out of the same window but never see the same thing. Still, one thing was clear. It was my job to stay alert. To pick up bleeps on my Merlin radar. And to stop him from tumbling through a hole in the world, like Alice.

After my last class one Friday, I was dashing to my car so that I could relieve yet another rattled and over-wrought childminder when I saw a mother silently sobbing by the gates of the private primary school next door. My heart lurched. I instinctively felt that she too must have a boy who didn't fit in. Perhaps the 'A' word had been bandied about? My emotions swelled with the recognition of her pain and angst and I found myself dashing to her side, arms open. 'What is it?' I said, brimming with fellow feeling.

'It's my son . . . He's five.'

'Yes?' I soothed, a hand on her arm, urging her to unburden herself to one who would understand.

'He's not taking to his French.'

I had an overwhelming desire to get into my car and back over her body repeatedly. And do you know what? A jury of mothers of special needs children would acquit me. For most mothers, their biggest worry is that their offspring won't eat anything which hasn't danced on television. I have seen mothers tearing their hair out over this. When my pupils' more aspirational parents tearfully complained about their wayward progeny not grasping *Beowulf*, I felt a grinding hollowness. The only remedy was to take a quick sniff of the classroom glue pot. I was tempted to commandeer Merlin's Postman Pat flask and start carrying something stronger in it than orangeade. Valium, say, with a heroin chaser – Mummy's 'little helper'.

I would have turned to my husband for comfort, but he had taken to imitating the Loch Ness monster: rumours of his existence abounded but there were no actual sightings. I understood that the shock of Merlin's diagnosis had sent Jeremy retreating into the world of high finance, where he could take solace from the solid predictability of percentages and equations, and at first I'd been patient. Jeremy's world has always been so certain. The only hard knocks he'd ever taken had been whilst playing polo. He'd perfected his French on frequent skiing trips to Verbier or Chamonix. Entertaining his parents' friends at dinner parties meant that he had learnt osmotically, from the cradle on, how to charm and disarm. Although professing members' clubs to be horribly outdated and unnecessary, he attends all the same and secretly relishes them. Having an autistic child was not on his life's shopping list. Consequently, my darling husband had become like a hostile witness, grunting and only answering in monosyllables.

He'd had a year to acclimatize and yet still refused to discuss Merlin's condition. The loud, contentious quality of Jeremy's muteness bounced off the walls of our ramshackle little terrace. The whole house seemed to be holding its breath. The plastic Philippe Starck garden gnomes he'd given me as a comedic housewarming gift stood back to back on our pocket-handkerchief lawn as though in a huff with each other. Yes, we'd bought our house cheaply as a 'fixer-upper', but it was us who needed fixing. We were falling to pieces. I felt I'd woken in my own home to find all the furniture rearranged. Disorientated, I had to reevaluate my surroundings.

I tried to make light of it. Against Jeremy's wishes I'd confided in family and a few close friends, but when other acquaintances, still oblivious to Merlin's condition, asked why Jeremy was never with us, I explained that he'd enjoyed trying to get me pregnant – 'He liked trying for that three times a day but contracted morning sickness – the *morning after the baby was born.*' After they laughed, I'd add, with a practised smile, 'He's just taking time to adjust. He'll get more involved when Merlin is older.'

When my husband missed appointments with our son's speech and occupational therapists, I told myself I wasn't stressed. I told myself that it was normal to add chocolate chips to a cheese omelette. When Jeremy didn't turn up to the interview for the special needs nursery I'd spent months lobbying, I joked with the headmistress that he'd muddled up the dates. 'The greatest mystery is how men, who are so universally stupid, got to rule the world. Dan Brown should write a thriller about *that*!'

When I had to forgo staff meetings because Jeremy was too busy to pick up Merlin from the latest child-minder, I commiserated with the other wives by delivering a stagey eye-roll. 'Ah, how wonderful marriage would be without husbands.' I jokingly took to wearing my wedding ring on the wrong finger so that I could quip at opportune moments that I'd 'obviously married the wrong bloke'.

When Jeremy didn't make it to Merlin's third birthday party, I philosophized, glibly, to the small gathering of family members, 'Do you know the one way to keep a husband at home?'

37

'Baking?' suggested my mother.

'Gymnastic sex?' volunteered Phoebe.

'Let the air out of his tyres,' I advised caustically.

My mother and sister exchanged concerned glances. My older sister is just like me, except she has a gentle disposition, an attentive, devoted husband, two normal children, a job she adores and a genuine love of humankind.

Our mother, although never the type to cut sandwiches into triangles and knit organic muesli, is also very loving. When she found out I was having a baby, Mum crocheted herself into a coma. Packages arrived from all over the world containing baby booties, mittens, beanies, cardigans, bedspreads, doilies and matinee jackets (one for the mornings and one for the evenings and one for any unaccounted matinee moments in between). Within weeks, my house was covered in crocheted things, as if a lumpy, multicoloured sauce had dripped over every surface.

After my father had died, naked in the arms of what my mum called 'a shady lady', my bookish mother had become a party girl. If there's a party on across town, she rings to ask if she can speak to herself as she can't believe she's not there. She would crochet her own party if she could. To complement her good-time girl image, she traded in her neatly knotted scarves for a feather boa which writhed about her throat like something tropical, exotic and most definitely alive. Mum had been a librarian by trade, which meant that the only excursions she'd experienced were flights of fancy. But then she discovered that my father had over-insured himself, which was amusingly typical of his inflated sense of self-worth and caused us to laugh through our tears at the funeral. Now Mum was always making up for lost time and was either off abseiling an Alp or doing a degree on volcanology somewhere unpronounceable or spending a small fortune saving lemurs. (Individually, I presume, at the price.) Most of my mother's conversations began with 'I'm just back from . . .', or 'I'm just off to . . .' It might be St Petersburg, or Bhutan or Belize. She was always either shark-diving or Turin-shroud authenticating, nude tap-dancing or off on a little trot around the Hermitage. 'Sorry, darling, but I don't have a weekend free till early October,' she'd say, gulping in the good life, every last drop, living the daylights out of every second. My own life just telescoped away to a blip of mundanity. 'Got a good deal on mincemeat at the supermarket,' I'd mumble in reply.

She communicated by postcard only. One arrived from Kathmandu with a yak on it and the scrawled message 'Madly in love with Sherpa.' Another arrived two months later from Brazil. 'Sherpa-ectomy. Now on dig for fossils – *not* the archaeologist, although he is fetching.' Merlin's diagnosis had brought her home immediately. Needless to say, my vibrant mother and Pollyanna-esque sister found my glib pessimism alarmingly distasteful.

39

But beneath my Teflon-coated veneer of repartee, my husband's indifference was cooling my ardour to arctic levels. Jeremy accused me of 'alienation of affection' – a legal term for losing the hots for someone. He said that attempting to make love to me was reminiscent of trying to shop in a small country town on the Sabbath. Nothing was open. When he complained that I never initiated sex with him any more, I wanted to tell him to go to hell but realized that, of course, by this point, single-parenting a child with autism, hell would be a major improvement on my own life.

My optimistic sister felt sure that Jeremy was suffering from some kind of post-traumatic stress syndrome. 'He'll come round. Basically, Jeremy is a decent, compassionate man.'

I laughed out loud. 'Calling Jeremy compassionate is like calling me a Peruvian pole-vault champion.' Bitterness had started to creep into my voice and lines of resentment were etching themselves on to my countenance. What had happened to the man I adored?

Jeremy began staying out later and later and then not coming home at all. And then when he did finally come home a week before Merlin's fourth Christmas, it was in a psychological suicide vest, judging by the grenade he threw into my world.

'I'm leaving you.' His voice was heavy with weary exasperation, his face flushed with drink. 'I need to find some peace of mind.'

What he found was a piece of a televisual domestic goddess called Audrey.

With Stevie Wonder's eye for detail, I hadn't noticed he was drifting into the arms and freshly lasered legs of a pulchritudinous daytime-TV chef. Finding a false fingernail in our bed should have been a clue, but no, I chose to put it down to an over-beautified babysitter. I trailed him and his suitcase out into the street, past the little Christmas tree I'd spent all day decorating. My face was a rictus of incredulity. 'Why?' We'd only been married for five years.

'Well, if you hadn't rejected me all the time . . . if you'd shown me the slightest bit of affection . . . but you've been so preoccupied.' The thin smoke of his breath was steaming away in the icy air, like a 1950s cigarette ad. 'All you can think about is Merlin. You've given up cooking. The house is a tip. You're so frosty in bed I feel compelled to keep checking your vital signs every half-hour.'

'Oh, forgive me, Jeremy. I'd love to screw your brains out but Audrey obviously beat me to it . . . judging by how much you've lowered your IQ to shack up with a woman who cooks cupcakes for a living. So, the way to a man's heart really is through his stomach? I always thought that was aiming too high.'

My sister Phoebe googled the TV temptress. Apart from a regular cooking spot on a daytime television chat show, where she pouted provocatively as though in a porn film, her only other claim to fame was a tabloid exposé of the time she sat in a plate of cocaine at a rock-and-roll party, giving new meaning to the phrase 'powdering your cheeks'. Photos revealed a scrupulously diet-conscious honey-blonde from the home counties with melonesque breasts, a minuscule waist and a cat-like languor. Her make-up was so consistently perfect it seemed she was permanently poised to receive an award on some imaginary stage for services to lip-liner.

Despite her prime-time habit of practically fellating the more phallic-looking vegetables before she baked them, the woman was so thin Yves Saint Laurent could use her as a straw. Her only large body parts were her breasts, which could easily be mistaken for a break-away republic. The posh trollop wore cashmere trousers – obviously to keep her ankles warm when my husband took her roughly by the hardy perennials in her herbaceous border. I suppressed a swift shudder of revulsion at the thought of my erudite Jeremy naked with a woman whose tan was the same colour as a carrot. One kiss and you'd have consumed half of your five a day.

When I broke the news to my mother by showing her Jeremy and Audrey's photograph in *Hello!* magazine (they'd been papped, ironically at some charity ball for disabled children), my mother gasped at the actress's stick-thin frame. 'That must be bulimia.'

'Yes,' I said sarcastically. 'Jeremy simply knows all the most interesting people. Her sister, Anne Orexia, is popping by later.'

I kept up this kind of feeble banter and brash façade for weeks. 'My husband gives reason to my life ... He's the reason why I'm broken-hearted, bitter, cynical and twisted,' I said to work colleagues.

'The trouble with women is that we get all excited about nothing and then we marry him,' I told my unimpressed principal, before taking a few days off on compassionate leave.

'Do you know what I call it when older m–m–men r–r–run off with younger, thinner women? Sylph fulfilment,' I slurred over cocktails with my sympathetic sister.

'We're having a little marital tiff,' I informed his family. '*I* wanted to celebrate our fifth wedding anniversary by having a lovely holiday in the Caribbean with our beautiful son, plus perhaps a new gazebo extension to celebrate Jeremy's pay rise at the bank ... but *he* wanted to divorce me and shack up with a TV cook named Audrey – sorry, *Tawdry* – and follow her to bloody America where she has a TV opportunity. Not even on a proper channel. Only on *cable* ... And, let's face it, the woman's *mammogram* is probably her best screen work. Is it any wonder I'm a Recovering Optimist?'

'My husband's birth certificate is an apology letter from the condom factory,' I told the childminder, the milkman, the social workers, the accountant . . .

But, privately, I howled my heart out. I wailed at the world. Like a dog tormented by wasps, I shook all over. I gnawed my pillow at night and curled into the fetal position in a paroxysm of self-loathing and 'if only's. *If only* I had paid Jeremy more attention. *If only* Merlin hadn't been born with autism. *If only* I'd never fallen pregnant in the first bloody place. *If only* I hadn't allowed Merlin's condition to seep into our marriage, our laughs and our love-making. (Believe me, no man can wake a woman who is pretending to be asleep. Even if you play amplified heavy metal into her earhole.)

I wrote and told Jeremy how I felt. I promised to do a cooking course, so that I'd never again use my smoke alarm as a timer. 'I've realized that "blancmange" is *not* the highest point in the French Alps,' I assured him by text. I baked him Yorkshire puddings. I cleaned the house top to bottom. I begged his forgiveness. I suggested having another child. I implored him to come back to us.

At first I felt sure he would, so tried to tease him out of his sulky silence: 'I would have answered your email sooner, only you didn't send one.' But after a month or two of wearing full make-up and silk lingerie, just in case he popped in, things began to feel a little Miss Havishamesque. I was tempted to wander around in my moth-eaten wedding dress, braiding my hair and drooling . . .

But there was no time for a nervous breakdown. Merlin was now at a local pre-school five days a week and I'd gone back to teaching full-time. Although single parenthood meant that I arrived at 8.55 and left at 3.30, which couldn't get me the sack as they were the hours I was contracted to do, it was considered a 'pretty poor show' by my colleagues. Keen teachers run drama and chess clubs after school and apply for advanced skill status, which I should have been doing by this stage. Yes, I am a career woman, I told anyone who would listen, but my tip for young women today . . . ? Just stick to the traditional investment path and inherit many hotels. I also gave up all ideas of penning a novel. It seemed a bit pointless – now that I was actually *in* one.

At home, I started to master my own DIY. Well . . . more or less, if you don't count the day I gave myself an impromptu perm in a bizarre electrical accident. I learnt to do housework in half the time. This involved a particularly athletic feat of changing both Merlin's sheets and duvet cover, flipping and airing the mattresses, and all without waking him once. Martyred domesticity dominated my days. I took to calling myself 'St Lucy' of Lambeth. I practically booked myself in for a halo fitting.

Minus Jeremy, life with Merlin became glutinous. Pushing through it was an effort, like swimming underwater against a tide. My second favourite mothering experience was talking to Merlin's pre-school teacher about my son's educational progress, my favourite being stubbing my toe repeatedly on the vacuum cleaner until it went gangrenous. In quick succession, Merlin was expelled from three nurseries, Montessori, Sure Start and Tiny Tots. Whenever the phone rang, I steeled myself for the voice of his most recent head teacher, dreading the four lethal words 'Could you pop by?' Whenever I was summoned to the pre-school office, a sense of trepidation as heavy as a winter coat hung on my shoulders. It appeared that Merlin's teachers wanted combat pay. I felt as though my son had been voted 'Kid Least Wanted in a Classroom' by teachers countrywide.

And I could understand why. Merlin's moods were a pendulum swing from dark to light, joy to despair. He'd gaze ahead in silent absorption, as if taking the pulse of the universe. For hours he'd just stare into space, as though he could hear secrets the wind was whispering. Then anxiety would creep up on him like a spy and there'd be an avalanche of frustrated rage for no obvious reason. Oh, where was my Owner's Manual? Then perhaps I could understand why his clothes seemed to scorch him. Each morning, as I tried to dress my son, he'd toss and buck like a horse attempting to escape from a saddle, leaving me bruised and battered.

Ah yes, you learn many things when you're the mother of someone with autism, like the fact that cats are not the only creatures with nine lives. There are also guinea pigs, goldfish, rabbits – even pet geckos are more durable than they look. (Although if put into the blender with the lid off, your kitchen will quickly achieve a new interior-design look you could only really call 'art gecko'.)

You also learn that embarrassment, like hair gel for a bald bloke, is a luxury not afforded to you. Nor is there any escape. Not only have you had a baby, but you'll *always* have a baby. What I mean is that your son won't grow into a man, he'll grow into a giant toddler. With a psychological umbilical cord that attaches you for life.

Merlin's volcanic tantrums turned him into Lana Turner, John McEnroe and Bette Davis all rolled into one fun bundle. After calming his meltdowns with cuddles and counselling, anointing his anxieties with 'You're so clever's until he felt better, I would be left as wilted as an old lettuce leaf. A lettuce leaf that was about to be arrested for child abuse – which would be the only conclusion the neighbours could reach, after all that hullaballoo.

The rest of my time I devoted to happy little hobbies like buying presents for nursery teachers or neighbours to apologize for Merlin's erratic, sometimes violent behaviour. To break the routine, I sometimes took a little jaunt outside to retrieve my many possessions which Merlin had thrown out of the window. Another leisure pursuit involved watching children evaporate away from my son by the swings. The sandbox invariably became a quicksand box. Angry parents, whose heads spun to stare at me judgementally, would half-hear my explanation before trailing off, fearing some AIDS-like contagion and abandoning me to a numbing silence. I spent the rest of my carefree 'me' time being told by shop owners that my son was a 'spoilt brat' and was no longer welcome in their stores, the crisp reprimand in their voices forbidding further conversation. If only there were a self-help book for social lepers.

I wrote 'to do' lists so that I'd stop jolting awake in the middle of the night because I'd forgotten to defrost the leg of lamb for the next day or to plan tomorrow's lesson on Sylvia Plath appreciation. I was developing my own Plath-ology – a desperate desire to take antidepressants. There's nothing wrong with taking Prozac, I convinced myself. Even God-fearing Moses took tablets, and look at the side-effects *he* had.

But my biggest note to myself was to stop yearning to put my head on my beloved husband's dearly missed prime pectoral real estate ... And then, more than anything else, trying not to mind when, aged four, Merlin said his first word since losing his speech at eight months. And that word was 'Dad'.

3
UFO – Unidentified Fleeing Object

The women in your life are your human wonder-bras – uplifting, supportive and making each other look bigger and better. My loving sister and mother kept me buoyant during this fraught time. Which is quite a feat when you consider Merlin's fifth year of life. Basically, things went downhill so fast I was amazed that the Olympic Bobsleigh team hadn't rung me for some top training tips. When Jeremy emptied our joint account, I realized that love really does end in marriage. My husband had never struck me as mean. He had always been the first to put his hand into his pocket … Unfortunately, now it was to play pocket billiards. The man I adored with all my heart had turned into the kind of guy who would stab you in the back and then call the police to have you arrested for carrying a weapon.

The first item on my 'to do' list was to kill UFO – Unidentified Fleeing Object, otherwise known as the Man I Mistakenly Took for My Loving and Committed Husband.

When Jeremy, who was now living in Los Angeles, filed for a divorce a year later, my hand flew to my forehead and I actually staggered backwards a few feet, like a heroine from a silent movie. I looked at the dashing arabesque of his signature – *Jeremy Beaufort* – on the dreaded document, which proclaimed that he wanted to dissolve our marriage. Then I vomited. All over the hateful, heartbreaking paperwork.

For the next few months, I tried to make my way through the Kafkaesque miasma of files and scraps of paper which is divorce court. But getting divorced is a vile maze of trap-doors, grilles and hatches. The locks and switches are coin-operated by lawyers. There are horrible spikes everywhere which lacerate your psyche. I joked to my sister that the day you consult a lawyer is the first day of the rest of your life savings. She replied that a divorce lawyer helps you get what's coming to him. But it was hard to laugh, being so painfully true. The man I had loved body and soul for seven years of my life was busily rearranging his finances to minimize payments to his only child. My uninspired, lacklustre lawyer said that Jeremy had diverted funds to another company which it would take a lot of time and money to trace – money I didn't have. But, surely, Jeremy's fast cars and Armani suits, and Audrey's dazzling, bling-tastic appearance, which was off the *kerching*-o-meter, were pretty good signs that my hubby had a healthy dose of affluenza? He was obviously practising moderation to excess.

'If you don't give me some money soon, Jeremy, I'll be washing your son's clothes by pounding them on rocks,' I emailed him. 'Luckily, the man who runs the corner store is Buddhist. I'll just tell him I paid for the groceries in a previous life, shall I?'

Jeremy replied that he was strapped for cash, having relocated to Los Angeles to help Audrey break into American television.

Cucumber-sandwich-nibbling, River-Cam-punting, Pimms-drinking, Wodehouse-addicted, sticky-wicket-cricket-loving Jeremy, moving country for a *woman*? And to La-La Land? A place where people say 'Have a nice day' and then shoot you? Well, it was as unthinkable as Lady Gaga giving up meat frocks and make-up. The sacrifices he was making for his floozy hurt me more than his infidelity. How had she made him do it? Obviously the woman was a vampire on a day pass. The other obvious fact was that Jeremy's mid-life crisis had started without him.

Jeremy went on to say that there was little left for him to give as I'd squandered all his life savings on quacks for Merlin because I couldn't accept that the child was mentally handicapped.

Striking while the irony was hot, I emailed back that what I couldn't accept was how he could be having a mid-life crisis when he'd never left puberty.

Jeremy responded with a list of complaints about me – unloving, sarcastic, obsessional, undomesticated, unreasonable – a list he would no doubt soon put to the court in the contested property settlement. Naturally, the judge, nauseous to the point of projectile vomiting at this catalogue of my flaws, would award him custody of all our possessions – except Merlin, whom he obviously didn't want. I comforted myself with the knowledge that my husband still couldn't sing all the lyrics to 'American Pie' from beginning to end, the rat. And he certainly put the 'ass' into 'Massachusetts'.

Because I was broke and bamboozled, Jeremy had duped me into signing a settlement that wasn't linked to the Retail Price Index, which is obfuscatory legal jargon for 'You're only getting a hundred quid a week no matter how much the cost of living goes up.'

When I discovered his treachery, I emailed Jeremy immediately. 'I obviously didn't sign in ink, but in my own *spilt blood*, you bastard!' When he didn't bother to reply, I realized that my darling husband had removed the word 'human' from his resumé. And it hardened me, I know it did. Merlin's diagnosis, coupled with Jeremy's betrayal, made me defensive. Pretty soon I had developed so many survival instincts I could easily have set off through the jungle with just a knife and a water bottle, my face set into a commando's grimace and impressively smeared with mud as camouflage against marauding predators. I became so tough that it got to the point where I would have received the news that I was about to be mugged with the mild annoyance of one who would have preferred to have got a parking ticket.

'Sarcasm can so easily segue into carcinoma,' my mother warned. According to Mum, the reason I'd lost my faith in humankind was because my ex turned out to be a megalomaniacal tosser with an ego the size of Ben Nevis. Only she didn't put it quite so nicely.

To spite Jeremy and to help me get over him, I decided to shear off my mane of long auburn hair which he so loved.

When Phoebe found me in her bathroom hacking at my locks with a pair of her kids' project scissors, she gave me a long, concerned look in her bathroom mirror. 'Maybe you need to take your mind off things. What about a hobby or something?'

'Well, I've tried meditation, Pilates, pottery, tango, musical societies and ski holidays . . . but I find pure alcohol is the best escape.' I swigged at the glass of red I'd positioned atop the toilet cistern.

My sister rubbed her soft knob of nose. Phoebe's strength is never allowing any room for negative thought. The light around her seems warmer somehow. Alluring. She's like a beacon I can ignite at any time. What's lovely about my sister is that she never arrives anywhere gloating 'Here I am!' She arrives saying '*There* you are! How *are* you?' I could never say anything nasty about my sister and, believe me, of late I'd developed a fondness for saying nasty things about everybody.

'Lucy,' she scolded, taking the scissors from my hand. 'I admire your stoicism. But I also know that you're putting on a bit of an act.'

'You're right . . . In real life I'm an eighteen-year-old catwalk model.'

She swivelled me by the shoulders to face her. 'Sometimes you can seem so in charge, so in control, that it can be hard to help you. But if you keep suppressing your anxieties, one day there'll be this volcanic eruption and you'll turn into a petrol-sniffing, shop-lifting, Nazi-memorabilia collector or something . . . Maybe you should go and talk to someone . . . ?'

'A shrink! Good God, no! I saw a shrink once. She told me that the typical symptoms of stress are eating chocolate, boozing and buying irrational clothes on impulse. The woman is obviously bonkers. I mean, that's my idea of a perfect day.'

'But Lulu, you've changed. You've become so . . . defensive. Brittle. Ruthless even.'

'Ruthless? Ha! I'm not ruthless! . . . Although, after I kill Jeremy and bury him in the garden, do you think I can claim him as a dependant?'

Phoebe's eyes widened in alarm. I thumped her affectionately in the arm. 'Come on, Pheebs, Stalin or Mugabe are ruthless. Not *me* . . . Why is it that a woman only has to stamp her stiletto once to be compared to a murdering psychopath?' I sighed and sagged on to the side of the bath. 'I just can't bear it when people say to me, simperingly, "I'm so sorry about your son." It makes me want to hide away.'

We were looking at each other in the mirror now. Phoebe has brown eyes, thin, arched brows, a smattering of freckles dusting her cheeks and centre-parted, wheat-blonde hair which curls around her face. I am olive-skinned and green-eyed. Our only similarity is our mouths. Jeremy always said my mouth resembled a split persimmon, red and luscious. I saw my sister's mouth curve into a compassionate smile and her eyes moisten. She briskly set about hiding her sympathy by fussing over my appearance.

'Lucy darling, if you're going to cut your hair off, let me soften your look a little, okay?' Having always been the practical, capable sister, she started snipping. 'Cut hair too short and you look like a Russian shot-putter cum Gestapo wardress. Too long and you look like an organic puppet-theatre manager . . . You need a Cleopatra-style square bob. Not blunt, because that could look too hard for your features, but slightly graduated . . . Maximum style with minimum effort . . . Oh,' she exclaimed, examining her handiwork fifteen minutes later. 'See how a bob brings out your beautiful eyes and high cheekbones and lovely long neck?'

I opened my eyes then glanced up from the auburn pool of my own hair around my ankles into the mirror

– and was surprised. The finished effect was clean and sculptural. 'Now let's tackle your brows, which,' she laughed, 'look like they've escaped from Afghanistan. I have seen more ruly caterpillars. *"Is ruly a word, Miss?"'* she imitated in the voice of one of my whiny pupils.

Phoebe had topiarized and tamed her own once-bushy brows into pencil-thin parentheses which gave her a slightly surprised expression, even when she wasn't. My fastidious sister set to with tweezers, triggering a volley of sneezes from me. 'There! You see? If you create more of an arch, it just makes your eyes seem so much more open.'

But my eyes had been opened too much of late. I hadn't wanted much out of life. A quality set of bed-linen and a solid set of saucepans. A loving husband and a happy baby. Was that too much to ask?

Heartache and anger consumed me for months. I wasn't exactly on the edge of the world, but I could definitely see it from here. It hurt every time I thought about Jeremy, like a nerve exposed to the air. Maybe I did need to see a doctor? *'Patient has absentee husband and handicapped child, but no other abnormalities.'*

But, eventually, there was a gradual blurring of Jeremy's memory. He became like a watercolour left out in the rain, smudged and faded.

And then there was just Merlin and me.

4

Asparagus Syndrome

By now Merlin and I were starring in our very own prime-time medical drama. All that was missing was the luxury trailer and the £60,000 per episode pay cheque.

Once Merlin had started talking again aged four, he just babbled away as garrulously as a brook. Words streamed out of him like traffic, a collision of stories and tangential, lateral lunacy. Trying to teach Merlin to do anything practical, like tie a shoelace or wash his face, and you'd have thought I was instructing him on how to fuel a nuclear reactor. He just stood looking at me in a dazed way. Yet by five he was asking me if he could keep a nit as a pet and if it was mandatory for caterpillars to turn into butterflies and whether God knew the Easter Bunny's phone number and did they chat with the Tooth Fairy and, if so, who invented

God? When his tooth fell out, aged six, he practically produced a PowerPoint presentation on primary orthodontics.

By seven, he wanted to know whether or not he could cry underwater. By eight he had memorized most of Hamlet's speeches and assured me that if Macbeth had booked in with a 'talking doctor' he wouldn't have killed Duncan.

'Why do people call psychiatrists "shrinks"? They should be called expanders,' he informed me earnestly.

My sister's son Dylan enquired if it would be okay to ask Merlin for some information on Shakespeare for an assignment. 'Would Merlin mind?' Asking Merlin for information on Shakespeare was like asking a haemophiliac for a pint of blood. He haemorrhaged information. Three hours later my nephew came staggering out from Merlin's bedroom, panting for air, food, sustenance.

By the age of nine, Merlin's encyclopedic obsession switched to the Beatles, Bob Dylan, the Big Bopper, Big Bill Brunsey and Buddy Holly. He knew more about them than their own mothers.

By nine and a half, he'd developed a fanatical fascination with the history of cricket. My son was Wikipedia with a pulse. I stopped keeping a diary, as Merlin's formidable memory meant he could recall where I was at any time on any given day of any given year ... And yet this same boy couldn't remember how to toast a piece of bread or brush his teeth. He also became hysterical about insects. You'd think a blowfly was an F1-11 jet trying to land on him, the way he screamed and thrashed. And the continuing panic-stricken frenzy that ensued whenever I tried to dress him would lead you to deduce I'd soaked his clothes in acid. Then there was his wardrobe fetish. While the rest of the male population seemed to be coming *out* of the closet, Merlin was determined to go *in*. The linen press became his favourite place to think. I often found him curled up between the pillowslips, writing numbers from one to infinity. He told me he was shunning sunlight, in case his brain melted. Dyspraxia, which is like physical dyslexia, meant that he couldn't sequence. Directions scrambled in his brain as soon as they'd been given. Remembering how to turn on the kettle or turn off the heating was like hieroglyphics to him. The poor kid regularly became so perturbed he'd hit his head on the floor until it bled. And I was the person upon whom he took out his frustrations. He'd hit and kick and bite me and then, at other times, cling to me as though lost on the big seas. Which we were, really. Cast adrift with no rescue or shore in sight, aboard HMS *Autism*.

But just when I'd resigned myself to accepting that my son was mentally impaired, he would dazzle me with his sudden aptitude. 'Why is there no other word for "synonym"?' and 'If onions make you cry, are there vegetables that make you happy?' and 'Is a harp just a nude piano?' and 'What is the speed of dark?' were typical Merlin-type questions. While teachers at his infant and primary schools made regular assessments that Merlin's IQ was below average, Merlin's own assessment was 'my vernacular capacities outstrip my peer group.'

In other words, I didn't worry about my son *all* the time – only on the days when the sun came up.

Living with Merlin was like living in a minefield. You never knew when you would touch a tripwire. When over-excited my son talked so fast, faster than an auctioneer on amphetamines ... Then anxiety would prowl through his psyche like a predator and he'd dissolve into a torrential downpour of tears, followed by hours of mute misery. One bleak day when he was about nine, he tried to throw himself off a window ledge. I talked him inside and then had all the windows locked shut, making our home even more like a prison. Which only increased my other anxiety – creeping loneliness.

With my flight attendant sister and globetrotting mother away so often, I tried to see more of my friends. But when all your friends' children are thriving and succeeding and getting A*s at school and going on ski trips and enjoying work experience at *Vogue* magazine and top barristers' chambers, it's like starving to death outside a banquet hall with the delicious aroma wafting through the windows to drive you to utter madness.

As for Merlin's friend front, well, basically I just pimped for my son. I bribed the kids from the council estates with free cinema tickets, cakes, trips to the zoo and funfairs. I tempted them to our house with a trampoline, table football and lemonade on tap. Merlin often ended up playing side by side with these kids – 'parallel play', the experts called it. He would make no eye contact and sit rocking much of the time, but at least there was the façade of friendship.

When he was five I'd had Merlin 'statemented' – which meant that he had a statement of special needs from the education department. Even though I couldn't bear to have his butterfly-like idiosyncrasies analysed and pinned down, this 'statement' promised to 'fulfil his educational needs'. The local education authority decided this meant 'mainstreaming' my son in a normal school, with two hours of support every day from an untrained, twenty-year-old assistant with the IQ of a houseplant. Even though the girl's only degree was in Advanced Eyeliner Application and she no doubt dotted the i's on her CV, the school hired her because she was cheap.

In other words, 'mainstreaming' meant shoving him into an already overcrowded inner-city classroom with the ambiance of a Dickensian debtors' prison along with forty other kids, many of whom were refugees and didn't speak English, including three other children with special needs (dysphasia, aphasia and dyspraxia – which sounded like three Russian models who'd formed a pop trio), plus *their* untrained helpers, meaning there were now forty-five people in the tiny classroom. A sardine would have felt claustrophobic in there. You needed a lubricant to get in.

The teacher, who was trying to master rudimentary Somali, Hindi, Zairian, Romanian, Russian, Tswana, Arabic and probably a few words in Klingon, was clearly headed for the loony bin. By the time Merlin turned ten, the only subject at which he was excelling was 'phoning in sick'. He could get an A in phoning in sick.

Still, it wasn't all bad. Merlin could be extremely, unintentionally funny. Describing the vacuum cleaner as a 'broom with a stomach' and a caterpillar as a 'worm wearing fancy dress' or asking how 'spies know they've run out of invisible ink' or explaining to his art teacher that 'mauve' was simply 'pink trying to be purple' made me laugh out loud.

But his bedroom had became a hard-hat area. Most mornings I had to drag him, shrieking and punching, out of his pyjamas and into school. We always planned to leave the house by 7.15 a.m. . . . and, like clockwork, we were usually out the door by 8.35. My son hated school so much he often just wouldn't get out of the car. Was it possible to have a car surgically removed, I would wonder, slumped on the kerb with my head in my hands, Merlin welded to the seat within.

'Only fish should be in schools. School doesn't work for me. It doesn't suit me. It's a prison for children.

How can you make me sit in that torture chamber all day?' he'd wail, his eyes the burning blue of a gas flame. A mix of bafflement and betrayal contorted his face into a daily mask of dismay. The one person he trusted was forcing him into a place where he was taunted for being different and beaten up so badly that, on one occasion, he needed stitches in his head. He once came home with a sign sticky-taped to his back reading 'Kick me, I'm a retard.' Trying to protect him was like trying to stop ice melting in the Gobi desert. Still, I had to keep trying.

Sending your special needs child to a normal school is as pointless as giving a fish a bath. But waiting lists for special schools have queues so long there are Cro-Magnon families at the front. For years I'd been lobbying and pleading with the local council to meet the obligations of Merlin's statement. As it was, with his assigned, untrained helper off sick or, as I suspected, back in rehab, and with no money for a replacement due to cutbacks, my son now spent the long school day silent, in the shadows. Other children were striving to learn maths and grammar. My son was striving to make himself invisible. If only there were an exam for sitting in the back of the classroom doing shadow hand-puppet workshops, then the kid would be top of the whole school, I'm not kidding you.

In time I understood that an educational 'statement' is really just an adroit piece of jargonized sophistry which promises much but delivers little. The system is designed with bureaucratic speed bumps to slow down a parent's progress. I filled in forests of forms and saw squadrons of educational psychologists. The technical term for this process is 'being passed from pillar to post'. I kissed so much arse, my lips chafed. Such officials are second only to mammographers in their ability to inflict pain.

Meanwhile, I kept on bankrupting myself with experts who swished in and out of doors in their white coats. But all the doctors with their stethoscopic minds couldn't really diagnose my son. The word 'Asperger's' was now being bandied about.

'Asperger's is a form of autism, but at the high-functioning end of the spectrum,' it was explained to me at £245 an hour. 'People with Asperger's are often of above-average intelligence. They have fewer problems with speech but still have difficulties under-standing and processing social situations.'

I burst with optimism. It felt like getting an airline upgrade. Or a prison reprieve. Or choking in a restaurant and it's George Clooney who gives you mouth-to-mouth. It also proved Jeremy wrong. It had been worth spending all that money on specialists. (My son's naïve but oddly perceptive definition of a specialist is simply a doctor whose patients never get ill at night or at the weekends.)

'Asparagus Syndrome', as Merlin called it, definitely explained why, despite showing many signs of autism, like the misreading of emotion and repetitive, compulsive, ritualistic behaviour, my son was always bounding up to me with Labrador-like affection, percolating with chit-chat.

But my euphoria was short-lived. Every expert agreed on one point – only in a small classroom with specialist teaching could Merlin ever reach his potential. Doctors, nurses, teachers, therapists, social workers, ed psychs and council officials all agreed that this was the case. But nobody wanted to pay for it.

All I could do was step up my lobbying of the local educational authority. (I was now purchasing arse-kissing ChapStick by the containershipful.) Finally, aged ten and a half, his name came up on some mysterious waiting list. Merlin and I practically skipped with joy to a grey office building in a grimy Southwark backstreet for the big interview. The electronic door *pssschsss*ed open. We watched people scurrying down a warren of corridors with white-rabbit expressions. Eventually we were greeted by a forty-year-old woman with a mopey face whose nametag read 'La–ah'. 'The dash is not silent,' Ladashah explained loudly.

She ushered us into a beige office, where we sat beside a pencil-poised male trainee. In some futile attempt to relieve the penal-institution atmosphere, La–ah's desk was smothered in Smurfs, Gonks and stuffed animals. It was to this menagerie I tried to explain how my son's understanding of the world was spinning round and round like a coin tossed in the air.

I wanted Mopy Face, the trainee and her Gonks to comprehend that Merlin's mind was a flutter click snapshot roll of Shakespearean quotes, cricket scores, music, facts, figures, dates and numbers, numbers, numbers – but numbers which didn't really add up to anything, as yet.

Throughout the consultation, Merlin gave the smile of an angel, benign but remote, the conversation going not over his head but around it somehow. His only contribution was to enquire what colour a Smurf would go if choked to death.

It was impossible to pinpoint the exact tone of the official's smile, but surely La–ah, with the non-silent dash, could see beneath my son's shifting surface to the brilliance below? But the colourless dough of her face and cold, indifferent gaze could have won her a bit part in *A Zombie Ate My Baby*.

'Well, thank you for coming.' She looked at my son as though he were some strange science experiment. 'There'll be a multi-agency meeting to discuss your case and then we'll get back to you as soon as a decision is made.'

I knew from my time in the teaching profession that a 'multi-agency meeting' is a gathering of Important People who think that individually they can do nothing . . . and together decide that nothing can be done.

'Can't we attend this meeting . . . ?' I asked.

'No, I'm afraid not.' She said this as though it were an edict from the Vatican.

'Why? . . . I mean, murderers at parole meetings get fairer hearings.'

La–ah was not used to parental insubordination. Her eyes slid over me like cold egg yolk. 'Don't you think discussing your child in front of him constitutes emotional abuse?' She threw a meaningful glance in the science experiment's direction. Merlin sat upright with rigid grace as he was dissected.

'*Emotional abuse* is leaving us out of the decision-making process.' I too glanced at my son. It was as though his face was a burden to wear. He kept re-arranging his facial features into smiles or expressions of absorption as though practising being human. 'Well . . . okay. I could always come on my own,' I conceded.

La–ah's nose, which was ample and slightly pocked, was now seriously out of joint. 'We often find that mothers self-diagnose. Which not only clouds the issue but is usually the very cause of the child's emotional delays . . . Perhaps the divorce is to blame? His behaviour could merely be a result of parentis incompetus,' she condescended with light malice. 'Which raises child-protection concerns . . .' the official added ominously, throwing her weight around, of which there was a hell of a lot. La–ah was the perfect weight . . . for a 25-foot-tall woman.

It took every ounce of self-restraint not to beat her to death with one of her beanie babies. 'Look, I'm a teacher myself,' I entreated, sick of the sound of my own pleading voice. 'Overcrowded classrooms demand conformity. Children on the autism spectrum are complex. Mainstreaming them doesn't work ... And getting help is a postcode lottery.'

But being white and middle class put us at the bottom of her list. If only I were a one-legged, lesbian, epileptic, agoraphobic Inuit who was also afraid of heights, I thought bitterly.

'There are two million children in Britain – that's one in five – with special needs.' A glance at her watch signalled that it was time for me to leave. 'The government believes that many of these children are wrongly classed as having learning difficulties to boost schools' league table scores, secure extra money or cover up poor teaching.' When I didn't take the hint she lumbered up from her desk and wrenched open the door. 'Very often a child's difficulties stem from problems in the home ...' she concluded coldly. This was a woman who curled her lip for a living.

In the corridor outside, a row of empty chairs lined up against the wall like a firing squad. After the interview, I sat there deflated for a good ten minutes. No doubt my ex-husband's New and Improved lover Audrey would have used the time productively to do 200 triceps dips and 3,010 bench presses, but I just watched the other dejected mothers filing past me. They all had the cheery look of people who've been wrongly condemned to a life sentence in a Congolese prison. The day was damp and dreary, grey as a graveyard. From behind La–ah's door came the indistinct murmur of voices deciding my son's future. Despair welled in my chest. I was failing my son. When it came to parenting, I obviously needed to wear a paper hat marked 'trainee'.

During the four-week wait for the department's verdict, I felt so relaxed I was only changing my underwear every half an hour or so. Minutes crawled past on their hands and knees gasping for water while we waited for the coveted placement.

When the letter with the cellophane window finally plopped on to the mat, I tore it open. Stark black type explained that there were just not enough places to go round at this time. My arms flopped at my sides. I began squeaking like a lost kitten. My eyes began to burn and my chin trembled. I packed Merlin into our decrepit VW, barrelled towards the Thames, double-parked and stormtrooped back into Mopey Face's building. Her office exhaled a stale, exhausted breath.

La–ah looked up, startled. 'Do you have an appointment?'

'An intelligent person, or even a reasonably bright fungus, can see that my son has special needs,' I blurted, tossing her letter of rejection on to the table. 'Unless you are wearing autism filters on your glasses, that is.'

'*Do* you have an *appointment*?' Mopey Face kept repeating like a dalek.

Merlin's expression was one of dizzying incomprehension. He gave the woman his famous candid stare, the pale-blue eyes wide, then frowned as though mentally calculating whether e really did equal mc^2. The kid could have been cracking the human genome for all I knew. My son was on the same planet as the rest of us, but in a different world.

'I'm at my wits' end . . . and it hasn't taken me that long to get here, either,' I carried on caustically. Merlin's now startled expression alerted me to the fact that I must have been talking more loudly than I realized. Loudly? Hell, judging by the amount of people gathering by the open door, I think I must have sounded as though I was in the final stages of labour.

Mopey Face nodded, but from a great distance. Like all flat-shoed, pudding-haircut bureaucrats, she did a great line in sympathetic head tilts and nodding. She could have been employed on the back shelf of a car, in lieu of a plastic dog. 'Well, I'm sure you can appreciate that there are a lot of children on our books' – her voice had a peculiar ventriloquial quality, as though someone else was pulling her strings – 'and only so many places on offer. The government wants to take at least 170,000 children off the special needs register.'

This made no sense to me, possibly because I've never been bludgeoned over the head repeatedly with a blunt instrument. 'But how can you take him off the special needs register when he has special needs?'

'We also think mainstreaming is a viable system.' She canted her head once more and kept on with the nodding. 'And possibly the best option for . . .' she glanced down at my crumpled rejection letter, 'Merlin . . .'

'The best option for Merlin is to find a place where he won't be beaten up or left staring out of the window all day. I know times are tough, but what a waste of his extraordinary intellect. With the right teaching, this is a child who could contribute to society.' My anger was bitter enough to taste. Unused to my raised voice, Merlin's smile was now flickering on and off like a faulty light bulb.

'Well, I'm sorry. But due to cutbacks, your son cannot be re-schooled at this juncture.'

'Really? Well, even though my son hasn't been accepted into a special school, which we've been end-lessly promised for five bloody years, I feel no resentment towards the education authority, who are obviously a *bunch of hypocritical twats*!!'

Watching his mother transmogrify into Attila the Hun made Merlin's knee jerk nervously, like the terrified beating of an insect's wing.

'Of course, if you're not coping' – the dough-faced woman stuck out her many chins and the hammocks of her arm fat wobbled with indignation as she reached for her phone – 'I could contact social services . . .'

Oh, was there anything as much fun as being

condescended to by a woman who obviously uses her body as a repository for fast food?

'I notice that he has quite a few bruises on his arms . . .' she noted menacingly.

Outside the window, the grey winter sky was low and bulging with dampness, but I was red-faced with indignation and rage. 'The bruises are from where he punches himself, through frustration about how much he hates his bloody awful school.'

'Many children who exhibit challenging behaviour end up on child protection plans, and care proceedings often follow,' said La–ah, with sinister sincerity. 'Violent behaviour means your son will be made the subject of a DoL – Deprivation of Liberty order – and taken to a care unit . . .'

I wanted to suggest that she sit on the paper shredder while it was going full speed, or perhaps just go bobbing for piranhas, but instead took Merlin's shaking hand in mine and strode to freedom, feeling her righteous gaze on the nape of my neck.

On the drive home I was in grave danger of feeling seriously sorry for myself. I could definitely compete in the Women's Long-distance Cross-bearing Competition. Life had lost its humour. Hell, the evening news was getting more laughs than me. '*Think negative and you have nothing to lose*' became my motto. Even my imaginary friend found me dull and ran off to play with somebody else. I reminded myself that I had a lot to be grateful for – Merlin wasn't vegetative, incontinent or in a wheelchair. But he still needed and deserved help and, if I didn't fight for his rights, who would? With the onslaught of cutbacks, kids with less severe disabilities like Asperger's or autism were losing out in the scramble for funds, which meant a future wasting away in a bedsit on benefits. I tried to rally my flagging spirits. Perhaps my luck would change? If so, I wouldn't just need a rabbit's foot but a whole *hare* dangling off a key-chain. But then, why bloody well bother? After all, it's not as though the rabbit's foot worked for the poor old rabbit.

To lift my mood, I spent an hour in front of one of those Jerry Springer-type 'I'm pregnant by my own son who is really an alien' TV shows, just to be reminded that there were people out there far worse off than us. And it calmed me, it really did. Our little drama wouldn't even rate on the Oprah-o-meter.

Relieved to be home again in 'our castle', as Merlin called our humble home, he pranced into the living room as though fresh from the Grand National. 'So, Mum,' he exclaimed, exuberantly, 'are you living the dream?'

The incongruity of his query made me splutter into a chortle.

'Mum, I have something on my mind I need to talk to you about . . .' Merlin lowered his voice and looked at me with searching eyes.

I girded my loins for a serious inquisition on his psychological condition, Deprivation of Liberty orders or his missing father. 'Yes, darling,' I replied gravely.

'Would you rather be buoyant or flamboyant?'

It was definitely a question I'd never been asked before. With his sky-blue eyes, wistful and wondering expression, blond curls and ruby-red lips, Merlin looked like an angel who'd fallen out of the frame of a Botticelli painting. 'Flamboyant,' I decided, and laughed out loud.

To celebrate our flamboyancy, I told him we could eat our spaghetti bolognese in front of the television. But just when I did actually start to feel more buoyant, a quick channel flick plunged me back into despair. The low, seductive voice of Tawdry Hepburn oozed through the TV screen and looped across the living room. This was how the husband-poaching predator lassoed her prey. My eyes darted to the screen and there she was, the curvaceous little writher, writhing after her own success with every sinew in her protein-only, no-carbs, silicone-coated, beautifully buff body. For the delectation of male viewers, she provocatively licked crème fraîche from her manicured fingertips before running her tongue over a hand-rolled sausage. '*Now, add a soupçon of innuendo, a pinch of double entendre and start stirring, until simmering.*'

Sick to my stomach, I watched as she batted her eye-lashes – lashes so verdant I suspected lost Amazonian tribes to be lurking there – and fluffed up her breasts in their cups. Breast-fluffing was a mannerism Tawdry employed to ensure that she was the centre of male attention at all times. As she displayed her latest gourmet concoction, I stared glumly at the bowl of spag bol on my lap. It looked as though something had eaten it already. It was clear that my only option was to walk the city streets and lie down in a few chalked outlines to see which one would fit.

When I told Merlin's teacher that I'd failed to find him a placement, she beamed at my son and said, 'Well, that's great, as I wouldn't want to lose him.' But her smile was thin and reticent. Like most people, she was wary of Merlin, as though he were benignly radio-active. 'Have you . . . considered home schooling?' she wheedled, a little desperately.

When Merlin played a football match and broke an arm – unfortunately, not his own but the arm of the school bully, who vowed vengeance – I knew that I had to get him out of there no matter what. I sat down with my bank statements.

I'm an English teacher and not that good at maths. I spend half the time worrying about addition, half the time worrying about subtraction and half the time worrying about division. As a kid I was more terrified of times tables than of werewolves. But even a math-ematical dullard like me knew that there was no way I could make my finances stretch to a private education. How could I make a quick buck? I only had two realistic options: become a prostitute or do a bank robbery. Obviously I could earn a fortune from my swimwear modelling, but was put off by the amount of waxing . . . If only sarcasm were a bankable commodity. Then I'd be rich as Croesus. Perhaps I could ask my head teacher for an advance on my salary – an advance of, say, *ten years*. As my mother had spent the last of Dad's death dollars before Jeremy left me, there was only one person to whom I could turn. As events go, I was looking forward to it only slightly more than I would have my own death by stoning in Tehran.

5

My Family and Other Aliens

Jeremy's mother glanced at my dusty skirting boards and cobwebbed light fittings and the crumbs lying around the toaster in a little landslide with the condescending contempt of a marchioness visiting the home of a plague-riddled serf. Although Veronica is the type of cook who boils vegetables for about a *month*, when I offered her packet biscuits instead of home-baked her eyebrows lifted high in fastidious disdain. My ex-mother-in-law's visits had always made me feel like a welfare case, but now even more so.

It had been six years since Merlin and I had seen her. After my son's diagnosis was confirmed, his paternal grandparents had become magisterially uninterested. Autism was a non-negotiable flaw. The Beauforts were not the endearingly eccentric, kipper-breathed, windswept and interesting toffs with comedy comb-overs who won boy scout badges in Trouser Tenting. No, these were the hard-bitten, born-to-rule, survival-of-the-fittest, landed-gentry types who ate Hail 'n' Hearty Cream of Gristle soup and Split Pea and Road Kill bisque, referred to their varicose veins as nature's pinstripes and didn't give a hoot that driving down the cobbled lanes of the local village with Bambi's mother strapped to the fenders of their Range Rovers might traumatize small children for ever.

I had never eaten anything at their home that they hadn't bred, stalked, snared, shot, plucked, stuffed or roasted with home-grown herbs and then gnawed from the bone. They culled things. They got rid of the runt of the litter. There was no sentiment about it. Derek Beaufort had the loving, affectionate nature of a piece of petrified wood. So it was no shock that, after the divorce, Merlin and I had been simply excised, as you would a tumour. But now, as my ex-mother-in-law gazed at my ten-year-old son, she could see that some of her genes whispered in his veins. Jeremy's genetic echo was right there before her, and I glimpsed her shock as she registered the fact. Although blond, Merlin was Jeremy in bonsai – slender, tall, tousle-haired, with the same flashing electric-blue eyes.

Merlin was the first to speak. 'Don't you find it amazing that you're my grandma?' He gave her a smile full of big, innocent teeth.

Veronica (better known as Moronica in my family

because of her obstinate stupidity) forced a saccharine smile in his direction. 'Hello, dear.'

'Oh! Don't give that cheesy grin.' Merlin flinched. 'Please don't smile at me! It unnerves me. That cringey grin. Ugh!' He covered his face, as though being zapped by death rays from a science-fiction stun gun.

It was Veronica's turn to recoil. She flushed red in the face, as if scalded.

'Merlin, why don't you go and write some of your numbers?' My curious son had taken to writing cricket scores for hours and hours. He'd memorized every player's career, every innings, run and test result from every major match ever played on the planet. He was as accurate as a computer . . . and yet still couldn't tell the time. My ex-mother-in-law watched aghast as I led Merlin into the hall, where he scrambled inside the linen cupboard. I closed the hall door and turned to face her.

'There are times when I truly believe Merlin to be an alien,' I said lightly. 'Sometimes, I feel that I didn't give birth to him at all but found him under a spaceship and raised him as my own.'

Veronica balanced her bulk on the edge of her seat and jigged her fat foot with impatience. Her legs were veined and bubbled, like blue and lumpy knitting. Her feet, more at home in wellies, were squeezed into tiny shoes, the ankles ballooning over the leather like cake mixture that has run over the edges of the tin. I sat opposite her and tucked my legs up underneath

THE BOY WHO FELL TO EARTH

me, to lend an informal mood to the proceedings.

'Single-parenting a kid with Asperger's Syndrome, which is the Latin medical term for "Your guess is as good as mine", takes the combined skills of a trapeze artist, a nuclear physicist, Freud, a car mechanic and an animal behaviourist,' I laughed, topping up her tea. (*Was I laying it on too thick? . . . Who was I* **kidding**? *I'd use a garden trowel if I could.*) I smiled to show that I was inviting friendship and intimacy and offered up the plate of biscuits.

She bit into a HobNob, the crumbs clinging to her lipstick. 'Nobody said motherhood was easy,' she replied cautiously. With her composure regained, Veronica's smile was once again as lacquered as her nails.

'Merlin's bright, don't get me wrong,' I went on, 'but his neural circuitry is just wired up differently. I live in a constant state of terror about what he might do. At the school fête, he's the one who will end up pulling over the table of juice or talking to the dog. My only survival technique is to turn around innocently and say to anyone in the near vicinity, "Who is this child and why is he calling me Mum?"'

Once again, my little attempt to charm her with humour was met with a ceilingward lifting of the eyebrows in finicky disapproval. Abandoning any hope of banter, I took a deep breath, like a diver going under, and tried a more serious tack. 'And then there's all his anxieties. He's worried the radio waves coming in through the microwave will warp his brain ... He insists on walking around the kitchen in a certain way for good luck ... And he takes everything literally. When I talk about the good scissors – "Has anyone seen my good scissors?" – he thinks there are bad ones, with evil, murderous tendencies. When I say "You'll have to fight me for the last cupcake," he squares up. Literally ... When I asked him to lock the door, as burglars might steal my jewellery, then came home to find the door open, he explained, perplexed, "Well, why would men want jewellery?"'

I flumped back in my lounge chair to await some sympathy.

But my ex-mother-in-law had mastered the upper-class art of remaining stoic in the face of someone else's misfortune. 'How ... quirky' was all she said.

'Calling my son "quirky" is like saying that a meteor hurtling towards earth is only a little life-threatening. "Quirky" is the kind way of putting it, Veronica. "Socially awkward" is another. Other mums get Mother's Day presents. Well, apart from the fact that I have no husband around to remind Merlin that it's Mother's Day ...' – (*I trowelled away. I was positively from Trowel and Co.*) – 'I constantly get notes from school suspending him for bad behaviour. Like this week. He interrupted class to ask the teacher if she was worried about the fact that glaciers move. Wasn't she concerned that glaciers had developed the ability to creep around? What if one stalked him? . . . You see, I think that's quite amusing in a tangential way. But his teacher thought it downright mutinous.' As did my ex-mother-in-law, by the way she rattled her cup irritatedly into the saucer. 'But he can also be hilariously charming,' I post-scripted, more positively. 'It's just that he has no filter. He always says exactly what he's thinking.'

The opposite was true of Veronica. She was trying to look empathetic, but her expression remained pinched. She wore the look of a woman who's just been offered a plate of lightly fried bat's brains on bubonic beef, in a nice nitroglycerine sauté.

'I know Jeremy has been paying child support . . .' (I had to bite my tongue not to add, *But not too bloody much . . . Let me get the latest cheque so that you can experience what an oily rag smells like.*) 'But what we didn't take into account at the time of the divorce is that Merlin is always going to be as dependent as a baby. I will always have to cut his toenails and sand-wiches, clean out his earwax and backpack. A mother's job is to hatch, match and dispatch. Correct? But I'll be bound to my son for the rest of my life – in the role of some indentured servant.'

'Perhaps he'll grow out of it?' Veronica volunteered crisply. 'Boys are notoriously late developers.'

My guffaw was like a saucepan lid dropped on a terracotta floor. The sudden burst of it made my ex-mother-in-law jump. 'With a kid like Merlin you can never delude yourself into thinking that he's behaving a little more normally . . . because that's the time he'll set fire to the headmaster's hair. Mind you, I'm sure he would improve greatly, if I could *just get him into the right school . . .*'

I let the statement float in the air like a verbal parachute. When she said nothing, I pulled the ripcord. 'The school he's at now is just a holding area for the nearest prison. The curriculum involves how to read, write and do a drug deal . . . Oh, well. At least it will teach him metric.' I smiled.

Still nothing. The door squeaked open and Merlin bounded back in holding a plate of cold fish fingers he'd retrieved from the fridge. He presented them to his grandmother with scrupulous courtesy. I'd been teaching him always to offer guests food and drink, even though *he* may not be hungry or thirsty, which was a very difficult concept for someone with Asperger's syndrome. Merlin gave Veronica a lobotomized grin. He'd also, of late, been teaching himself to smile. My heart lurched with affection for my brave little boy.

Veronica's eyebrows did their usual airborne leap towards her hairline. 'Do you think fish fingers are an ideal meal, nutrients-wise?' she demanded in a BBC wartime-broadcast voice. Veronica's most memorable feature is her nose – possibly because she's always looking down it.

'I'd like to be a perfect mother, Veronica, I really

would, but I'm too frantically preoccupied bringing up my son *on my own*,' I replied pointedly.

Merlin gave his grandmother a look that was both polite and sullen, his eyes bright but unreadable beneath an overlong fringe.

'No . . . thank . . . you . . . Merlin.' She separated each word as though he were hard of hearing or had recently arrived from Gdansk, then smiled up at him, which made him cringe all over again. As I steered my son back to the second shelf of the linen press, he looked me straight in the eye and said, with the kind of perspicacity which occasionally took my breath away, 'A smile can be a trick, Mum.'

When I returned to the living room, Veronica was examining a framed picture Merlin had drawn of himself, with a tiny body dwarfed by a huge head, massive ears and eyes and over-sized hands. It was a pictorial expression of his over-stimulated senses. Experts called it 'sensory defensiveness', a profound sensitivity to visual stimuli, smell, taste, touch and sound. Veronica's expression as she examined this clumsy crayon creation was as rigid as an Easter Island statue.

'Dear' – she spoke slowly, as though soothing a small and irascible pet – 'it's obviously terribly hard.' Her words were crisply enunciated, like those of a TV presenter. 'And it's obviously too, too much for you.'

I let down my guard for a moment and replied, genuinely, 'It is. It bloody is. But you know what motherhood is like. Just when you think your tooth-paste tube of devotion is all squeezed out, there comes along another dollop.'

'But seriously, Lucinda . . .' Her eyes shifted around the house, taking in the dust and the debris.

'Lucy,' I corrected her, for, oh, only about the six millionth time in my life. Although I was christened Lucy, she had always introduced me to her friends as Lucinda, to make me sound posh enough for her son.

'What do you think Merlin's prospects are?' The word – 'prospects' – held all the pernickety con-descension of a Victorian aunt.

'Well, if I can get him into a good school – and by that I just mean a school where he isn't mugged, stabbed, sexually propositioned or sold large quantities of Class A drugs on a daily basis – he does have potential and prospects. He's bright and original.' A wave of weariness washed over me. It was time to send the Beauforts on a little excursion – a one-way ticket on a guilt trip.

'Look, I know you and Derek don't like to admit that there's anything wrong with Merlin, because everyone knows that autism and Asperger's are genetic. But have you searched back through the family tree? There must be a few other defective branches? Maybe it would be worth employing a genealogist? . . . That's someone who traces your family back as far as your money will go,' I said, lamely, in an attempt to lighten the awkward atmosphere. 'But I do think it's time to find out why Merlin's like this ... Have there been other idiot savants like him in the Beaufort clan? I mean, take Derek. Highly intelligent, yes, but socially awkward and insular ...'

Medusa-like, Veronica's livid gaze nearly turned me to stone. 'There's absolutely no history of any mental weaknesses on *our* side of the family,' she said categorically, implying that it was my side of the egg-quation which had brought about this chromosomatic catastrophe. 'What history of mental illness is there in *yours*?'

'Well, my father was a sexually incontinent B-grade actor who took up tantric yoga late in life and died astride a Polish prostitute and part-time druid priest-ess and my mother then frittered away his life insurance globetrotting with toy boys ... but otherwise, no, all relatively sane in the relatives department.'

'Are you certain?' Her voice was furiously measured. 'Actually, this is the very reason I agreed to come here today. I had a rather distressing call from some kind of ... *social worker*.' She used invisible tongs to hold the words to the light.

'The educational psychologist? Yes. I gave her your number to set up an appointment for some family therapy.'

'They were doing some sort of psychological back-ground report. A complete invasion of privacy. As an

MP, Derek is in the public eye. This kind of intrusion is potentially very embarrassing.' She put down her cup with such determination that it wobbled precariously in the saucer.

Ah, yes, I thought to myself. The great parliamentarian Derek Beaufort would not want any shame brought on the family brand. If a tractor could mate with a Doberman, the result of that union would be my former father-in-law.

'There is only one solution to the Merlin problem,' Veronica continued through lips as thin as a paper cut. 'He should be sent away somewhere. I could write you a cheque for £100,000 right now, today – if you let me take Merlin with me and have him looked after properly. In a private care home.' She placed her crocodile-skin handbag on her lap, where it writhed like something alive. She opened its jaws and extracted her chequebook. 'And you could start a new life. Jeremy started again. Why shouldn't you?' Her smile was as sharp and sweet as icing.

I looked at her, agape. 'You're serious?' My heart gave a wrench of protective love and my throat restricted. 'But I'm all Merlin has to keep him from crashing through life like a falling stone.'

'I could make it £200,000.' Her voice rang out harshly in the still room as she snapped open her chequebook. 'There's an institution near us, in the country. So we could visit him . . .'

How kind, I thought. The woman obviously

took skimmed milk with her human kindness.

'Microwaves warping his brain, talking to dogs, evil scissors, punching you to get a cake, violent episodes . . .' The superfluity of Veronica's flesh quivered like custard '. . . It's clear the boy needs professional help.'

If my eyes could shoot out lethal beams like Disney superheroes, she would have been annihilated there and then. My anger boiled over like milk. 'You're trying to *buy* my *son*?'

'Well, it's clear you're not coping.' Jeremy's mother's hooked nose suddenly gave her a hawk-like, predatory air. 'Your anger gives you away. Do you want things to deteriorate to the point where Merlin's taken into care by social workers? Imagine the scandal. You've just told me that you think your son is an alien, that you often pretend he's not your child, that you find him an embarrassment, that you resent the idea of him living with you for ever, as if he were some feudal lord . . . It's clearly impossibly awful for you,' she concluded with calculated cruelty.

I looked at her string of rubies, which I'd earlier admired. They now seemed to cluster around her neck like bubbles of blood. 'Yes, raising Merlin is hard. But it also brings me infinite joy.' Even though my voice was querulous with outrage, I tried to stop my face shattering like glass.

'What about the psychotic episodes? Setting fire to the headmaster's hair? Letting the burglars in? The pages and pages of numbers he writes, like some kind of Rain Man . . .'

I understood the numbers. The numbers provided a vessel Merlin could pour himself into. It gave him a shape. It contained him. But how to explain this to a tweedy, beige battleaxe like Mrs Derek Beaufort? A woman who looked as though she spent her leisure time bludgeoning baby seals?

'In an institution they can get him on to the right kind of medication,' she added.

Yes, I mused. As certified by the Albanian Food and Drug Administration. I squeezed as much hauteur into my voice as possible and replied, 'I don't want to drug my son into submission.'

'There's a very innovative doctor working at our local facility. He's pioneering a new treatment for autistic children. He dissuades them from behaviour deemed dangerous to themselves or to others with the use of electrodes. It's only a two-second electric shock to the skin, no more than thirty times a day.'

I looked at her, dumbfounded. Not even the Hubble telescope could locate this woman's sense of compassion.

'I'm not sending my child away to be tortured! Truth is, I totally blame you for my marriage break-up. If you'd shown Jeremy the love he was owed, if you'd taught him how to communicate instead of banishing him away to boarding school aged seven, where he wasn't even allowed to take his teddy bear, he would never have abandoned me. He just didn't have the emotional maturity to cope. No wonder he moved to America. He just wanted to get as far away from you as possible.'

My ex-mother-in-law gave me a contemptuous gaze, her face screwed up with fury. '£300,000 then.' Her pen was poised above the chequebook. 'I'm only offering because I feel sorry for you, Lucinda.'

'You don't have to feel sorry for *me*. I feel sorry for *you*. And, it's Lucy, by the way, *Moronica*.'

6
The Coven

That went well, I told myself, as I sandblasted the last traces of the ex-mother-in-law's lipstick off the rim of my best china cup. Glancing up, I caught my reflection in a mirrored cabinet. If you look like your passport picture, it's a pretty good indication that you need a holiday. My expression seemed held in place, as if for an invisible photographer. Little fjords had appeared either side of my lips. If I'd glanced in the mirror more often over the last five years, I might have noticed how my mouth had started to turn down and the glint go out of my eyes.

When had my heart started to harden? I hadn't realized that I'd changed so much until I walked right through a department store on Oxford Street and nobody, not one spruiker, offered me a free puff of perfume. But it was only when I screamed at a stranger during the meditation section of my peace and tranquillity yoga class (Phoebe's husband was minding Merlin so I could 'unwind') that I admitted that perhaps I wasn't coping as well as I thought.

'Lucy!' My sister yanked me by my leotard up off the floor and out into the changing rooms. 'What is the matter with you?' she stage-whispered.

'Well, that woman wouldn't move an inch because she wanted to be "close to the plant", which meant that I was contorted in the doorway, with no mat and lying in a tiny patch of somebody else's sweat trying to do a downward dog,' I explained, peeling off my lycra condom.

'So you swore at her?' My incredulous sister flicked on the shower knob and had a perfunctory paddle. 'In the *relaxation* bit?' Keeping her hair out of the jet stream meant craning her neck sideways, which gave her the look of a peeved giraffe.

Later that night, when the Chinese takeaway hadn't been delivered and I rang to demand, 'Where's it coming from exactly? *Beijing*?', my mother was summoned back from her adventures. With Dad's life insurance money all spent, my enterprising mum was now taking National Trust working holidays, where you help to protect some of Britain's most beautiful historic houses. In exchange for labour, the Trust offered her hundreds of different activities, ranging from goat-herding to archaeology. Mum was currently tending the medieval knot garden at Norbury in Derbyshire before heading off to run a food fair at the Godolphin estate in Cornwall. She arrived in a dazzle of May sunshine, decked out in so much animal print she would have blended into the Serengeti.

'I'm sorry I've been away so long, darling,' she said, sitting herself down at the rickety little table in our overgrown garden. 'Now, what's going on?' My mother gazed at me with an expression that was both tender and concerned. 'These outbursts are so out of character, sweet pea.'

It was wine o'clock, so Phoebe cracked a bottle of chardonnay as we half-watched my ten-year-old son re-enacting Shakespearean tragedies with plastic action figures. My mother sighed. 'Lucy, darling, I was just like you, when your father died. I felt that I could never, ever be happy again.'

My mother, who had spent her life tethered by her apron strings to the kitchen, cooking and cleaning and catering for Dad's every thespian whim whilst, more often than not, supporting the family on her librarian's wage, was decimated by his death. It took her a year but she finally found her feet again. 'Life is in two acts,' she'd told me at the time. 'The trick is to survive the interval.' Well, the woman was having a hell of a second act. She was only fifty-three when Dad died, so she decided that instead of having hot flushes, she'd have hot tropical holidays. And who could blame her?

'The secret to happiness, Mother, is limbo-low expectations,' I told her.

'Darling, nobody's saying you should be happy all the time. If you were happy every day of your life you'd be a breakfast television weather presenter,' my mother philosophized. 'But the occasional bout of mirth is allowable, dear, surely?'

'I'm fine,' I stressed.

'Oh, Lulu! You are so schizophrenic,' my exasperated sister butted in. 'You pretend to be all strong and independent, but secretly you're so lonely.'

'Hey,' I jibed. 'I may be schizophrenic but at least I have each other.'

My family didn't even dignify my verbal sidestep with an eye-roll. I didn't mean to hide behind glib comments all the time, but it had become my default setting – a protective shell.

'You've isolated yourself from friends,' Phoebe went on. 'I mean, when Mum and I are away, who are you going to call if you wake up in a hotel room with an overdosed gigolo?'

'I would *never* wake up in a hotel room with an overdosed gigolo. Do you know me at *all*??? . . . And I'm not lonely. I'm thinking of joining a new social network called Faceless Book – for people of a certain age who believe that their private lives are no one else's fucking business.'

I could almost hear Phoebe poking out her tongue behind my back. My mother gave her Resigned Mother look.

'Dear, what I diagnose is chronic AAADD –

Age-activated Affection Deficit Disorder. You have got to start dating again. Your bed, my love, is emptier than a supermodel's refrigerator.'

'Dating again?' I cringed. 'But I haven't done anything wrong! Why must I be punished?'

'Not just for you, darling. But for Merlin. He needs a male influence in his life.'

'Not having to worry about men any more is the secret benefit of death,' I reasoned.

'Yeah, sure.' Phoebe poured more wine into my glass. 'You love being single . . . except for the no sex, no late-night laughter in bed, no rubbish taken out for you and no big and burly love god to hit the burglar over the head. Yes, it must be joy. Paradise.'

'My darling daughter, how do you ever expect to meet Mr Right if you don't go on the odd date?'

I looked at my mother and sister in alarm. The reason I'm such a pessimist is because my family are such bloody optimists. 'Mr Right? Who the hell are you all of a sudden, Mother – Julie Andrews? The idea that there's someone for everyone is mathematically impossible. I found my Mr Right and he ended up being a Right Bastard. As did yours,' I added.

My mother talks with her hands. When she sprained her wrist whilst skydiving (don't ask) it was as though she'd developed a speech impediment. She folded her hands in her lap now and looked down at them, and I instantly regretted my barbed outburst. What was wrong with me? When had I soured so? What happened to the frisky, free-spirited girl I used to be? The one who could do handstands whilst yodelling, and (in the right circumstances) naked? The only thing I had faith in now was that there was nothing to have faith in.

Phoebe stroked my mother's arm reassuringly. 'Being hurt by a man doesn't mean a woman has to keep her heart wrapped in crime-scene tape, *does* it, Mum?'

'How *is* Jeremy?' My mother imbued his name with utter contempt.

'Who?' I shrugged. As far as I knew, Jeremy was still living in LA indulging his inalienable right to the pursuit of life, liberty and leggy domestic goddesses. Tawdry's US cable cooking programme had just won some kind of television award, worse luck. It was impossible to avoid the picture of her in the tabloids clasping the statuette to the fluffed-up fleshy soufflé of her breasts.

'But darling,' my mother rallied, gesticulating again, 'it's been over six years since he walked out on you. You're a gorgeous-looking woman, Lulu. Pretty *and* witty. If you would just use your feminine wiles you could . . .'

'Feminine wiles!' I interrupted. '*Feminine wiles* means nothing more than whiling away wasted hours being pathetically feminine. It's not for me.'

'You see what I mean, Mum?' Phoebe sighed. 'She's become so anti-male people are going to start thinking she's a lesbian.'

I snorted with laughter. 'Just because I hate men doesn't make me a lesbian. It makes me a realist.'

'Darling, ours is a happy family,' my mother reprimanded. 'We don't do dour.'

I looked at my mother with love. Since my father's untimely departure, her mantra had become 'Live simply; laugh often; love deeply'. Mine, I suddenly realized, had become 'Live complicatedly; cry often; hate always'.

Phoebe is equally blessed with hopefulness. Ever since we were children, she'd collected wounded birds, frogs, lizards, squirrels . . . then, later, men who were all no-hopers and losers. She put them through college and helped with their visa applications and found them jobs. They all left her eventually, as soon as they'd become strong. Except for her painter-decorator husband. Danny was so devoted to my sister, he'd happily build kennels for all her underdogs.

'You've perfected this kind of casual contempt for men, Lucy,' Phoebe persevered, refusing to give up on her only sister. 'But think about how this will rub off on Merlin: "*Mummy, when I grow up, I want to be a miserable misanthrope like you.*"'

'Being misanthropic and cynical is all a part of my mystique,' I replied. Merlin was squatting in the grass, his face vivid with excitement. '*As if we were villains of necessity, fools by heavenly compulsion, knaves, thieves, and teachers, by spherical predominance,*' he said, parroting Edmund in *King Lear*, with no real comprehension of the meaning of the words, which I knew, from my librarian mother, related to astrology. *Merlin*'s sign read 'DO NOT DISTURB', with Asperger's in the ascendency. I touched his golden head and he beamed up at me. His smile was painful in its nakedness and I felt a stab of remorse at the thought of his sweet face becoming tutored in moroseness by my example.

'You see why I'm worried, Mum?' Phoebe threw up her hands in frustration before flouncing off to the kitchen for more alcoholic reinforcement. 'This is why I made you come home from your medieval knot gardening,' she called back over her shoulder.

'Medieval knot gardening? . . . You know there's a very fine line between a hobby and mental illness, Mother.'

'Oh, sweet pea.' My mother's voice dropped an octave. She stood behind me and brushed my hair, the way she did when I was little, even though it was so much shorter now. 'I'm sorry I haven't been around as much as I should. Single-parenting has exhausted you. When Merlin says jump, you jump – and, as a result, you've now got a strained back and have to lie down with a toyboy for, oh, I'd suggest about a month or two.' I couldn't see her, but could hear the twinkle in her voice.

'I think celibacy is the only dignified attitude for a career woman in her mid-thirties, don't you?' I said trenchantly, trying not to be depressed by the fact that my pensioner mother was obviously more sexually active than I.

'Celibacy is not dignity, Lucy, dear. It's lack of opportunity. You're so famished for love, petal, that you'll soon start sexually harassing yourself.'

'So what if I do?' I jibed. 'Porn – so much cheaper than dating.'

'But can a deluxe, top-of-the-range vibrator talk to you, cuddle you or change your flat tyres?' my straight-talking mother asked plainly. 'Sex is going to rear its ugly purple head at some time or other, darling.'

I shuddered. 'Do you know the best contraception for a woman my age? Nudity.'

'Do you know the best way to avoid wrinkles? Take your glasses off,' my mother touchéd.

'I'm not like you, Mother. I can't get naked in front of a stranger. I've become such a prude. Even when home alone I don't walk around my bedroom naked.'

She sighed. 'Sometimes I think you're adopted, Lucy, I really do. Orgasms are a minor pastime of mine I rate just before eating and drinking and waking up each morning,' my bohemian mother espoused. 'Your vagina has become the Howard Hughes of sexual organs. No visitors and never goes out. A little casual sex would do you the world of good . . .'

'There's nothing casual about casual sex, Mother. It's incredibly stressful. You have to get your roots done, your facial hair tweezed . . . Casual sex? God! Nothing could be further from the truth. "Casual sex" is when you're married and half-heartedly make love with the telly still on.'

'Well, sweet pea, you simply must have sex soon before you sag. My skin has sagged so much my tattoos are no longer legible.'

I swung around in my chair to eyeball her. 'You have tattoos? When did you get a tattoo?'

Mum ran a hand through her helmet of dyed red hair and waved away my query. 'I went out to dinner with your father and his actress friends once and we spent the entire time establishing which of us had the perkiest breasts. Sadly, it turned out to be your father.' My mother fired off a laugh of affection for her long-lost husband. It amazed me that he'd betrayed her and yet she still found it in her heart to love him.

'Do you know that our mother has a tattoo some-where on her body?' I interrogated Phoebe as she returned from the kitchen with a platter of antipasto.

We both looked at our parent with amused awe. 'Show me!' Phoebe insisted.

'I'm not showing either of you until your romantically challenged little sister promises to date again. Merlin needs a male influence in his life,' Mum reiterated, in the same tone someone would say 'May Day. Abandon ship. Right now.'

'Lucy, our mother has a tatt. Just promise to date again,' Phoebe beseeched me. 'Come on. Don't you want to see it?'

'Perhaps I'll date again, later . . .' I shrugged, with a mouth full of taramasalata.

'How much later, dear? You'll still be hot, yes, but only due to your menopausal flushes. You'll be wearing support fishnets. And an orthopaedic G-string, as your vagina will have dropped because you didn't do those pelvic-floor muscle exercises I keep telling you two about,' my mother chided. 'Do them now, girls, for God's sake.'

We all sat silently for a few minutes, contracting and holding and counting. Cold was creeping into the garden. The best of the day was behind us.

'Mum's right. I love you so much, Lulu. But you're becoming curmudgeonly,' Phoebe said, ruffling my just-brushed hair. 'You need an outlet . . . Merlin needs an outlet. Your relationship is too intense. You need a man in your life. Do it for your child.'

'I can't believe you're serious, Phoebe. Where can a 36-year-old woman with a special needs child find a sexy, intellectual, evolved male who is interested in her? Let me tell you. In a bookstore. Under "Fiction". Besides, Merlin would hate it if I dated men.'

'Merlin!' my mother called in her imposing voice, a voice that could not just quell a school library of unruly illiterates but no doubt command a battleship. 'Come here, darling!'

My mother gestured for him to come closer. But, of course, he couldn't just walk over. He had to walk towards us in a certain way, for luck. Anti-clockwise, it turned out today. 'So that I can go on living,' as he put it. Five minutes of anti-clockwise circumnavigation later, he threw himself at me, launched himself really, like a fleshy Exocet missile. He hugged me with debilitating enthusiasm, the kind of hug that would require a chiropractor to reset my bones.

'So, what's been on your mind lately, Grandma?' Merlin said experimentally, trying to fit in.

'Merlin,' my mother chirped, 'don't you think it would be a good idea if your mum had a boyfriend?'

I awaited his howl of protest, but instead his eyes sparkled. 'Why does a woman marry one man and have babies and then stay that way for life? I find it lacking in ambition. It's like being the teacher's pet. I like the French approach. You don't have to think I'll be upset if you get a boyfriend, Mum. I would find it intriguing.'

As I prised myself free of Merlin's vice-like grip, I looked at my son's slender, toned body and, for the first time in a long time, missed the bulk of a real man.

'It's not a man's world. I don't think father-pride. That's the old style. But it would be enthralling to know what happened to my real father. Is he a time traveller?' His face lit up with puppyish eagerness. 'A moonwalker? Or an International Man of Mystery?'

Sadness settled on me like a soft deposit of giant snowflakes. I could be the best mother in the world but my son would still be furtively seeking a father's hand in the dark.

'Look,' I acquiesced, 'even if I wanted to go out with men again . . . I'm a single mother. I mean . . . how can I date?'

'Because,' my mother stated grandly, 'I am going to Merlin-sit. I've put away my leopardskin luggage for a while, to stay with my adorable grandson,' she said, placing a big, juicy, coral-coloured kiss on his cheek.

'Grandma, how old are you exactly? Were you alive during the reign of William the Conqueror? Did you date Harold Godwinson before he was speared through the eye by the Normans?'

My mother laughed. We knew better, in my family, than to be perturbed by any of Merlin's remarks.

'I'm not entirely sure exactly how old I am, petal. I just round my age down to the nearest decade. And keep a Happy 50th Birthday card around at all times.'

'Fifty, eh? Yes, fifty is a fabulous age for a female . . . especially if she happens to be sixty-six!' I rebuked. 'But you're really not gallivanting off around the globe for a while?' I asked her, amazed.

'Only if you give a definite yes to start seeing men again.'

'I could give you a definite maybe . . .'

It was this tipsy sentiment, plus a glimpse of the Rolling Stone-inspired 'lick me' tongue tattoo on our mother's left hip bone, which prompted me to allow my sister to create my dating profile on Match.com.

'Now . . . which photo to post?' my mother pondered. 'You need to look flirtatiously at the camera, show some toe cleavage and be doing something interesting like playing a ukulele. Under no circumstances have a pet in shot. Especially not a cat.'

'I don't want to contemplate why you're an expert in internet dating, Mother, it will only give me nightmares. Internet dating is unsafe.'

'Why? Because it doesn't have a fire exit and wheelchair access?' my mother poo-pooed.

'Just some friendly advice –' Phoebe admonished, cracking open her laptop – 'maybe telling a man on the first date that you define marriage as a "legal contract which sanctions rape" might not be the best way to attract a mate.'

'Ugh . . .' I sighed. 'Dating was bad enough at sixteen, but at thirty-six it's ridiculous. You're both lobotomized to think computer dating could ever work. *Maths-obsessed cross-dresser in Manolo Blahniks and Prada A-lines seeks slightly soiled health-food fascist for mismatched evenings worrying about the sugar content of M&Ms* . . . No, thank you.'

'Must have GSH,' Phoebe typed in my profile section, 'as *I* definitely don't have one.'

'Ha ha.' I biffed her good-naturedly. 'GSH . . . LTR . . . Every personal statement decodes as the same thing: *Depressed suicidal failure seeks gullible female with more money than me to shag for free until the police arrest me for skipping bail*. The trouble is,' I admitted in a bout of honesty, snapping closed my sister's laptop, 'I don't think I'm as nice as I used to be. That desire to please, to take the crap and hold my tongue is gone. Merlin-wrangling will do that to you. Plus your husband dumping you for a domestic goddess. I feel as though I was born with a set allocation of patience and it's all used up.'

My mother and sister exchanged sympathetic looks. Phoebe rallied first. 'You've just forgotten how foxy you are. A little makeover and you'll look better than any famous young telly chef.'

'I don't want to look like a famous young telly chef. Are you kidding? Those women don't win a TV statuette unless they weigh less than it does.'

'You're slim enough, Lulu, you just need to tone up a little. Why don't you take up jogging?' Phoebe pointed into the lane, where a Lycra-clad gent was galumphing along, panting.

'He looks as though he's chasing the fat he lost last week,' I grunted.

'Phoebe refuses to take you to yoga ever again, but what about Pilates?' my mother suggested. 'Get in touch with your body.'

'Funnily enough, I heard from my body just the other day. *"How'd you like to go to the six o'clock pump class in vigorous bum-toning?"* I asked it. And, clear as a bell, my body said, *"Listen, witch . . . do it and die."* Besides, I'm already athletic. Do you know how many trays I've run up to Merlin's bedroom for nothing more serious than a hangnail?'

'More proof that you over-pamper him. Merlin

needs the robust influence of a man in the house. I'm booking you into my salon for some' – Mum chose the word carefully – 'grooming.'

'Grooming? Isn't that what paedophiles do on the internet you say is so safe?' I retorted.

'Beauty fades,' my mother said, 'but implants last for ever.'

'You haven't!' I gasped. Although nothing about my mother would surprise me.

'Not yet.' She winked. 'But I am scrupulous about eyebrows, bikini line and underarms. I've glimpsed your underarms, dear. The last time I saw anything like that, the whole herd had to be culled. And your pubic hair looks as though you're harbouring Brezhnev's escaped eyebrows in your knickers.' Her laughter was vibrant with affection. 'Any man down there will feel like one of those tigers in a Rousseau painting.'

'I like my pubic hair, Mother. It's like having a little pet in my pants.'

But my mother would not be dissuaded. She'd given up her National Trust working holiday for this, after all. 'I had a feeling you'd say that.' She then extracted some goodies from her handbag. 'My secret armoury. Stay-up stockings, to hide veins. And crotch-less panties, for the times you haven't waxed.'

My mother then pressed a few hundred quid into my palm. 'And buy yourself a little something. You look as though you were dressed by Helen Keller in a dark room.'

I had been concealing heartbreak beneath wise-cracking stoicism, gritting my teeth in preparation for pain and constantly poised for disappointment for so long, I'd forgotten how to yield; the pleasure to be had in letting go.

'Use it or lose it, honey,' were my mother's wise words. 'Believe me, the worst thing about old age is that you grow out of it.'

'Don't worry about life after death, you should worry about life *before* death, as in, *will you ever have one*?' Phoebe reiterated.

Exaggerating runs in my family. We are the world's most brilliantly over-the-top, unbelievably world-class exaggerators known to humankind or the entire universe – with no exaggeration. If my father got a parking ticket, it would turn into an armed arrest, a full body search and a possible prison break-out. If my mother so much as singed the toast, by the time she'd honed the anecdote, the entire kitchen had burnt down and she'd been fondled by the fireman. But maybe this time my loved ones weren't exaggerating my plight? Maybe I had turned into an alien from Planet Doom?

It was definitely true that things which never worried me before were suddenly proving profoundly irksome: logoed clothing, 4×4s, nose rings, Western women converting to Islam, piercings, Botox, corporate jargon, loud *doomf doomf* music, personal trainers, people famous for just being famous, upward inflections, incorrect grammar – but also Conan the Grammarians who corrected other people's grammar ... Instruction manuals, leaf blowers, stupid names like Satchel, Sage, Moon, Starlite, Melody and Apple ... Oh my God! I *had* become a curmudgeon. Phoebe was right. It was a wonder I hadn't started wearing brown, crumpled corduroy and tweed knickers, writing letters of complaint in green ink and over-boiling vegetables.

The realization made me laugh out loud. Admittedly it was the kind of desperate and deranged laughter that normally goes with a straitjacket. But it was laughter. 'Okay. I give in. What am I saving myself for?' I snatched up my mother's crotchless panties, not a mother–daughter bonding moment you'd see in a Doris Day movie. 'Whatever I've got left, I'm giving away to whoever will take it. And in the process, finding a father for Merlin.'

My sister re-booted the computer. 'What shall I put on your dating profile? Non-smoking atheists only?'

'Oh, darling,' my mother chirruped. 'There's no such thing as a male atheist. They all believe they're gods!'

I chortled out a suggestion. 'What about *Don't assume I'm not into meaningless, degrading sex.*'

Although by then none of us could type, because we were bent double, cackling like a coven, our ribald laughter crunching like cars on gravel.

7
Relationship Roulette

Relationship roulette, I suppose you'd call it. Over the next five years, from the time Merlin turned eleven, I dated a minestrone of men – a manastrone. Not that I did so with any fervour. My mother and sister took it in turns to drag me to cocktail parties, barbecues, charity bike rides and polo matches, anywhere there might be single men. I would spend the whole time sighing despondently and looking around me with all the enthusiasm of a cross-Channel swimmer on a rainy winter's day. But, for Merlin's sake, I persevered and was eventually jolted from my sour cynicism by a lightning bolt of lust.

Potential Father for Merlin No. 1. The Polo Player
There are a number of props which increase sexual

arousal, particularly in women. Chief among these is a man in jodhpurs. Polo players are, well, perfect. *Too* perfect. They look like the type of male you inflate by blowing into his toe. Mahogany brown, glittery eyed and muscular thighed, the jodhpured Adonis taking tea in the marquee was way out of my lust league. Watching him tilting back dangerously in his chair, one booted leg casually crossed over the other, I searched in vain for those 'womanly wiles' my mother had talked about, but feared I had whiled them away. I was like a circus whose animals have forgotten their tricks. The younger women were *all* 'wiling away'. This seemed to involve pretending to chat to each other whilst flicking their hair about a lot and slyly looking over their shoulders to gauge their effect on the guests. But when I found myself next to the Adonis in the Pimm's queue, I did manage to muster a few rusty rejoinders.

'Polo. That's the thing which lasts in your mouth all day, isn't it?' I then enquired if the female groupies ever got nosebleeds from all that social climbing and whether their dress code read 'boob jobs'. 'Bimbos should check in their breast implants at the door to level the playing field. Forget foxhunting protesters. You male players need an anti-husband-hunting league. It's cruelty to dumb animals really, isn't it?'

'Are you calling me dumb?' he asked, astounded.

'Well, you're upper class, so I imagine you are probably educated beyond your intelligence.' I threw in a few comments about horses being more intelligent than humans, because they don't bet on people, and then asked if his huge mallet meant he was compensating for some other shortcoming. Intrigued, the heterosexual hunk proffered the cake plate, which the stick-insect women going whoosh whoosh with their hair were avoiding like anthrax. I accepted ravenously, explaining that eating was the second best thing a girl could do with her lips.

'S–second?' he stammered, beguiled.

A tease that jodhpurs are surely a contraceptive – 'Once you get into them, you can never get out again' – and he was driving me home.

My nerves were sizzling filaments, stretched to twanging point. Something was going to give, and I had a feeling it could well be my lacy black knicker elastic . . . Not much later I was savouring the weight of his thigh as he rolled me on to my back and pinned me against my bedsheets. I felt the corners of my mouth lift as though they'd been hooked over my ears. Pretty soon a smile covered my face like sauce.

'Christ,' he panted, some hours later, 'if you were a praying mantis, I'd be dead now . . . How long has it been?'

'Seven or so years,' I confessed. 'But who's counting?'

'The seven-year itch, eh?'

'Yes . . . Could you scratch it again?'

* * *

'The man's sex drive is phenomenal,' I confessed to my sister the next day. 'We don't have much else in common. But ohmygod. I have definitely broken the drought.'

We were sitting at my kitchen table trying to unknot Merlin's shoelaces. My son's dyspraxia had been explained to me by the doctor as a retardation of his 'gross motor skills'. Even though that sounds a lot like driving a tacky car, it's actually an ostentatious term for clumsiness. Lack of co-ordination meant that Merlin didn't ever undo a bow. He just knotted another on top of the last one. The end result was a lumpy macramé a foot or so long on each lace. I showed Phoebe a snap of Octavian on my mobile phone, resplendent in mud-splattered joddies and leather knee-length boots.

'My God,' Phoebe drooled. 'If he were a horse, he'd need gelding.'

'He's only twenty-six. I had to keep the lights low so he wouldn't notice that I'm more than ten years older than him. We made love by Braille.'

'Well, love is blind,' Phoebe clowned. 'So are you going to see him again?'

'I don't know. Like I told you, I don't really like casual sex.'

'So? Wear a tiara,' my mother's voice boomed as she sailed into the room in some kind of paisley kaftan and matching turban. 'Just train Merlin to lower his age, dear,' she advised.

I put my fingers to my lips to indicate discretion. None of us had noticed that my son was sitting under the table. But a few muttered numbers suddenly alerted me to the fact that he was ensconced there, writing cricket scores in his notebook.

'*Girls*,' my mother whispered, glancing at the photo on my phone, 'the simplest toy, one which even a senile woman can operate, is the toyboy. A toyboy as sexy and handsome as Octavian only comes along three or four times in a woman's life. Enjoy it, dear.'

My sister and I exchanged bemused glances. Despite feeling a little queasy at the realization that my mother knew how to operate a toyboy, I had to admit she was right. Tempus was fugiting like there was no tomorrow. I would leap into that sexual saddle and ride the man ragged. Yesterday's orgasmic interlude was so beneficial I felt sure I could claim my himbo as some kind of medical expense.

But all too soon I was thrown from my mount. It was only our second encounter. I had just mixed Octavian a gin and tonic, the preferred tipple of the polo classes, lured him to the couch and begun to feel his penis thickening in my fingers when the back door boinged open. Merlin didn't ever just enter a room. He spurted into it.

'I thought you were at Grandma's tonight,' I spluttered, gathering my silk kimono more tightly around my breasts. 'Um . . . this is my . . . friend, Octavian.'

I didn't introduce Merlin in the hope that he would evaporate but, trained by me in social skills, my polite son extended his hand and said formally, 'So, how is your private life developing? I am Lucy's exuberant son, Merlin.'

'You have a son?' I could see Octavian doing a quick bit of mental arithmetic.

'Child bride,' I explained, with mock-lightness, scrambling to my feet.

'*Am* I actually your son?' Merlin's wind-tangled hair blurred wildly around his face. 'It's amazing, isn't it? . . . I find it astonishing that I'm your son. Who introduced us? How did we meet? Did we meet at a party? It was back in the nineties, wasn't it, Mum?'

'Darling, shouldn't you run back to Grandma's?' I urged.

'I forgot my Hansard book.' Merlin, unaware of the nuances and undercurrents of normal conversation, continued brightly, 'I'm nearly eleven, but Mum wants me to pretend to be younger. She keeps the lights low so you won't see how old she is.'

'I will have you know that I am at the pinnacle of my senility,' I jested in a hearty voice to camouflage my acute embarrassment, wishing, in fact, that I were anywhere else in the world – including Guantanamo naval base. I hugged Merlin to me, glowering at him in the hope that he would understand my body language and shut the hell up. 'Oh look, Merlin' – I fingered his soft face – 'you're growing a moustache.'

My son gave me a measured, objective once-over. 'Well, so are you,' he said, matter-of-factly.

I could have deep-fried chips on my cheeks. 'I've told you a million times, don't exaggerate,' I joshed desperately.

Once more, my son turned his studious countenance towards me. 'I'm not exaggerating. Look. See all the hairs on your top lip? There's millions of them. You have one or two on your chin as well.'

'If only I'd taken a tip from mother nature and eaten my young.' I laughed a little too loudly. The slight age gap between Octavian and me suddenly widened into a Grand Canyon chasm.

'You must be the one she doesn't have anything in common with, who has a good sex drive,' Merlin continued, oblivious to my distress. 'Although I'm not sure what that means . . . Does that mean you drive here for sex with my mother?'

Gin and tonic spurted out of my nose.

'So, um, Merlin' – Octavian's polite private school education kicked in and he tried to tack into calmer conversational waters – 'what do you want to be when you grow up?'

My eleven-year-old son took a long, serious look at my toyboy. 'Why? Are you looking for some ideas?' he said, without a trace of irony. 'Actually, when I grow up I want to be taller,' he then added logically.

The air had become too thick, too hot, too rich – like broth. I kissed Merlin with urgency. 'Off you go! Grandma will be so worried about you . . .'

'Gosh, Mum . . .'

I spasmed with fear. Hair follicles prickled up all over my body in a premonition of disaster. 'Y . . . Y . . . yes . . .' I whispered, in a voice that screamed NO!

'Your breath smells so much nicer now. When you're in bed in the morning, it smells like poo.'

When Merlin was safely dispatched, my jodhpured Adonis rose to erotic ardour with all the enthusiasm of a giant panda at London Zoo glumly coaxed to do his duty.

After he'd faked some equestrian-related phone call that demanded his immediate departure, I threw on some clothes, put on my sunglasses, even though the sun had long gone in, and stomped the block and a half to my mother's home.

In the gloom of the hall, I excavated a space on the book-lined stairs, sat Merlin down and attempted to explain to him that it wasn't always best to tell the truth.

His blue eyes lasered into me. 'You want me to lie?'

'Well, yes. Sometimes. For example . . . if I said to you "Does my bum look big in these trousers?" it would hurt my feelings if you said yes.'

'But your bottom *is* far too big for your trousers.'

'Merlin! That's not the point . . .' Losing my train of thought I stood up and craned over my shoulder to scrutinize my reflection in my mother's hallway mirror. 'Do you really think my bottom looks too big for these trousers? It just looks a little peachy, doesn't it? Oh,' I sighed in exasperation with myself and with him, and flumped back on to the stairs. 'Look, there are just some things it's not nice to say. Like, okay, you should never say anything to a woman that even remotely suggests you think she's pregnant unless you can see her waters breaking and she's lying on a birthing table with her legs up in stirrups.'

'Why?'

'Why? Because she might just be fat. Do you understand?' I snapped, trying hard to keep the frustrated fury out of my face.

Merlin shook his head.

I looked at my eccentric son in disheartened despair. As usual, I longed for some operating instructions. 'Oh, Merlin, just sometimes can't you try to act normal? Okay? Just for my sake. Like, smile occasionally. Not glower. And don't just volunteer information. Try to ask questions about *them*.' My voice was raised in irritation. '*Will you promise to at least try?*'

Merlin just looked up at me with the huge, sad eyes of a dog that didn't understand why he'd been kicked by his master. Just as well I wasn't doing yoga any more, as I'd be crying into my hair during headstands.

My mother and sister were waiting for me in the kitchen with a glass of what my mum called 'lady medicine'.

'Darling, we are crossing Outlandishly Handsome Men off our list. Beautiful men always leave you. Of course, an ugly man may leave you too, but ... who cares?' my mother chortled, topping up Phoebe's Sauvignon blanc.

'Having a drop-dead gorgeous toyboy on your arm merely distracts from your designer handbag' was my sister's verdict. 'Why not opt for an older man?'

'Oh yes,' my mother enthused. 'Older, uglier men are just so damn grateful.'

Octavian had left me feeling a little genitally gun-shy, so for the next eight months or so I declined my family's matchmaking machinations. After turning down Phoebe's tenth invitation, she regarded me with an expression of bemused sadness. 'If you don't get a date soon, we're going to organize a telethon to help you,' she warned.

There was a good chance I'd have remained in romance rehab if I hadn't been summoned to Merlin's headmaster's office. When I rushed in, late, having slipped out of my own school during a frantic lunch hour, Merlin's smile came out like the sun. The headmaster, who'd only been at the school for about a month, made his sombre Stonehenge face and steepled his hands. He seemed to have some kind of AstroTurf glued to his head. Perhaps he was planning a game of miniature golf for pygmies up there? I tried not to stare at his hair transplant as he droned on about Merlin's disruptive behaviour, absenteeism, pathetically low grades in his Key Stage 2 plus exams and lost homework.

I attempted to strike a chord of schoolteacher camaraderie. 'Oh well. We all lose things. Especially we teachers. After all, we're the ones who lost the square root of the hypotenuse. Otherwise, why are we always telling the kids to find it?'

Stonehenge refused to be mollified. 'We know there's an intelligence there. Which is what makes me think your son is just indolent. And an attention-seeker.' His searing stare bored into me like a drill. 'He put Mrs Crimpton's shoes in the class bin today.'

Merlin's smile had seeped away. His hands were fluttering in his lap like a trapped butterfly. Despite the overheated stuffiness of the room, he sat hunched into himself as if cold.

Screw teacherly comradeship. 'He was probably just trying to get her attention, as he tends to sit in the back of the class all day, ignored. One thing is clear' – I could hear my voice spiralling up into a peeved shriek – 'if my son stays in your school much longer, the only good mark he'll get will be in Copying Off the Exam of the Asian Kid Seated in Front of Him.'

In truth, I was more furious with myself than with the headmaster. Not getting Merlin into a special needs school meant that I'd officially forfeited my shot at Mother of the Year.

The headmaster gave me another scalding look. 'Perhaps if Merlin had more constructive support from home . . .'

I pictured my nightly homework battles with my

son. If only we could harness the steam that came out of his ears as he sweated over the incomprehensible comprehension we could power the whole of London. 'It's not that we don't try. But Merlin's got special needs.'

'Yes . . . he *needs* to be in school more often! . . . ADD! Dyslexia! Asperger's! Why do you parents insist on making excuses for your children? Your son's not special. He's just lazy and underachieving. Or, as we called it when I was a child, *naughty*.'

Merlin's face crumpled like a paper bag. I wanted to swat the headmaster like a fly, but controlled myself. The last thing I needed was for my son to be suspended. If I took any more time off work I was pretty sure my own headmaster would suspend me too, possibly on a permanent basis. Being struck off by the General Teaching Council is not exactly a good career move for a single mother. And so I took a deep breath and smiled; the most genial parent in his educational parish. Trying not to look at the dandruff silting his shoulders, I promised to try harder and departed as fast as possible.

Walking down the corridor, Merlin turned his face up to me, a mask of despair. 'Did my father leave because I'm lazy, indolent and underachieving?'

'Darling, no, of course not!'

'Why did my dad leave? Male seahorses give birth. But male polar bears eat their cubs. As do the Hanuman langur male monkeys in India. Male lions also perpetrate infanticide. As do male mice. Is my father a polar bear-monkey-lion-mouse type?' he asked in a tremulous voice, on the brink of tears. 'Or a seahorse?'

I didn't need David Attenborough to tell me that it was time to nab a new dad to take his mind off the old one. It was no coincidence that later that night I found myself paying up to join the internet dating site Phoebe had recommended. My eighty quid for two months promised me five contacts. The experience was not unlike going to an estate agent's office and asking for a decent, three-bedroom brick bungalow in a quiet neighbourhood but being endlessly shown dingy bedsits in need of a makeover, next to noisy abattoirs. Every day I would request a six-foot-tall non-smoker in gainful employment. And be offered a five-foot-four, unemployed nicotine addict. After a while, I started to wonder exactly why I was being matched with men who were drug-dependent, on social security and/or looking for a dominatrix. A panic-stricken thought hit me – maybe this was the calibre of man a single mother on the wrong side of thirty could expect to attract?

Eventually, after I'd weeded out the cross-dressers, necrophiliacs, and blokes who possessed swastika pyjamas, secret love bunkers and the exact knowledge of how and when the world was going to end, I would correspond by email. Do you have children? What are your favourite things to read, do, see? What do you do for a living? If he didn't list his occupation on his tax return as 'Crazed Loner', I would then decide whether it was worth the excruciating embarrassment of an encounter.

The internet dating rule is to arrange to meet for coffee somewhere public so you can leave quickly, in case his opening line is 'Does this look infected to you?' or 'I'm not *just* a scientologist, I also sell genital wart cream.' I can't tell you the number of times I excused myself to powder my nose – in another café. I also never met anyone I hadn't seen a photo of first. But let me tell you, few potential Romeos even remotely resemble their headshots. In real life, I'd seen better heads on a pimple. Except for Bob, who proved even more handsome. Bob was far shorter than Octavian but powerfully built, with muscular arms matted with fine dark hair. His throaty chuckle belied his studious appearance and his melancholy face was full of ironic kindness. Our coffee encounter went so well we agreed to a date. Which is how I ended up at a barn dance.

Potential Father for Merlin No. 2. The Dentist

The barn dance was in Wimbledon. Obviously, Wimbledon has everything in common with the Wild West, except for language, sunshine, climate, ambiance and dress code. My bachelor number two, a forty-year-old orthodontist named Bob, was about as Wild West as, say . . . cucumber sandwiches, cream teas and Coronation chicken. Despite his Stetson and checked shirt, the man looked as if he would be more at home in a bank than a barn.

'Actually, I'm not much of a cowgirl myself. Although I have been known to mount my high horse occasionally. The only cowboys I know are of the corporate kind – my ex-husband, for example.'

'I'm so glad you said ex,' Bob twinkled.

I twinkled back. I may even have twirled a tassel in his direction. 'I only know two types of dances, though,' I warned him. 'One of them is the go-go . . . and the other isn't.'

'With barn dancing, you don't have to be able to dance. You just hold on to *me* while *I* do,' he parried.

And so I did – and I liked what I held on to. Every time we passed each other in the do-se-do or the do-se-don't, or whatever it's called, we continued our verbal quickstep. 'Barn dancing is like a game of chess, with sweat,' I panted as I was passed on down the line.

'It's like indigestion – it just *repeats* on you,' he countered, next time we met.

'As does the music. I keep thinking it'll turn into a tune but, um, it doesn't . . .'

'And it doesn't help that the singer is singing with his mouth, through his nose . . .'

It had been so long since I'd had fun I'd forgotten how good it felt. By the end of the night, I just wanted to lasso the man, hogtie him to my bumper bar and bring him on home.

But Bob, a widower and devoted dad, wanted our children to meet before we undertook any duvet pursuits. I deferred this encounter so often that Bob eventually just turned up on my doorstep with pizzas, a bottle of wine and his two teenage daughters. With trepidation, I introduced Merlin, begging him with ocular semaphore to behave.

Merlin gangled in the kitchen door, all legs and elbows. I looked at my son, standing there as stiff as an accountant at a garden party, with a smile spackled across his dear face as he tried hard to be normal, and sympathy welled up in me. As Bob introduced his teenage daughters, making small talk about school and exams, I saw Merlin select 'interested' and then 'amused' from his Rolodex of facial expressions. My son's luminous eyes fleetingly held mine, seeking re-assurance that he was behaving the right way. I beamed encouragement as Merlin laughed at Bob's minor jokes.

Post pizza-feast, I suggested that Merlin take the girls into the garden to use the trampoline, then fell into Bob's embrace. I had a feeling Bob would be so good in bed his headboard would need an airbag. My salivary glands had just shifted into 'drool' when the girls erupted back into the room.

Bob and I leapt apart as if electrocuted. The girls went into a whispered huddle with their father. I began to sweat. Small beads studded my skin like diamonds. Merlin appeared and, trying to be hospitable and normal, manufactured a smile which was poignant in its transparency.

'Is everything okay?' I finally asked, knowing full well that things were not. The younger girl was pleading through hiccoughing tears that she wanted to go home.

I was now sweating more than Paris Hilton doing a sudoku.

Bob took me to one side. 'Apparently,' he said sternly, 'your son asked my daughters how old they are. When they said thirteen and fifteen he commented that they must be growing breasts and, now that he's hit puberty, it would be very educational for him to see them.'

How I wished we had eaten something else instead of pizza – say, a Dr Kevorkian's suicide McNugget. I glanced across the room at Merlin. The multicoloured lozenges of his eyes were summery with laughter, obviously oblivious to the drama. I wanted to be cross with him, but he was wearing his beanie at an absurdly touching angle and I felt the usual fierce onrush of tenderness.

'Well, I did warn you over coffee that my son was a little eccentric . . .'

'Eccentric might be putting it a bit mildly. He then asked them about their' – Bob lowered his voice with embarrassment – 'clitorises.'

Bob's older daughter interrupted, scandalized, 'He asked me if my clitoris was long or short. Or if all girls have the same size.'

'And then . . .' sobbed the thirteen-year-old '. . . then he asked me if I was a virgin . . . or not yet? He said it must be awful to lose your virginity and why couldn't I back it up on some kind of disk.'

'Why do women get embarrassed when you tell them they have nice breasts? It's a compliment,' my son volunteered, perplexed. His face was scrunched into the expression of agonized self-loathing he wore when he knew he'd done something wrong but had no idea what. 'I know it's not right to touch a female on the chest but I don't know why it isn't. People touch me on the chest and I don't mind.'

I tried to explain, as quickly and calmly as I could, about intimacy and privacy. Merlin hung on every word as though I were Moses delivering the commandments. Most boys only want to discuss the word 'period' if it's next to 'Hellenic' or 'Jurassic'. But my son wanted every fact and figure in exhausting detail. I'd been chiselling at the coalface of the Sex Talk for a good fifteen excruciating minutes when my mother walked in with a tray of cupcakes she'd baked.

'Grandma, why does my penis keep making me touch it?' Merlin non-sequitured.

'Oh darling!' my mother guffawed. 'That's a question women have been asking since the dawn of time. If we had the answer to that, sweetheart, we would have solved the world's problems.'

Oh, where were a pair of ejector knickers when I needed them?

As Bob and his distraught daughters made their excuses to leave, Merlin remembered his manners and extended his hand. 'Bob,' Merlin began, 'your daughters are very sexually stimulating. I found it quite physically arousing meeting them ... But tell me, does *your* penis make you keep touching it?'

Bob regarded Merlin's outstretched hand with distaste, shook it limply and then dived outside so fast he practically left a huge dentist-shaped hole in the wall. And another boyfriend bit the romantic dust.

It became clear that casual dating with Merlin around was the equivalent of a kamikaze mission. By the following March, I was ready to give a call to the pope to see if he needed any tips on celibacy. I was then given an abrupt and brutal reminder why I'd embarked on this father replacement quest in the first place ...

It was a day of icy drizzle. I arrived home from work to find my son sitting on our front steps in the rain, a funereal droop to his shoulders. As I leapt out of the car and ran towards him I saw that his shirt was ripped and face filthy. I knew who the culprits were. The local boys on the council estate wore three-inch shit-kicker shoes and walked with a swagger that suggested not brawn so much as haemorrhoid tribulation, but they terrified my son. And no wonder, as they bullied him so often on the way home from school. This time they'd stolen his wallet where he kept his house key and rubbed dogshit into his face. 'Merlin, darling! Are you okay?' I cradled him to me.

He just sat in mute horror, shrinking into himself.

Fury surged through my body. Why did they bully him? What joy could they get out of it? It was like taunting a fieldmouse.

'They called me a retard,' Merlin whispered, grief-stricken. 'They said if only my father had settled for a blowjob. What does that mean? Am I a retard, Mum?' His wide blue eyes filled with tears.

My heart gave one huge thump in my chest. 'They're the retards!' I spat. He burrowed his cold, wet head into my lap, his face twisted up in anguish. I stroked his cheek, wiping off the excreta with a tissue. I tenderly traced the outline of his cheek and said soothing words until the desolate weeping subsided.

The mother of a special needs child has to be his legal advocate, fighting his educational corner; full-time scientist, challenging doctors and questioning medications; executive officer, making every decision on his behalf; and, also, full-time bodyguard and bouncer. After Merlin was showered and cosied up with hot chocolate, I marched down to the estate and fronted up to the kids hanging around the rubbish-strewn stairwells. It was like downtown Mogadishu only without the glamour. 'Have you no shame?' I demanded in my best headmistress voice. It was as effective as squaring up to Voldemort armed with a butter knife. They laughed in my face before scattering and I wasn't fast enough to give chase. It was then I found myself longing for a tall, broad-shouldered bloke who could explain to these blockheads that many a nose has been broken by a mouth.

I would just have to do more internet dating – otherwise known as relying on the kindness of passing serial killers. But then I was saved from having to bat an eyelash at yet more random blokes, because very soon after I bumped into Chris – literally.

Potential Father for Merlin No. 3. The Pilot

I was returning from an 'Assessment for Learning' conference in Dublin put on by educational bigwigs for smaller wigs like me – although who was I kidding? Careerwise, I was nothing more than a lanky hair extension. But it was whilst waiting in the taxi queue that my bag locked wheels with a captain's suitcase. 'I hope your flight ran more smoothly,' he smiled, cute little cap rakishly askew.

'I hate flying. I don't know why you made me pay for a whole seat when I only used the edge of it. I want my money back,' I replied.

The pilot's eyes narrowed with keen interest – hazel eyes topped with thick, curved lashes, I now noticed. He laughed and we began to banter. Chris's voice was deep and moist, like warm mud slipping between your toes. He didn't look like a captain at all. His collar-length, ruffled dark hair and long, lean body lent the man the elegance of a matador. Four dates

later, he suggested a little trip. 'Vanuatu is a bit far' –
his soft brown eyes caressed me tenderly – 'Positano
with a side trip to Ravello maybe?'

'Sounds fabulous,' I purred. 'But a girl's favourite
destination is a cosy little spot which goes by the name
of G.'

'I know that place. Hard to find but well worth it
when you get there. The views are magnificent.'

And I wasn't disappointed. By the foreplay *or* the
wordplay. When we pulled away from each other in
bed he fondled the lace on my lingerie before referring
to us as 'basque separatists'. The man was as thin and
as straight as a pencil. But there was a lot of lead in it.
And oh, it felt so good to be kissed and caressed again.

Two months into our love affair, we introduced our
children. He was a recently divorced father of a
fourteen-year-old girl, and this time I took the
precaution of telling him about Merlin's quirks. I felt
confident that, forewarned, the social cogs would turn
more smoothly. After all, Merlin was now educated
about sex. What I hadn't realized is that there is such a
thing as being too educated . . .

My mother cooked her famous paella dish. While
the rest of us noshed happily around my kitchen table,
Merlin remained taut as an archer's bow. His hair was
falling into his eyes like the mane of a shy pony. Chris
cheerily asked Merlin if he was going to start shaving
soon, now that he was a teenager and, as there was no
man in the house, would he like some lessons in the

next year or two? My spirits rose at this intimation of commitment and I beamed at my beau. Then I looked at Merlin, wriggling my brows in encouragement.

My son moves sluggishly through social situations, as though encumbered in an old-fashioned diving suit in deep water. His lips were stiff with the effort not to say the wrong thing, but he also knew he was expected to say something.

'I don't understand the point of shaving,' Merlin finally replied. 'It only grows back. Body hair is very confusing.' Sweat began to tingle in my armpits. I suddenly felt there was a time bomb ticking beneath the conversation. 'I used to look at my mother in the bath and think "Have you got a willy? Are you sure? Under all that hair?"'

Silence swooped down and tightened its grip around the table. Chris's teenage daughter was ogling my thirteen-year-old son with horrified fascination. Forget Paris Hilton's sudoku attempt, I was now sweating more than George Bush trying to play Scrabble. Merlin lit up, smiling at me blissfully, convinced I'd be proud of his effort to be sociable.

'Who'd like more salad?' I squeaked, telepathically begging Merlin to shut up, a grin plastered to my face.

'I've read all the books Mum gave me,' my son persevered with undiminished zest, his words crashing into the low-key conversation, colliding and smashing and ricocheting off the walls, 'although I do have many questions. For example, do dogs do it "people-style"?'

Merlin's confused reaction at the lack of response was to crank up his enthusiasm level. 'But I know now that on girls hair first grows on the labia before filling the pubic triangle and then the thighs. Pubic hair grows to stop chafing.'

A sharp elbow in the ribs is the accepted international signal to abandon a topic. But not to my son. He just said, bemused, 'Why are you elbowing me, Mum? That information is correct.' In his nervousness he began to speak faster. Like a skater on thinning ice, he accelerated to save himself from drowning. 'I'd actually like to make an important announcement,' he declared formally.

I quailed inwardly, suggesting with brittle urgency that he hurry up and finish his meal so we could have dessert.

'I'm having wet dreams!' my son exclaimed triumphantly, as excited by this discovery as a Labrador in a pork-chop shop.

Little black dots danced in front of my eyes. It struck me then how ironic it was that I'd spent so much money getting my son speech therapy when all I wanted him to do was shut up.

'Merlin,' my mother spluttered, 'don't you think that might be private information? Something you might want to keep to yourself?'

Merlin looked at my mother, scandalized. 'But

you're my grandma. Surely you should want to know everything about me?'

Merlin's words stood in the air, like skywriting. I could only wait for them to evaporate. The silence was broken by Chris's daughter, who made a face of a snail being poisoned on a slug pellet before fleeing outside to their car. Merlin, trying to appear friendly, gave his best and brightest high-wattage smile, a grin which could laser four layers of skin off your face. But his eyes were full of a helpless, painful expression. He wanted to atone for his unconscious mistake but couldn't, not knowing what it was. And my heart went out to him.

As Chris departed, he patted my son gingerly on the back, as if he were an exotic pet which might bite his fingers. 'I'll call you,' he said to me. But soon started flying long-haul.

Now I don't want you to get the impression that this was a non-stop sexual gymkhana. By the time Merlin was in his third year in secondary school, I had resigned myself to the solitary, sexless life of an amoeba or some other single-celled organism. Lambeth had changed in the sixteen years I'd lived there. Our square was now full of yummy mummies who did yogalates, baked bread, wore zodiac-inspired toe-rings and bought those beautiful educational wooden toys that kids so adore . . . well, kids named after pieces of fruit or large landmasses anyway. Our 'renovator's dream' house had never been renovated. As all the properties around us had undergone architectural facelifts, mine looked even more faded and jaded. Although not on the inside. I used to think that any woman who said she got high doing housework was inhaling way too much cleaning fluid. But over the last few years I'd become obsessed with cleaning. My sister said it was obviously a way of exerting some control over the chaos of my life, which seemed to be getting increasingly chaotic. Merlin's outbursts meant that the neighbours were polite to us but looked at him as though he had just won the right to represent earth in the Intergalactic Weird Alien category. I did explain that Asperger's wasn't infectious, but the parents of all those Apples and Peaches and Chinas and Indias just didn't feel we fitted into their gastropub and power-plate world.

I was also the only mother on the square whose child wasn't attending a private school. Local education authorities allocate children to state schools in random and mysterious ways. The authority, who'd obviously attended the Mad Dog Gaddafi School of Reason and Logic, had rejected my first-preference secondary-school request for Merlin to be enrolled where I taught, enabling me to protect him. At the start of each school term I'd push again for a special needs school, which involved the annual trek to La–ah's office for the ritual flagellation, fasting, sacrifice of virgins, etc. But I had to face the fact that it was more likely that the Amish community would introduce a lap-dancing club than that Merlin would get the placement he'd been promised. I could sue the education authority for not fulfilling the obligations of Merlin's statement, but it would cost around £25,000 for a lawyer, plus £20,000 for all the medical reports and assessments. Or it meant joining another interminable queue, this time for legal aid. (And people say you can't have it all!)

Merlin's secondary school had proved to be even worse than his primary. The wiry, pale young boys in his class had hair cropped to stubble and were muscled like fighting dogs, with eyes sharp as knife blades. Merlin proved very sweet meat to them. The newspapers were full of stories about the increase in London's prison population. And I was pretty sure most of them had been pupils at my son's secondary school. There were so many local thugs and felons, Hallmark cards needed to put out a new line for exclusive sale in our area with messages which read 'To a man of many convictions' or 'Condolences on losing your appeal' or 'Here's hoping you get the top bunk!'

When Merlin had his head flushed down the school toilet for the second time, I made an appointment with his latest headmaster. I tried to hold out hope that he would be more sympathetic and effective than the last two or three, but Merlin and I set out to see him like prisoners off to our own execution.

'This is all a test, isn't it, Mum?' Merlin asked me dejectedly. 'You're giving me marks out of ten, aren't you? To see if I can pass as normal.'

When the new headmaster began the interview by steepling his fingers, I knew there was no hope of help. Finger-steeplers are nearly always substandard head-teachers. As he droned on about lack of proof to punish the perpetrators, I looked at my vivid, original son and longed to shelter him from the world.

'It keeps going round and round in my head, what those bullies said to me,' Merlin confided on the way home. 'About being a spastic and a cretin and a retard. If the body's designed to vomit up anything con-taminated, why not the brain? Why can't my brain throw up, Mum?'

Forget brain. Brawn, that was what I needed. And I determined there and then to bloody well find it any way I could, through the internet, blind dates – hell, I'd stand on a street corner if needs be.

Potential Father for Merlin No. 4. The Gardener
Hackney is not a wealthy neighbourhood, but it is full of men more at home with a computer keyboard than a chainsaw. For ridiculously reasonable rates, Django would trim treetops and de-leaf rain gutters and dis-pose of rats. He was now Phoebe's odd-job man too.

'You'll like him,' she enthused. 'He's from Bahia, in Brazil. Macho, but sensitive. His ex-girlfriend told me he often cried during sex.'

'Yeah, well, pepper spray will do that to you,' I scorned.

Django's clients were throwing him a small surprise party in the local pub to celebrate the Home Office granting him citizenship. The pub was called The Queen's Legs. 'I'm waiting for The Queen's Legs to open so I can get a drink' is how Phoebe's husband Danny explained it to me. I entered expecting the worst. It was the sort of bar where even the water is watered down. I walked in as though I already wanted to leave.

'The English don't do anything spontaneous without a warning ... which is why I'm kind of surprised to be at a surprise party,' I said when my sister introduced me to Django. His exotic name was matched by exotic looks – ebony eyes, silky skin as dark as imported Swiss chocolate, wild Medusa hair, a powerfully built body, each bicep the size of Arnold Schwarzenegger.

The white crescent of his smile was dazzling. Even more dazzling than the sex, which was so hot it only just fell short of igniting my pubic hair. But we had little else in common. While I preferred conquering the great indoors – galleries, theatres, restaurants – Django liked to kayak, canoe and rock-climb.

'Um, I'm British. I'm only slightly more mobile than a pot plant or a fire extinguisher,' I assured him.

Django threw back his head and guffawed at nearly everything I said, which I found so beguiling that I was soon kayaking, canoeing and rock-climbing. Best of all, he liked Merlin. Even when we arrived at his flat in Hackney and the first thing Merlin asked was 'Which bathroom should I use for poo?'

But Django's teenage boys didn't share their father's magnanimity. Two hulking, big, streetwise boys bedecked in bling hunched over their Cokes, they eyed Merlin warily. As we sat around the table sharing chorizo and fresh fish, nerves made me flutter my hands aimlessly. Merlin was also jumpy, playing jerky drum solos with his knife and fork. A variety of emotions scudded like clouds across my son's face. Every hour of every day for Merlin is like being a gymnast trying to balance on a beam. He can never relax, in case he falls. My nagging meant that he now kept constant vigil on what he was saying.

'I'm sure I'll give a flawless performance at dinner tonight,' he'd told me bravely on the drive over, before adding perspicaciously, 'The trouble with talking too fast is that you might say something you haven't thought of yet.'

I watched now as my son selected a warm smile from his repertoire of facial expressions and then, in his desperation to please me, attempted some light repartee.

'So, where are you from? Africa?'

'Hackney,' the boys replied in broad Cockney accents, eyes narrowing suspiciously.

'No, no,' Merlin corrected them. 'You must be from

Africa . . . So, have you played Othello?' he asked. 'I used to think that all black men were Othello.'

Both boys sat stock still, their faces rock hard. Confused, but determined to act sociably, Merlin beamed so broadly you'd think he'd just been given a vitamin B12 shot. 'You do have quite splendid pectorals.' He then leant over and squeezed the biceps of the sixteen-year-old boy, oohing and aahing appreciatively. 'If I were gay, I would find you very attractive because of your exquisite musculature.'

It was then that the younger one punched Merlin hard enough for my son to require a three-hour wait in casualty with a chronic nosebleed. I spent the time contemplating emigration to Iceland, and Django, the dishy gardener, decided to sow his wild oats elsewhere.

One thing I learnt in my three years of disastrous dating is that when Cupid closes one door . . . he slams another in your face. Who knew that Asperger's was sexually transmittable? But it must be, judging by the way men bolted at the first glimpse of Merlin. I didn't even bother buying full packets of condoms any more as it was just a waste of rubber. But my mother didn't give up. For my fortieth birthday, she bought me a membership to the Tate Galleries. 'A lot of women I know hang around in museums to meet men. Any man who collects old masters also collects young mistresses,' she counselled.

'Mum, the kind of men you meet hanging around in museums belong in them – as exhibits.'

Besides, my entire life was taken up with the exciting activity of educating my son. Primary school had been tough enough, but secondary school was giving me a ride like a bucking bronco. Every second day there were letters and phone calls chastising Merlin for being insubordinate. His latest misdemeanour was to explain that the reason he was always late to school was because he liked to stay in bed to play with his penis. 'Don't *you*?' he'd asked the pinstripe-underpanted headmaster matter-of-factly. This won him three detentions and a loss of privileges. Basically, if I'd been in an aeroplane I would have been adopting the crash position.

Of late, a lost look had come into my son's eyes. He retreated behind a habitual veil of forlorn exclusion. 'Did my father not love me because I'm insubordinate?' Merlin asked me one afternoon, on the drive home after his sixth detention in a row. 'Was he lucky to be rid of me?'

'Any man would be lucky to have you as a son,' I assured him. And I was back on the hunt, armed with everything bar a net and tranquillizer dart, to track down a father figure for my bewildered boy. My first stop was a favourite watering hole in the urban jungle – an art gallery, just as my mother had suggested. And, in a triumph of hope over experience, I started dating again. It was to be two weeks from mojito to finito.

Potential Father for Merlin No. 5. The Film Director
Dennis was strikingly handsome, in a historical way, like a carved monument, although, judging by his physique, there was nothing crumbling behind his ramparts. Yes, he was older, but there was a reassuring bulk and gravitas to the man. Dennis sidled up to me and gazed with quizzical good humour at the work of art I was appraising.

'In my experience, if you have to stand on your head to decipher it, then it's modern art. What did you think of the Gauguin?'

'So good you have to Gauguin and again and Gauguin,' I replied. When he smiled, I recognized him from the Hitchcockian cameos he made in the movies he directed. 'So did you have to perform sexual favours for yourself on the casting couch to get those parts?' When he laughed, I greenlit the project.

Over dinner we exchanged basic information – favourite author, least favourite word, what you would be if you could have any other job, attitude to children (answers: Emily Brontë, 'fecund', opera singer, adore kids). A few days later I found myself in his Thames-side apartment, which was seared with light. I raised the cut-glass flute to my lips as champagne bubbles gossiped to the surface and felt as effervescent as they did. Okay, the guy wasn't perfect; he only wanted to see obscure films with subtitles about one-legged albino transvestites looking for the meaning of life. I teased him about his footage fetish

. . . but it turned out he had other kinks as well. He was particularly keen on a nondescript French tickling implement with feathers which was not designed to dust things. Still, as I confided to my sister, the great thing about bondage is that you can tie the man up and get control of the remote. 'It's love with strings attached,' I punned. We laughed about his occasional mistimings with Viagra, taking it too early and becoming priapic at the opera, or too late and pole-vaulting on his own penis to breakfast, but agreed that I should keep having fun.

Dennis's passion for the wilder reaches of sexual behaviour aroused and repelled me in equal measure. But I definitely wanted to explore them in more detail. But my experimentation with nurses' uniforms, rubber catsuits and being fastened to the hotel bed by the cords of two complimentary bathrobes whilst he videoed the encounter ('Don't worry. It will be like the rest of my movies. Nobody will ever see it') was cut short. And you don't have to be Einstein to work out by whom.

'I heard Mum telling my aunt that you're in your sixties and possibly always have been,' Merlin blurted when they accidentally met at the door one evening before I'd had time to brief either one of them. 'What does that mean? How old are you exactly? Were you alive during the reign of Henry VIII?' Ignoring my frantic interruptions and eye rolls and hand signals, Merlin, pleased that he could think of something to say, just kept parroting our private conversation. 'My aunt Phoebe is worried about your age difference. She says that impotence is nature's way of saying "*No hard feelings*" ... I don't get that, but they laughed like hyenas ... Do hyenas really laugh? Or are they just pretending to get the joke?'

Self-esteem? Don't leave home without it. If only it came in a spray can so I could replenish Dennis's supply. Dennis, who had seemed so dashing, suddenly exuded the charisma of a sachet of instant soup – expired.

I didn't wait around to see the end credits.

When Dennis and I broke up, Merlin wrung his hands, utterly at a loss. He reprimanded himself over and over – 'I must try not to say what I'm thinking without thinking!' – but I was under no illusion. The chances of finding a father figure for my son were looking a little remote. Introducing Merlin to anyone filled me with dread. I constantly felt I was looking into a gas tank with a lit match.

By the time my son was fifteen, I'd accepted the fact that there would only ever be Merlin and me. 'Well,' I told anyone who enquired, 'I've tried computer dating, speed dating, blind dating, even carbon-dating in Dennis's case, but I find a good vibrator works best. My new motto – reach out and touch yourself.'

So, you ask, why didn't I move to some cave some-where and take up whittling? Or commit myself to a little light calligraphy in a nunnery? Because Merlin started asking more and more questions about his father: 'Does he like marzipan?' 'Is he a man of man's experience?' 'Is he a corporate cowboy or a space cowboy?' And then he got badly beaten up on his way home from school. When the police showed little interest – 'People with special needs are routinely targeted,' the constable told me. 'I'm afraid it's the price of disability' – I knew I just had to endure another whole host of disastrous internet encounters. They usually fizzled out two sips into our first cappuccino when my prospective partner either revealed a habit of wearing 'Home of Big Ben' boxer shorts, arrived carrying a tub of coconut love butter, proved to have problem flatulence or a penchant for hanging upside down naked in gravity boots.

'Your standards are too high,' my sister sighed over my shoulder as I dismissed man after man on the dating website.

'Yes,' my mother chorused. 'If you want to stay a spinster, look for the perfect man.'

'I'm not looking for the perfect man. At this point, I'm looking for any biped who has his own teeth and some hair and no psychopathic tendencies.'

To be honest, I wasn't just looking for Merlin's benefit. My sexual frustration had become so chronic I'd taken to strip-searching myself. I'd practically worn off the fingerprints of my right hand. But every possible romance was accidentally sabotaged by my son.

Like the time Merlin said to my doctor, as he was about to take me into his office for a cervical smear, 'So, what does Mum mean when she says you're bonkable?' Or reporting to the priest who'd been defrocked for insubordination, 'I heard Mum telling my grandmother that she's dreading the day you suggest doing it in the missionary position, in case she lies down on her back and you bugger off to China ... So exactly what is the missionary position?'

Then there was the dinner when, with cartoonish inevitability, my son asked my very shy new boyfriend, an acupuncturist, what hair colour he puts on his driver's licence, as he's bald. Before then enquiring if he'd ever noticed that his chin looked like 'upside-down testicles'?

The acupuncturist's response? 'Take two thumbtacks and don't call me in the morning.'

'Have you ever thought of not saying things, Merlin?' I begged him, time and time again, my head in my hands. 'I really think it's an option we should explore.'

But shortly after, when I'd been home six Saturday nights in a row, I felt myself falling into a trance of desolation. The day was dying in the wet window. The evening was seeping away, and my stamina was dwindling with it. Merlin had now taken to truanting. He was tired out with the effort of deciphering the world whilst smiling fakely at the foe. And I was tired too, with trying to mould him into a world where he didn't fit.

As always, my mother had something to say. 'Why have I given up my adventuring if you're hell bent on becoming a Trappist monk?' was her comment. 'I mean, what do you want, Lucy?'

'I want it all, Mother – and I want it drizzled in truffle oil with a caviar chaser. But that's not going to happen, is it? It's not easy to find someone to share your life with when you're a cynical, bitter, twisted divorced mother of a kid with special needs secretly harbouring a desire to maim all men.'

Well, not all men. As I hadn't yet met Adam.

Final Potential Father for Merlin. The Tennis Instructor

The probability of being observed by a gorgeous man is directly proportional to the stupidity of what you are doing at the time. I know this from personal experience. I was trying to demonstrate to a squealing Merlin why hitting my head with my hand would not give me brain cancer (by hitting my head repeatedly with one hand) and why walking around the car in one direction would not bring him good or bad luck (by circling the car clockwise and then anti-clockwise, faster and faster, whilst hitting my head) when I noticed Adam leaning on a tree in the sports-complex car park, watching me.

Adam had a tennis racket slung over one shoulder. Because he coached at the local sports complex, he'd

met Merlin many times before and wasn't discombobulated by his candid outbursts. Mid-thirties, he
was muscular with a wrestler's handshake, but so
elegant he would have fitted very snugly into a tango
dancer's tux. His good looks suggested arrogance, a
misconception dispelled by his ready laugh and
ebullience. Adam was so funny and upbeat that, after
a few morning coffees together, I felt my attention shift
towards him like a sunflower turning to the sun.

'I like him. I don't know why. It's just that when I'm
with him – well, it's corny, I know – but I feel like a
shrub that's just been watered,' I told my mother and
sister. I liked Adam enough to allow him to talk me
into things I hated, like camping. *'Camping?* In the
countryside? The countryside contains large quantities
of nature, doesn't it?' I shuddered.

'I thought Merlin might enjoy it.'

Adam was the first man in my life who wanted
Merlin to share our time together. Which is why I put
up with mosquitoes the size of sumo wrestlers and
living off the land, i.e. half-cooked innards of roadkill
garnished with bugs the size of racehorses. If Adam
had offered me plutonium on rye I couldn't have been
more appalled but I liked the guy so much I wasn't
going to let the threat of a painful death by salmonella
spoil things. He had moles like splashes of mud on his
broad back. And I loved every one of them. They were
a constellation I kissed on a regular basis.

With my head on his warm, broad chest, bathed in

the flickering light of the campfire and soothed by the cadences of the waves on the rocks of the Cornish coast, contentment coursed through my veins. I found myself telling Adam that he was my Only One.

As Adam's long-term girlfriend had turned out to be a compulsive liar and sexual kleptomaniac who slept with all his best mates, this declaration of monogamy meant a lot to him. His hazel eyes shone. 'Merlin!' Adam threw his arm around my son's shoulders. 'Your mum has just told me I'm the only man in her life! Besides you, that is.'

Merlin, who was roasting marshmallows, looked puzzled. His famously blue eyes blinked and blinked. 'Well, technically, that's not entirely accurate.'

Before I could stop him, Merlin then recited, with computer accuracy, the dates and names and duration of every relationship I'd had in the last five years.

'2006, 22nd May till 26th May, Octavian, polo player. Finding out how old Mum is meant Dr Love left the building. Bob, a dentist, 3rd March 2007 till 20th April. The affair sank without trace because of his sexual prudery. Ditto Chris, the pilot. 22nd June till 1st September 2008.'

'Merlin! Okay. That's enough, darling.'

But he yabbered on with more zeal that an Energizer bunny on crystal meth. 'Then there was Django, gardener, Brazilian, 6th February till 10th June 2009, ended because of violence in the familial home resulting in hospitalization.'

'Merlin. Stop!' But my protests had as much effect as a feather in the path of a category five hurricane.

'Dennis, the film director, 3rd January 2010 till 18th February, couldn't face up to his encroaching senility and impotence. Tuesday 29th July, a promising development in her private life was prematurely terminated when Dr Kureishi, who my mother said was "bonkable", determined that she just wanted him for sexual intercourse . . .'

Pundits are always claiming that conversation is a lost art form. And, right then, how I wished that were true, as I frantically tried to silence my son with a Marcel Marceau repertoire of gestures and grimaces. But Merlin just talked on and on like a demented typewriter, his staccato jabs laying bare all names and numbers. He finally concluded his bravura performance, bursting with pride at his accomplishment, 'The rest of 2010 and the beginning of the year 2011 proved a mixed romantic bag of one-night stands and broken hearts, including an ex-priest, a policeman, a shrink, a poet, a plumber, an acupuncturist . . . concluding with you, 6th March 2011 till now, 28th April 2011. But you have definitely been my mother's favourite partner in her career so far.'

I tried a mock-laugh. 'Oh Merlin, you're such an exaggerator . . .' My stomach churned and my head pounded.

Adam shifted his body out from beneath my head, which clumped on to the blanket. There was a cold shift in his attitude too. 'Merlin never gets a fact wrong,' he said, jerking to standing. 'You told me that you gave up on men after your husband left you. You lied to me.'

'Mum says that it's okay to lie. She says that lying is good.'

'No, darling, I didn't quite put it that way . . .'

'Merlin cannot tell a lie,' Adam admonished me. His eyes were narrowed to half-slits, his lips zipped shut.

'Adam . . .' But my voice was plaintive with defeat.

The man I thought I could possibly fall in love with shuddered theatrically like a child being force-fed Brussels sprouts. I think he finally saw a downside to camping – it's so hard to storm out after a fight, as you can't slam the flap.

I tried hard to redeem the situation, but when Adam kissed me goodbye at Paddington station the next day it was with all the zeal of a tree sloth searching for a bit of wilted algae.

Bobbing our way home in the back of the taxi, Merlin, oblivious to the truly baroque bedlam he'd unleashed, enthused, 'Wasn't that a great weekend!'

I was hit suddenly with a severe fatigue, which I only experience when talking with my son. I felt as if my ears were going to shrivel and my mouth fall off.

'Oh Merlin,' I post-mortemed, 'why did you blurt out all those dates and names? That was private information. You frightened Adam off. He thinks I'm some kind of floozy. Just call me Hail a Hooker! He won't be back, thanks to you!'

Merlin, still unsure of what he'd done wrong but aware that I was really upset, gripped my shoulders fiercely, as though I were the rudder of a boat in a big sea. Unable to fathom the reason for my anger, he lashed out at himself. 'I bet you wish you'd never had a child! I bet you're regretting it now! . . . Why did you make me this way? I'm a fucking freak! I can't do the things other kids can do. I hate it. I hate myself!' Merlin tilted his face up towards me. He had such a serious, befuddled expression. 'Why did you make me born with this disease? It's your fault! Will I ever have a girlfriend? I *won't*, will I?' he wailed desolately. 'Why can't I be *normal*? I *hate* fucking Asperger's. I hate it, hate it, *hate it*!!!'

'Sshhhhh . . .' I held him to me, chastising myself for my outburst. A profound melancholy pervaded then, as soft and persistent as Irish rain. As a forty-ish single mother, I no longer expected to be asked to pack only a change of lingerie for a private plane flight to a tropical hideaway with an heir to the throne . . . Or to take a quick impromptu stroll down a Parisian catwalk in Prada. Or to do a little light wrestling in jelly with Brad Pitt before being tossed casually over his shoulder and then ravaged in his penthouse apartment jacuzzi . . . but I wouldn't have minded the company of a man now and then. With a world-weary sigh, I resigned myself to the fact that this was never going to happen.

Five years of dating and dashed hopes had been character building ... but if I had wanted to build character, I would have gone off to plant rice for the Peace Corps or plotted the overthrow of Ahmadinejad or Mugabe. Besides which, Merlin had quite enough character for one household already.

But just when I was tempted to see if I could shove my son back into the condom vending machine for the refund, I found this card on my pillow.

Dear Legendary Mum, I have thurally enjoyed and taken advantage of being your son and I hope it will continue in the same quality trend. Its been a tremendous plessure to be in your company these sublime 15 years. Every 15 year old that I know would kill to have a mum like you, which is why I try to embrace every moment I have with you. You have been an insperation for me as a mum and a witty, enthusiastic, karismatic goddess. You are an interlectual giant and I am in oar of you. I think you have lots of panash in just about everything. You where the most trendy outfits, which make you look about 30. In my mind you have an exquisite physeque and a dazzling, flamboyant and

extravagant personality. You are my
favourite woman who walks the earth and
I think you are a creative, articulate and
artistic genius. Your smashing.
Love from your wity and at times
compelling son Merlin.

There and then I put a sign on the dating website my sister and mother had set up for me four years earlier.

ALIENS ARE COMING TO EARTH AND THEIR MISSION IS TO ABDUCT ALL GOOD-LOOKING AND SEXY PEOPLE. YOU WILL BE SAFE, BUT I'M JUST EMAILING YOU TO SAY GOODBYE.

From now on, there would always just be Merlin and me . . .

Part Two: Archie

Part Two Alone

8

There Came a Tall, Dark Stranger . . .

The trouble with being a woman at the beginning of the twenty-first century is having to be so damn strong all the time. Fixing fuses in the middle of the night, fending off muggers, changing car tyres in the torrential rain – any more of this equality was going to put me in a psychiatric ward, I thought to myself, as I missed the nail I was attempting to hammer into a broken drawer and whacked my thumb instead. I'd been attempting my own DIY for years, but the instructions were always so complicated. I invariably ended up super-gluing my elbow to my earlobe or making a bookcase out of myself. It was early one school morning and I was now sucking my throbbing thumb and leaping about in a fury, hopping from foot to foot as though in some hot-coal initiation ritual in Lower Volta, when my mother's email plopped into my inbox with a *boing*! Now that I'd given up dating, Mum had given up Merlin-minding. She had rented out her flat to fund her adventures and was currently cruising the Great Barrier Reef with a wealthy widow who called her floating retirement home HMS *Panty Liner*.

> Sweet pea, sorry to let you down but I just can't
> make it home for the summer, as bloody families,
> totally impervious to the economic Armageddon,
> are bunging up planes with their half-witted 'yuh-
> whatever' offspring and I can't get a cheap flight
> out of Cairns. But am sending a substitute – your
> cousin Kimmy's husband, Archibald. He needs a
> place to stay in London for a few weeks and has
> offered to do all your DIY, burglar-bashing and
> Merlin-chauffeuring in exchange for your spare
> room. Could work well? Toodles. Must away –
> we're counting tiger sharks for scientific research. ☺

Of course you are, I mused sarcastically. Hadn't marriage to my father been dangerous enough? The reply – 'No way' – was typed and ready to be sent when an ominous thump and a stream of expletives erupted from Merlin's room upstairs. I checked my watch. Seven a.m. He was having his usual meltdown about Guantanamo Bay, which is what he called his school. Every morning I had to endure an exhausting war of words. Even though my son was now nearly

sixteen, it could still take me an hour to haul him out
of bed, and only then with a mixture of cajoling,
begging, pleading, blackmailing and, finally, sheer
rage. By screaming till the paint peeled off the walls, I
could usually half-stuff him into his uniform, but not
before he'd trashed his room in the process, often
slamming doors so hard they came off their hinges.
My brilliant mothering skills became strikingly apparent when I would then run back to my room and sob
into my pillow. Eventually I would drag him, as he
cursed and cussed, to his school gates, before dashing
to work, all distraught and dishevelled and panda-
eyed from mascara leakage. The daily ordeal left me
more depleted than Our Lady of Put-upon and
Exhausted, the patron saint of single mothers.

I abandoned the broken kitchen drawer I'd been trying to fix and trudged towards the stairs. I felt like a
pilot about to fly up into a tornado. My nightie billowed
out around me like wings as I climbed up into the
storm. It was then I suddenly found myself fantasizing
once more about how restful it would be to have a man
to do a little light Merlin-taming. Plus the odd bit of
light-bulb changing and carburettor tuning . . . The very
thought of it was like a holiday. A male guest would be
like having a boyfriend, only without the snoring and
boring bit.

When I'd finally got Merlin to school that morning
and was lying, worn out, in the fetal position on the
back seat of my car gnawing at my nails and

whimpering, I typed an answer to my mother's email on my BlackBerry: 'Okay.'

Over the next few days, against my better – i.e., my more sceptical – nature, I found myself starting to imagine what this Archibald might be like. My mother sent another email explaining that Archie had been a famous rock musician in Oz in the eighties, before he became 'spiritual'. A picture of an erudite, easy-on-the-eye, wise and witty muscular love god, possibly sitting cross-legged on a flying carpet, began to gel in my addled mind.

I was in front of my terrace house in my pyjamas one warm June morning a few days later, attempting to stamp the recycling into the green plastic box and remember my mother's recipe for the cake I had to bake frantically for the school fête, when a taxi pulled up and a middle-aged man with a greying ponytail, torn T-shirt and pointy boots alighted carrying a guitar case, a rucksack and an amplifier. He got out of the cab the way a cowboy dismounts his horse, with an understated swagger.

'How's it hangin'?' The stranger spoke in wide, skidding, languorous vowels, vowels so elongated and laid back they were practically lounging in a hammock.

I stood and gawped at the Neanderthal figure with his prognathous jaw, minimalist forehead and broken nose. Acne scars corrugated his cheeks. Stubble had worked through the cratered surface. He was dressed head to toe in black. The satanic image was enhanced by scuffed riding boots, a tattooed python coiled on one bicep and a cockily angled cowboy hat. Disappointment clung to me like a clammy raincoat.

'Flew here on Virgin. Was worried I'd have to swim the last hundred miles 'cause they wouldn't go all the way.' The man's green eyes puckered into an amused squint. His face had more ridges than corduroy. His tanned neck was seared by pale creases where his V-neckline began. As he extended his hand for a shake, I glimpsed underarm hair which resembled an adult yak in hibernation. Steel-wool curls encrusted a chest emblazoned in a sloganed T-shirt reading 'Elvis is dead, Sinatra is dead but I'm still bloody well here.'

I must have flinched, because his next words were 'Hey, don't go by appearances . . . I'm even sicker than I look.' He doffed his hat. 'Thanks for letting me stay till I find my feet. That's real nice of you.'

'I gather you're the "famous" rock star?' I said, a little haughtily, to hide my disappointment.

'Yeah, what's left of him.' He gave a rich chuckle. 'Doan worry. I won't believe everythin' I've heard about you, if you don't believe everythin' you've heard about me.' Without waiting for an invitation, he re-shouldered his rucksack and guitar and barrelled past me, carrying his amplifier into my hall. His scuffed boots rang out on the naked wooden floorboards.

I trotted after him, into my living room, welling up with indignant rage. 'Hey, rock 'n' roll man!'

The interloper jammed his hands into the pockets of his obligatory black moleskins and swung around to face me. 'I'm not in a rock band any more. I've gone freelance.'

I eyed him with the disdain of a Victorian aunt, despite the fact that I was wearing shortie pink PJs. 'Oh, so you're unemployed.'

'Naw.' He drilled me back with a stare which was just as judgemental. 'I'm currently developin' some fascinatin' projects.'

'Oh, so you're *long-term* unemployed,' I decoded. 'I've done internet dating. If I meet a man who tells me he's a solo artist, I immediately ask him which supermarket shelves he's stacking.'

'Listen, toots,' said my cousin's husband. 'Music's not what it used to be. Endless Deep Purple covers, crowds of pissed dickheads, duff equipment, only one speaker out of four workin' so the whole bloody audience has to list to the left to hear the music. Oh fuck. And the *music*. "Mustan' Sally/Guess you better slow your mustan' down" . . . "Rockin' All over the World" . . . "Brown-eyed Girl" . . . "All Right Now",' he medleyed. ' "Johnny Be Good" . . . "Pretty Woman" . . . I used to love "Maggie May" but I can't stand it now. I've sung it every Friday and Saturday night for twenty friggin' years. I'd rather crawl through my own vomit. But' – he shrugged off his rucksack –

'there's no money in new material. So you just end up whackin' away in the erection section . . . the rhythm guitars,' he explained. 'I just need to spend some time not hearin' fuckwits yellin', "DI it into the PA, man" . . . Direct input it straight into the public address system,' he deciphered, clocking my confused expression.

'If you hate it so much, then why did you become a rock musician?' I asked superciliously.

'To get my cock sucked by bimbos, of course.' His chortle disintegrated into a smoker's cough. 'If you'll pardon my French.'

'So, it was a vocational calling to a higher art form then,' I replied scornfully.

'Hey, is it my fault that when you're a rock star you can have any chick in the world?'

'And in your case, you did, judging by the way the syphilis has rotted your brain.'

'Hey, toots' – he shrugged with his eyebrows – 'if you've got it, flaunt it! When I was born, I got a choice – a big dick or a good memory . . . I can't remember what I chose.' The Neanderthal then gave me the most lascivious wink. 'Nice place, by the way. Anyway, once again, thanks for havin' me.'

It was clearly time to Tipp-Ex my mother off my Christmas-card list. What had the woman been thinking – or rather, *not* thinking. 'So, Archibald . . .' I infused his name with total contempt.

'Archie.'

'. . . why are you in London really? Let me guess. You've jumped bail and are on the run?'

'No offence, love, but your mum warned me that you're a hard arse.'

'Hey, I used to care, but I take pills for that now.'

'What? Bitchy pills?' he laughingly enquired. 'The reason I'm in London is that I had to make a pilgrimage to Abbey Road at some point. And I just love that Princess Anne. She always gives the impression that her horse is tethered, like, two feet away. Jeez. I'd just love to saddle up some member of the royal family and ride her round the block. Yee-hah! Giddy-up, girl!'

I looked at him as though he were something I'd walked in on the bottom of my shoe. 'Well, I don't know what my deranged mother told you, but I am not a halfway house for recovering celebrities. So, I think you'd better find somewhere else to stay.'

Archie flexed a heavy forearm as the muscles in his jaw tensed and twitched. 'The reason I'm here is that I need to lie doggo for a while. Whatja mum tell ya? Bugger all, by the looks of things. I met your mum through your cousin, Kimmy, my wife. They went off to some solstice yoga tantric retreat together or somethin'. Anyway, my wife started usin' the rhythm method . . . literally. She started rootin' my drummer. Which kinda put the kybosh on the band. I'm tellin' ya, just lately, if it was rainin' palaces I'd get hit by the dunny door.'

His voice, ragged with emotion, no longer sounded harsh. It was more like ruined velvet. His obvious pain made me relent a little. 'Well, I know what that's like. To be left, I mean. My ex-husband left me when our son was three. It took time, but I've now expunged him from our lives . . . In fact, I'm writing to the pope to confirm that Merlin is the product of immaculate conception.'

My visitor scratched forlornly at his five o'clock shadow. 'Divorce is like a haemorrhoid: in the end, every arsehole gets one.'

I was about to suggest a few cheap hotels when a cacophony of swearing erupted from upstairs. I could hear books thumping to the floor, lamps being thrown and doors slammed.

'What the bejesus is going on up there? A poltergeist?'

'The Immaculate Conception. He hates school.'

'Can't blame him. Is he chuckin' a sickie?'

'Daily.'

'You mean he does his block like this every bloody mornin'?'

'Well, it does save on gym fees, being attacked by a teenage male on a regular basis. Dodging hits and kicks is quite aerobic.'

I thought this revelation would be enough to send the antipodean rock-and-roller scurrying off to a B and B. But the interloper took off his hat and swung his feet up on the coffee table as though he lived here.

'Little bastard! Jeez, that must be bloody exhaustin'.'

My barbed veneer was momentarily cracked by his sympathy. 'It is actually,' I sighed wearily.

'You must want to wring the little bugger's neck.'

'Some days, I really do!' I confessed, with shocked relief.

I sagged into myself. Suddenly my shortie pyjamas felt too big for me. The grey stuffing was coming out of the sofa, like a brain spilling out after a road accident. The house really was on its last, wood-wormed legs. Whatever money I made teaching was eaten up by tutors, 'talking doctors' and occupational and cognitive therapists. I looked beyond Archie to the garden, which had grown knotted and wild, and felt momentarily overwhelmed with fatigue. My shoulders slumped just thinking about getting Merlin dressed. I was like a punctured balloon with all the air slowly leaking out. It was 7.30 and I hadn't yet made the cake for the fête. In my experience, only two things seriously upset teachers, the disappearance of coffee mugs and the health of the photocopier. But not con-tributing a cake to my school fête would be a definite mark against me in the staffroom – a fête worse than death, I murmured to the cat, the only creature who seemed to appreciate my Wildean wit. Unfortunately, the last time I baked was when I fell asleep on the beach, which meant a last-minute dash to the shops . . .

I turned back to the big, bulky shape on my sofa. He wasn't gym-toned, like my ex-husband, but his body was corded by hard work and heavy lifting. Muscles and sinews strained against his shirt.

'So,' I heard myself saying, 'can you do DIY?'

'Sure. It's easy. You just use WD40 for everythin'. Even on the foreskin,' he twinkled impertinently.

It was a mistake. I knew it as I offered it. 'Okay, you can stay. For one week. A trial only. And you can start by persuading the Poltergeist to come down for breakfast.'

Archie opened his guitar case, cocked a leg up on to the coffee table like some kind of conquistador, plugged his guitar into the amp and hit some gigantic chords which sounded a lot like a nuclear explosion. By the end of the chord sequence the windows were shuddering.

'Shit, I've never played this badly before!'

'I didn't realize you *had* played before,' I shouted, covering my ears and cringing. But before I could renege on my offer, Merlin's head thrust itself around the door.

'My brain is leaking through my ears,' my son announced.

I felt panic rising in my chest. Was he having some kind of haemorrhage?

'Yeah? My brain leaks through my ears all the time, mate. It's normal,' Archie counselled, between twangs. I looked up at Merlin. And Merlin was grinning.

I took stock of the bedraggled, ponytailed, cowboy-booted 50-year-old ex-rocker sprawled incongruously across my living room. He was an odd bird. But still, he was also a bird in the hand. Merlin was so entranced by Archie's strumming I was able to take off his pyjama top and button up his school shirt without any violent resistance. For that moment, I dared to let myself believe that having such a man around the place might actually make things easier. That maybe this maniac had ridden to the rescue of Merlin and me . . .

But what I'd forgotten about a bird in the hand is that it's bound to crap on you.

9

You Say Tomato

'The man's as useful as a bloke at a lesbian festival,' I moaned to my sister. It had taken only three days for Archie's charm to wear thin. We were sipping tea as we watched my fifteen-year-old son trying to make a sandwich. We'd been watching in an agony of impatience for twenty minutes as Merlin laboriously but haphazardly laid out the ham on the bread. The simplest request, like making his own sandwich, left him rubbing his temples as though dazed from a fistfight.

'Merlin, do you like Archie?' my sister asked.

'Oh yes. I find it quite relaxing being around musicians. Musicians see the world in a very placid way,' he replied. 'I prefer being with musicians than lawyers or accountants and other grown-ups.'

'There!' Phoebe said to me, sitting on her hands so

she wouldn't be tempted to help my son slice his tomato. 'Surely it *is* kind of relaxing having a man around the house?'

'Relaxing? Well, I guess it's more relaxing than getting gang-raped by a horde of bikers with gingivitis, but that's about it.' My perplexing son was now staring at the tomato as if attempting, through the power of his gaze, to make it slice itself. 'Hold the tomato with one hand, honey, like I showed you, and then cut slowly.'

'Archie's wife is dead,' Merlin said matter-of-factly. 'He said he didn't realize at first, because the sex was the same, but the dishes started to pile up in the sink.'

Phoebe spluttered into her tea with inappropriate laughter. Merlin laughed his head off, too, before stopping abruptly and confessing, 'I don't really get it, Mum.' Whenever he didn't get a joke, he would laugh immoderately to cover his confusion, concluding in a bewildered, lippy grin.

I glowered at my sister. 'It's not funny. Archie says these things and Merlin takes them literally. Kimmy left him for the drummer in his band.' I glanced back to Merlin, who, panic-stricken, was now holding the big round tomato as though it were a hand grenade. 'Merlin, darling, why don't you try to slice the tomato the way I've shown you . . . only, like, *a million times*,' I reiterated, under my breath.

'Because knives make me nervous. What if the blade goes into my brain?'

'How can the knife go into your brain when it's in your hand, nowhere near your head?' I asked, my heart shrivelling up like a raisin.

Phoebe topped up my tea to distract me from the glacially slow sandwich-making. Merlin's movements were so sluggish it would be faster to move things telekinetically. 'But Merlin told me Archie's been busy about the place,' my sister said encouragingly.

'Oh, Archie does his best to appear productive to the untrained eye. But in reality his approach to DIY is that if you can't fix it with a hammer, you've got an electrical problem. He reckons that you only need two tools in life – WD40 and duct tape. If it doesn't move and *should*, he uses the WD40. And if it shouldn't move and *does*, he uses the duct tape.' I rattled the spoon in my teacup with irritation at Merlin's snail-like progress and made myself look away. 'I mean, what was our mother thinking? I am going to kill her. Do you have any idea where she is, by the way?'

'I think she's helping to save a butterfly habitat in Darwin. Or is it Darfur? Or Alpha Centauri? I simply can't remember.' Phoebe laughed fondly. 'You'll have to send a smoke signal or a homing pigeon to find her. Um . . . Lucy . . . ?' Phoebe broke off to point a painted nail in Merlin's direction.

I turned to see my son trying to dislocate his jaws, boa constrictor-style, so he could fit two slices of bread wedged around a huge, whole beef tomato, into his gaping maw.

'Oh Merlin, you can't eat the sandwich like that! You have to *cut* the tomato. I've been trying to teach you this for months.' My frustration erupted vesuvially. Then, as usual, overwhelmed by his dependency and despondent at his helplessness, I commandeered the knife and effortlessly sliced through the tomato. I then layered the slices neatly into the sandwich and shoved it at him. 'You're like a giant toddler, do you know that? You're nearly sixteen now. You have got to try harder!!'

Merlin's face was stricken with anxiety. 'It's not easy growing up. Why can't I be a baby again? Do you know how hard it is for me . . . that there are only sixty seconds in a minute? It's like some kind of punishment. Why does time have to only go in one direction? Why can't it go backwards?' he demanded. 'Who decided a minute should be so short? Where does time go? It's just blasting. Like a jet plane. How old would you be if you didn't know how old you are? I don't want to be an adult, ever, ever, ever!!!!'

As usual I instantly regretted my outburst. My patience was fraying. I needed help, goddamn it. And with no partner, my mother off somewhere on the planet being what she called a 'Sassy' – 'single, sexy and sixty' – and Phoebe flying long-haul, there was only one person who readily came to mind . . .

I prodded at the bulk lying prone on my couch. A snort let me know it was alive. I shoved harder this time, prompting an even more guttural outburst. Archie peeled open one eye, grunted and rolled over. I picked up the glass of water on the table and poured it over Rip Van Winkle's head.

'Fuck!' my antipodean lodger spluttered, jerking upright as though tasered. 'You've got to be the worst landlady in the freakin' world!'

'I doubt it. That would be too much of a coincidence . . . I agreed that you could stay here for a week, Archie, in exchange for help around the house. But when I said "Make yourself at home" I didn't mean lounging on the sofa all day eating all my crisps. I meant cleaning my oven, de-leafing the gutters and getting the mould out of the grout.'

'Bloody hell, your hospitality knows no bounds.'

'You're half man, half sofa.'

'Well, you're half woman, half prison-camp wardress. I've never seen a woman clean so often. You're so anal you'd put newspaper under a bloody rocking horse.'

'I'm not *anal*. I'm just trying to discourage rodents . . . although it didn't work in your case.'

It struck me then that even though I'd only known the man for a few days we were arguing like an old married couple. The instant familiarity was unsettling but felt strangely natural. Sparring with him was infuriating but compulsive – a bit like the way you pick at a piece of torn nail quick or jiggle a loose tooth with your tongue. In retrospect, I can see now how much I was craving adult company. Archie was exasperating, but he was also an inoculation against loneliness and so much more conversational than the cat.

'Housework's a complete waste of bloody time,' Archie continued, yawning. 'As soon as you finish it, you have to do it all again, like two lousy months later.'

'It may have escaped your notice, but I'm a wage slave. I'm a teacher. Not a princess living in a castle.'

'Even if you built a castle in the air, you'd spend all bloody day cleanin' it,' he scoffed. 'And anyway, I do some housework,' he said, looking around. 'See? I'm sweepin' the room with a glance.'

I rolled my eyes in exaggerated annoyance. 'So, who does the majority of cooking and cleaning? Feel between your legs. Are there testicles there? Then it's obviously not you. Didn't Kimmy domesticate you at all?'

He took the feather duster from my hand. 'Chill out, woman. I tell you what, no bloke ever got the horn for a chick 'cause her carpet was well vacuumed. "*Oh, look, there's no dust on your skirtin' boards. I want you now, you comely wench.*" He made a playful grab for my waist.

I lacerated him with a cutting stare. 'Oh, by the way. The 1970s rang. They want their manipulative chauvinism back . . . I'm beginning to see why my cousin traded you in, Archibald.'

My words obviously stung, but he countered with a

caustic comment of his own. 'You say "manipulative chauvinism" as though that's a bad thing. Ah, women,' he sighed, 'can't live with them – can't force them into slavery.'

'You see, that is exactly the kind of crack you make in front of Merlin, which he thinks you're saying seriously.'

'Babe, I *am* saying it seriously. Hey, I understand the concept of feminism, but just not how it applies to me.'

'Well, see how *this* applies to you.' I raised a combative eyebrow. 'You are on a one-day probation. If I don't see an improvement, you're out on your arse.'

As I was jogging back from the park the next morning, I paused to text Phoebe, who was on an overnighter to Berlin. 'That's it. I've put a sign on Archie's door with his check-out time.'

But, turning the key in my lock, I was astounded to see the old rocker up and about and not in his boxers. 'Well, what do you know. It walks and it talks.'

'Housework's bloody exhaustin'.' I watched him disembowel one of the croissants I'd just put on the table. 'I haven't stopped since I got up this mornin'.'

A glance at my watch told me that it was 7.30 a.m. I curled a disapproving lip in his annoying direction. 'Don't forget to wipe your mouth, Archie ... there's a little bit of bullshit on your lips.'

'I even took out the rubbish. So, can I stay now?' he asked, spraying crumbs.

'That's what I hate about men. Unstack one dishwasher and you practically take out an ad in the paper proclaiming your huge achievement.' As he took another croissant, I wished I'd purchased a home autopsy kit instead. 'I've got to get to work. Why don't you get Merlin up and off to school today, do the laundry, get supper and then we'll see, eh?'

Archie stopped eviscerating his pastry in alarm. 'Dinner? Christ. Would Madam like her Vegemite on toast medium or rare?'

'Vegemite can be used as a toast spread, yes . . . or an industrial solvent,' I griped. 'No, I mean a balanced meal, Archibald.'

I staggered home after six hours of trying to teach iambic pentameter to a classroom of kids who couldn't even read their antisocial behaviour orders to find the whole house pulsating with bass notes. The windows of my ramshackle Georgian terrace were rattling as if reliving the Blitz. Angrily subduing my umbrella, I marched into the living room, silenced Led Zeppelin on the stereo, then strode past a recumbent Archie to the washing machine.

I felt the beginnings of a headache zigzag across my cranium. 'I thought I asked you to do the washing?' I demanded, mentally rehearsing my eviction speech.

'Toots, I figure you're about fifteen weeks behind in the washin' department. No point launderin' all

Merlin's clothes now, as he's probably outgrown them.'

'And what about dinner?' Seething with resentment, I stomped around a kitchen littered with bowls enamelled with crusty food.

'I thought we'd have leftovers,' he called from the couch.

'Left over from what? Where is the original meal? Who cooked that? And when?' I was shaking so much I might well have been in the advanced stage of Parkinson's disease.

'Hey, behind every successful woman is a microwave and a ready meal.' He laced his fingers behind his neck and flexed his muscled arms. 'Oh, and a bloke checking out her arse,' he added, craning to get a good view of my rear.

I looked with contempt at the shepherd's pie packaged in plastic on the counter. 'Do you remember what I said about a balanced meal? Where are the vegetables?' I pulled on the rubber gloves and started slamming plates into the sink.

'We had a very balanced lunch, Merlin and me. We had both white *and* dark chocolate, didn't we, Merlin?' he called.

I was about to berate him over the chocolate meal when I realized what I'd heard. 'For *lunch*?' I froze. 'You mean he didn't go to school?'

'Hey, don't do the dishes today – you've been hard at work.' I thought for one irrational moment that

Archie was going to offer to wash them, but then he added with a sly grin, 'Why not do them tomorrow? Or, better still, let Merlin do them. Hey, Wizard!'

'Wizard?' I cringed.

My son bounded into the kitchen and squeezed the breath out of me in his typical bearhug, his face vibrant with exhilaration. 'You are such a gorgeous woman!' he enthused, but then his expression changed into puzzlement. 'But are you my real mother?' Emotions chased each other across his face. 'Is this whole house a set? Are you all actors playing people from a rehearsed script?' The blue eyes transferred their focus from my face off into infinity. I often felt he could drown in his own brainwaves.

'Merlin, why didn't you go to school?' I began, but then stopped short, astonished, as my son picked up a knife and sliced through a tomato. Four, five, six slices. I watched agog as he made himself a sandwich. I wasn't just *a* gog, I was several gogs. I was thrilled at his accomplishment but also detected a small ache of unexpected jealousy.

'That's fantastic,' I said in a brittle voice. I tried smiling at Archie, but it was just a waste of facial muscle, because I didn't mean it.

But to Merlin, I said, 'Darling, that's the most beautifully sliced tomato I have ever seen.' I hugged him, with tears in my eyes. Anyone would have thought he'd just completed a round-the-world solo yacht trip.

' "You say tomato, I say tom-ate-o . . ." ' Archie sang

in a surprisingly mellifluous and melodic voice. 'You say fellatio, I say fell-atio. Tomato, tom-ate-o, fellatio, fell-atio . . . So, can I stay?'

My instincts screamed no, but I nodded yes. A humble tomato had won Archie a stay of execution.

'Is fellatio some kind of gelato?' asked Merlin curiously. 'It would be mesmerizing to try it.'

'You kill me, kid. I love the way you think outside the box.'

Merlin looked at him, mystified. 'There's a box?'

This set Archie off again. He slapped his thigh with mirth. 'After dinner, how 'bout I teach you a few more chords on the guitar? Maybe even how to play with your teeth.'

I groaned inwardly. What had I done? I knew even then that letting Archie stay was as logical a decision as opening a glassware shop in downtown Baghdad. All I could do was wait for the crash . . .

10

A Walk in the Park

Since Merlin's diagnosis, I'd often got the feeling that the whole world was against me, even though, in my more rational moments, I knew it wasn't true ... I mean, Switzerland is neutral, right? I had thought Archie would prove to be some kind of saviour, but the opposite had turned out to be true. His reprieve lasted exactly four days.

'He has to go!' I grizzled to my sister yet again. We were in the garden hosing out Merlin's school back-pack, in which I had just found five rancid sandwiches, whose 'use by' date, judging by the pong factor, obviously read *When Dinosaurs Roamed the Earth.* 'Do you know what he said to Merlin yester-day? He told him that women have evolved smaller feet because it allows them to stand closer to the kitchen sink,' I said in a froth of indignation. 'He asked my son how many men it took to open a beer, and answered, "None. It should be open when she brings it." He told him that the tattoo above a girl's arse is called a beer mat . . . Merlin takes these things literally. He'll repeat it to some woman and end up on a sexual harassment charge.'

I upended the rucksack to drip-dry in the warm June sunshine.

'So, do you think Ape Man will swing down from the forest canopy long enough for me to meet him?' asked Phoebe, intrigued.

'He'll be at Merlin's sixteenth birthday party. But I have to warn you, Moronica is coming. Her ladyship has taken to seeing her grandson once a year on his birthday. She wants to give him his gift . . . Hopefully, his father's head on a plate.'

'And you still never hear from Jeremy?'

'No.' Merlin's father never rang or wrote to his son. I tried to minimize the pain with a glib remark. 'When a woman marries, she should pause and think – is this the name I want to see on my monthly maintenance cheque?'

But my loving sister wasn't fooled. She suddenly held me close; her warm arms wrapped me tightly, as though I were a present. 'I don't know how you do it, Lulu.'

'Alcohol and drugs,' I replied flatly.

On the afternoon of Merlin's sixteenth birthday party, I set the table with sombre sadness. There were so few people to invite. Merlin and I were now to social occasions what myxomatosis is to bunnies.

Apart from me, my sister and her husband Danny and their two children, who came under sufferance, there would be my snooty ex-mother-in-law, Merlin's addled and raddled teacher Penny and her boyfriend and Archie the interloper. It broke my heart that Merlin didn't have one friend his own age. He should be roaming the streets in a noisy whirlpool of boys, chiacking and having shenanigans. But, I gave a melancholy sigh, there was only ever Merlin and me.

'So, where's Cro-Magnon man?' my sister asked, as she employed her years of intensive trolley-dolly training to fold napkins into swan shapes. I'd been in Doris Day overdrive, cooking and cleaning since the early morning, and Phoebe had just dashed in to lend a hand. She'd come straight from the picket line at Heathrow, where BA employees were striking for better pay conditions.

'Archie promised to help, but he's so unreliable. If he says he'll turn up at two on 21 June, that means four o'clock some time in September.'

It was actually five o'clock when Archie finally staggered into the living room, wearing little more than a smirk. 'Thanks for all your help,' I said scornfully.

'Sorry. I was suddenly taken drunk,' he replied, hoicking up his skull-and-crossbones board shorts. 'I seem to remember waterin' your lemon tree with vodka. That means all we need to do in future is squeeze the lemon into the glass.'

'Pure genius,' Phoebe laughed.

Archie turned to eye up my sister. 'Boom chicka wah wah,' he exclaimed suavely, giving a whistle. 'And *you* are?'

'Lucy's little sister,' Phoebe lied, scoring an eyelash-batting average which would put Donald Bradman to shame.

I looked at her askance. I couldn't believe she was flirting with the old fart. She was suddenly the Flirt Master General.

'If I'd known we had company,' he drooled, 'I wouldn't be free-ballin' . . . No Speedos under me board shorts,' he explained.

'Archibald, do you think you could try not to be an arsehole for five minutes and help set the table or peel the potatoes or put out the nibbles or something?'

'Hey, being an arsehole is all part of my manly essence . . . My housework technique is to answer the door to guests and say, "Shit! We've just been robbed. And the house has been trashed. Look at the bloody mess they've made!" With any luck, the guests then clean up, out of sympathy.'

Phoebe, still in her BA uniform, giggled coquettishly as she perched up on a kitchen stool to show off her shapely legs.

I groaned. 'I'm warning you. The reason Archie likes sophisticated women is because opposites attract.'

'So, Phoebe, tell me all about yourself, toots. Everything you've heard about *me* is true, includin' the slander and lies.' He spluttered into a hacking cough, which slightly ruined his Casanova routine. 'Bloody hell. There has got to be a better way to start the day than coughin' your lungs up.' Archie reclined on the kitchen armchair, muscly arms knotted behind his neck, the hair on his chest sprouting from the V-neck of his white sleeveless vest.

'It's evening, actually,' I said curtly, thrusting the potato peeler into his hands. 'And it would be nice if you could get dressed before Merlin's grandma arrives. Oh, and by the way, excessive use of the tongue when kissing my ex-mother-in-law hello could cause a drop in your popularity.'

'So, where's birthday boy? He's been showing me his lists of cricket scores. The kid's memory's bloody awesome.'

Where *was* Merlin? Whenever my son was quiet in his room, I worried that he was hacking into the Pentagon and sparking a computer-generated international missile exchange which would herald the next world war. Dashing upstairs I found him writing pages and pages of his cricket-related facts, every run from every match catalogued from memory, every batting average remembered down to the last decimal point. I knew nothing about cricket, except that my own marriage seemed to have lasted less time than a test match. But my son's complicated head was teeming with numbers. Which was ironic, as he could never get the right change from the corner shop. When I let him get his hair cut on his own, he left a tip big enough to send the barber and his extended family on a trip back to the old country.

'Merlin, darling, I want you to try to be nice to people today. Try to do what people ask you, even if you don't want to, because that's the polite thing to do. That's what a good host does. Put your shoulders back, make eye contact and when people ask how you are, reply "Fine, thanks, how are you?" Can you do that for me, love?' I ruffled his hair affectionately before going into my maternal mantra. 'Thanks, darling. You're a very good boy, you know. And a lovely person. And I love you very, very much.'

'Don't sneak up on me, Mum! I'm really sensitive to noise because I think people are after me . . . Are you really my mother?' he reiterated for the thousandth time. 'You still haven't told me if you're being paid by a TV studio.'

An expression of fondness mixed with fatigue suffused my face. Déjà vu – the gift that just keeps on giving, I thought wryly to my weary self. Of late he'd become so paranoid that if I was walking in front of him, he'd think I was following him the long way round. 'If you're really paranoid, Merlin, you should move to Iran or China, so that your fears are justified,' I joked, kissing the crown of his poor, addled head. 'Of course I'm your mother, love.' Me and whatever alien

185

life form beamed you down to planet earth, I mused, descending the stairs.

I returned to the kitchen to find Archie pre-boarding an air hostess. No more potatoes had been peeled but, following my orders to smarten up, he'd changed into the tracksuit he'd bought from the local charity shop. It was so fluorescent I was worried guests would assume he was an exit sign and leave early. He was leaning on the counter next to my sister and smiling lasciviously.

'I told him not to wear it,' Phoebe fizzed flirtatiously. 'People will think you're a fun-fair attraction and want to ride you.'

Archie winked, a cigarette dripping from his lips. 'Feel free, ladies.' He raised his glass in a toast. 'Hair of the dog . . . ugh,' he winced after taking a sip. 'That dog has mange!'

'You're drinking already?' I chided in my best school-ma'am voice, before stubbing out his fag.

'Of course not. My body is a temple,' Archie mock-bowed.

'Yeah . . . the Temple of Doom.'

And doom was pretty much how I was feeling about the impending party.

Looking back, it's hard to say which bit of the birthday dinner was more toe-curlingly embarrassing. Was it Archie's idea of 'making a sartorial effort', which proved to mean wearing a cummerbund across the fluorescent tracksuit pants? Or was it the way he held forth to my left-wing brother-in-law about Obama? 'What's all this fuss about America havin' a black president? Zimbabwe's had one for ages and he's an absolute fuckin' disaster.'

Or perhaps it was his soliloquy on global warming? 'There'll be some good things. Meltin' polar ice caps make for much better surfin'. And those long queues at Disneyland will be totally reduced by sunstroke. Plus, you can use "bogged down in road tar" as an acceptable excuse for missin' work.'

Or was it what Archie said to Merlin's teacher, Penny, a dedicated feminist? 'Women should always pay for dinner on a date. You chicks fought for equality! So it would be wrong of me not to allow you to pay. In fact, it'd be downright sexist. Hey, Merlin. What do you get if you cross a group of feminists with an Oxo cube? A laughing stock.'

Or was it when he realized that Penny's boyfriend was Korean. 'Jeez. Hope you're not hungry. I didn't tell the neighbours to hide their dogs.'

But no. The honour of Worst Remark Imaginable must have been his introductory conversational gambit to Moronica. As my ex-mother-in-law offered him a pale cold cheek for a perfunctory peck, Archie winked and said, 'Maybe you'd prefer an Aussie kiss?'

'What exactly is an Aussie kiss?' she asked in her angular, prodding, metallic voice.

'The same thing as a French kiss, only down under.' Archie leant over to pat her formidable posterior.

'My girlfriends call me "the Pussy Whisperer".'

He later told Merlin's very grand grandmother, whose usual sucked-on-lemon expression had become even more sour, how much he liked unwaxed pudendas. 'I love it when the pubes kiss-curl out of bikini bottoms. Talk about a fringe benefit,' he chortled. 'My ex-wife – well, she's still my wife, only she's screwin' my best mate – anyway, I satisfied her so much in bed she often had a double orgasm.'

The skin on Moronica's smooth cheek tic-ed. Despite the silence that fell like snowdrifts around the table, I'd drunk enough to allow me to snort with laughter at his sexual ineptitude. 'Double orgasm! Huh!'

'I think you mean multiple,' Phoebe half-whispered to Archie.

'Hey, take a multiple and double it,' Archie rejoindered, before slurping, with succulent indecency, on the oysters he'd brought home from the fish market the day before.

'What's an orgasm?' Merlin asked, putting his shoulders back and making eye contact, as instructed – only the person he was making eye contact with was his totally flummoxed grandmother. Moronica busied herself by poking suspiciously at her gazpacho, as if it were evidence at a crime scene.

Archie proffered the plate of oysters to Moronica. 'Eat one. Then you'll know what it's like to be a lezzo,' he smirked.

'What's a lezzo?' Merlin asked, attempting to show Interest and Engagement, as I'd insisted.

Optic muscles were now in overdrive as guests played frantic eye-tennis. In floral Laura Ashley, my ex-mother-in-law rustled into a more straight-backed position and sipped at her soup like some old sequestered duchess. 'Delicious,' she said blandly, her face a mask of malice. 'Cold soup. What a ... courageous idea.'

But Archie did not take the hint that the subject had been changed. 'J'know why God invented lesbians, Merlin?' my boarder persevered. 'So that feminists wouldn't breed.' He chuckled heartily, then slugged back another beer.

Merlin's teacher, Penny, excused herself and left before dessert with her allegedly dog-famished boyfriend in tow. Moronica patted at her corrugated perm and re-applied cerise lipstick whilst surreptitiously consulting her watch. I hurried things along by launching into a loud rendition of 'Happy Birthday'. Merlin, shoulders back, making eye contact and determined to be a gracious host, rose to his feet. 'I'd like to make a speech.' My toes curled up in my shoes like dead leaves in dread at what my un-predictable son might say.

'It's delightful to have my grandma here, even though my mother and my grandma haven't had the ideal relationship. In fact, I'm rather surprised they're in the same room. Mum says you're two-faced,

Grandma, but if so, why would you be wearing *that* one?' he asked without a trace of irony.

While the guests' silent eye-tennis became more frenetic, Archie guffawed out loud.

'It's always a delight to see my cousins, with whom I share a fascinating genetic inheritance,' Merlin continued, unabashed. 'Even though they think that I'm a geek and a freak because I worry about things like whether you can use yo-yos on the moon. Thank you for my iPod, Aunt Phoebe, and I just want to say that you are nearly as ravishing as my mum. You have beautiful clavicles. And are definitely on my list of the World's Smoking-hot Babes of your Generation . . . Thank you for the paints, Grandma, but I'm retiring from art. Artists are too selfish. Name me one artist who isn't selfish. They think they're gods. I know there's a lot of pressure on me to become a genius because I have Asperger's. But I'm not a genius. I'm not a philosopher either. I think you all want to turn me into a philosopher. Nor am I a discoverer. But I do think I'm at the most handsome point of my career and a legend of society. It would make me feel amazing inside if a woman loved me. It would be so majestic . . . Why do no love goddesses ever want to ask my age and chat with me? Women make me feel sugar sweet and electric. Women are my number-one priority at the moment and I hope to get a girlfriend soon . . . Archie is going to teach me how to do this because he tells me he is an animal in bed.'

'Yeah, a hamster,' I whispered tipsily to my sister. But the aside died on my lips as I turned back to see the guests gawking at a stash of lad magazines Merlin was pulling forth from a plastic carrier bag.

'Which is why he's given me these educational magazines . . .'

'Dylan,' Phoebe called urgently to her son, 'why don't you take Merlin to the park to take some photos with his new digital camera?'

Merlin pocketed his new iPod, slung the digital camera my mother had sent from Suva around his neck and slipped on the hideous maroon cardigan Moronica had given him because she thought I didn't dress him well enough. 'And don't forget your phone,' I called out after him.

As soon as Merlin had left, I rounded on Archie to deliver the routine lecture circa 1970 on how pornography tells lies about women and the truth about men . . . or maybe just to point out that he was obviously the only living brain donor in medical history. But before I could speak, Moronica's thick, jewelled claw of a hand was on my arm.

'I am shocked to find Merlin fraternizing with such a creature. Who *is* this hideous man?' She spoke as though Archie weren't even in the room. 'How can you allow such unsavoury people to live in your home?'

Archie responded with a loud and melodious belch.

'He's my cousin's husband,' I said helplessly, gathering up the offending gazettes.

Moronica's expression was vinegary and her angry voice rose half an octave, losing much of its well-bred intonation in the process. 'Well, it's clearer than ever that Merlin needs to be somewhere more suitable.' That word 'suitable' held all the glacial condemnation of a judge's pronouncement of sentence. 'My offer still stands.'

As Moronica mounted her high horse and set off at a gallop, she gestured with a peremptory sweep of her arm for the table to be cleared, forgetting momentarily that we were not her servants. But Phoebe and I leapt at the excuse and made a beeline for the kitchen, a bemused Archie in our wake, leaving Danny to bear the brunt of her complaints. Archie switched on the insinkerator to help drown out my ex-mother-in-law.

'You see, you can't kick me out, Lucy,' Archie grinned, shouting above the grind. 'I'm just so good in the kitchen.'

'Yeah, you can just graze there for hours. But you can't seriously think I can let you keep living here after your appalling behaviour today? Not to mention giving those degrading magazines to Merlin without my permission. For that alone, you leave first thing in the morning.'

When Phoebe and I finally sat back at the table some forty minutes later, Moronica stopped berating a now desperate-looking Danny and turned her attentions back to me. 'You know you can put a carrot into a mould of, say, Great Britain and it will grow into the shape of Britain? Well, a child is the same. Experts in an institution can mould him.'

'You want to turn my son into a deformed vegetable?' I enquired. Phoebe giggled, insubordinately. I might have explored my former mother-in-law's hilarious horticultural intentions a little further, except that Merlin suddenly thundered into the house. He slammed the door behind him, as though a pack of wild dogs were hot on his heels. The boy was all wide eyed and upset . . . and only wearing his underwear.

'Darling, what's happened?' I asked, leaping to my feet as though electrocuted.

His face was a blur of misery. 'My camera. I dropped it. And my iPod. Plus, Mum, my phone . . .'

I felt panic punch my chest. 'Merlin. Where are your clothes?' I hoped that my voice didn't betray the detonation of fear I felt inside.

'This man. In the park.' His voice was plaintive with despair.

I felt my throat clamping. 'Go on, darling.' I moved to his side and ran a reassuring hand through his turbulent hair. 'It's okay,' I soothed, as calmly as I could.

'This man. In the park. He asked me how I was and I remembered to do what you said. I put my shoulders back and made eye contact and asked him how *he* was. He told me that he was a tourist and that he would like to take a photo of a Londoner . . . I remembered what you said . . . about being polite to people and not just thinking about myself all the time . . . so I said yes. He said let's go into those shrubs over there so I can get a good photo of the foliage. I said it would be my pleasure.'

Merlin's eyes were darting everywhere and flinching from everything. His words ran into each other like raindrops down a window pane.

'He started taking photos of me. Then the stranger said, "It's so hot. Why don't you take your shirt off?" He said that I had such a good body, would I take my jeans off for the photo too . . . Then he asked me to take all my clothes off . . .'

In my mind's eye, I could see the predator's slow, lazy blink as he spun his nasty web, and an involuntary shiver gripped my spine.

'I didn't want to be rude, Mum, because you said I should try to be more sociable and try to do what people ask even if I don't want to. Because that's polite . . . But it didn't feel right to take my underpants off. And then he tried to pull them off and . . .' Merlin clung to me like melted marshmallow. 'It was so confusing.'

I was gasping in and out, like a fish on a shore, dreading what was going to come next.

'And then it just entered my mind that he could be a' – he searched for the right word – 'podiatrist. Or even a murderer. He said I had good muscles and could he feel them.' Merlin waved his hand back and forth like a windshield wiper to sweep away the images in his head. 'I know you told me to be nice to people but I think eye contact is overrated . . .'

The normally lethargic Archie sprang up like a ninja. 'What did this bloke look like? Skinhead? Posh? Young, old, middle-aged?'

'He spoke like Prince Charles. I think he was aged about in the middle,' Merlin said into the suffocating silence. 'Trousers – a jaundiced mustard colour. Shirt' – he pondered for a moment – 'crushed strawberry.'

Archie was on the street before Merlin had finished his sentence. The front door banged against the hall wall then shuddered backwards, gaping open.

Merlin drew himself against me like a small animal in need of a place to hide. I stroked his hair. In the next half an hour, with the calming comfort of cups of tea and gentle assertions that Merlin had done nothing wrong, I ascertained that the man had tried to coax Merlin back to his flat.

'But I just had this bad feeling that this was not going to go very well,' Merlin reiterated, putting on the clothes Phoebe had fetched for him, 'and ran home ... Was that rude?' he asked, mortified that he may have made another faux pas.

Not getting a joke, not knowing what to say then saying the wrong things, being told off but not under-standing why, doing your best but still getting it wrong, feeling confused, frightened, left out, out of synch, all day, every day, this is the world of the Aspergic child. I hugged him fiercely. The relief that he hadn't been abducted, bashed, raped or killed was so intense it almost felt like pain.

Merlin went on to explain that his cousin had left him in the park as soon as they'd got there and gone off to meet his mates. Phoebe, fuming, was already on the phone to ground her son, which would only make Dylan resent Merlin all the more, I noted sadly. 'Merlin is *not* a retard!' I heard her seething at my nephew down the phone.

Throughout it all, my eagle-eyed ex-mother-in-law watched from the sidelines. Her eyes were aglow with a chilling triumphalism. 'You see?' she announced, with a smug note of certainty. 'This is why Merlin would be better off living in a protected environment full of people just like him.' Moronica's hand shot out like a tentacle and suctioned on to my arm. 'A place where these things can't happen.' Her lips moved like a pair of scissors, as she spat out her cutting comments.

I was about to call the police to report the incident when Archie strode back into the house. He was carrying an expensive-looking camera. His shirt was torn, there were grazes on his knuckles, a scratch on his arm and some skin off his nose. 'I took a photo of the slimy bastard with his own camera to show the cops. I told him that with each mugshot taken, he would get two complimentary wallet-sized prints ... just before I punched the ratbag's lights out.'

'You retrieved my iPod!' exclaimed Merlin ecstatically. His smile lit up like neon.

'Yeah, and your phone, clothes and camera.' Archie

lowered his voice a few decibels. 'I decided to leave the cardigan.' He winked at me. 'Happy Birthday, kiddo!' Archie then popped a can of beer and took a good long swig. He picked up his guitar, snuggled the curve of the wood across his knee and started to play a medley of Beatles hits, successfully silencing my ex-mother-in-law once more.

Merlin was soon happier than a germ in a jacuzzi. My heart stopped knocking about in my chest, my breath slowed down and I began to regain my senses.

'It's just as well you're here, Archie!' Phoebe enthused. 'I'm so glad you came to stay. Merlin and Lucy really need a man around the house.'

I struggled with a hundred emotions. I too felt over-whelmingly grateful for Archie's protective stance for my fatherless son, but was also profoundly disapproving of his bad influence. 'What? Phoebe, no! Archie's not staying. Who said so?!'

But as Phoebe and her husband Danny backslapped Archie, singing his praises, in between harmonizing along to his guitar medleys, nobody took note of the fact that it was not what *I* wanted. 'No, no, he really can't stay,' I reiterated. '. . . Is anyone listening to me?' I felt as though I were having a heart attack in a game of charades. 'I mean it!' . . . But I was speaking to thin air.

11
Train of Thought

It wasn't just that Archie stepped over the line. He didn't seem to understand that there even was one.

Despite the man's tomato-slicing tutorials and paedophile-pounding, 'He's got to go' became my refrain all through the summer. 'He's a lazy bum, a total sponger and comes home half-drunk every night.'

'Well, he's obviously trying to soothe his broken heart,' Phoebe volunteered, ever willing to see the good in people.

'The only reason he comes home half drunk is because he's run out of money at the bar.'

'He told me his money transfer from Australia has been held up.'

We were at the post office, queuing up to have my intrepid mother's mail redirected. We hadn't heard much from her, except for a postcard explaining that she was now crewing a tall ship in Vanuatu, buddying less able-bodied crew members in exchange for another sailing holiday. 'Girls, I adore ship life. The endless opportunity for semen jokes!' she wrote. And then, three weeks later, another postcard saying that she was now washing elephants at a wildlife rescue centre in Thailand: 'Always have your photograph taken beside an elephant. It makes you look soooo much slimmer and, of course, much less wrinkly!' she advised.

'I've fed and housed the man for weeks now, and he still shows no sign of getting a job or making his "*album*",' I complained to Phoebe as the line shuffled forward. 'He did a one-man show at the pub the other night and, believe me, there were more people on stage than in the audience.'

'But he's so good with Merlin. Hot flush, hot flush.' My 47-year-old sister leant back on the post-office wall and fanned herself frantically. 'Ugh! I'm having my own weather.'

I passed her my chilled bottle of mineral water, which she held to her perspiring forehead. 'I don't suppose *you'd* take him in?' I asked tentatively.

'Are you kidding?' she said, her face beetroot red. 'In my hormonal state? I'd either fuck him, eat him or kill him.'

After a quick Thai meal with my sister I drove home, steeling myself for battle. It was time to turn into Attila the Landlord and eject my interloper. I slid the key into the lock of my darkened house with slight trepidation. Usually Merlin would be playing air guitar with Archie to Pink Floyd or Rolling Stones tracks. The silence was ominous and the darkness eerie.

'Merlin?' I called out, my voice giving a good impression of a Viennese choirboy, octave-wise.

'Shhhh!' The deep-throated, hushed admonition came from the living room. 'And don't turn on the lights.'

I brailled down the hall towards the voice. 'What the hell's going on? Has the fuse blown? Gosh, if only I knew a *handyman* anywhere in the near vicinity,' I drawled flippantly.

'It ain't the fuse.'

'Then why are you sitting in the dark?'

'I don't want the neighbours to know that I wasn't invited to the openin' of the new Rock 'n' Roll Hall of Fame.'

'You know the *neighbours*?'

'Course.' Archie nodded casually. 'I always leave their parties before midnight too . . . So people think I have to get up early in the mornin', you know. Because I'm workin' on somethin'.'

'You've been invited to my *neighbours*' houses for *parties*?' I said, amazed. 'I don't even know the names of those yummy mummies. And anyway, why *aren't* you working on something?'

'Work, ah, yes . . . work fascinates me,' Archie said, wistfully. 'I can look at it for bloody hours.'

'So I see,' I snapped, noting the pile of washing-up in the sink and stacks of empty plates on the table. Oblivious to our conversation, Merlin was contentedly surfing on his laptop . . . probably breaking into some Nassau secret site for which he'd be arrested, extradited and sent to an upstate maximum-security prison for the rest of his natural life, knowing my luck.

'Hard work doesn't make you a better person. It's total bullshit. Hard work has killed millions of people. Indolence is the way to go.'

'Archie, what are you? Fifty-two, three? Fifty-six maybe? Your life is not a rehearsal . . . Although, in your profession, you could definitely have done with a few.'

'It's not that I'm eschewin' gainful employment, toots. It's just takin' time for me to break into the British music scene.'

'Along with only about 3 million other people.' I flicked on the light, flooding the room with harsh yellow neon.

Archie flinched at the sudden illumination. 'Better than just karaoke-in' your way through life. Like you.'

'Archie, I'm telling you this because you've been nice to my son and I appreciate that. You need another game plan besides sitting on a private plane demanding only yellow Smarties and pink poodles and Jack Daniels, because that's Never Going To Happen.'

'No animal products are used in the manufacture of Jack Daniels, you know. It's practically a friggin' health drink.' Archie took a swig from the bottle he was holding then leaned forward to salt his plate of chips.

'Save your breath, Archibald. You'll need it to inflate your next girlfriend. You need to get a job so you can find your own place to live. And, can I just give you a word of advice? In England, it's generally considered tacky to take an Esky to a job interview.' I impounded his bottle of whisky. 'And get your hair cut. It's simply sitting there on your head like roadkill.'

'Exactly what kind of job ja have in mind?' he asked, slouching further back on to the couch. 'An office job, no doubt. A tie is a noose a man hangs himself with.'

'Any job will do. Windexing the sneeze hood over the salad bar. Pouring drinks in a wine bar . . .'

'Come on. Is it a credible hypothesis that a rock star would work in a wine bar, for Chrissake? I won a gong for one album . . . Well, I would have, if the lead singer from Navel Fluff hadn't got an embolism. That bastard.'

I wasn't sure if he was joking or not, but shook my head at him with pity. 'The only award you'd ever win is at Crufts – the dog show. Because you are an animal.'

'Obviously, in your eyes, I'm nobody. But, as Nobody is perfect, you forgive me, right?' Archie chortled, before adding plaintively, 'For your cousin Kimmy's sake, you should just let me stay here till my money comes in. You were quite matey when you were kids, right? Hey, I could be your toyboy. Now there's an attractive idea. Especially when you're wearin' such a tight T-shirt and no bra. Five people killed in Lambeth from high-velocity nipples!' he deadpanned. 'Boom chicka wah wah.'

With immense irritability, I shrugged on a cardigan. 'Archibald,' I said icily, 'I would rather extract my own fillings with a pair of pliers than go anywhere near you.'

'Baby, I taste so good you'll want the recipe.' Archie, whom I only really recognized perpendicular, now stood up and moved towards me with a panther-like pace, his weathered boots ringing out on the wooden floor. 'Why don't you come out to the pub with me for a drink? Goin' out with me is like makin' love. When it's good, it's very good and when it's bad . . . it's even better.'

'You're not getting this, are you? *I'd rather have tent pegs hammered into my nostrils.*'

Archie cocked one leg behind him, resting his foot flat against the wall, and eyed me slowly up and down. 'Why doan cha go slip into somethin' a little more comfy . . . J'know, you've got such a great figure. If you didn't have that bitter and twisted, totally cynical "All men are bastards" look in your eye so bloody common to single mothers, you could have been a model.'

I moved rapidly towards the stairs. 'Spoken like a true chauvinist. Do you know what chauvinists are,

Archie?' I flung the comment over one shoulder. 'Mother nature's way of promoting celibacy. You're moving out. Tomorrow. Kimmy or no Kimmy. Blood is thicker than water, but not whisky.' I took the stairs two at a time, slammed my bedroom door and lay on my bed, exhausted. What with work hassles and Merlin and my unwanted house guest, I would have loved to take up Archie's offer of slipping into something more comfortable, preferably a coma.

By the next afternoon, I had packed up all Archie's various possessions and dumped his guitar, amp and rucksack on the front steps. Phoebe had come over as back-up.

'I know the guy's complexion is rough hewn and craggy. But there's something attractive about that kind of lived-in face,' Phoebe mused in a whisper, as we surreptitiously observed him pack up his CDs.

'Lived-in! That's a face which should be closed down for demolition.'

Archie sauntered into the kitchen towards us, looking pretty much exactly the way he had when he had first crashed into my life. 'G'day, Phoebe. So you heard the bad news?'

'Let me guess. Angela Merkel and *Playboy* magazine have agreed terms?' she suggested playfully.

'That your sis is kickin' me out,' he said sadly. 'I'd love to have a heart-to-heart with her about it, but what would *she* use?'

I rolled my eyes with pantomime theatricality. 'I'd love to respond but I left my spontaneous barbed ripostes in my other handbag. Sorry.'

Archie ignored me and bent over my sister's hand and kissed it tenderly. 'It's been great meetin' you though, Pheebs ... I'll just wait to say goodbye to Merlin.'

I checked my watch. 'Really? Must you? He's at the British Museum,' I told my sister. 'He's started going there every Saturday. But he'll be home at 4.30 on the dot. He's incredibly punctual.' A wave of relief washed over me. In an hour or so the intruder would be out of my life and then, once again, there'd just be Merlin and me ...

It was half past five when I realized Merlin was missing. I'd been so distracted fumigating my spare room that I hadn't noticed the time. Merlin knew the train route. I'd escorted him at least ten times, until it was ingrained in his brain. When he'd turned sixteen, I'd allowed him to travel on his own. He had his mobile phone. And money for a taxi if anything went wrong. I punched his number on my speed dial. No answer. I rang the British Museum and convinced them to page him. I contacted the police. But the officer said that they didn't investigate missing teenagers for at least a week. He might be a runaway. Were there troubles at home? The thought of my gullible son out there in the rollercoaster world, full of dangers and strangers, made my stomach heave sourly.

At 6.30 I rang the transport police and explained about my son's Asperger's. They offered to put out a description to their station workers, but in a city like London it was needle-in-a-haystack territory. By now, panic was fluttering in my chest like a moth. Had he been mugged down some ruinous alley? Kidnapped by another paedophile? Had he fallen on to the tracks? My throat was on fire with misery. Archie asked for the route Merlin took to the museum and set off on foot.

At 7 p.m., I gunned the car and big-dippered over local speed bumps to get to the tube station. No sign of my son. I churned the streets, double-parking during dashes into Merlin's favourite haunts – a couple of cafés, a bookshop, HMV on Oxford Street . . . As the minutes crawled by, my heart hammered against my ribcage.

I rang Phoebe, who was waiting at my house in case Merlin had turned up. No news. At 8 p.m. I steered my car away from the museum towards the British Library, a place he also frequented. The city seethed with people. When the rain fell they hurried faster, like caged mice. As I drove through the drizzle, the wiper blades made frantic arcs, then, as I cut the engine, staggered to a halt, like two collapsing marathon runners. Darting on foot through the trundling buses, I inhaled the diesel belches of taxis, then slalomed through the throng pouring in and out of King's Cross tube station. But still no Merlin. I even searched St Pancras station, as he'd recently told me that it had enjoyed a 'much better career than Euston'.

Back in the car, in my confusion and panic I took some wrong turns and ended up careening through the City. Buildings needled the sky like giant syringes. At 9.45, I left the glittering pincushion of central London for Lambeth.

By the time I got home, my nerves were shrieking like unoiled hinges on a derelict barn door. In between rain showers I took to pacing up and down the road. All I could hear was the sound of puddles sploshing and hissing from passing car tyres. By 10.30, my mind was clattering. By eleven, I was about to call Jeremy for the first time in ten years. Then Archie and Merlin sidled into view.

I flung myself at my son and held him to me. 'Are you okay?' I quavered. I clung to him, paralysed by love. A brittle sob of exhaustion escaped my lips. Fear, danger and elationfought for emotional supremacy. Finally, a wave of outrage rose in my chest. 'Merlin! Where have you been? Why didn't you call?'

Merlin pushed away from me, distraught, his nerves stretched taut. He waved his arms around in an agitated way as though conducting Beethoven's 5th symphony.

'I looked all around Russell Square. Every café, bookshop, park. Then I finally thought I'd check the tube station. And that's where I found him. Sittin' on a platform. Apparently he'd been sittin' down there since four o'clock,' Archie said, as we squelched inside, out of the rain.

'Why?' I thought once more of all the dreadful fates that could have befallen him. Still oppressed by the residue of terror, I held Merlin close once more.

'Well . . .' Archie scratched his chin stubble '. . . it's got somethin' to do with tube germs and a sex change. I brought him home by bus.'

'I just knew that if I got on any t-t-t-train, the germs from the carriage would give me a s-s-s-sex change,' Merlin stammered, gripping his hands together convulsively, the way he did when traumatized.

I felt the colour drain out of my face. 'Why didn't you just leave the station and get a taxi?'

'I just kept hoping I could get the courage to get on the next train . . . I was trying to make myself . . . But the sex change! The germs!' He fell into a state of hand-wringing anxiety.

I took him by the shoulders and looked into his startled eyes. 'But you know that's illogical, Merlin, don't you?'

'But how do I know it couldn't happen? Tap water has female hormones in it too.'

Archie carted his bag back to the spare room he'd vacated earlier, to change into some dry clothes. Merlin and I went on in this circuitous vein, with me trying to explain the impossibility of such a scenario, lecturing him on genes and chromosomes and trying to point out that, if this were the case, why didn't every commuter change sex all the time? But Merlin just became more and more fraught.

'Perhaps people do change sex? Maybe you were a man once?' he asked me suspiciously, questions whirring around his head like hornets.

I now experienced a more brutal fear than the realization I'd lost him earlier in the evening. Merlin's mild angst seemed to have morphed into something more serious. Was this the beginning of a darkening of his moods? Would he now be endlessly fleeing down some descending labyrinth of the mind, at the end of which his own demons lay in wait?

I stroked his arm and tried to rationalize away his terror. But Merlin remained lost in his own private torment. I looked into his face pityingly, all the time talking calmly and quietly. But my son's expression remained one of baffled incredulity. Merlin took a shuddering breath and screwed up his eyes, as if in pain. Anxiety was always with him, the shadow on his psychological X-ray. There was no cure. His condition was constant, like tinnitus. It was just *there*. Always.

Merlin and I could have gone on and on in conversational circles till dawn if Archie hadn't short-circuited the situation. I looked up to see him standing in the doorway draped in an old designer wrap dress Jeremy had bought me all those years ago. He wore a floral hat and a slash of red lipstick. His big hairy feet were half wedged into my sling-back stilettos, his heels sticking out the back like lumps of Parmesan. We all gaped at him as he pranced about in my purloined high heels.

'Oh, look,' Archie said in his earthy, twangy drawl. 'I must have got on to a train carriage and changed sex because I feel like a woman.'

He grabbed his guitar and broke into a Shania Twain song, 'Man, I Feel Like a Woman', segueing, with hip wiggles, into Dylan's 'Just Like a Woman' and Alice Cooper's 'Only Women Bleed'.

I looked at Archie, dumbfounded. How could he be so psychologically crass? This would only confuse Merlin all the more. But then I noticed that Phoebe was rolling about laughing. And so was Merlin. Great, heaving belly laughs that he wasn't putting on.

'Archie, as a woman? *I don't think so,*' my son guffawed. 'I suppose it is a pretty deranged theory.'

And then I laughed too. With relieved abandon. I laughed until I started crying.

Fortified by success, Archie then asked if he could unpack his bags.

'Okay.' I shrugged docilely, wiping tears from my eyes. There were worse things that could happen than Archie moving back in, I thought to myself . . . But then why did I feel as though I was using a hammer to swat a fly on my forehead?

12

Nothing Risquéd, Nothing Gained

After sixteen years of raising Merlin I could qualify for a Ph.D in angst. If nail-biting adventure had been what I was looking for, I would have tried jumping over the Grand Canyon on a motorbike, diving with sharks, crossing the English Channel on a Lilo or taking a job as a BP oil-company executive. Trying to conquer Merlin's condition all on my own was as effective as attempting to kill Genghis Khan with a paper cut.

My main worry about my son involved mugging. After failing all his exams, Merlin was repeating his GCSE year. In the course of his first week back at school in September, he was beaten up on the school bus, all for £1.50. On the way to the cinema he was mugged at knife-point to extort fifteen quid and his iPod. On the way to the British Museum *by bus*, he was cornered in the shelter by a gang who humiliated him by holding a lighter under his chin and filming it on their phones. For Merlin, leaving the house was as hazardous as Scott leaving his Antarctic base camp. He was held up so often that Archie started giving marks out of ten for the robbery. Plus extra money. 'Here you go, kiddo. Money for the bus and a bit extra for the mugging.' He also started teaching my son how to kickbox and some other forms of self-defence. 'But screamin' like a girl and runnin' for the hills is also good,' he advised, chortling. 'That's my motto, kid. Do unto others . . . and then run!'

As Mother was currently helping street children in Peru before trekking to Machu Picchu on the Inca trail, as you do, there was little choice but to trust Archie to keep an eye on Merlin after school. I'd planned to be deputy head by this age and, in my spare time, win the Orange Prize for literature, presented, of course, by Daniel Craig, preferably wearing his James Bond budgie smugglers . . . But all that going home as soon as the bell rang and popping out at lunchtime meant that I hadn't even been promoted to head of department. Now that the hairy old rocker was earning his keep, I was trying to make up for my poor performance by running the after-school drama club and poetry appreciation. If opportunity doesn't knock – get a doorbell. That was my new motto.

'Sure. You can trust me,' Archie said – words which had the same striking ring of authenticity as Iran saying it wasn't developing a nuclear weapon.

'Okay,' I quizzed, as I threw together a packed lunch to take to work, 'if Merlin was choking on, say, an ice cube, what would you do?'

'If he was chokin' on an ice cube, I'd simply pour a cup of boiling water down his cake-hole. That should do the trick ... I'm jokin',' he said, to placate my horrified reaction.

But it wasn't such a funny joke when I arrived home after drama rehearsal to find Merlin urinating in the bathroom basin. 'Merlin! What the hell do you think you're doing?'

'Archie told me the best way to avoid arguments with women about leaving the toilet seat up is to pee in the basin.'

'Archie!' I stormed through the house looking for my hapless boarder. I found him stretched out in my bath-tub beneath a blanket of bubbles, with the door ajar. 'Why did you tell Merlin that!!! About the basin??' I was stopped in my tracks by an unmistakably pungent odour. 'Are you smoking dope?'

'I smoke drugs to forget I smoke drugs. Just like I have casual sex to forget that I have casual sex,' he teased.

How could I let him know just how displeased I felt? Perhaps if I turned on my hairdryer and tossed it into the bath? 'What kind of example are you setting my son?' I pulled the plug on his bubble bath. But the symbolism that I was about to pull the plug on a whole lot more was obviously lost on the miscreant because he then said, 'Hell, I can set a good example. Merlin!' he called out. *'Some advice, son. Say no to drugs, so you'll have more time to drink.'* Archie sank below the frothy surface then blew a stream of water vertically through the suds, like a sperm whale.

I waited impatiently for him to reappear. 'And if you think casual sex is satisfying you need to have both your heads examined.'

Merlin's tousled cranium popped around the door. 'So,' he asked us, grinning like the cat which had not only licked the cream but also eaten the canary, 'are you two having the ideal relationship?'

Archie's laugh came from deep within his chest and rattled around the tiled bathroom. Merlin mimicked his chortle all the way down the hall.

'What other life tips did you give my son?' I demanded to know, averting my eyes as the water drained away. 'Besides the fact that Iron Man is a superhero and that "Iron Woman" is a command.'

The bath water had drained, leaving my boarder beached on the white enamel, his body hairs glistening. I'd imagined Archie to be so hairy that he'd make Chewbacca look waxed. I thought he'd be as bulky and white as a fridge, with an IQ to match. But, naked, he was alarmingly manly. Not to mention his obvious potential for a very lucrative jockey underwear endorsement deal.

'You're right, Lou. I feel totally remorseful . . . but I

reckon I have the strength of character to fight it,' he scoffed.

'You see, *that*'s the kind of statement you make as a result of controlled substances being in widespread use. What you don't understand is that Merlin takes everything literally.'

'You're so friggin' overprotective. I can't believe you let the kid out . . . Out of your womb, I mean.' Archie hauled himself up on to his feet in an avalanche of foam. He faced me, his muscular legs planted in a V-sign. I turned my back on him before the foam evaporated.

'Of course I'm overprotective! Most parents expect their kids to have all the things in life they couldn't afford so it'll be nice to move in with them in old age. But my son will never leave home.'

'Bullshit. How will you ever know if Merlin can cope in the outside world when you never let him in it? Every time he leaves the bloody house you'd think he was emigratin'. The fuss, the cryin', the worry, the long hugs an' heartfelt goodbyes. It's nauseatin'.'

Fury bubbled up in me. 'What do you know about it? Someone has to make sure he's charged his mobile phone, that he has enough money on his travel card . . . Someone has to make sure he eats his vegetables. And that person is me.'

'The way you get a kid to eat vegetables is to coat them in chocolate,' he jibed.

'Do you mind getting a towel? You naked is a sight

people pray they don't live long enough to witness,' I lied.

'The kid's sixteen. In two years he can vote, for Chrissake.'

'You've heard what Merlin says! He doesn't want to grow up. He wants to stay a teenager.'

'Well, who wouldn't?' he said, towelling off. 'You get to take drugs, get pissed, stay out all hours, never work and not pay taxes. Seems perfectly sane to me. In fact, I want to stay a teenager too.' Togaed in a towel, he sauntered downstairs to the kitchen to help himself to some of my food.

'You know what?' I complained, trotting after him. 'I think I'd rather take grammar lessons from George W. Bush or, I dunno, grooming lessons from Motorhead's Lemmy than parenting tips from you.'

'Truth is, toots, the kid doesn't need a babysitter. At his age, *he* could babysit. Besides, j'know what Merlin said to me about babysitters? He told me that he doesn't understand why adults hire teenagers to act like adults, so that the adults can go out and act like teenagers. Pure genius,' he chortled. 'Strewth! The kid's shavin'. But look at the instructions you leave when you go out.' He picked up my list of emergency phone numbers. 'It's longer than War and bloody Peace.'

I was outraged by his ill-informed audacity. '*She'll be right, mate,*' I mimicked his accent. 'That's your answer to every angst, from parking tickets to a tracheotomy.'

Archie gave me a reproachful stare. 'Merlin's like a bungee-jumper. That invisible umbilical cord keeps snapping him back to you. Cut the kid free. Let him glide, soar . . .'

'Does the word "splat" mean anything to you?' I carped coldly. 'I think you'll find that a mother knows best.'

'Bullshit!' He rounded on me. 'Mothers get stuff wrong. My mum told me that good things come to those who wait, that the meek shall inherit the earth and, oh yeah, that money ain't everythin'. What a steamin' pile of horseshit. For your information, sweet-cheeks, your son thinks you're an interferin' snoop . . . But I'm sure you've already read that on his Facebook.'

'I *need* to interfere. It may have escaped your notice, Einstein,' I castigated, 'but my son is not normal . . . unless you count it normal writing thousands of cricket scores on the bedroom walls, blogging about his wet dreams, wearing a Batman mask on the tube and a bike helmet to bed in case his brain melts out of his ears, and wanting to live in a communist country so that he doesn't have to make any decisions.'

'You want Merlin to be normal, but what the hell is normal? Are *you*? Am *I*?' Archie cast an amused eye over me and then, much to my surprise, laughed right into my face. 'It's abnormal to be normal. Everyone seems bloody normal until you get to know them.'

'You're not getting this, are you? When a woman's

pregnant, she's always wondering, when will my baby move? Well, the answer is *right after he's finished college.* But my son will never go to uni or have a job or move out. He can't concentrate in class. He failed every one of his GCSE exams. Examination papers are like Swahili to him.'

'Seems to me that Merlin has this photographic memory – which has yet to develop,' he punned. 'But I have a feelin' the kid's gonna grow into his brain . . . Meanwhile, you've gotta let him make mistakes, get drunk, get laid . . .'

'Laid?' I snapped, appalled. 'He's not a carpet, Archibald.'

'You're the only woman in his life and it's gettin' a little bit like a Greek tragedy around here.'

'Don't be obscene! There's nothing inappropriate about Merlin's feelings for me.'

'Maybe not in *Tasmania.*' Archie's amusement grew as he took pleasure in my discomfiture. He was practically cocking his elbow on an invisible car window ledge and whistling a tune.

'You disgust me!' I slapped the lid on some Tupperware and burped it tightly – my emotions similarly concealed. Furious, I retreated into martyred domesticity, peeling vegetables and rattling saucepans, little tornados of steam fuming ceiling-wards.

I didn't speak to Archie again until Merlin bounded into the room straight from his tennis lesson at the local gym, all limbs and jerky wild movements. He hugged me as usual with the kind of fervour that could result in hairline fractures.

'Oh Mum, you are such a gorrrrgeous woman. You have such a *fab*ulous figure for a woman your age. You have such a curvy arse. Your arse is soooooo peachy. Do men *crave* over you?' my tall, muscular son boomed, squeezing me to him again. 'Do you take your pelvis seriously? And your *skull*! Mmmmmm . . . You have such a firm skull. We're so lucky to have shoulders, or our heads would just roll off . . . Do men ask if you're single at parties? Great guns, Mum!' he enthused, squeezing my biceps. 'They feel *really* good. Isn't my mother sexy?' he asked Archie. 'She has such a sexy body. She has the most silky' – I looked at him in alarm and only relaxed when he added – '*earlobes* . . . Do men tell you that you have beautiful breast—' I glanced up again in horrified Oedipal anticipation. '. . . bones?' he concluded, running his hand along my neckline. 'Great clavicles, Mum. Mmmm. I *love* the smell of your marzipan skin. It makes me feel so electric.'

Archie erupted into a rich chuckle and raised an 'I told you so' brow.

I gave my son a long, measuring look. For the first time I noticed a light dusting of acne across his chin, and then saw that there were more pimples plotting to break out on his forehead. He was jangly with bio-chemicals as adolescent hormones coursed through his veins. 'Merlin, darling, it's not really appropriate to talk to your mother that way, sweetie.'

'Why not? I've known you since you were twenty-six. You're one of my oldest friends, Mum. I keep asking, but you never tell me, who introduced us? Am I bisexual? I might be bisexual. Or I might just be a lover of the world. What do you think I am?'

Merlin pulled his T-shirt up over his head. His torso was honey-coloured and smooth. I saw the ridges of muscle on his taut stomach and marvelled at just when my lithe little boy had morphed into this contoured, chiselled specimen? His fine, delicate jaw was lichened with incipient stubble. He was becoming a man, whether he liked it or not.

'I do think I could keep a girl in a contented dazzle-ment of surprise. This is a message to all smoking-hot babes,' he foghorned. '*Come and join me in my magic world, where relationships are at their quirky best.* Dr Love is in the Building!' But then his face clouded over and his voice softened. 'Will I ever get a girlfriend, Mum? Or will I always just be wandering in the wilderness?'

I was surprised by the desolation in his voice. No matter how fast Merlin ran, his dark moods chased him, casting long shadows that would occasionally fall over him like a net. 'Of course you will, darling.'

'I won't. There's this dance at school. But nobody's asked me. I'm not into those phoney Heath Ledger movies, which is why I'm not going.' The atmosphere in the room became cloudy, as Merlin started pacing and squeezing any objects within reach. 'I'm a high-functioning autistic. I don't want to make the transition to adult. I don't want to grow up. People aren't really adult. They're in adult disguise.' Anxieties were buzzing around his brain as insistently as wasps. 'You always build me up to be some ladies' man, Mum, telling me how handsome I am. Well, I'd like to give a woman a good seeing-to and get some rambunctious fluff – some tang on the side. But it's never going to happen. It really hurts me when you compliment a girl and tell her how delectable she is and she shoots you down. It happens a lot and, most importantly, I don't know why. Will any woman ever throw me a lifeline of love?' Merlin scrunched his eyes closed and smacked the heel of his hand against his forehead. 'Anyway' – his voice darkened – 'women are a waste of time. If women are so great, why aren't there many female world leaders? Tell me that then? I bet you wish you had a penis, don't you?'

Upset, he avalanched out of the room, a tumble of limbs and flying wild hair.

Archie gave me another of his knowing looks. 'Believe me, if that son of yours doesn't get laid soon, he's gonna become a full-on misogynist,' he counselled.

'Oh, unlike *you*. A "good seeing-to"? "Fluff"? "Tang on the side"? I wonder where he got *that* phraseology. Anyway, it's a ridiculous idea. He's still so young . . .'

'Mmm. Nice breast *bones*,' Archie mimicked.

Unable to protect my son in an enshrouding embrace, I hugged myself around my waist instead.

'*You* should get laid too,' Archie chuckled. 'You're just sooo uptight. Right now, your favourite sexual fantasy is – a partner, am I right?'

'No, you are not!' I gave the man a withering glance straight out of the facial repertoire of Mrs Danvers in the draughty drawing rooms of Manderley. But, in truth, I was so sexually frustrated I was starting to have romantic thoughts about my electric toothbrush. Just last week I'd found myself cooking anatomically correct gingerbread men.

'I'm actually havin' interestin' thoughts about you right now . . . Maybe we can grab a bite – then have dinner?' he said, with a playful smirk. 'Merlin's right. Men do crave over you. I for one would love to slide my hand over the sweet contours of your peachy arse . . .'

'Well, I wish you'd stop *talking* out of yours.' I turned up the volume of Classic FM and let Wagner's great wash of strings sweep his crassness from my mind.

With the pressure of having to complete my School Action Plan (an activity so riveting I'd had to remind myself on an hourly basis that there were worse jobs – say, starting the cars of Colombian judges) I completely forgot about the school disco until Archie informed me that he'd organized Merlin a date. When he told me she was a 22-year-old backing singer called

Electra, my instinct was to smother the idea with an emotional emergency fire blanket, but Merlin was incandescent with excitement.

'All right,' I finally acquiesced. 'But I need to establish what time he's expected back. I think 11 p.m.,' I suggested.

'Really?' said Archie. 'I was thinkin' Monday.'

'Monday!'

'Although I will point out that it's Electra's responsibility to get the kid to school on time.'

'I'm so worried Merlin's going to do or say something wrong . . . Archie, why don't you just take him?'

'No bloody way. The only way you can get me to dance is to shoot at my feet.'

The night of the school disco a week later, Merlin appeared in the doorway and I did a double take. There was my son, dressed, pressed, suited, booted, scrubbed and rubbed. I was ambushed by feelings of tenderness for my handsome, idiosyncratic boy. Maybe he would add up to a whole person one day? Then he spoke.

'Why does my stomach have feelings? Are there really butterflies in there? Do they fly in formation? Were they caterpillars once? . . . I like being on my own actually . . . What if my date makes a cheesy grin and unnerves me? What if she's all talky-talky yakkity-yak? What if she doesn't like my moves?'

Merlin launched into an eccentric choreography, which consisted of 'The Chopping Board', where he mimed chopping a tomato; 'The Typewriter', which was similar but with more dervish-like thrashings of arms, and 'The Angel-wing Dance', involving an inversion of his hands behind his back and then a lot of mad flapping. I had seen him dancing at family gatherings, and his total lack of inhibition made for a rather funny but also slightly terrifying performance, especially when he ripped off his shirt and twirled it above his head with increasingly explicit groin thrusts. It was as though his feet had taken steroids.

'The music moves me, but it moves me ugly!' Merlin exclaimed, sliding on his knees across the carpet. 'I'm going to sweat bullets on the dance floor!'

I was so eaten up with nerves that he would make a faux pas or lose his temper or become a laughing stock when he leapt too high and grazed his nose on the glitter ball . . . but Archie let out a chuff of laughter, a raucous, kookaburra volley of squawks which made me laugh too.

I walked my son to the door. 'Have a great time, Merlin. And don't forget to tell your date how pretty she looks and—'

'But what if she doesn't look pretty?' Merlin asked, perplexed.

'Just tell her she does anyway,' I coached.

'She's a backin' singer in the band I'm playin' with down the pub. Believe me, she's hot. Have fun, kiddo. Come and I'll introduce youse.'

Electra was gunning the engine of a red rust-bucket. The roof of the car was peeled back, so I could see she was wearing a sequinned dress which was so short I was worried her ovaries might catch cold. The backing singer had rouged cheeks, iridescent green eyeshadow and stilettos sharp enough to disembowel a ferret. I swallowed hard. Merlin introduced himself with the words, 'So, are you a woman of experience?'

By the look of her, she definitely was – and no doubt charged for it by the hour.

Archie led me back inside before I could call the whole thing off. 'You need a glass of fizz,' he declared, popping open a bottle of something French he'd bought for the occasion and filling the flute to the brim. I glanced at the rain pattering on the window, twisting my rings this way and that. I calculated I had five or six hours of worry ahead of me.

'I wish you wouldn't look at me at all times as though I've got a red-bellied black snake tied to my dick,' Archie said, pouring more champagne. 'Don't worry about Merlin. I've paid Electra not to mind anythin' he says or does. She's gonna get him such kudos with the other kids.'

I nodded my head mutely but all I could think about was Electra's ramshackle car and the slick, wet road with its treacherous bends . . . not to mention the conversational collisions awaiting my son. 'But what if he says something inappropriate to one of the boys and gets head-butted?' I blurted, slumping into the couch. 'Or what if he asks some other girl the size of her clitoris? Or to show him her breasts for educational purposes? And then she hits him with a sexual harassment charge? What if Electra doesn't bring him back safely?'

'I know a pretty good cure for insomnia,' Archie said with a lopsided grin. 'Sleep.'

'I'm going to stay awake all night,' I pronounced resolutely. The pile of thirty-eight essays I had to mark on the use of the pathetic fallacy in romantic literature (which, pathetically, was the only place I got any romance these days) nagged me from the kitchen table. My headmaster had recently hauled me over the career coals about failing to hand in my action plans on time, meet targets and provide leadership. That's the trouble with opportunity. Sometimes, when it knocks, you're out in the forest trying to trap a rabbit to get its foot.

As I was thinking all this, Archie leant down, slipped off my shoe and swung my own foot up into his lap.

'What the hell are you doing?' But as he kneaded my toes an intoxicating lassitude took hold of me. When he lifted my other foot into his lap and ran his strong musician's hands up and down the arch, I wafted into a dreamlike state.

Some time later, I jolted back to consciousness. 'Oh my God, did I drift off?'

Archie gave me an impertinent wink. 'Yep. I think

you exhausted yourself *staying awake all night*,' he teased.

'What time is it?'

He checked the TV screen, where a football match was playing softly. 'Ten thirty.'

'Oh my God. I'm not cut out for motherhood. I just don't have a big enough capacity for alcohol. Have you been rubbing my feet for two hours? I hope I didn't snore or anything.' I sat up, startled.

'No, but has anyone ever told you how cute you look with drool coming out the corner of your mouth? Christ! Pins 'n' needles!' Archie rose and stretched before shuffling to the kitchen for refreshment reinforcements. 'These jeans are so bloody tight. Your cupboards are bizarre. You hang somethin' in your wardrobe for a couple of weeks and it shrinks two sizes.'

'Is that right?' I snickered. 'You don't think it's got something to do with the fact that the older you get the tougher it is to lose weight, because by then your body and your flab are really good friends?'

It was Archie's turn to laugh – a rich chuckle that he really meant. His walk back from the kitchen with the crisps and wine was pure panther.

'Why are you walking in that sexy way?' I asked him, slightly alarmed.

'Sexy?' he growled in his granulated voice. 'I'm just trying to hold my stomach in. Although I want you to know that this is not a beer belly, it's a' – he read the label before he poured – '*Beaujolais* belly, since living with you. Ironic, isn't it?' he drawled. 'I began by dropping acid and now I'm dropping antacid. I'm just getting way too old for rock 'n' roll.'

'I thought you were giving up on rock 'n' roll because everyone is selling out to conglomerates?'

'Truth is,' he sighed, 'I'd bloody love to sell out, only nobody's made me a bloody offer.'

After months of bluster and bravado, his confession was as alarming as his nakedness a few days earlier. 'So why did you come to London then? Oh Christ. You're not really skipping parole, are you?'

'Nope. After my wife buggered off, I skedaddled. I mean, life in London still has no meaning, but I'm less likely to run into people who can't wait to tell me that they just saw my missus sittin' on the face of my best mate.'

'You'll find somebody else,' I platituded.

'Naw. Women are too complicated these days,' he said with a playful smirk. 'I can't read the signs. You're, like, I want you to take me, slap me, rape me and cuddle me all at the same time, without touchin' me. And I want you to do it right now! Except I'm pissed off you didn't read my mind that I wanted all that.'

Whether it was the alcohol or the nervous tension, I laughed so hard I thought I'd rupture a key internal organ.

'Life went bad for us blokes once they invented

wheelie bins. As soon as they put wheels on the dustbins, we men weren't needed any more.'

His rough-and-ready charm softened my resentment like sun on butter. 'I don't know. I could definitely have done with a man around while I've been raising Merlin. His father pissed off at the first diagnosis.'

'Yeah?' His gaze was like the touch of a warm hand and I felt myself unclench.

'We met on a plane. Phoebe got me a birthday upgrade to New York. Jeremy was the most self-centred, arrogant smart-arse I'd ever encountered.'

'So you got up the duff by accident?'

'No. I fell completely and utterly in love with the bastard, got married and had his baby.'

'And what a baby.' Archie raised his brows. 'It must have been bloody hard yakka. You should get a medal. How could the 24-carat pissant abandon youse?'

'My ex-husband is a selfish, mean-spirited, low-down snake . . . but I don't say that in any disparaging way. To know him was to love him . . . until you really got to know him and then you wanted to kill him,' I added.

'There's only two types of people in a divorce. Those who screw you over and those who get screwed. If you're unlucky enough to be the one gettin' shafted, they do it without lubricant in every orifice, with no foreplay, and then cut you open with a chainsaw and shove maggots in your weepin' wounds.'

'Divorced people – you can spot us a mile away,' I agreed. 'We get that tortured, soul-destroyed, shell-shocked look of prisoners of war who have just tunnelled to freedom . . .'

'Yeah, only to find ourselves smack bang in the middle of the Battle of the bloody Somme.'

'Exactly. Anyway, if it makes you feel any better, I'm a much bigger failure than you, Archie. I'm a teacher who has failed to teach her own son. I should also be deputy head by now, but instead I'm trying to teach English literature to teens whose reading material is limited to takeaway menus. My GCSE-level English class told me recently that they hate books, especially when they have to read them.'

'Literature should be banned. It's the only way to make reading popular again,' Archie teased.

'Yes, besides the kind of books which have a sex goddess on the jacket and no jacket on the sex goddess . . . And whatever happened to my own Great Novel?'

'Well, what the hell's stoppin' ya? Just put the word "memory", "road" or "ghost" in the title, which means that it's gonna have a shitload of war and torture in it, and then it'll be shortlisted for every bloody prize goin'.'

As I laughed, Archie switched off the football match and turned to face me. 'By the way, foreplay for Australian men is the technical term for turning off the telly,' he said, and then he leant forward and kissed me.

I gave the surprised gasp of a warm body entering

a chilly sea. I felt an instinctive sexual quickening within me, an unexpected fizz of exhilaration. He tasted like coffee beans, a smoky, burnt flavour of amaretto and caramel. His spicy, musky tang of sweat and wine and smoke enhanced my senses. His beard was rough on my face. I savoured the weight and bulk and muscle of the man. An electric current ran from my tonsils to my toes and quite a few places in between. I stopped fretting and felt myself vanish into the moment.

When we broke apart, Archie gave me a look which was both tender and lascivious. Even though my heart was beating insubordinately, I decided to utilize Archie's Aussie foreplay technique in reverse and flicked the telly back on. Confused, I slunk to my end of the couch and pretended to be riveted by a re-run of a Romanian darts final that had come on. Big emotional displays were no longer my forte. These days I was better at bitterness and sarcasm. I sat in taut, bamboozled silence until Merlin rattled his key in the lock. He practically Nureyeved down the hall.

'My first date!' He was helium-filled with happiness. 'What a majestic evening. I had a very special moment in my life. The atmosphere was electric. I ripped off my shirt and started busting out some phenomenal moves. It made me feel immortal . . . I think I have a mesmerizing personality, don't you, Mum?'

I laughed. 'Yes, darling, you do.' My son seemed to

have ripened and grown almost luminous. He launched himself at me for his usual bearhug, squeezing the breath out of me as though I were a fleshy accordion. His shivering delight transmitted itself to me.

'Lucky Merlin,' Archie said softly, an audible smile in his voice.

I wished Archie goodnight with the formality of a French courtier and retreated to my bedroom. Shortly after, a note was slipped under my door.

> Just got a very interesting call from the chairman of
> the International Missed Golden Opportunities
> Commission. I think they want to honour you at
> their next big gala. I gave them your number.
> Signed, YRRGC (Your Resident Rock God Chum)

I lay in bed, wide awake, Archie's touch whispering away on my skin. I found myself wondering how he would move in bed, how he'd smell, how his powerful legs would feel wrapped around me. And then I heard music. Soft, liquid notes lured me out into the corridor and Pied Pipered me to the top of the stairs. A cascade of melody spilt into the hall below. It was Archie, accompanying himself on acoustic guitar. The surprising poignancy of the composition and the tender timbre of his voice gave me goose-pimples on my goose-pimples. By the time the song concluded, Archie had gained an entire new dimension. There was a fascination about him now. Retreating to my bed, I realized that the man was not a Neanderthal after all. He'd positively moved up the evolutionary scale to Homo erectus. It was obvious to me that Archie had been putting on an act . . . As had I.

13

Dr Love is in the Building

I awoke next morning to a stripe of warm, syrupy sun
across my bed. I had a busy yet boring day ahead –
grocery shopping, taking Merlin to Alexander
technique swimming class and the torture of trying to
help with his school assignments – but the thought of
Archie's kiss and the melody of his song kept a smile
in my eyes all afternoon, even in the supermarket
express lane, where the queue was so long you could
get a pap smear, a manicure, pedicure and divorce and
still not lose your place in the line.

Why, I wasn't sure. Archie was the opposite of what's
usually required for the role of romantic hero. He was
the very antithesis of the Sensitive New-age Gladiator
with a portfolio of capital venture investments tucked
up each sleeve of the kind currently favoured by
fashionistas. The rangy old rocker had a muscular build,

but it was going a bit soft in the middle. He had a good head of hair, yes, but lassoed into a ratty ponytail. The man had a face only a mother could love – a blind mother. And yet I astonished myself with an impulse to kiss him once more.

I began to find his sayings oddly enchanting. When I saw him on the street, I would suddenly start waving wildly, as though summoning rescue. Obviously, my libido was not reporting to mission control but following some kind of renegade X-rated sat-nav system. I began to linger and stall over the kitchen table, pouring yet another cup of tea, hoping that he'd pull me into an embrace. And pretty soon there were quite a few heated entwinings on the landing, in the hall, by the washing machine.

Merlin was predictably pragmatic. 'I saw you kissing Archie this morning. Are you two actually having sexual intercourse?' he asked, in front of my sister, who nearly fell off her chair with shock.

'Of all men? I thought you said he was an animal?' Phoebe asked, bug-eyed with amazement.

'All I can say is, God bless the wild kingdom.'

'But, just last week you loathed him.'

'I still do, in some ways! I'm astounded people don't stop him on the street to ask if he's the guy who played the man-eating Alien from Planet Yuk in "The Extra-terrestrial Cannibals are Coming". The list of reasons not to fancy Archie is jaw-droppingly long. Maybe it's simply the fact that he likes Merlin and that Merlin likes him?'

'Well, I think you'd better go to bed with him and find out,' Phoebe suggested, grinning her head off.

And later that night, when Archie brushed a fingertip along the back of my neck, the liquid heat of desire flowed through me. I felt myself slip inside the moment as though it were a warm bath. We lay on my bed and the heat of his body radiated into mine. The soft night was charmed, as if some kind of spell had been cast, and a short time later, we were sweating away joyfully in the nude.

When I woke, Archie was leaning up on one elbow watching me. His smile broke on me like a big, warm wave on a rock. 'Boom chicka wah wah,' he enthused, his eyes closing reverentially. 'What a ride!' He flopped back on to the pillows. 'I'm gonna start puttin' bets on you at the Grand National.'

'You're one to talk! Those sexual techniques of yours are not for amateurs. People shouldn't try them in their own homes, unsupervised,' I replied with wonderment, lazily pulling on my knickers. 'If you were a snooker player, you'd be blowing on your metaphorical snooker cue right now.'

'I've applied for a patent on my recipe – seventy-three minutes of witty conversation, sixteen jumbo-sized compliments, *zero* references to footy or sports cars and some elaborate, laboratory-tested tongue-work which I cannot divulge at this point – but

I do have a rival in Brazil, apparently.' And then he returned the compliment. 'But, Lou, *you're* so good in bed even the next-door neighbours are havin' a cigarette.'

Within seconds we were going at it again, me pressed back on the bed, my lace panties around one ankle and my ankles around his ears. Even the neighbours' *pets* would be lighting up this time. And this is pretty much how we remained for the rest of the weekend.

On Saturday afternoon, Merlin arrived home unexpectedly early from the museum and burst into my bedroom. His face was twisted into amazement, as though he'd been struck by some gargantuan hammer. 'I'm flabbergasted!'

I yanked the covers over my breasts and stiffened, awaiting a body blow.

'I was in the museum when it suddenly hit me. About the nature of time! Time is the universe's way of stopping everything happening at once!' He wrung his hands in wonderment and sighed dramatically. 'I've also worked out that when a person smiles it's just a thought appearing on your face, isn't it, Mum? I couldn't wait to tell you. Oh,' he sighed, 'the trouble with factoids is that there's just so many of them.' Then he climbed into bed with us, beaming cheerfully. 'So, what are we going to do now?'

I erupted into a fit of relieved giggles which in turn made Archie guffaw. And this pretty much set the tone for the next few days. Our house became a cosy cocoon of love and laughter, full of thrown-together bubble-and-squeak meals and impromptu comic mayhem as Archie mucked around with Merlin. The happy pandemonium was soundtracked with snatches of music, as Archie twanged away at kitsch country-and-western ballads. The songs became even funnier when we had to explain their meanings to Merlin. 'I Hate Every Bone in her Body, Except Mine' proved particularly tricky. As did 'I Ain't Ever Gone to Bed with an Ugly Woman, but I Woke up with a Few'. And 'It's Hard to Kiss the Lips at Night that Chewed My Ass All Day'. I felt a spreading thrill as I watched Merlin blossoming in the domestic fug of all that friendly warmth and comforting camaraderie. No longer was I earthed by the gravity of all life's obstacles and impossibilities. Instead I found myself buoyant with optimism.

'If there's a happy hour in bars, does that mean there's a sad hour too?' Merlin asked me earnestly, as I kissed him goodnight later that weekend. 'The American Constitution says you must pursue happiness. But how do you know when you've caught it?'

How indeed? Ecstatically entwined in the small hours soon after, I did feel a shiver of pure joy. It was a feeling it took me a moment to recognize. Could this rough-and-tumble, ramshackle man really squeeze all the misery out of me and fill the hollows of my bones with happiness? Could he really turn my prose deepest purple like that? Just as well I *wasn't* writing that novel, because 'The Colour Purple' had already been taken as a title.

Later I heard someone uttering a heartfelt endearment which included the word 'adore' and realized, as Archie's tongue flicked back and forth across my nipple, that it was my own voice. A light of hope crept into my eyes like a timid guest. Could I really fall for a man again? I advanced towards the thought on tiptoe, as if I were afraid to wake it. Maybe life was making it up to me? Maybe this old rocker was the joyful twist in a tortured narrative? Over the years, I'd become a tough crowd of one. But something about the man made me let down my guard. Who would ever have thought that Archie would be the citadel-storming, moat-swimming parapet breacher?

A 4×4 vroomed past shuddering with *doomf doomf* bass and I didn't even care. My mood was so elated that I suddenly found myself kindly disposed towards logoed clothing, nose rings, Western women converting to Islam, piercings, Botox, corporate jargon and personal trainers. People famous for just being famous no longer irked me. Nor did upward inflections, incorrect grammar, Conan the Grammarians, instruction manuals, leaf blowers and stupid names like Satchel, Sage, Moon, Starlite, Melody and Apple. I seemed to have undergone a curmudgeonectomy.

Archie rolled over on top of me. Looking up at his

warm, smiling face it suddenly didn't seem so strange to love him.

When a knock roused me from bed early on Friday morning, I had to tear myself away from Archie's embrace as though the man were made of Velcro. In the crystal autumnal morning, the golden-tinged leaves shimmered outside the window as I padded blissfully down the stairs.

But if I'd been in a movie, the water in my vases would have started to quiver and shake in warning that something monumental was about to happen. Oblivious, I trotted to the front door, all dishevelled, reeking of the rich, sweet-and sour scent of love-making. I opened the door wearing nothing more than Archie's shirt and a satisfied smile – to find my ex-husband standing on the threshold, his arms bedecked with flowers.

'Lucy. I'm so sorry for abandoning you. The truth is, I love you. I've never stopped loving you. And Merlin. And I want to dedicate the rest of my life to making it up to you. I want you back, darling. Desperately.'

Part Three: Jeremy

14

The Born-again Human Being

I ascertained that I hadn't wet my pants so, all in all, I was pretty proud of my response. Blood beat in my ears. I looked at my ex-husband for a silent eternity: twenty seconds, a decade – who could tell? It was the same Jeremy, the same sharp cheekbones, firm jaw, blue eyes just deep enough to drown in and the dashing smile of a gambler who plays for high stakes. The tailored shirt and black trousers, the obligatory Rolex, yes, he had everything . . . *bar the bolts sticking out from the side of his neck*. I reminded myself that this was the monster who'd abandoned me all those years ago. Tearing my eyes away from his, I tried to speak, but my lips felt Novacained.

My only survival technique was to revert to my default setting of caustic flippancy. 'I should have guessed you were in the vicinity, as all the neighbourhood animals are running around in circles,' I finally commented, though my heart was percussing wildly against Archie's shirt. 'What do you want?' I had grown strong enough by now to absorb any blow.

'I behaved appallingly.' Jeremy said this gravely, like he'd just disclosed that he had testicular cancer. There was that voice, familiar in a strange way, strange in a familiar way. We stared at each other across the abyss. He then launched into a prepared speech. 'Men should be made to sign emotional pre-nups. Grooms are always so worried about finances, but what about feelings? . . . It's *feelings* a woman is banking on. If only you'd made me sign an emotional pre-nup, things would probably have been fine: *I promise to keep trying to make you laugh. I promise to keep laughing at your jokes . . . I promise to tell you all the things I love about you, daily, starting with your lovely laugh . . . I promise to never leave you in your hour of need . . . I promise to be a good father.*'

My face froze in a rictus of incredulity. I rolled my eyes so high I could see my own hairline. 'So, you expect me to believe that, after all these years, you've suddenly changed?'

Jeremy's brow wrinkled like the skin on cooling custard. 'I *have* changed. I can't believe what I put you through. I had to come and tell you how I feel.'

'How you feel? You don't emote, Jeremy. The closest you get to showing your feelings is when you say "This gave much pleasure to 100 per cent of our focus group."'

'That's the old Jeremy! I appreciate it's a little late in the day to realize these things, but I've learnt that career and work are not everything.'

'Spoken by a man who has been known to call out at the point of orgasm, "Oh God! The Dow just went down 2 per cent. Yes! Yes!! Yes!!!"'

'Yes, I *was* like that. I admit it. But I now know that friends and family are more important than anything else.'

'Great! Let's celebrate. I suggest we invite all your friends . . . I'll book a table for one, shall I?'

'My father died,' Jeremy said suddenly. His voice was thickened by buried emotion.

'Oh,' I said, the wind momentarily taken out of my vitriolic sails. 'I'm sorry.'

Jeremy discarded the bouquet and slumped down on to the low brick wall separating my dilapidated terrace from the gleamingly renovated abode next door. 'I loved my father, Lucy. But I do partially blame my parents for our marriage break-up. If they'd shown me the love and affection I was owed, if they'd taught me how to communicate, I would never have abandoned you. But my parents preferred their canines to their kid,' he said bitterly. 'They kept the dogs at home and sent me off to that high-class kennel called Eton. After Merlin's diagnosis, well, I just didn't have the emotional maturity to cope. It's too late to tell my father how I feel.' He hung his head despondently. 'But I've told my mother. She's desperately sorry too.

She wants to see you both again, so badly. As do I.'

He looked up at me then with such pleading candour that I momentarily dropped my guard and lowered myself on to the rickety wall beside him.

'I just drifted into fatherhood, a boat without a rudder. Then panicked and dived overboard and swam like crazy for the shore. And I've been shipwrecked all these years.' He put his head in his hands.

I wanted to believe him, but the divorce lay between us like a big, black bruise. '*Your divorce settlement will be fair and equitable . . . Now bend over*,' pretty much summed up the experience. Instead of putting a comforting arm around his grieving shoulders, I performed a slow handclap. 'Very touching, Jeremy. Almost a Victorian novel. By the way, even if you're certain you're included in your father's will, it's considered a tad rude to arrive at his funeral with a removal van, you know.'

Jeremy's red-rimmed eyes sought mine. 'Oh my God. You really think so little of me? Well, who can blame you?' He sighed bleakly. 'I behaved disgracefully. My mother has told me all about Merlin's problems. It's not his fault that he can't make the right emotional choices and responses. I've been reading up on Asperger's. His cognitive empathy – being able to understand what others are feeling – is impaired, I know, but experts say it's a—'

I raised my hand. 'Um, I'd like to put in a request to interrupt your soliloquy, Jeremy. This is a warning that

I will be getting a word in within the next few minutes, and that those words will be *I don't give a damn what you think.*'

Jeremy persevered, regardless. 'But it's clear to me that Merlin inherited the condition from my side of the family. Oh yes. We are very adept at emotional blindness in the Beaufort clan. Just look at my father. He never once told me he loved me, do you know that?' he groaned miserably. 'Maybe he had undiagnosed Asperger's? Who knows? But with him as a role model, is it any wonder I've been such a terrible father myself? Which is why I've come back to help. Merlin will benefit from intensive support within the family and professional input, which I can pay for. And, most important of all, a father's love. It's the least I can do.'

I looked at my ex with a mix of astonishment and suspicion. In the last decade, asking my husband for money had been like asking a corpse for a pint of blood and yet here he was offering a cash haemorrhage. 'What do you want?' I demanded coldly.

'Forgiveness. Another chance. Merlin needs to learn to build on his core social skills. And so do I. My dad dying, well, it forced me to rethink my life. An epiphany, I suppose you could call it. I have vowed to become a good father. And sworn to stay faithful to that promise.'

'Huh! Which is more than you did to me ... How *is* Tawdry Hepburn? How did her career on American cable pan out? I did see her on some cooking show recently. She looks more animated in still photographs actually. Too much Botox, I suppose? Still, Audrey does have two very impressive assets, which she flaunts in every programme. I keep hoping one tit will flop into the frying pan. Braised breast of tartlet. Do you think, if it was important to the integrity of the show, that she would ever consider keeping her clothes *on* for an entire episode?'

My marriage was now only visible to me in painful flashes of memory; most of the time it was just a blur of gloomy shapes and noises. But the pain of Jeremy's betrayal was suddenly seared into my consciousness once more.

'It's over with Audrey.' Jeremy looked down at his hands and his shoulders drooped.

'Let me guess. You got bimbo burn-out,' I commented belligerently. 'Can't be helped when you shack up with a girl whose sun protection factor is higher than her IQ.'

'It's just that, well, Audrey didn't share my beliefs. When I was younger I was looking for this magical meaning of life. I thought it was success, social status, financial rewards. But, in truth, it's very simple. The meaning of life is to make the lives of others meaning- ful . . . by doing something of lasting value. Which is why I'm going into politics.'

I heard a rattling sound as the penny dropped. He was just going to sashay into that charmed political space warmed up by his dear departed dad. 'You? In politics? You're a banker. Your morals are harder to find than a small-business loan.'

'Not any more. I fell out with my American business partners. Did my mother ever tell you that I eventually set up my own hedge fund company in LA? But the blatant greed of my partners, the tax dodging, the Ponzi schemes . . . it turned my stomach. It made me want to dedicate myself to public service. I'm on the party's shortlist. They vote next week. The chief whip's called a by-election. I want to give back to society.'

'Oh really?' I said stonily. 'I know the way your family gives back.' I jack-knifed to my feet. 'You'll initiate a slight tax increase which will cost normal people like me £200 a year and then a substantial tax cut which will save us twenty pence.'

'I'm standing for the Liberal Democrats,' Jeremy said, with sombre sincerity.

I reeled around to look at him. 'Really?' Now I heard a groaning sound as Jeremy's Tory father turned over in his grave. 'And what? You think your change of political heart will soften my view of you? I do have a soft spot for you, actually . . . face down in a bowl of custard.'

My ex-husband's face sank in with sadness. 'Oh my God, Lucy. Look how cynical you've become. You used to be so optimistic and positive. That's why I fell in love with you. Did I do this to you? If so, I can never forgive myself . . .'

'Did you do this to me?' I guffawed. But my laughter turned very abruptly into hot angry tears as the pain of the past hit me square in the chest. 'How could you have just abandoned us?' I yelled at him, and then saw fists flying through the air and realized as they pummelled Jeremy's chest that they were attached to my own arms.

Jeremy took each blow until I'd run out of steam. 'I deserve it. I hate myself for what I've done.' His voice cracked. 'And I want to make it up to you, Lucy.'

'Why should I believe you?' To my own ears I sounded vulnerable, in spite of my Muhammad Ali impersonation.

'If *you* can change so much, Luce, then so can *I*. Won't you let me see my son?'

'Oh, *now* you want to see him? But what about all the times *he* needed to see *you*? Where were you during your son's banging-his-head-on-the-ground stage? And where were you when he tried to jump off the window ledge? And where were you when he used to punch himself in the testicles with self-loathing frustration? Where were you when he was getting his head flushed down the school toilets?' I stomped on the bouquet by my feet. 'Where were you then, you bastard?'

Jeremy had the look of a man who has just accidentally run over the Easter bunny and has come to break the news to the kids. 'Oh Lucy. I'm so ashamed. I don't know how you've coped.'

'Oh well,' I said, my voice dripping in sarcasm. 'Any slight frustration I might occasionally have felt was simply alleviated by locking the door and screaming into my pillow for hours and hours and hours . . . If it weren't for my family, I'd be in an institution by now, braiding my hair.'

Jeremy faced me, open-armed. 'Let me make it up to you. I want to take care of you and my son.'

'Oh, the way you took care of us in the divorce? You told me we would split everything down the middle. Except that there was nothing left to split. You hired a crack legal team who managed to hide all our assets and write off most of your income. I didn't stand a chance.'

'Divorce is the equivalent of asbestos removal – delicate, fraught and highly toxic. My father handled it all through his lawyer. I can see now how bad his advice was. How cruel they were. But, Lucy, we were so in love once, don't you remember?'

'Yes, we had so much in common . . . *You*.'

'Do you remember our beautiful wedding?' he coaxed.

'Yeah, it was a fairy-tale marriage . . . rewritten by Quentin Tarantino.'

'There are five golden rules to a happy marriage.' Jeremy attempted a wry smile. 'Unfortunately, nobody knows what the hell they are.'

'Oh, I do. Gin, tranquillizers, vodka, Xanax and sleeping pills. The reason we broke up is that you did

251

not regard matrimony as an exclusive carnal arrangement.'

'Men are weak. Inferior. Not worthy. Your own father turned out to be a priapic fancier of underage masseuses and lap-dancers, but you forgave him. If you forgave your father, can't you forgive me?'

I looked at my ex-husband with forensic attention to detail. It was the same Jeremy, but he wore an unfamiliar expression – remorse. It may have moved a less battered woman. But the only thing I didn't doubt was my doubt. 'No.'

'I was wrong ever to leave you,' he said in a thick voice. 'I've never loved any other woman but you.' In the shade of the building, his eyes no longer seemed blue but dark and soft, like liquid chocolate. 'You cut your hair? It suits you.'

'You are dead to me, Jeremy.'

His eyes were now full of a sensitive schoolboy's baffled hurt. 'As is my dear father, with so much left unsaid. But I still have time to make it up to *my* son . . . Do you think Merlin has any feelings for me?' he asked tentatively, as biddable as a baby.

'Like me, I'm sure he worships the ground you're buried in.'

'Oh, Luce, how can I prove myself to you?' He glanced up at my paint-peeled, crumbling brick terrace, choked by ivy. 'Let me buy you a new house. Would you like me to do that? What would you like me to do?'

Locking him into a sewage canal with a cadre of syphilitic sex criminals seemed a reasonable choice under the surreal circumstances. 'Just stay away from us,' I said angrily.

'So I suppose there's no point in asking you to marry me again then?' He flashed me his most seductive half-smile.

'Marriage to you was like having an autopsy performed whilst still alive.' I moved back inside the doorway of my house.

He hung his head. 'I'm so sorry, Lucy.'

I savoured the full depths of his shame. 'I think it's time for you to return to the sulphur-scented depths which spawned you.'

I felt a warm, firm hand in the small of my back and Archie's breath on my neck. 'What's goin' on?' he asked sternly.

'My ex-husband's managed to be reincarnated while he's still alive – I must rush upstairs and email Shirley Maclaine.'

I felt Archie's body stiffen. 'So you're the maggoty dip-shit who deserted her in her hour of need. I think you'd better leave now before I make headlines for doing somethin' violent.'

The door shivered on its hinges as Archie kicked it shut in my ex-husband's startled face.

15
Daddy Dearest

Botanical gardenfuls of flowers started to arrive the very next day. The house was soon heady with trumpet blasts of blooms bursting from brightly coloured paper. This was followed by vineyards of champagne. A new laptop for Merlin came next. And then, opera tickets. I returned the tickets with a note. 'When it comes to the effect these gifts have on me, think of the world stage and then think of yourself as Tuvalu or Liechtenstein.'

Real estate brochures came special delivery, with chirpy little cards:

Why do they call it real estate? They should call it *un*real estate, because who can afford it? Well, thanks to my inheritance, I can! I'm sorry I never fixed up our 'fixer-upper'. Let me make it up to you now. Call me and we'll go and view a few properties for you and Merlin.

When I ignored him, Jeremy started turning up 'accidentally' to places I frequented – the supermarket, the gym, the local library, the park in our square – pretending it was a coincidence. 'Hey,' he'd say, casually, 'didn't I marry you somewhere before?'

'Yes, and haven't I yelled degrading comments at you somewhere before, too?' I'd retort, or something similarly caustic, before storming off.

'Please let me meet my son,' he pleaded over the phone. 'I know I don't deserve any sympathy. But do it for Merlin.'

'Absolutely not.'

'Has he ever asked about me?' he begged, his voice quavering with penitence.

'No,' I lied, hanging up.

The five-star grovelling went on for weeks. My sister and mother, returned from her travels, were astounded by his contrite reappearance. 'Jeremy apologized?' they chorused, agog.

'I know. Incredible, huh? The only person he's ever apologized to before was the business partner he once bankrupted – and that was court ordered.'

'Don't be fooled,' Phoebe warned. 'Your ex is an aggressive, foul-tempered, selfish megalomaniac . . . And I don't say that in a castrating way.'

'She's right. That man's moral integrity you could

stuff into the navel of a fruit fly and still have room for three caraway seeds,' my mother stated, eccentrically.

'He wants to buy us a bigger house.' I proffered the brochures. 'How crass to think that he can purchase my forgiveness.'

My sister, who was back on the picket lines, snatched them up and devoured the details. 'Notting Hill Gate? Have you checked out prices around Notting Hill Gate? I can't even afford to buy enough *drugs* to allow me to *hallucinate* that I could afford to live around there. Maybe you could just take Jeremy's money but have nothing more to do with him?'

'Stay away from him, dear,' my mother warned. 'If only you'd taken tips from the black widow spider – mated with him once . . . then eaten him.'

But I didn't need convincing. If Jeremy tried to wheedle his way into my affections, I told the cat, all he'd be courting was disaster. But my Early Warning Parental Anxiety System must have been on the blink, because I had totally underestimated my ex-husband's tenacity. To say Jeremy was persistent was the biggest understatement since bin Laden said to his wives in his Pakistani hideaway, 'I think someone's at the door.'

Merlin and I were swimming in the local pool the following Saturday, with my son breaststroking in the wrong direction in the fast lane, as usual, bumping into everybody and causing mayhem as lappers capsized all around him, when Jeremy swam straight up and introduced himself. 'You must be Merlin. Hello. I'm your father, Jeremy.'

Spluttering with rage, I must have swallowed half the pool as I dog-paddled, aghast, beside my son. Like *this* could be a chance meeting, dodging jellyfish globs of phlegm in the deep end of the local verruca-encrusted council baths. What my family calls 'the cesspool' is really just a crowd of people with water in it. It's like sharing your bath with a hundred strangers. 'What the hell do you think you're doing?' I finally fumed at him.

But Merlin gave his widest Cheshire cat grin. When my son met his father for the first time in 13 years, he said, in no particular order: 'Do you remember the day we met? Are you a man of experience? Do you sleep with a teddy bear? Do you have any gay friends? Do all women have to have sex to make a baby? So, that means you had sex with my mother? That's the most off-putting smile. It's so cringe. Do you moisturize? It's incredible that you're my father. Are you getting any fluff lately? Any tang on the side? Do you have children with another woman? Are you living today for tomorrow? Do you have any communist values? When you saw my mother again did you sink to your knees and cry happy tears? Do you like my rambunctious style? Your hair's so grey and white. Are you a polar bear? Do you perhaps transform through the fridge, to your polar-bear family in the North Pole, which is why you haven't been around and why I haven't met you before? Can I meet your polar-bear family? Have you had as many wives as Henry VIII? How many wives have you actually had?'

'Apart from his *own*, you mean? All his friends' wives and colleagues' wives no doubt, judging on past performance,' I interrupted, my crisp voice peppermint cool with condescension.

'Are you really my father?' Merlin asked, still treading water.

'From now on, all day, every day.'

I would have yelled at Jeremy to fuck off and leave us the hell alone except that Merlin's every facial expression shimmered with joy. My son had the look of a traveller who for years has read of the existence of the spotted silver-backed mountain cheetah but never expected to be this near to one.

As we clambered on to the side of the pool, I noted that Jeremy's taut body had filled out only slightly. He wore tight black swimming shorts which hugged a posterior so pert that it would cause cardiac arrest in a sloth. If only he'd gone bald or developed hideous eczema all over his body. But the man oozed charm and sophistication. Judging by the admiring glances of the other mums, he also proved an instant antidote to the anodyne, baby-faced pastiness of the teenage lifeguards. I found myself remembering how good my ex looked naked. Shocked, I dashed the image from my mind's eye and harrumphed on to the bench by the life-rings. I saw Jeremy appraise my figure with what

I took to be appreciation, before he draped his arm tentatively around Merlin's shoulder and asked how he was feeling.

Merlin replied that his mood felt like dense particles from an exploded star which had sucked in all the positive energy from the known universe, only not as fluffy.

'Oh,' Jeremy said, 'right.' I saw him try to suppress the slight tremor of his upper lip and resolutely steady his mouth.

After Merlin had run off to get dressed, Jeremy exhaled with relief. 'God, that was nerve-racking. My stomach's been so knotted I thought I had an ulcer. Ugh . . .' He put his hands on his abdomen in obvious pain. 'I feel as though I'm having a turn right now.'

'Really? I'm so concerned. I must summon an ambulance. Let me send a message in a bottle,' I mocked. 'Or maybe a carrier snail would be faster? How dare you just turn up like this! Merlin will be so traumatized.'

'He's so handsome,' Jeremy enthused, embroidering his comment with 'Thank God he got your looks . . . Although I don't know how he smells anything, walking around with my nose on his face.'

I glared at him with unbridled hostility. 'For the millionth time, we don't need you! Just get dressed and fuck off!' In my mind, each word was a bullet, aimed at his heart. I flounced off to the changing room then dashed towards the showers. I needed to rinse off the stench of chlorine, but there was a queue. After an impatient wait, I resorted to a slapdash wash at the sink. With no time to blow-dry my hair, I just scrambled, still wet, into my clothes, as hastily as I could. But I still wasn't fast enough. By the time I emerged into the café, buttons misaligned, one jean leg tucked into a half-mast sock, Merlin was happily ensconced at Jeremy's table, gulping down hot soup and thick wedges of fresh bread and butter, babbling away, laughter bubbling into his eyes.

Merlin could feel disproportionate joy at the smallest things, only for his spirits to plummet with vertiginous haste. Anointed by magic as he now was, he could just as quickly be assailed by demons. So I bit back my anger and let Jeremy know of my fury in veiled terms. 'I'm amazed you haven't wilted,' I seethed at him, through a gritted smile. 'There's garlic in that salad. I thought vampires couldn't handle garlic?'

Archie, who'd been pushing weights for the last hour, powered into the café ten minutes later. Since our love affair had begun, Archie had swapped the booze for bodybuilding. His muscular frame now won lascivious glances from the local yummy mummies in our square. Their heavily mascaraed eyes would super-glue to his manly thighs whenever he kicked a football around the communal park with Merlin. When Archie spotted my ex-husband he gave Jeremy a measuring, suspicious look and flexed his biceps menacingly.

'Archie is commander-in-chief of my mother's affections,' Merlin explained happily. 'He's the shogun of rock who plays with finesse, flair and flamboyance. He's a music wizard. The Shakespeare of the guitar.'

'Accolades indeed.' Jeremy rose and extended his hand. 'Nice to be properly introduced. Jeremy Beaufort. The commander-in-chief of abasement,' he added for my benefit. 'Charmed to meet you.'

Archie looked at Jeremy's hand as though it were infested with fleas. 'Who are you again? Oh yeah. Right. You're the scumbag ex who dumped his wife once he realized his baby had special needs, then ripped her off in the divorce ... I'd like to tell you what a piece of scum you are, but of course I would never say anythin' shitty about you in front of your own son ... Come on, kid.' He shot an impertinent wink in Merlin's direction. 'Game's on in ten.'

'True love asks for nothing,' were Merlin's parting words to his newfound father before bounding out of the door.

As we walked home behind my son, who was leaping ahead of us with giddy abandon like a kangaroo on crack, Archie kicked at the autumnal leaves. They crunched beneath our feet as though we were strolling through a giant bowl of cornflakes. He took my hand and squeezed it. 'Jeez, that dickhead lays on the charm so thick it's like having blancmange syringed into your ears. Trouble is, a banker without a forked tongue is like, I dunno, Charlie Sheen without a hit of crystal meth and a hooker. Im-bloody-possible,' he said, in that crushed-velvety voice of his.

'I know. I could have killed him there and then . . . except for the thought of that orange Day-Glo prison jumpsuit. It just wouldn't match my skin tones,' I joshed, to mask my uneasy apprehension.

'Not to mention the pressure of which gang to join once you're in the slammer . . . And the agony over what tattoo to get, of course,' Archie deadpanned.

'Still' – I cut the banter and turned to face him – 'Merlin so enjoyed meeting him. I loathe the heartless bastard. But surely a son has a right to know his own father? Maybe I should have a more open mind?'

'An open mind? That only lets the bloody flies in. Not to mention the cold winds. Slam it shut immediately,' Archie advised vehemently.

I squeezed Archie's hand in agreement. He was so right. I believe that everything is possible in life, except maybe skydiving in stilettos, scuba-diving in rollerblades and an ex-husband changing his psychological spots. Hell, I'd rather go on a blind date with Hannibal Lecter than let Jeremy back into my life. Merlin's father may have thought he was offering a window of opportunity. But I would simply draw the blinds.

16

Paying Lip Service to Love

In actual fact, my mind wasn't closed or open. It turned out to be merely ajar. Despite my antagonism, Jeremy rang the next day to suggest driving Merlin and me to his mother's house for lunch. As the Beauforts are sticklers for etiquette, I tried to phrase my refusal in a polite manner: 'I'd rather be shackled into a jacuzzi with a school of piranhas.' Jeremy went on to explain that his mother wanted to discuss setting up a trust fund for Merlin, including payment of all future fees at a top special needs school. I declined. After he'd abandoned us, we'd learnt to cope quite well on our own, thank you very much. We didn't need help from anybody.

I would have remained resolute, if I hadn't been called in by Merlin's headmaster to discuss my son's imminent exclusion. Merlin, who was repeating Year

Eleven, had spent more time on detention and suspension than he had in an actual classroom. Of late, my son was in hot water so often he could have been a teabag. Most of the time, I felt like a sidecar on an out-of-control motorbike. Things had got so bad, I was contemplating attending Parent–Teacher night under an assumed name.

Throughout Merlin's school life, my heart would sink with dread whenever I picked up the phone and heard my son's name mentioned. But, recently, the situation had become much more serious. When his chemistry teacher had asked the class to name two things commonly found in a cell and Merlin had apparently replied 'Asian British black and Afro-Caribbean,' I was summoned to the office.

'Inciting racial hatred is a crime,' the headmaster told me coldly.

Merlin turned his dream-clouded eyes upon me and smiled mistily. It was no wonder he liked to retreat into his own world. I rubbed my thumping temples. 'He's not being racist. He's being literal. Merlin regurgitates facts. After Caucasians, that's an accurate description of the majority of the prison popu—'

'It's not an isolated example either,' the headmaster interrupted. 'Commenting on people's height, weight, looks or sexuality is a civil wrong.'

I came up for air, spluttering about how kids with Asperger's don't have a psychological filter nor the cognitive ability to defend themselves. I pointed out how the other kids know they can coax a reaction, so goad Merlin by calling him names, sneaking up behind him and poking him like a dog then running off. 'Yet it's always my son who is punished.'

The headmaster's response was to ask me what I thought was the appropriate action for Merlin's disruptive behaviour. I suggested towing the local education authority out to sea on a decommissioned naval frigate then sinking it in the deepest, darkest part of the Arctic ocean. The headmaster preferred exclusion.

The word 'exclusion' hit me like a 100-watt shock. Merlin was still wearing his Sphinx-like smile, his eyes fixed on something I couldn't see. 'I am pleading for my son's life here,' I begged. 'You hold it in your hands. If you exclude him, what's he to do? Leave school with no qualifications? Or get shut away in a Pupil Referral Unit – otherwise known as "Losers Anonymous"? And what kind of education will he get there? Unspecialized teachers trying to control feral, violent kids . . . That unit is a stepping stone to prison. The government's just announced 3,000 fewer prison places, so I'd better hurry and get my son's name down for one!' I said sarcastically. 'Do you know what kind of career that unit will prepare Merlin for? Licence-plate making. With tutorials on how to pick up the soap in the shower without bending over,' I ranted.

'Then your son can test out his cell theory,' came the headmaster's cold reply.

Surely clobbering such a man into unconsciousness with a hardback copy of *The Curious Incident of the Dog in the Night-time* would only be a Class B misdemeanour?

Walking back to my car, Merlin said in a tiny voice, 'Mum, it must be so hard when you have a son you don't think is amounting to anything.'

'It's your school that doesn't amount to anything,' I griped, driving home at break-neck speed. I checked my watch. With only ten minutes till the end of my own lunch break, I didn't even have time to stop the car. I just flung Merlin on to the pavement outside our house, like a mailbag, so I could dash back to work before my own headmaster noticed my absence and put *me* on exclusion. I'd had so many notes of chastisement this term, I'd taken to calling my boss Captain Memo.

Cutting the engine in my allotted space in the school car park, I sat for a moment and watched other mothers chatting at the gates. They seemed totally unaware that they were the lucky winners in the genetic lottery. I thought of Merlin trying to fend for himself in the disorienting, dizzying school environment, unsupervised at lunch and unprotected at play. I could hear the staccato of mocking laughter he suffered every day. What was my child's future? Given the six Fs and three 'Unmarkables' on his last GCSE school report, and a CV on which playing air guitar in my living room was the high point, I had a vague suspicion that the answer was Fuck All. The chances of my eccentric son surviving one hour in a dreaded Pupil Referral Unit were as likely as a spelling bee at the Playboy mansion. It was then that I suddenly found myself dialling Jeremy's mobile phone.

'Re: lunch,' I said abruptly. 'Okay, we'll come. But only if your mother can keep her foot out of her mouth for long enough to apologize to her only grandson for the way she's treated him.'

Even though I had told Archie that I was looking forward to the excursion only slightly more than a visit to the gynaecologist for a cervical smear, I was aware of a gruesome, voyeuristic desire to see Jeremy again; a masochistic curiosity to know what had happened in his life. Yes, I had told Jeremy that he was dead to me. But in some weird way, over the last few weeks my interest in him had kept growing . . . like the toenails on a corpse.

When I told Merlin we were going to his father's house for Saturday lunch, he gave me a look fizzing with joy. All the way to Cheltenham, purring along in Jeremy's sleek black Mercedes, my happy son swooped from thought to thought like a monkey through the treetops. As he chatted excitedly from the back seat about spin bowlers and the nature of time, I noticed how he had started mirroring his father's behaviour and language. Eager to please, he was laughing over-loudly at Jeremy's every comment, a technique he'd cultivated to cover his confusion when he was in situations that overwhelmed him. I sat in silence, sending my ex-husband slit-eyed glances of distrust. Jeremy wanted me to believe he'd changed. Sure, I mused sarcastically, and Britney Spears is actually a painfully shy recluse who will go to any extremes to avoid media attention.

Even though Archie thought of the English country-side as a cold, drizzly place where rabbits and deer hop around uncooked, he had offered to speed down deep into gin-and-jags territory to pick us up in my car at the slightest hint of unpleasantness. I had his number on my SOS speed dial. 'Time may heal a broken heart,' Archie had texted protectively, 'but not a heart which has had a stake driven right through it. Which is what will happen if that flash bastard upsets you or Merlin in any bloody way.'

The gravel on the Beaufort drive was loose and wet and crunched under the tyres of Jeremy's car, which gave a low growl as it turned into the forecourt. Two-hundred-year-old hedges all topiaried into fanciful shapes of tigers and peacocks loomed in a sinister and predatory way in the encroaching mist. Climbing out of his Mercedes, I looked at the statues of Merlin's long-forgotten ancestors, their feet in inky water, cold as ice on this wet October day.

The Tudor roofbeams of Jeremy's familial mansion arched above us like the blackened ribcage of a whale. I felt I'd been swallowed whole. And then, I really was being devoured. Not only were the Beaufort hounds leaping and licking at my legs, but Veronica was also suddenly suctioned on to my arm. She deposited an out-of-character kiss on my startled cheek.

'Welcome back into the family, Lucy,' my ex-mother-in-law said grandly. She dabbed at a wet eye with a lace hanky. 'And Merlin! Oh my dear boy. How you've grown!'

Her reunion speech was interrupted by a melodious fart. 'Why does hot air come out of my arse?' Merlin enquired of her cheerily. 'Does hot air come out of your arse too?'

To conceal her embarrassment, Veronica threw her arms around her grandson. Rolls of fat encircled her wrists like ivory bracelets. Merlin stood statue-still. Finally realizing that he wasn't going to hug her back, she unshackled herself and tried not to appear humiliated. A life-long mastery of her emotions had given Veronica an air of supercilious calm. But to my surprise, she didn't give her usual soliloquy disguised as conversation but tried to engage Merlin in chit-chat about his latest obsessions. She didn't even flinch or nostril flare when he asked her over lunch why men had nipples and God had invented lesbians. What had happened to the woman, I marvelled. Had she been abducted by aliens and replaced by a Pod Person? Jeremy's mother had become so sweet, half an hour in her company and we'd all have diabetes.

When Jeremy took Merlin out to the court for a game of tennis, Veronica moved her chair closer to me, settled down companionably and took my hand in hers.

'I can't tell you how wonderful it is to have Jeremy back. When Derek died' – her lips, a slash of glossy crimson, turned down and quivered with a rare display of emotion, which she struggled to control – 'well, obviously, an opening came up in the local party. A safe seat. Jeremy has always wanted to go into politics. I presumed he'd take his father's place. And it was a bit of a shock when ... But he's his own man.' She shrugged. 'Needless to say, the local Lib Dems snapped him up immediately.'

Yes, I thought to myself, with the family money to bolster his campaign, I bet they snapped him up faster than a condom at a chlamydia convention. As Veronica spoke I looked at the familiar sporting trophies marching across the mantelpiece. This was a family obsessed with achievement.

'And there's no doubt he'll be a huge success in politics,' Veronica continued, trying to conceal the smug note of certainty in her voice. 'He's getting a lot of press attention already. He's very busy, doing the rounds, knocking on doors, holding public meetings ... But Merlin's his priority. He wants to make it up to both of you. He's a changed man. His father's death . . .' There was a crack in her Formica face and she took another moment to dab at her eyes again. 'Well, it's made him question his values in life. And me mine. I was wrong to judge you so harshly,' she said tightly, 'and I want to make amends. Oh, how I rue the day I welcomed Audrey into this family!'

Satin blouse creaking irritably, she went on to talk in agricultural terms about her initial delight in Audrey's 'good stock' but then gradual dismay at her refusal to 'breed'. She poked absent-mindedly at the cashews curled up in their dish like pale little foetuses. 'As a TV personality, she didn't want to ruin her figure. I mean, *really*!'

Of course she wouldn't, I thought to myself. Having sold yourself as a Ferrari, you have to maintain yourself like one. Starting by not stretching your vagina the customary five kilometres and getting *National Geographic* boobs from breastfeeding. Veronica went on to complain bitterly about how Audrey forced Jeremy to live in 'that soulless city' while she waited for her 'big break' and then, as soon as she got the prime-time cooking programme she'd always coveted, ran off with her male co-presenter. 'She calls him her gastronomic love god, apparently,' she shuddered. 'How *common*.'

I flashed back to the devastation I'd felt when Jeremy traded me in all those years ago. Unable to bear the pain of all that remembering, I leapt at my mobile when it shrilled.

'How's it goin', sweet-cheeks?' It was Archie's voice, reassuring, solid. 'Why doan I drive down and save youse from that old witch. At least I know where to go when I want my warts cleared up.'

I laughed. 'We'll be home soon, Archie. And thanks for the call, *darling*,' I added for the old witch's benefit.

Jolted by Archie from my sad reverie, I glanced pointedly at my watch. 'Well, it was nice to see you again, Veronica,' I platituded. 'And yes, Merlin would love to take up your very kind educational offer. But as it's a long way back to town . . .'

'No! Why don't you both stay the night? It's so lonely rattling around this big, empty house.' She looked old all of a sudden. Shrunken. Like a once-formidable battleship about to be scuttled. The ancient mansion gave off a supercilious, haughty air. It felt cold in the big dining room, as if the sun had never stolen in. 'With Jeremy back and you three joyfully reunited, we can make it a happy family home once more.'

That would put the 'fun' into dysfunctional, I thought sarcastically. Veronica was delicately conveying a piece of cake to her mouth on the tines of a silver fork. 'That was my boyfriend on the phone.' I waited till the fork was just near her mouth before adding, 'You remember him . . . The man who asked you for a French kiss, but down under.'

The cake wobbled precariously and then cascaded carpetwards in a shower of crumbs. Veronica's face fell along with it, but before she could locate her vocal cords, Merlin and Jeremy tumbled into the dining room, all sweaty bonhomie. Jeremy switched on a great constellation of chandeliers and standard lamps.

Merlin bounced into a chair. One skinny leg wrapped itself around the other about seven times, an elbow plonked on to a knee and then his face landed on a waiting hand. My son was trying so hard to be likable he was going for gold in the Fixed Smile Event. My protective love caught me off guard. His awkward eagerness to please his father tore at my heart.

After cake and scones, Veronica announced that she was taking her grandson on a tour of the house. Jeremy caught my eye as his stout mother wrestled with the sleeves of her cardigan. She looked like a Doberman trying to get through a cat flap. As we both tried not to titter, Jeremy handed me a clinking glass of gin and tonic and, in unison, we said, 'Mother's little helper.' I felt a half-smile twitch at my lips. I'd forgotten that there had been good times.

As soon as they'd left to look at heirlooms and artifacts, an activity which Merlin would find as interesting as watching hair recede, I swigged down the whole glass of gin. Alcoholically fortified, I then rounded gleefully on my ex.

'So Audrey dumped you for her co-presenter. Ha! Just as well she didn't ever co-star with Willy the Whale. Or Mickey Mouse. *Oh, I just couldn't resist his animal magnetism.*'

'Why do you always begin a conversation as though we're in the middle of an argument?'

'Because we are.' I thrust out my glass for a top-up. And then downed that in one go, too.

Jeremy sighed deeply. 'Shall we take a stroll?'

No way, I thought, but found my legs moving out on to the billiard-baize lawns, which meant that the rest of me was forced to follow.

'Are you ever going to forgive me, Lucy?' Vast swathes of grass stretched down to an artificial lake dotted with architectural follies. The soft scent of wet soil wafted up from freshly turned beds. 'I've grovelled so much I've got gravel rash of the knees.'

'It's just that you turning up out of the blue like that . . . well, it opened up old wounds. Actually, the wounds have never healed. You broke my heart, you bastard. At least now you know what that feels like.'

'My heart's not broken over Audrey. It's broken because I left the only woman I've ever truly loved . . . I guess it was the shock, the depression, the grieving for the child I thought we'd brought into the world, alongside the crushing realization that all the old certainties in one's life are no more . . . Yet you refused to accept Merlin's diagnosis, running around from doctor to doctor . . . I felt as though you'd shut me out. And then I met Audrey, who seemed so bubbly and luminous. And our life was so dark at the time . . . I realize now that my attraction to her was nothing more that a case of arrested development. Some pubescent fantasy. When she turned thirty we had a secret birthday party, as nobody was allowed to know. Can you believe that? I suspect that when Audrey was born, even her mother kept it a secret from her.'

I felt a smile welling up in me. I tried to bite it back but it was all so habitual, strolling here in the manicured gardens of his family home, past the nooks and crannies where we'd hidden away and even once made love on the moonlit lake. Everywhere I looked, I was soothed by pleasant recollections.

'I wanted to be footloose and fiancée-free,' Jeremy punned, 'but my father's passing has taught me the importance of belonging. I want to belong to a son, a wife, a home. I want to be a committed father. Not the doofus dad from situation comedies and ads for ready meals who is always peering baffled at the pantry. I want to make educational sock puppets – well, he's too old for that now, but you know what I mean.'

'A regular Socrates,' I scoffed, to cover up the confusion I felt. The change in him was new and stupefying. It made me raw with mixed emotions. My eyes swept over him assessingly. Was he sincere?

'I made a mistake. The worst mistake in my life,' Jeremy admitted mournfully. The lawn was sprinkled with a shiny confetti of wet leaves the colour of burnt toffee. Swivelling to face me, he suddenly lost his footing and slipped on the slope, sliding down the embankment on his arse in a skid of grass stains. I squawked a laugh at the sight of him sprawled, prone, beneath me. 'Take me back,' he said self-deprecatingly. 'You'll never find anyone like me again.'

'Which is why I'm so glad you don't have a twin,' I replied tartly, but my mouth was wide with mirth.

'Seriously, Lucy, we could get back together again. It'll be just like our marriage, except we'll be happy and still talk to each other and want to have sex.'

Leaning up, he yanked me down on to the mossy bank and threw one warm, lean leg over mine, half-pinning me to the leafy lawn. I was aroused, alarmed and strangely titillated in equal measure. 'Don't try anything, buddy. You may be stronger than me but you forget that I know where all your old sports injuries are.' I tweaked his hamstring till he yelped.

We exchanged a tentative glance. No longer adversaries, we were unsure of how to speak to each other. The gin had gone straight to my head. Old feelings of affection for him glowed briefly, like a blown-out match.

'You have no idea how hard it's been,' I blurted. A flood tide of grief lay just behind my tonsils.

Jeremy took my face between his palms. 'I know.' His voice was melodious, the vowels soft. 'I'm so, so sorry, Lucy.' His hands now warmed mine, rubbing at my fingertips. 'I hate myself for what I did to you.'

My prejudices about Jeremy wavered in the heat of his scrutiny. Perhaps he really had metamorphosed back into the man I had fallen in love with? Then he sang 'American Pie' all the way through, word perfect. His hand moved on to my hip. It felt so familiar. Being with him was like walking back into a house you once lived in decades before – you think you've forgotten it but still remember where all the light switches are, which floorboards creak and windows stick. Instinctively, I shrugged myself deeper into his embrace and inhaled his familiar aroma. As I nestled in the crook of his arms like a baby, he placed his hot lips against the skin of my neck and gooseflesh as big as acne erupted on my arms and legs as I was ambushed by naked memories.

I felt the wild, vertiginous panic of losing my moorings. Somewhere in the back of my befuddled mind I thought vaguely that now might be a good time to give Archie that SOS call on my speed dial. But instead my lips just drifted in a trancelike state towards the mouth of my ex-husband . . .

17
The Ham in the Man Sandwich

A journey of self-discovery starts with a single step . . .
But so does falling down a flight of stairs. This is what
I thought when Jeremy dropped us home later that
night and I clocked Archie's anxious expression. As
soon as Merlin had loped upstairs to bed – vowing to
sleep with his cricket bat to 'bring me good luck in
the morning' – my boyfriend said eloquently, 'So
how is that dingo-dicked, lyin', cheatin', two-faced
jerk-off?'

'You could just say "your ex-husband".'

'As long as he still is that?' Archie asked crustily.

'Believe me, ex does *not* mark the spot,' I replied. It
was true that Jeremy's kiss had caught me momentarily off guard but then I'd broken away, reminding
myself that my ex-husband could charm anyone and
anything, from an ocelot to a tea cosy.

'And how's that hatchet-faced, bible-bashin' old battleaxe? A woman who has no vices will have a lot of irritatin' virtues, I'm tellin' you. The old gorgon probably thinks it's a sin to have meaningless sex on a Sunday.'

'The way *you* make love, it's a crime any day of the week,' I teased him, pinching his posterior.

'Obviously I need more practice.' Archie nuzzled those words into my ear. As he savoured my neck and throat, lust fluttered beneath my skin. Unclasping my bra, he fixed his mouth to my nipple and kissed me in that dizzyingly slow way of his. I was suddenly jelly-legged with longing, so it was just as well the old rocker then threw me over his shoulder. By the time Archie lay me down on my bed, I was pulling at his boxers – tasteful Calvin Klein, but I wouldn't have cared, at this stage, if they were neck-to-knee tweedy long johns. But then my pillager paused.

'Lou . . .' Archie's voice, a semitone lower than most other men's, dropped even further now as he plummeted into unchartered emotional waters. 'After Kimmy ditched me, I didn't think I could ever love another woman,' he confessed, plunging to Jules Verne-ish depths.

'I don't believe in love,' I countered, in an attempt to bring him back to the surface. 'I don't even believe in evolution. If evolution were true, mothers would have developed eyes in the back of our heads by now, no need for sleep and about ten hands.'

'You can't just say that you don't believe in love. Love is like South America. You can't trust the tourist brochures. You really have to go there and take a walk around.'

I looked up at him, all barrel-chested and piratical, and decided that I liked him too. A lot. I don't know why I found him so oddly enchanting, but I just glowed in the unexpected light of his gruff adoration. If love is a drug, then Archie had become my all-night chemist. I'd taken such comfort in the warmth of his arms every night for the past month. Guilty about my unexpected kiss, I hesitatingly owned up to it now. Archie took a beat or two, then said that it was only natural to have unresolved feelings about an ex.

Relief flooded through me. 'That's what I like about you, Archie. You still love me, despite my faults and foibles.'

Archie feigned huge astonishment, widening his eyes in mock-shock. 'You have faults and foibles?'

His muscular leg parted my thighs. It felt so natural, it seemed we'd been deliberately designed to fit together in this fashion. Whether it was a reaction against lunch with the Beauforts, a place where hors d'oeuvres are speared in the middle and people in the back, or the mischievous glee in Archie's eyes, I don't know. But a throb of expectation warmed my body.

'Some bloody experts were rabbitin' away on the radio today that the G-spot doesn't exist. The bloody experts are idiots. Not only can I find your G-spot in a jiffy,' he said in a granulated, sexy voice, 'but the search for the G-spot *is* the G-spot. It's not the destination but the journey.'

And with that, he gnawed his way through my panties.

The journey was sublime and the arrival even more so. I lay in his huge, hairy arms and marvelled at the curious symbiosis I shared with this incongruous creature. The night filled up with soft noise, the wind whipping through the trees, pattering rain, the odd cat mewling – and a long-forgotten sense of serenity branched through my being.

When I woke, late Sunday morning, Archie was perched on the edge of the bed with a tray of eggs, bacon, coffee, fried tomato and toast.

'See what fun it is to have a lodger? It saves you so much time.'

'Okay, if you're so keen to save me time, you can start by taking out the rubbish. Don't forget' – I winked at him – 'it's the journey not the destination.'

He gave an explosive bark of laughter, so contagious I too was soon hooting into my pillow. I vowed not to let Jeremy slide under my emotional radar again. Some old gravitational pull had drawn me to him out of habit. The only answer was to stay out of his orbit. If his mother wanted to pay Merlin's school fees to make amends for her neglect, then that was fine. But it didn't mean I had to spend any time with them. And I would have kept my promise too. Except that Merlin had other ideas . . .

'To my gorgous, snazy, mystifous mother, the one and only Lucy,' read the note shoved under my bedroom door some time during the night, in his big loopy scrawl, with erratic punctuation and spelling. (It took me a good few minutes to de-code 'mischievous'.)

> Horay joy for the world i had the time of my life i am so gratful to you for finding my father i love and adore my entire family. I feel as though i deserve this magical treat. love from your histericle son Merlin.

On the flipside was a note addressed to Jeremy.

> Dearest legendary Dad,
> I have had the tremendous pleasure of knowing you on and mostly off for 16 years. You've already had an increadable and remarkable life and ther are so many apsects of your character and demina to admire. Your academic acheevements are top notch. You are a supirior legend of banking and the Andrew Flintoff and Ricky Ponting of politics. I hope you have a sublime and mesmorizing election. I would love to embrace the years ahead of our

quality relationship. From your favourite son Merlin.

When Jeremy rang that night, Merlin shimmered with excitement. After a marathon conversation, my euphoric son hung up and then jumped from foot to foot as though doing a demented rain dance. For the rest of the night and all the following day, he nagged me relentlessly about having his newfound father over for dinner. He was like the human Hadron Collider, such was the speed of the words that came crashing out of his mouth. 'We would have such an awe-inspiring and robust evening,' he assured me. A week later I finally gave in. Jeremy arrived that very night laden with bottles of Krug, foie gras, an Xbox 360 and a Nintendo Wii.

I overheard Merlin explaining Jeremy to Archie. 'You, Archie, are a gorilla. But can you see my father's grey salt-and-pepper hair? And see how he wears a grey and white pinstriped suit? That's because he's a polar bear. He's been raising his other family in the North Pole. He transforms through the fridge. Mum, do you think a polar bear could live in this house? Would polar bears and gorillas try to eat each other?'

I didn't need to consult *National Geographic* to fathom the answer. Archie crunched Jeremy's fingers in a chiropractic handshake. I saw Jeremy wince but say nothing, not wanting to lose face.

'Archie is a legendary character of masculinity. He's

also a composer,' Merlin elaborated. 'The secret to being a successful rock star is to remember a tune that nobody else has thought of.'

'Ain't that the bloody truth,' Archie chortled. 'No rock-'n'-roll composer can have all work and no plagiarism. God, you kill me, kid,' he said appreciatively, before placing a proprietorial arm around Merlin's shoulders and leading him into the living room to rig up the new electronic toys.

Jeremy poured champagne into my flute with fastidious care. It hissed in the glass, but not as loudly as my ex. 'I know it's none of my business, especially after the appalling way I've behaved. But are you really *intimately* involved with *him*?' He made the words 'intimate' and 'him' sound like puppy vivisection. 'My mother told me about his racist and sexist behaviour. What do you see in the man? I don't want to say that he looks evil exactly, but his features most closely resemble a dark lord of torment last seen in a cautionary fourteenth-century gargoyle. Did you see how hard he shook my hand? He's clearly borderline insane.'

'I dunno, Jeremy. Raising a kid with autism all on your own tends to recalibrate one's view of sanity,' I said severely. 'Archie's the kind of man who grows on you.'

'Yes. Like plankton.'

I thought of Archie's panty-gnawing expertise and gave a secret smile at all the private pleasures only the two of us knew about. 'Archie has hidden charms. Besides, Merlin adores him.'

Jeremy bristled. 'That was before he had a father. I'm determined to make it up to our son by being the best dad ever.'

Through the rest of October Jeremy sneaked back into our lives so stealthily he might have been wearing camouflage combat fatigues.

He turned up at Merlin's speech day and sat next to me in the back row. When Merlin was the only kid in his class not to be awarded a certificate of any kind, the boy who had failed every maths test commandeered the microphone and told the audience that 'the difference between two positive numbers is 5 which has a massive arse like a peachy woman, and that the difference between their square is 55, which is two peachy arses, and then the sum of those two numbers is 11, which is skinny like two women on a diet.'

The maths teacher gawped at Merlin, flummoxed, his amazement clearly indicating that Merlin's deduction was correct. Jeremy and I looked at each other with bewildered pride, and a fleeting feeling of tenderness for our strange son passed between us.

The next week Jeremy gave up the campaign trail once more to attend Merlin's tennis tournament, cheering from the sidelines, even when our son startled his opponent by delivering a five-minute lecture at the net about friends who had fallen out: 'Wordsworth and Coleridge, John Lennon and Paul McCartney, Banquo and his murderer Macbeth, David Copperfield and Steerforth, Buzz Lightyear and Woody, Falstaff and Prince Hal.' He then segued on to friendships that had endured: 'Celia and Rosalind, the fellowship in *The Lord of the Rings*, Laurel and Hardy, Holmes and Watson and . . . my mum and dad,' he concluded, beaming at us. When Jeremy and I saw the happiness spilling from our son's eyes, something altered in the air between us.

Archie must have picked up the slight softening of my attitude to my ex, because he suddenly developed a passion for housework. Watching Archie trying to be domesticated was like watching a Masai warrior attempting to Morris dance. But he persevered. Vegetable stews and curries were suddenly simmering and sheets flapped on the line. He also took up gainful employment as a guitar teacher.

Jeremy retaliated by sending round a handyman. Within a week, nothing in the house leaked oil, spilt water, smoked when you plugged it in or made a funny clunking sound, and all without WD40 or duct tape.

Archie, who had always suffered from a terminal case of languor, responded by vacuuming the carpets so thoroughly he practically sucked the skirting boards right off the walls.

Even lunch became an opportunity for one-upmanship. At a Sunday barbecue, Archie bayoneted a hunk of fried chorizo.

'Can I have a bite of your sausage?' I asked him.

'I thought you'd never ask,' he replied lasciviously.

'I take that entendre and I double it,' Jeremy said tightly, handing me a whole snag.

Every time the two men met, the conversational version of jousting ensued, minus chainmail and medieval hosiery. When they weren't scoring verbal points off each other, Merlin became the football they tossed about between them. While Jeremy took Merlin to Paris, polo matches and film premieres, Archie whisked my delighted son off to a Pink Floyd reunion concert, a paintballing park and camping. When they got back on the Sunday night they were both so desperately in need of a shave they resembled a two-headed Yeti. But despite emitting a damp fungal reek of eau de mildewed sock, my son was effervescent with joy.

The average wait for a table at one of the country's top restaurants is, oh, about 35 years. But not for Jeremy. He took Merlin to Heston Blumenthal's The Fat Duck, twice, in one week.

Archie responded by queuing in the cold for five hours to get tickets to the taping of *Top Gear*. 'The taping is three bloody hours long. I'll die of boredom,' Archie texted me from the TV studio. 'Yeah, the show is filmed in front of a live audience – at first!' he joked. But, upon their return, it was clear that Merlin's obvious rapture had meant Archie had secretly enjoyed the jaunt.

Jeremy enrolled our son in a private special needs college. When my ex came over to discuss Merlin's assimilation (and who wouldn't assimilate into a classroom of only six pupils?) Archie's guitar would plaintively twang a pointed medley from my living room. 'While My Guitar Gently Weeps' melted into 'I'm Gonna Wash that Man Right out of My Hair' or 'D.I.V.O.R.C.E.' When that ploy failed to move me, Archie started making up his own songs with lyrics along the lines of 'I've got tears in my eyes from lying on my back crying over you'.

When I insisted that my boyfriend come along on Jeremy's planned family excursions to Greenwich or Hampton Court, Jeremy would unlatch his car door with the reluctant generosity of a kid whose parents are forcing him to ask if anyone else wants the last hot chip before guzzling it down himself. But even though his eyes were screaming 'Must This Caveman Come Everywhere with Us?!' Jeremy was so determined to prove how much he'd changed, he just smilingly acquiesced and invited Archie to 'climb on in'.

Archie's testicles were also in a twist. 'Must that needle-dicked, pillow-biting ponce hang around us all the bloody time?' he finally exploded when I told him that Jeremy was coming over for Sunday lunch, again.

But Merlin was determined to make a happy family of the four of us. We hadn't even finished the entrée when he pushed up on to his feet to make another of his famous speeches.

'People with Asperger's have trouble recognizing other people's feelings. I have a scheduling problem. I also have trouble organizing my thoughts and processing information. Breaking things down is more convenient for me. So, let's break down our intriguing family. First, there's my mum. You are the best mum in the whole world and I love spending time with you and your lovely clavicles.' He squeezed my shoulders until my head nearly popped like a pimple. 'I like squeezing. It helps me to think.' He then addressed the two men. 'Mum brightens up my day and she makes my day. She does this by making my dreams come true. Meeting my father is a dream come true. I never thought I would be so fortunate in my life. I cherish my life that my lovely mum and dad gave to me.'

His words dripped honesty, like clear honey. I was touched by the sweetness. A wash of autumnal sunlight, pale as the flesh of a lemon, fell on his beautiful face, and I blinked back a tear.

'And Archie has taught me to embrace life and live in the moment. I am allergic to history and I have also been diagnosed with a serious case of an allergy to mathematics. But Archie says that I don't have to be the top, star student. I just need to give it my all and pursue life robustly. So, I just wanted to thank you all for this mesmerizing, spectacular and sublime day.' He sneezed then and rubbed his nose vigorously. 'My nose keeps attacking me. It has feelings. Sometimes I can show my feelings and sometimes I can't. But I do think I've given a flawless performance over the past few weeks, don't you?'

I leant over and kissed his sweet head, tenderly. 'Yes, darling, you really have.'

The same could not be said of Archie and Jeremy. On the personality palate, they were oysters and custard. And no amount of meltingly sweet Merlin monologues could give them a taste for each other.

'So tell me,' Jeremy asked Archie two nights later when he came in for a drink after taking Merlin to the opera, 'are those clothes donated?'

Jeremy was clad in one of his immaculate pinstriped bespoke suits. I knew for a fact that Archie only ever ironed the backs of his shirts if he planned on taking off his leather jacket.

'Spoken by a bloke who can't find his prick without a pair of tweezers. Mind you, there's nothin' wrong with you that a hitman couldn't cure.'

Jeremy opened a bottle of Montrachet. He poured a glass for me then half-turned in Archie's direction. 'Would you like a taste?' he asked, before adding sarcastically, 'Although drinking straight from the wine bottle might bruise the bouquet and could lack a little *savoir faire.*'

'*Savoir faire* . . . That's knowing which fork to use to dig out your earwax at the dinner table, ain't it? Shame we can't all be sophisticated banker types like you. So, tell me, which particular slug do you base your business techniques on?' Archie enquired contemptuously.

'Please, no fieriness!' Merlin begged, putting his hands over his ears. 'Fieriness makes me nervous. It's so Latin American.'

I rounded on both men. 'Merlin's right about the pointless arguing. You're both so megalomaniacal it'd be impossible to dent either ego without a year or two of carpet-bombing.'

I might have taken a relationship raincheck on them both, except that very night I found a curious score sheet in Merlin's room. At first I thought it was his cricket calculations. But, upon closer inspection, I realized he'd been rating Archie and Jeremy as Possible Fathers, using tennis-scoring techniques. 15–love to Jeremy. Then 40–15 to Archie. Then deuce. And so, despite the tensions, I allowed our contrapuntal existence to continue. Jeremy took Merlin and me to string quartet concerts at the Wigmore Hall and orchestral recitals at the Festival Hall, and penned poems full of atonement, secreted in bouquets of fragrant red roses.

Archie telling me he wanted to be reincarnated as my G-string was about as romantic as the Aussie rocker ever got . . . but who needs romance with a sex life so hot you require asbestos condoms? In bed, Archie was clit-tinglingly, tantrically, erotically eccentric to the point of orgasmic female blast-off. I felt such a heated attraction for the man that, as soon as I saw him, I wanted to shove him back on to the sofa and ride him rodeo style, with an insouciant toss of my hat in the air.

My mother always said that the only time a woman could change the male of the species was out of nappies when he was a baby. But it seemed to me that both men had changed substantially. Jeremy had become a born-again human being. And Archie was such a new and improved version, I found myself scanning his temples for electrode scorch marks.

But the situation was proving very confusing. I needed some advice. But I was about to learn an important lesson. Advice is like herpes – better to give than to receive.

18

A Rip in the Designer Genes

When my mother realized that I'd allowed Jeremy back into my life, she told me that I should be documented in one of those Oliver Sacks books on weird psychology cases, as I obviously had a rare head injury. It was a Friday night in late October. Phoebe, Mum and I had just sat down to dinner when Jeremy's next shipment of Harrods hampers filled with truffles, exotic olive oils and oysters arrived. An iPad for Merlin had been couriered over earlier.

Merlin was so excited he spun me into his arms as though we were dancing the flamenco. 'What do they mean on TV when they talk about a free gift? Aren't all gifts free?' he asked, puzzled.

I laughed. Sometimes there was an epic simplicity to the things he said.

'I'm going to my room ... When you're on your

own, all your annoying habits disappear. Have you ever noticed that, Mum?' And then he was gone, in a blur of hair and limbs.

I cracked open the can of caviar. 'It's funny, you know. When Jeremy left me I lost faith in my own judgement. But he's been so charming and kind, so thoughtful to Merlin, that it's a, well, it's a relief to remember why I loved him. I mean, do you remember how hard I fell for the man?'

'Yes, like a condemned building,' my mother stated crisply.

'But you liked him too in those early days. And he's back to being the man I remember, Mother. He's changed.'

'Light bulbs change, tampons, minds, weather – but men, never.'

'Well, this caviar has changed *my* mind about Jeremy. I've been thinking, Lulu . . . would it be so bad to take up with him again?' my sister chirped pertly, her teeth blackened with roe. 'He's obviously still attracted to you. And *I* am very attracted to his bank balance!' she squealed, discovering a tin of foie gras at the bottom of the wicker basket.

This comment was so out of character for my sister that I commandeered the vintage Veuve Clicquot that had arrived thoughtfully pre-chilled, presuming she'd drunk too much. I offered my mother a glass. But she shook her head abstemiously and pointedly filled her glass with tap water or 'Château Thames', as she called it.

'I still don't trust Jeremy,' she said emphatically. 'His smile doesn't quite reach his eyes.'

'Oh, Mother. Lighten up.' Phoebe eye-rolled. 'You've become such a social worker of late. It's a wonder you're not wearing Birkenstocks and a cheese-cloth smock.'

'Talking of cheese, free cheese is only found in a mousetrap,' my mother philosophized. 'Believing a man like him can change, well, you might as well believe in UFOs, fairies and politicians' promises. And what about Archie?'

'Gosh. What's that sound?' My sister put a hand up to her ear in melodramatic shock. 'Oh, it's the sound of the bottom of barrels being scraped. Look, I like Archie, but what can he offer you, security-wise? Zilch. We're not young any more. BA are laying off staff. An old cart tart like me will be the first to go. We girls need to become more pragmatic.'

'How much have you actually drunk, Phoebe?' I enquired, seriously disturbed by the change in her.

'It's true you can't keep stringing both men along, darling,' my mother admonished.

'And the decision you make should be based on one fact – what is best for Merlin. And the obvious answer to that is Jeremy,' Phoebe added.

'You're undervaluing Archie. He's been wonderful for Merlin too. I know I didn't like him in the beginning. But over the past few months, feelings for him have seeped into me, like tea from a teabag,' I said fondly.

'Switch to coffee,' my sister advised, retrieving a bag of expensive Colombian beans from the hamper.

My mother and I studied Phoebe with concern. All my life, my sister's buoyant spirits had known nothing of Sir Isaac Newton and his gravitational theories. She'd always been optimistic, happy, bounding with energy. But, of late, my beloved sister had been in danger of having to remove the trophy for Patron Saint of Loveliness from her mantelpiece. Phoebe was now like a domesticated, docile family cat that suddenly starts flashing claws and going feral.

'I like Archie,' my mother stated. 'He's a durable man. And honest. What you see is what you get. Jeremy, on the other hand, should have a Buyer Beware sticker stamped to his forehead.'

'That was the old Jeremy,' I corrected her. With each bite of mouthwatering pâté and sip of vintage champers I felt a pleasurable emotional vertigo, tugging me towards a defence of my ex.

'But Archie has made you so happy,' my mother counselled. 'And if his song lyrics are anything to go by, dear, he can do a lot more with a Mars bar than the packet implies.' My mother winked. 'Actually, I never understood what your cousin Kimmy saw in Archie, until I glimpsed him eating oysters . . . But, oysters or no oysters, even these ones from the Harrods food hall' – she speared a mollusc from its shell and regarded it suspiciously as it dangled from her fork prong – 'if you let Jeremy back into your life, you'll require worming tablets. The man is vermin.'

'Even if Jeremy doesn't speak from the heart, he speaks from the hip pocket,' Phoebe declared, gulping the mid-air oyster with greedy relish. 'And I'm liking the language.' She paused to rummage through the rest of the hamper and squealed with delight at the discovery of individually wrapped crème brulées. She cracked a toffee top with the back of a teaspoon and savoured a bite. 'Mmm. If this crème brulée were a man, Mother, you'd whip your clothes off and make love to it. Don't you want a nibble?'

She thrust a spoon of dessert into my mother's face. There was an uncharacteristic aggression in Phoebe's action which my mother, although startled, chose to ignore. She gently pushed my sister's hand aside then added earnestly, 'Lucy, dear, listen to me. If someone betrays you once, it's his fault, but if he betrays you twice, it's your fault. And your fault alone.'

Then my gentle sister, who has only ever won an argument with herself, rounded on our stunned mother. 'Taking your advice on love is like taking flirting lessons from a eunuch. Or, I dunno, discretion lessons from Wikileaks. At your age you should be radiating a mix of authority and dignity, not belly-dancing with naked toyboys in Tibetan ashrams.'

'Phoebe . . .' I placed a calming hand on her arm.

'What on earth's the matter with you? You're starting to make Vlad the Impaler look like a librarian,' I joked.

But my sister refused to be mollified. 'I'm serious, Mother.' She shook me off. 'What kind of financial security can an ageing, fading rock star give your poor destitute daughter?'

'I'm not destitute. And, anyway, Archie does have a job now,' I defended him. 'Plus he's working on an album.'

Phoebe squawked a laugh. 'The gap between Archie's aspirations and his achievements has the same cargo capacity in metres as, say, Idaho. You're exhausted from single motherhood, Lulu.' Under fizzing brows, she glowered at our mother before adding vehemently, 'And the reason she needs financial security is because you've spent all our inheritance, flitting around the world like an irresponsible teenager.'

My mother's pale complexion went an even more arctic colour. 'As you will one day discover, Phoebe, the difficult thing for women my age is not downshifting a career but upshifting. Just when a mother comes blinking out of her murky, milky years, liberated from the school run, the three meals a day, the laundry and taxi services and housework slavery, all ready for action, society hands you Invisible Man bandages. I don't want to be a runner-up in the human race.'

'Why not?' Phoebe rejoindered bitterly. 'Your daughters are. Thanks to you.'

A chasm opened in our tight-knit little family circle. My mother was stricken with anguish. After a few minutes of staggered silence, she tried to defuse the situation.

'I think I'll write a screenplay next, dears. Everybody else is. Mine will be the touching, auto-biographical story of a hardworking woman with a philandering husband who raised her children and then tried to forge a small life for herself before she kicks the bucket but whose daughters don't appreciate all the wonderful things she's done for them. Julia Roberts will play the mother and the kids will be played by hideous, troll-like George Lucas special effects.'

But her attempt to heal the rift with humour fell flat. My mother is a one-woman task force. It was un-nerving to see her emotional resilience faltering. In our family, we usually just argue and argue until my mother is right. But not today.

'Phoebe, darling, I'm sure all this anger and negativ-ity is merely because your hormones are leaving the building. The good thing about the menopause, dear, is that you can warm your own dinner plate on your forehead. The bad thing is it turns you into a raving maniac.' She smiled, attempting one more stab at levity, but her lovely singsong Somerset lilt had lost its spring and sounded uncharacteristically dull and flat.

'*You* have fun all the time, but when *we* get a little pleasure you rain on our happiness parade. How I wish it were *you* leaving the building instead of my hormones.'

My mother bade her grandson goodbye and left before dinner ... And Phoebe wouldn't let me run after her.

19

Dr Love Has Left the Building

All men make mistakes, but live-in lovers find out about it sooner.

'I hope you're aware that motorbikes are society's way of promoting the funeral business?' I said when Archie sauntered in one Saturday afternoon, his head encased in a bike helmet.

'A mate lent me his Harley.' Archie levered the heavy helmet off his cranium. 'Thought Merlin would like a spin so I picked him up from the museum.'

Merlin bumped into the room next, giving a mumbled exclamation, his helmeted head bobbing with glee.

My synapses snapped to attention. 'Oh my God, Archie! Did you leave several major brain lobes as a deposit? What if he'd fallen off?'

Archie cast an amused eye over me and then, to my

surprise, laughed right into my face. Why was he laughing at me? A spasm of irritation darted raggedly through my temples.

'Don't make me kill you,' I seethed. 'I haven't had my afternoon coffee yet.'

'It's smother-love. You never let the poor kid out the door without sufficient items in his backpack to set up a wilderness homestead.'

I liberated my son's head from its casing.

'What an exhilarating and intoxicating adventure!' he exclaimed. Merlin's hair was on end as though a couple of wild animals had been grazing there.

I swallowed my anger and said as sweetly as I could, 'Darling, run upstairs and have a shower. Your father will be here soon to take you to the theatre.' Jeremy, who'd been absent for a few days in Paris at a conference organized by the British Council, was bursting to see his son.

Merlin grimaced. 'But I'm theatre-intolerant. I go into actor-phylactic shock.'

'Why?'

'You have to sit there with a cramped, stiff arse, staring at the stage with a straight face pretending to understand what's going on whilst trying hard not to think about other things in your life and the universe.'

'What about Shakespeare? I thought you adored him?' I queried, amazed.

'I've retired from Shakespeare,' he said, drawing his

shoulders together defensively. 'I get tired of Dad expecting me to be a genius. Creativity is associated with a variety of cognitive disorders suffered by high achievers, like Newton, Orwell, Charles de Gaulle, Thomas Jefferson, Enoch Powell . . .' He was talking faster and faster, wringing his hands nervously. 'But not everyone can be a creative genius, you know . . .' He trailed off, glancing sidelong at me in sudden embarrassment.

'No one expects you to be a genius, darling.' In truth, Merlin's 'genius' was like a planet that sometimes sparkles into view or a mirage that shimmers in the sun – there one minute, gone the next. Totally intangible. 'Just give this a go. It's a musical. Sondheim. You might like it. And here . . . can you put away your clean clothes for me? I've labelled the drawers so you won't get mixed up, okay?'

Merlin's dyspraxia meant that his brain fused when it came to logical practicalities, so socks often ended up in the shoe cupboard, shoes under his pillow, the spoonerisms in the mixed-metaphor drawer.

When Merlin had left the kitchen, arms laden with freshly ironed jeans and T-shirts, I rounded on my irresponsible boyfriend. 'I know that some people like to sit astride 500ccs of throbbing horsepower screaming down the highway with the wind in their hair . . . *Most of these people are now dead*. How dare you take a risk with my child's life without even checking with me first!'

'Life's a risk, toots. You've gotta start preparin' him.

Merlin is maintained, enclosed, fed, watered, caged . . . He's no more than a very expensive pet,' replied Archie mulishly. 'Ya gotta let him get drunk and get laid and . . .'

'You keep going on about that. And what if he gets some girl pregnant? I'm to be a grandma, am I?'

'The hottest granny in town.' With a carnal smile on his fleshy lips, Archie sauntered over and squeezed me to him.

'It's not funny. After all that sex education, he asked me the other day whether girls poo . . . What am I supposed to do? Give him a vasectomy? Who am I? *Hitler?* . . . Because he'll never figure out how to put on a condom,' I objected, pushing Archie away. 'And even if he does, he won't remember.'

'This new special needs school of Merlin's – well, the girls are bound to be just like him: crazy, wild, hot-to-trot chicks with margarine legs – easily spread. It could happen, Luce. Face facts. If you'd let me take him to a brothel, the girls could teach him. Nothin' like some hands-on experience.' He ran his fingers up my leg under my dress and gave me a playful spank.

'Archibald, you are *not* taking my baby boy to a brothel.'

'Well, you can't take him. You'd make such a fuss about whether there were nuts in the chocolate body paint and if the duck-down pillows were hypoallergenic . . .'

'He's only a child!'

'Look, that slimy ex of yours might be able to pay for Merlin to go to a posh private school and take him to eat in fancy-shmancy, courgette-up-the-bum French joints where five people can eat for the price of a small Mercedes. No way can I compete with that. But I can equip the kid with some street-smarts.' Archie's face wore a mutinous expression. 'Ridin' motorbikes, swearin', smokin', sleepin' around ... The reason teens are so vile is so you won't be upset about the empty nest once they go walkabout.'

'You don't get it, do you? There will never *be* an empty nest. Merlin is with me for life. Like psoriasis. Or rheumatism. Or a heart murmur or something. I just hope he dies before I do, because who is going to look after him? The worry of it keeps me awake at night.'

Archie's thumbs sunk angrily into his jean pockets. 'You should have more faith in him ...' And, by implication, more faith in my boyfriend, I duly noted. 'People think Merlin's weird, the way he can't make small talk and eye contact. But he thinks *we're* weird. The hours we spend being nice to people we don't even like ... If it weren't for the Merlins of this world, human beings would never have got out of the bloody cave.' Then Archie's smile grew mischievous and he shifted into a more irreverent gear. 'And you *don't, do* you?' he mocked.

'What?'

'Poo!' He winked. 'After all, you are a goddess. Hell,

you look positively underdressed without a plinth.'

Turning my back abruptly, I busied myself in the kitchen. I was nursing my coffee cup in both hands, mulling over what Archie had said and wondering if perhaps I could advertise Merlin on eBay – 'one strapping, quirky youth in need of older, understanding cougar' – when Jeremy arrived. It was only when I went to open the door and saw the pile of Merlin's clean clothes dumped on the floor that I realized with a jolt that he'd obviously loitered there in the hall and overheard our argument. A small alarm bell went off in my head. I called his name. No answer. Rifling through his coat pocket, I discovered his wallet was also missing. My face took on the pallor of someone who has just stepped off the Daredevil Thunder Mountain ride at a theme park. 'Oh God, Archie. I think Merlin overheard our conversation.'

'What conversation was this exactly?' Jeremy asked, striding across the threshold.

'We were having a tiff about me treating Merlin like a little boy and not letting him grow into a man by' – I paused, searching for the least inflammatory vernacular, 'keeping pace socially, pharmaceutically and sexually with the other kids.'

'Merlin is socially immature. I too had a low emotional IQ,' my ex-husband admitted humbly. 'But I've changed. And, in time, he will too, Lucy, I promise you.' He held my hands reassuringly.

Archie rolled his gooseberry eyes up to the ceiling.

'The only reason Merlin is immature is that you two drongos keep mollycoddlin' the poor little bastard. Youse never let the kid out the door without instructions on what to do if there's an earthquake, tidal wave, nuclear attack or alien invasion.'

'Oh God, Archie,' I said with sudden insight. It was no longer a small alarm bell ringing in my head but the giant boom of Big Ben. 'You don't think he went to a brothel, do you?'

'How would he have the dosh?' Archie asked practically.

'Jeremy, you gave him a few hundred quid the other day, didn't you?'

'Yes. For books . . . But a brothel? It's preposterous. How exactly in God's name would he know where to find such a place?'

'Well, um . . . when I was lookin' around for gigs, I popped into that nightclub down on the high street . . .'

'What nightclub?' Jeremy demanded.

'It's called the G-spot – which explains why you've never found it, Beaufort,' Archie wisecracked. 'And, um, Merlin was kinda with me at the time.'

'You took my son to a lap-dancing club!' I shrieked.

'They're not lap-dancers. They're singers.'

'Yeah, right. She's gyrating on the stage in a black basque cut to show off her singing ability.'

'And there's this sauna out the back which I kinda explained to him . . .'

Jeremy has a lot of flair. Most of it in his nostrils. 'Let me get this right,' he flared. 'You took my son to a lap-dancing club and then encouraged him to frequent a brothel? You know how they say you should live every day as though it's your last? I suggest you take advantage of that adage immediately.' Jeremy pulled himself up to his full six-foot-two height and squared up to Archie.

'Somebody's gotta teach the kid to be a man. And what the fuck would you know about that, you poncey git? You're probably wearin' padded jockey shorts. Wonder Y's – the wonder pant for wimps,' Archie chortled. 'Or Disney boxer shorts from "It's a Small World After All".'

Jeremy's glare was as loud as thunder. 'Lucy, have you ever quizzed this man on his dating history, excluding pets and other animals?'

If it were possible to smug an opponent to death, Jeremy would have won the ensuing skirmish. But, when he threw a punch, Archie intercepted it with expert ease, effortlessly clipping Jeremy across the cheek.

Archie only had time to land that one punch before I inserted myself between their bristling forms. 'Did you both have a bowl of bile for breakfast? My son is missing! Archie, take me to that club immediately. Jeremy, wait here, in case Merlin comes back,' I instructed. 'Call me immediately if he does.'

Archie drove my car towards the high street. The

yellow, lopsided moon had a greasy ring around it, like a badly fried egg. I felt so angry I could have fried an egg on my head. Archie tried to lighten the atmosphere by making some flippant remarks about where to park outside a brothel – 'in an erogenous zone?' But I just sat in tense silence as all around me the world was exclaiming. My eyes raked the Saturday-night throngs. Archie parked in the grounds of a dilapidated housing estate then led me into the lap-dancing club. Patrons jerked back and forth on the dance floor as though being electrocuted with invisible cattle prods, while semi-naked girls gyrated on podiums above them. I searched through the dancers as they writhed in the multicoloured lights, but there was no sign of Merlin.

Archie then steered me down a side alley which straggled beside the railway line. The brothel's windows were painted black. A hot-pink electric sign reading 'SAUNA' spluttered on and off like a dying fly.

The outside was positively grandiose compared with the interior. The dimly lit reception was malodorous and musty smelling. A desultory gaggle of girls broiled prawn-like in the glare of naked pink neon. Their velvet glances slid over me and on to Archie, accompanied by a pantomime of half-hearted preening and pouting. The girls started introducing themselves to him. They all had the names of alcoholic beverages – Chardonnay, Tequila, Brandy – only they didn't mix well, practically elbowing each other out of the way to get to new male meat.

I approached the desk and spoke to an older woman whose hair was piled high into a platinum-blonde halo.

'I'm looking for a boy . . . Tall, blond, slim . . .'

She shrugged noncommittally. 'Yeah? Well, I'm lookin' for Brad Pitt naked on a bed of lettuce.'

'No, you don't understand . . .'

'Why don't cha just tell me what you want, I can tell you to fuck off, and then our lives can go on?' she said, gimlet-eyed.

'I've come for my son . . .'

'Oh, and I thought it was to steal my Rembrandts.'

Archie disentangled himself, strode over to the desk and gave his most raffish grin. 'Hi, sugar tits,' he crooned, much to her pleasure. 'Thing is, the kid's underage, which wouldn't look that good on your rap sheet. So maybe we could just take a quick Captain Cook – a look,' he clarified, winking.

I didn't wait for permission but bounded up the stairs, trying not to trip on the moulting shagpile. Where was my son? I stood on the landing beneath a dangling bare light bulb, surrounded by an aureole of dust. 'Merlin! Merlin! Come out here immediately.'

A door squinted open and an inquisitive head peered out. I strained to see through the frugal lighting, but it wasn't my child. I banged on the walls further down the hall, calling his name. A finger of light probed forth from a door which was ajar. The chapter headed 'Recovering Your Teenage Son from a Brothel' is curiously absent in most child-rearing manuals. With no other course of action suggesting itself, heart in mouth, I just peeked inside. And there was Merlin. His face had the bewildered look of some-one stuck on a crossword puzzle, but he was at least fully clothed. Relieved, I flung the door wide.

A shabby chenille bedspread lay unruffled atop a lopsided wooden bed. A red scarf draped over a bed-side lamp gave the room a post-Chernobyl glow. On the bed, clad in pink baby-doll pyjamas, was a podgy woman in her thirties with pale papery skin and sunken, kohl-rimmed eyes.

The relief of finding him overcame me momentarily. Then I remembered where we were. 'What's happened?' I demanded. 'Tell me. I'm his mother.'

'No shit?' she responded, eloquently. 'Well, lemme see. So far we've nattered on about, like, time travel, Shakespeare, astronomy an' that. Oh yeah. And why it's better to live in a communist country where no one gives a toss about material possessions,' she rasped out in a voice that was just one packet shy of lung cancer.

'Merlin, we are going home right now,' I said, as though auditioning for the role of Miss Jean Brodie.

Merlin bent over the woman's hand and kissed it. The prostitute guffawed at the polite incongruity of the chivalric gesture, yet blushed, as if secretly flattered by the gallantry.

'Come back again, kid,' she smiled, then added a postscript addressed to me, 'Hey, no tip?'

'Yes. Get a wax,' I advised her.

'So, kiddo,' – Archie ruffled his hair affectionately as we walked back to the car, 'I hope you didn't have a good time. It was supposed to be educational.'

I suggested to Archie that if he didn't shut up I'd be tempted to see how long it would take for his head to explode if I backed my car repeatedly over his skull. 'Like Jeremy said,' I concluded, 'I hope you didn't have any plans tonight that involved living a little longer.'

Archie was undeterred. 'Death is the greatest kick of all – that's why they save it to last. Right, sport?' He winked at Merlin in the rear-view mirror. Nobody spoke again until Archie was reverse-parking my car into a spot outside our house.

'So . . . the women at a brothel, they don't really love you, do they?' my son finally asked.

Archie laughed so hard he bumped into a red Saab behind him. 'Oh bugger. J'have a piece of paper so I can write a note? Doan worry. If there's any damage, I'll pay for it.'

'You bet you will.' I rummaged in my handbag. The only paper I had was the price list from the sauna which I'd picked up from the counter. 'So, did you pay that woman any money?' I asked Merlin tentatively, dreading the reply.

'Oh yes. She commandeered it all.'

So much for their pro-communist, in-depth discussion on the unimportance of material possessions.

'She also asked me if I was old enough to open a bank account. And would I take her to the cash machine . . . How do you open a bank account? With a key? Do you unlock a box and there's lots of money? An account is invisible, isn't it?'

I glowered at Archie. How could he have taken this child into a den of iniquity? And yet, the man wasn't all bad, I thought, watching him scrawling a note of apology.

Jeremy, who'd been observing our arrival through my living-room window, pushed a glass of whisky into my hand the minute I walked through the door. 'Is he okay?'

As they'd now missed the theatre, I persuaded Merlin to bound upstairs for a shower – although I would have preferred soaking him for a week or two in a vat of penicillin – then replied, 'Yes. Thank God. For a while there I thought we were in some French subtitled movie. All that was missing was Charlotte Rampling or Gérard Depardieu and perhaps a crack team of existentialist philosophers spreading ennui . . . But nothing happened,' I concluded with relief.

'I can never forgive myself for abandoning you to the likes of that cretin.' Jeremy gestured out of the window at Archie, who was tucking his apology note beneath the windscreen of the red Saab. 'All the pressure I've put you under, raising Merlin alone, well, it's all just been too stressful. Especially when you're working. How can I ever repay you? Why don't you give up work, Lucy? Become a lady of leisure?'

'I'm not sure I could fill either part of the equation, Jeremy.' I gulped at my whisky and winced at its bite.

'You could come on the hustings with me. The by-election's coming up and I could do with your wise counsel. I would put you on the payroll, so you'd be totally supported financially. With no real workload.'

I looked at my ex. Working full-time whilst trying to look after Merlin meant that life was incredibly busy – which was really just a euphemism for total chaos and please don't fire me. I said nothing but, in truth, Jeremy's offer was as comforting as a thick winter blanket.

Archie, who was hanging up his leather jacket in the hall, gave a snorted guffaw as merciless as a sneeze. 'So, the Beatles were wrong. Money can buy you love.'

'Only in a brothel,' I snapped angrily. 'Say what you will about Jeremy, but he would never have exposed Merlin to something so crass.'

'Jeez, Lou. You're such a bloody hypocrite. You worry about Merlin going to a brothel, but you'd consider going on the road with a politician? Screwin' people comes as naturally to your ex as breathin'. You want justice, go to a brothel. You wanna get fucked, go to a pollie.'

Jeremy touched his eye, which was now oystering up with swelling. 'Well, we can't all be as moral and upstanding and perfect as you, now can we? I need to wash this dried blood off my face,' Jeremy said dramatically before striding from the room.

'I'm amazed it's not blue,' Archie called out after him. 'You could have washed it off while we were away, you wily prick, but then you wouldn't have got the sympathy vote, right?'

Alone now, Archie and I stood facing each other. The air between us crackled with tension. After an awkward silence, he said, 'Look, I know those places exploit women. I never said my feminist conscious-ness was evolved. It's evolv*ing*! It's an ongoin' thing, right? As a bloke, I'd just like to apologize for everything, okay? But you've gotta give the kid points for havin' the balls to even get into the joint. I mean, that took a lot of initiative and guts.'

I turned my back on him. Right now I would have preferred the company of a Somali pirate or even Berlusconi wrestling in jelly.

'So,' a refreshed Jeremy said, re-entering the room a few minutes later, 'Lucy says you grew up in Tasmania?'

'Yeah. People always laugh when I say I'm from Tasmania, possibly because Tassie has 22,000 people and only seven surnames. Do the maths,' Archie chuckled, in a valiant effort to soften my mood. 'That's the reason I want to move back there one day. 'Cause everyone has the same DNA, meanin' you can never get caught for a crime.'

'I think you'd make a rather hopeless criminal, actually, as the good ones never do get caught.' Jeremy flourished a piece of paper I recognized as the price list from the sauna. It was the note Archie had put under the windscreen of the red Saab. In a bad imitation of an Aussie accent, Jeremy read out what was scrawled on the back.

G'day. Sorry, mate, but I accidentally hit your car.
The woman I have the horn for is watching me
write this note so I'm pretending to write down my
details. An oldie, but a goldie! See ya!

Archie's expression was that of a man who has been contemplatively collecting driftwood on a beach and has just caught a tsunami in the back of his neck. 'You lowly piss ant,' he said to Jeremy.

'You're plagiarizing from Byron again, aren't you?' Jeremy condescended.

Archie's face was as weary as an unmade bed. 'Jeez, Lou. How can you take any advice from a man whose cufflinks and ties are funnier than he is?'

Archie's deceit impacted like a blow to my chest. 'Oh Archie,' I sighed. 'How can I ever trust a man who could write a note like that?' My words felt heavy and sour.

'You don't seem to have any trouble trusting the president of the Slime Committee here.'

'But Jeremy has taken responsibility for his mistakes. You can never even admit that you've *made* one. Like taking my son on a motorbike and to a brothel.'

'But what makes you think the scumbag isn't gonna shoot through again? How can you trust a bloke who talks as though he's pouring syrup on a pikelet?'

Jeremy insinuated himself between us and spoke in a voice that was sinuous and exact. 'What is so saintly about you, Lucy, and why I love and respect you so much is that you have always put Merlin first. His life was endangered tonight. Twice.'

'He wasn't endangered!' Archie bellowed. 'Why don't you quit workin' yourself up into seven types of arsehole and keep out of it . . . Lou,' he entreated. 'Talk to me. Say something.'

Before I could respond, Jeremy then reached under the coffee table and upended a rucksack I recognized as Archie's. Its alarming contents spewed across the table. 'I took the liberty of going through your things while you were at a *brothel* with my *child*. And look what I found.' Jeremy poked through the offensive debris with forensic fascination. 'Amyl nitrate, hardcore porn, marijuana, and what I presume to be ecstasy tablets . . .'

'You talk so much shit your teeth must be brown,' Archie seethed. 'None of that crap's mine.'

'No wonder you're encouraging Merlin to keep pace pharmaceutically with the other boys, because you're his dealer.'

'You fucker. I can't believe you left out a sex tape of me and Paris Hilton or, I dunno, a clubbed seal. Lucy, come on. You can see it's a set-up. You do believe me, right?'

Angry and discombobulated, I said nothing. That very day I'd checked on Merlin's score sheet. They'd been deuce for a while, but today it was definitely advantage Jeremy. And I felt inclined to agree with Merlin.

'Archie, old man, I think it's time you found your way back to Australia, don't you? It's 4,000 miles wide, bright red in colour and surrounded by sharks, so you shouldn't have too much trouble finding it.'

'Why don't you stay out of it, you gangrenous ball sack!' Archie fumed. 'This is between Lucy and me. Lou' – he took me by the shoulders – 'you know I love ya. If I stuffed things up, I'm sorry. But don't throw me aside. Nobody will ever know you so well,' he persevered. 'Gimme a test. The "How Well Do You Know Her?" test. What is your favourite pizza topping? How many squares of chocolate will you eat on the day before your period? What food do you secretly want me to order so you can nibble it off my plate? How often do you like to be spanked? And, for advanced lovers: at what velocity?' When his spiel failed to amuse me, he changed conversational key and added sombrely, 'Lou, if you ever ditched me, the bum would just drop out of my world.'

I didn't know what to believe. It felt as though the

wild animal I'd picked up in the street and taken home and fed and loved out of kindness had swerved around and bitten my hand.

Jeremy shoved the contraband into the backpack and thrust it at Archie. 'I've heard of slow readers but you're a slow listener. Read my lips. YOU'RE NOT WELCOME HERE ANY MORE.'

Archie might have decked him there and then, except that a freshly showered Merlin suddenly burst into the room. We stopped talking and all looked at him in unison. My son stood there with one leg up behind him like a flamingo, squirming with embarrassment. 'I don't always know what to say, you know. I can't just be yakity yak all the time.'

'I'm sorry to disillusion you, Lucy. I really am. Especially when I behaved even more atrociously in the past,' Jeremy added regretfully. 'But I know you'll do the right thing.'

My years of expertise perfecting a flinty exterior came in handy now. 'Merlin,' I said with ambassadorial diplomacy, 'Archie has some gigs to go to. He's going away for a little while,' I concluded in a voice of clotted-cream consonants modelled on the late Queen Victoria.

Merlin's wet hair dripped on to his T-shirt while he absorbed this information. 'It's not going to end like this, is it, Archie?'

'I don't know, Merlin.' Archie took me by the waist and looked deeply into my eyes. 'You are seriously lettin' that dip shit influence you? Who the hell have you turned into, Lou?' When I said nothing, he added, 'Why don't you get back to me when you've talked it over with all of your personalities.'

Archie then let out a chuff of laughter; it was the most tired laughter I'd ever heard. He lowered his head, his eyes vanishing from view beneath the brim of his conniving black hat, and then he and his backpack, guitar case and amp were gone, with just a cartoon plume of exhaust smoke left behind in his wake.

I felt suddenly, miraculously, absolved of all responsibility. I sank into Jeremy's arms with the exhausted relief of a cross-Channel swimmer flopping on to the shore.

Part Four: Merlin and Me

20
Sexual Politics

It seems to me that people only attend political meetings because it's illegal to masturbate in public. When
I'd told Jeremy that only one thing had heard more
inane comments than a political meeting – a painting
in a museum – he'd laughed.

'Artists, writers, journalists seek to interpret the
world. But politicians change it,' he replied, before
promising to prove me wrong ... Which is how I'd
ended up at his local town hall on election night, one
crisp November evening.

In a far corner of the castellated structure of sooty
Victorian brick, with paint-clogged woodwork and
flowery plaster ceiling decorations, the candidates
and their tellers watched the vote-counting. The
mayor then called the three candidates together and
whispered the results. I tried to ascertain the outcome

from Jeremy's expression, but his handsome face remained impassive. The candidates then followed the mayor up on to the stage. When the returning officer announced the voters' verdict, a hearty cheer surged up through the onlookers. When Jeremy was declared the duly elected member for Wiltshire North, the first Liberal Democrat ever to win in this Tory stronghold, I remembered what it was I had loved about him. The man gave off a rich, dark glow that made others seem pale and faded by comparison. He glittered in public, he shone. And not just because of his 100-watt smile, a smile so dazzling it made you reach for your Polaroids.

Jeremy graciously acknowledged the attributes of his competitors. But before he could launch into his victory speech, a dissenter's voice demanded to know if we'd 'all soon be carrying the contents of our desks out into the street in cardboard boxes, like all you wanker bankers?'

Jeremy became quieter than Sarah Palin after a question on European geography. Then he responded, with thoughtful calm, 'You're right. I was a wanker banker. I thought I had complete control over the world. I was arrogant and opportunistic. But it's never too late to turn into the person you might have been. And, even more joyous than winning this by-election tonight is that the love of my life is here to share it with me. Lucy not only allows me to be myself, she enables me to be a little bit nicer as well. There's been a lot of interest from my constituents and the media about my private life. I'm not saying my phones are hacked, but I don't recall buying that white van that's parked in my drive and I have noticed that my new paperboy looks a lot like Michael Moore. Plus, men sporting headphones and Sky News jackets keep emerging from the shrubs asking to use my loo . . .' He waited for the appreciative laughter to fade. 'So let me announce right here and now that I lost my . . . appetite for life in America,' he hinted, in a subtle reference to the domestic goddess. 'And I'd like to renew my marriage vows with the mother of my child, if she could ever forgive me.'

I flushed with embarrassment as people swivelled and craned their necks to locate the lucky woman. But their attention was quickly drawn back to the stage because Jeremy had started speaking with passion about all the ways he wanted to make the world better, including helping children with special needs.

'Disabled people are of equal worth. They may not contribute in conventional terms but that doesn't make them less valuable people, and it's up to us to help them flourish.' His voice played up and down the diplomat's scales: reassuringly deep and then flirtatiously light and coruscating. 'Working out a child with special needs is like trying to put together a huge jigsaw puzzle without the benefit of having a coloured picture on the box. But that just makes the challenge more exciting!'

It was then I found myself looking at my ex-husband with new, warmer eyes, as though I had borrowed Merlin's vision. Listening to his mellifluous tones, licentious feelings crept up on me, like fish twining through seaweed. I felt myself moving towards my ex, as if drawn by the inexorable pull of a thread.

'Lucy, dear!' A voice that was all smiles and cinnamon buns interrupted. 'Isn't it thrilling! Lib Dem headquarters have already called to say they're going to fast-track Jeremy. He'll be PUS, Parliamentary Under-Sec level, at first. That's just two rungs below Cabinet. But, as they're in coalition government, a Cabinet promotion isn't far off. They're talking about slotting him in at DCMS,' Veronica continued in her political patois. 'Culture, Media and Sport, or whatever they call it now,' she decoded. 'In no time at all he'll be sharing podiums with Nobel Prize winners, shaking hands with Obama, playing charity tennis matches with Nadal and kissing Angelina Jolie. You wait and see!' And right then, I could see it. I really could.

Acolytes and admirers washed back like a tide to make way for Jeremy to leave the stage. Constituents were bowing before him as though about to ask him to dance. Later, when all the well-wishers had pumped his hand, Jeremy made his way to my side. The warmth of his fingers on my arm spread across the surface of my skin, pulsing downwards. I felt myself sink and inwardly fold in his direction. I watched his mouth move as he thanked me for coming and told me about his most recent trip to Paris a few days earlier. His appearance at a conference a month or so earlier on 'The Future of Politics – British and French approaches' had gone so well, he'd been invited back for media appearances. I tried to listen, but all I could think of was how much I wanted to slide my tongue over those sensuous lips.

When I did so, he kissed me back, with grave tenderness. And he didn't stop kissing me all the way back to his family mansion. The tornado that was Jeremy's life had whirled me around and deposited me once more in the Jacobean four-poster bed where we'd first lain down together all those years ago. He took my face in his hands.

'I've waited thirteen years to make love to you once more and I'm not going to let you go again,' he said.

Whereas Archie was reckless and hungry, all muscle and sinew and frolicking, rollicking fun, when Jeremy caressed me it was as though he were laying fine silk threads across my skin. In my dreamy state, my body fell back into old rhythms, rocking against him. He was like slipping back into a favourite pair of jeans.

'You're too old for jeans,' my mother said when I rang to explain why I needed her to stay the night with Merlin.

'If you'd heard Jeremy's speech, Mum. It was inspirational.'

'How can you *fall* for what a Tory *stands* for?' she punned. 'And what about poor Archie?'

I couldn't bring myself to think about Archie, so sidestepped the question. 'Jeremy's not a Tory, Mum,' I repeated wearily. 'He's a Lib Dem.'

'Same thing.'

'I keep telling you, the man's reborn.'

'I used to believe in reincarnation, dear, but that was in a past life. You need to come home. I'm seriously worried about Merlin. His behaviour's deteriorating. He's obsessed with not hitting his head. When I asked him why, he said it's because he wants to be able to think for ever. When I enquired why he wanted to be able to think for ever, he explained that he's got to keep in perfect condition. "*I want to be perfect, for my father,*" he keeps saying. "*I don't want anything to happen to me before I see him again. I need to be perfect.*"'

'What did you say?'

'I said, "Why? Your father's not perfect. He's a perfect bastard, actually."'

'Oh, that's helpful! Mum, he hates change. Merlin's behaviour's a little erratic right now because of his new school . . . Jeremy's being so kind to him. You should see all the presents he's brought him back from Paris this time. For you, too. A new translation of Simone de Beauvoir's love letters, a Chanel lipstick . . . Although, Jeremy says the way to really annoy a French person is to only kiss one cheek,' I giggled.

But my mother didn't laugh along. 'Going back to

your ex-husband is like having your tonsils put back
in. It's just wrong, dear. And I'm not happy about it.'

'But *I* am happy, Mother.' And I really was, I
thought, climbing back into bed and curling into
Jeremy's warm back. Sure, it wasn't the kind of
euphoric, serendipitous bliss I'd experienced when I'd
accidentally fallen in lust with Archie. But it felt
comforting and safe. Everyone's aiming to land on
cloud nine, but cloud eight has just as good a view and
is so much less further to fall.

But I was soon to find out that, either way, I just
didn't have a head for heights.

21

BitchesRUs

Beauty may be in the eye of the beholder, but so is conjunctivitis. That's what I told myself when I got home a day later to find Tawdry Hepburn perched prettily on the doorstep.

Even though I was bad at maths, a quick mental calculation told me that the domestic goddess, twenty-two when they met, must now be thirty-five, although she looked years younger. I'd never seen her in the flesh before and was peeved to discover that she was even more beautiful than in photographs. Her honey-blonde hair tumbled over toned shoulders which were starkly outlined in a tight pink cashmere jumper. The woman was wearing so much mascara she looked like a partially sighted lemur. Her long legs, fetchingly crossed beneath a panty-skimming black leather mini concluded in a Himalayan-high pair of Laboutin stiletto boots. Her lips, a slash of glossy crimson, were forming a sentence.

'You're Lucy, aren't you? I need to talk to you.'

'Why?' I asked, trying to swallow the sour taste of envy in my mouth.

'It's personal,' she said, her big brown eyes darting up and down the street suspiciously. Like all celebrities, no matter how minor, they feel irritated when you recognize them and furious when you don't. She was probably paying the paparazzi to prowl after her in a predatory fashion to prove to people that she was A-list material.

On automatic polite pilot I led her into my humble home. 'Do you have any food?' she demanded. 'I totally forgot to eat today.'

I looked at her askance. Now, I've forgotten many things – my mobile number, my mother's maiden name, my car keys. But I've never forgotten to eat. You have to be a special kind of stupid to forget to eat. Especially when you're a chef. I delved in the fridge and retrieved some ham, cheese, butter and bread.

Tawdry shuddered with revulsion at my wares. 'Oh, I have to keep to this totally strict non-dairy, vegetarian, organic-only diet.'

'Really? Does it make the Botox work faster?' Up close and under the harsh kitchen fluorescents I could see the traces of fillers around her mouth, the collagen implants in her rosy cheeks, plus the tiny hairline trace of a brow lift. The woman had a body more preserved than Lenin's. I was tempted to tell her that it might be faster and less painful just to have a DNA transplant but decided instead to cut straight to the chase. 'I have thirty-seven essays to mark on the use of language, form and metre in metaphysical poetry, which, as you can imagine, I'm simply *dying* to get back to. So, just tell me, what is it you want?'

'My boyfriend back.' She had a high, piping voice, her home counties, Kate Middleton accent contorted a little by Californication.

The melodrama of the situation – the woman who stole my husband turning up thirteen years later to beg for him back – cast my nemesis as a crayoned caricature. Five minutes before I'd been in awe of her pneumatic, gym-toned body, but she now looked to me like an inflatable doll, her curvaceous breasts blancmange-like in their obvious sexuality.

'It's a bit late, Audrey, after you traded him in for a wealthier model.'

Her succulent lip trembled. 'Is that what he told you?'

'Jeremy gave me the impression that you drove around Hollywood with a casting couch strapped to your roof rack.'

'He left me! Not the other way round. He was supposed to be helping me make the transition to network TV but came here instead to pursue a political career. I was convinced he'd come crawling back . . . I am a trophy girlfriend, after all!' She paused for a moment, to preen and pose. 'And then I found out that he was seeing you and the boy. And that's when it hit me that I totally love him. So, basically, that's what I came to tell you.' Her voice dropped an octave. *'Back off, bitch.'*

I figured ripping out her femoral artery with my teeth would be the most appropriate reaction but said instead, 'The only reason Jeremy left me all those years ago is that he was too immature to cope with having a handicapped child. The way I see it, he was running away from home when he stubbed his toe on a rock, looked down to see what would crawl out . . . and it was you.'

'The only stone I've ever been under is Mick,' she retaliated, pouting provocatively.

I'd always presumed Tawdry to be little more than a predatory blonde from BitchesRUs – a monument to the cartoonish simplicity of male desire. Five minutes earlier, I'd been tempted to ask her if all those word balloons put pressure on her head. And if she knew that Khmer Rouge was not a cheek highlighter . . . But, despite the store-bought boobs and acrylic nails sharp enough to fillet a fish, there was a savvy intelligence to the woman which totally unnerved me. The wide-eyed, moist-lipped flirtation was a front. I suddenly realized that it takes a lot of brains to look that vacuous.

'He's over you,' I said stoutly.

'Really? Is that so? 'Cause he was under me the day before yesterday.'

My heart stopped with a queer jerk.

'In Paris,' she purred, in her honey-buttered accent. 'I'm shooting a series on French cooking.'

What a waste of exquisite cuisine, I thought. Tawdry was so thin she probably ordered one crouton for dinner – then shared it.

She looked me up and down with pity. 'Of course he could never take you to France, for fear you'd be arrested at the Gare du Nord by the Chic Police for not being, like, suave enough.'

Ignoring her barb, I allowed the full impact of what she'd said to hit me. 'You've been meeting up in Paris?' I said, stunned.

'It's not like he hasn't asked me to marry him. He has. A squillion times. But I wanted to seem available to my fans. When he called my bluff like that, well, I realized that my career is secondary to my man.'

'Yes, how goes your illustrious rise to fame? I'm sure your televisual fellating of various vegetables has been of great importance to men serving life in prison,' I bitched.

'. . . Which is why I've finally decided to accept his proposal,' she continued, as emphatic as her lip liner. 'Because we're soul mates, Jerry and I.' Emotion contorted her face and her shoulders shook.

I thought of my passionate encounter with Jeremy the night before in his four-poster. I dwelt on all the loving declarations he'd made to me, post coitus. 'You're lying.'

334

Tawdry Hepburn lasered me with eyes that were glistening wet with tears. 'Listen, sweetie. I'm a TV presenter with two expressions – looking happy and less happy. That's it. I do not cry on command, believe me,' she said, thick-throated with sobs. It was then that I glanced down at her breasts. My nemesis is famous for fluffing up her breasts in their cups on a regular basis to ensure that she's the centre of attention at all times. But there they sat, not even half fluffed but sadly deflated.

'Rule number one in the How to Keep a Man Interested manual,' Tawdry enlightened me, 'is to play hard to get . . . Well, I did that. I kept right on filming my show . . . I didn't change my plans to film in Paris. Rule number two in the How to Keep a Man Interested manual – if that doesn't work, *hack into his emails*. I knew from the papers that Jerry had announced our split. But I didn't know till this week that he was,' she looked me up and down once more, 'reheating leftovers.'

'You hacked into his emails? I think you'd better leave now,' I asserted, frogmarching the fembot to the door. It was my turn to give her a glacial once-over. She reminded me of roses you buy at a service station – beautiful but with absolutely no fragrance. 'I suspect the French Chic Police have an arrest warrant out for *you*, because despite your rounded vowels you're nothing more than a tacky, scheming little lowbrow. You probably left your posh little private school without even one O level.'

'Lowbrow?' Her cosmetically lifted eyebrow vaulted so high it practically left the stratosphere. 'Do you know what Jerry liked about me when we met? That I'm a self-made career woman. Do you know what he says about university? That it's just a place where women go until they can get alimony.' She sniggered, with sour glee. 'So, don't think all your fancy talk of metaphysical poetry or whatever impresses him, sweetie. Jerry maintains that the only way you can get something intelligent to come out of a woman's mouth is if she stops sucking Einstein's dick.'

I felt momentarily unable to contribute to the conversation so slammed the door in her perfect, pouting face. I stood there in the hall in a state of disbelief. I told myself she was lying . . . But a few minutes later I was running for the tube. I thought I'd finally got my life on the right track, but apparently I was tied to it and there was a train coming.

22

Smuggery, Buggery and Skulduggery

Experience is a wonderful thing. It enables you to recognize a mistake when you make it again. This is what I thought as I sprinted up the tube escalator, two steps at a time. Leicester Square was grey and gloomy. In the distance, dark clouds roiled like a blossoming bruise. Jeremy's PA had told me he was lunching at the Garrick Club, a place for Old Etonians raised on smuggery and buggery and other types who send their shirts out to be stuffed. I stomped up the green-veined marble steps into the cavernous foyer and made a dart towards the grand oak staircase. An epaulette-adorned doorman barred my way.

'May I help you, madam?' He glanced with disdain at my jeans. 'Who are you meeting?'

'Jeremy Beaufort.'

'I wasn't aware he was expecting any lady guests,' he said, consulting his luncheon list.

'Well, he's not exactly expecting me . . .'

He placed a restraining hand on my elbow. 'This club is for male members only, madam.'

'Is that so? Well, I've got a lot of testosterone. Not only am I very bossy and self-sufficient,' I snapped, 'but I also have a hair growing out of my chin.' And then I just shoved him aside and bolted up towards the first-floor dining room. Musty, fusty men were rumbling and grumbling over their claret and pork chops. I spotted Jeremy straight away, dining with a bunch of pinstriped people, one or two of whom I vaguely recognized as Cabinet ministers.

'How can you belong to a club that bans women as members?' I spat at him. 'No bloody wonder so few women reach the top judicial and political ranks when they're excluded from this cosy little enclave of all-male networking. You might not have joined your father's party but you've still turned into him.'

Jeremy looked up, startled. 'Has something happened?' he asked, springing to his feet in alarm.

I picked up a knife from the table. 'Well, I'd say, in a romance scenario, lunging at your lover with a carving knife is not a sign that things are going all that bloody well, wouldn't you?'

The chrome-domed group of Tory grandees stuffed into leather chairs too small for them gasped in consternation. 'Sorry to interrupt. But I've come to bury my ex-husband,' I told them. 'A task made slightly more difficult by the complicating fact that he isn't *dead yet*.'

The antique doorman was now at my elbow, panting asthmatically. Jeremy excused himself and strong-armed me out into the foyer and then, after a brief aside to the gathering security men, into a secluded, book-lined room which had 'Empire' stamped all over it. As Jeremy disarmed me, I now noted that the weapon I'd seized was only a lowly butter knife. Oh well, I suppose I could have slathered him to death with margarine or mustard.

'Lucy, what on earth are you so angry about?'

I recoiled from him as though he were a plutonium-riddled Russian spy. 'You might think that I sound bitter, but that's because I am!' My voice was so shrill it practically shattered the stained-glass windows. A huge mahogany desk now sat massively symbolic between us. 'So apparently you think that university is just a place where women go until they can get alimony? At least that's what your girlfriend told me!'

'My girlfriend?' He leant his arms on to the desk and loomed across at me. 'What on earth are you talking about, Lucy?'

'When you said you were laying all your cards on the table, I should have taken a quick peek up your sleeve – no, your trouser leg. And, oh! What would I have found there, but Audrey.'

'Audrey?'

'Yes. She paid me a little visit.' Over the last couple of months I'd allowed myself to become happy and optimistic again. Now mistrust radiated from me in zigzags that I felt sure were visible to the naked eye. 'Apparently, the whole time you've been declaring your undying love for me and our son you've been secretly meeting with her in Paris. It's a wonder the fire department hasn't closed down your bedroom due to overcrowding.'

The puzzlement dissolved from my ex-husband's features. Jeremy smiled at me tolerantly, as if I were a sulky child. 'And you believed her? Lucy, the woman is delusional. She's been leaving all kinds of deranged messages for me at the office. Obviously, things didn't work out with her celebrity-chef lover and La Stupenda of the Blender has realized she's lost her meal ticket.' He picked up my abandoned butter knife and laughed. 'No wonder you were tempted to do a little cleaver-wielding of your own.'

He strode around the table and pulled me to him, hugging me hard. I resisted for a moment, like some heroine from a Victorian melodrama, but then the spreading, pleasurable sensation of his equatorial embrace engulfed me. Jeremy was a fire that had never gone out. He just stoked the embers and my feelings for him flared up accordingly.

'I so want to believe you,' I said, summoning up all my strength to push him away again. 'But then why didn't you let her know you'd come back to us? She said she only found out by reading your emails.'

'What?' His eyebrows collided in fury. 'She's hacking into my emails? That's a criminal offence. I'll have her prosecuted. Oh my God! How was I beguiled by her for so long? It makes me doubt my own judgement.' His voice was thick with self-loathing. 'Leaving you for that calculating creature was the biggest mistake of my life,' he reiterated. 'You're the only woman I've ever loved. You and Merlin mean everything to me.'

'Merlin is fragile enough at the moment, Jeremy. The last thing I want is some half-baked, cake-cooking, egg-whisker stalking us.'

'I'll take out a restraining order if necessary. I'll call the police right now. Where is she? Scuttling back on the Eurostar, no doubt, before I can have her arrested.'

I sagged like a day-old soufflé. 'I'm sorry I over-reacted. It's all the stress about Merlin. I'm so worried about him,' I confided. 'His behaviour's been spiralling downwards since he started this new school. He's washing his hands compulsively. He has all these issues about fate and luck and rituals and lock check-ing. He has to do things at exactly the same time every day in the same way, measuring, counting, checking . . . He won't go near the microwave in case it ignites his brain. He won't put his knuckles near his ear, in case it makes him go deaf . . . Getting him to school in the mornings means fortifying myself with so much coffee I end up passing everybody on the road – when I'm not even in a car.'

Jeremy kissed the top of my head with great tenderness. 'You know what? Why doesn't Merlin come and stay with me for a few days? If he wants to, that is. And you could go to a spa and de-stress. Take your mother and sister. My treat. My secretary will organize it. You can get a taste of what it will be like to be an LOL ... Lady of Leisure,' he deciphered. 'I would come too, but I have so much work to do now. Delegation is for second-raters.' He winked. 'Let someone else do it.'

I tried to smile at his little joke, but it went crooked, as though it had been hijacked on the way by some unseen emotion. It had been a very topsy-turvy day. Outside the big bay windows a mass of grey and white clouds sloshed across the sky like jumbled washing. It made me think of housework and how much I didn't want to be doing any right now. A spa sounded so tempting. Single mums can never make a declaration of independence, especially the mother of a kid with special needs. But there's no reason we couldn't enjoy the odd bit of Life, Liberty and the Pursuit of Happy Hour.

'I'll think about it,' I said.

23

Life, Liberty and the Pursuit
of Happy Hour

I didn't have to think for long. By early December Merlin's behaviour had become more and more erratic and disturbing. He developed a preoccupation with his head. He went into a panic that he'd injured his brain because he nearly hit his head on the door. He spent days punishing himself for this near-miss. He begged me for a brain operation. No matter how much I explained the lack of logic in his angst, he remained convinced that *almost* hurting himself meant he had. He drove himself mad by looking in the rear-view mirror of his mind, wishing he'd done or said things differently, going over and over his mistakes then chastising himself for his inadequacies.

The poor kid was constantly apprehensive. I could feel it coming off him in waves. His anxieties were like a Mafia gang of thugs in his head. They waited for his emotions to come strolling down the street, then they'd mug them, hold them hostage and beat the living crap out of them.

One morning, pre-dawn, my distraught son woke me in a panic about which shirt to wear. 'Short-sleeved shirts will give me bad luck in the cold weather. It's all about luck,' he said, gnawing fretfully on the inside of his cheek. When I walked past his room, it was festooned with shirts. He had tried on every single item in his entire wardrobe.

During breakfast he balanced himself on the edge of his chair, ready to leap up at any time, jiggling his knee up and down and wiggling his toes. He drummed his fingers on the table in time to some secret rhythm in his head.

'What's the matter, darling?' I asked nervously, preparing myself for a postcard from a parallel universe.

'I get worried about glass. I worry about my knuckles going near my ear. I worry about fingernails and toenails. I worry about Archie. Where is he? Was he a paid actor in a script?'

I often thought about Archie too but then reminded myself that it wasn't just that we weren't on the same page, we weren't even in the same library, let alone the same book.

'I just want to be able to think for my whole life and hear. Clenched fists and closed eyes are also a bad idea. I think I need an ear operation because my knuckles went near my ears.'

My son's face registered such intense apprehension it was almost parodic. 'But darling, you know that's irrational, right? Look, my knuckles are near my ears, I'm banging my ears with my knuckles and I'm not deaf. Am I?'

'No! No! Don't,' Merlin shrieked, catapulting to his feet. 'Now if you go deaf it will be my fault. I used to think that my brain ruled my body, but then I started to think about what was telling me to think that.' Merlin lowered his voice, glanced around conspiratorially, then mouthed, 'My *brain*.'

Whenever I tried to help, he would round on me, aiming with malicious precision at the areas where I felt most vulnerable. 'Not as young as you used to be, eh? Doctors are wrong. Wrinkles do hurt, don't they?' ... 'Thought you'd be a head teacher by now, didn't you? But no. You're still only a lowly English teacher. You've never quite lived up to your potential, have you? And whatever happened to the Great Novel you were always talking about?'

The shrink Jeremy had hired assured me that Merlin was just projecting his negative feelings about himself on to the person he loved most. I told myself not to get upset; that things could be worse. The female turtle swims thousands of miles to lay gazillions of eggs and not one of her offspring sends her a mother's day card, right?

By mid-week, when Merlin woke me again in the middle of the night to ask why countries go to war with other countries to show them that going to war is wrong and announced that he was going to stick a knife into Tony Blair for getting us into the Iraq war under false pretences, I actually felt nostalgic for the days when I only worried about him accidentally hacking into a Pentagon computer whilst looking for evidence of the existence of UFOs and getting extradited to the US to serve a sixty-year jail sentence for cyberterrorism.

By Thursday, my nerves were so shredded I decided to take up Jeremy's kind offer. Trying to map a child with Asperger's ... well, in charting the unknown, it equals the feats of Columbus, Captain Cook and Cortez.

While we waited for Jeremy's car to cruise into our street, Merlin turned to me, sombre-faced. 'Isn't it good to have a big smile on your face?' he asked me glumly. 'I'm going to have a big smile on my face all day. And it's a stunningly beautiful day,' he added, in a desultory monotone. Misery was rising off him like steam. 'You know how my father transforms through the fridge to the North Pole to be with his polar-bear family? Well, I think the polar bear thinks I'm a seal and wants to eat me.'

'Don't be silly, darling. Daddy loves you. As do I. You're a wonderful, quirky, clever, original, unique person, with so much to offer the world.'

He pulled the sleeves of his shirt over his hands, a wintry gesture at odds with the glitteringly sunny late-autumn day.

When Jeremy's Mercedes purred to a halt outside our house, Veronica lumbered up out of the front seat to greet Merlin. 'How is my little Mark Zuckerberg in the making?' she exclaimed, tweaking his cheek. The once-surly Veronica had become so sweet she could spontaneously trigger tooth cavities.

Merlin greeted them both with scrupulous courtesy. As he loaded his rucksack into the boot, Veronica patted my hand consolingly. 'All masterminds are overwrought. They're highly strung. It's normal. Did you know that H. G. Wells was so gawky and insecure at school that he had only one friend? Albert Einstein took a job in a patents office because he was too disruptive to work in a university! Isaac Newton was able to work without a break for three days but couldn't hold a conversation, apparently,' she informed me cheerily. 'Today's Asperger's is tomorrow's genius!'

I tried to interrupt to explain that Merlin's 'genius' was like a comet, infrequent and brilliant but also accompanied by a lot of space garbage, but she was too busy bustling her 'gifted grandson', a category she obviously felt comfortable explaining to her bridge buddies, into the car. I knew what Merlin meant now. When you have Asperger's Syndrome, the expectation that you're a genius is as limiting as the assumption that you're stupid. For his next birthday, Veronica would probably give him a set of Mattel Nobel Prize action figures to play with.

Merlin's face in the back window of the car was a mask of misery festooned in an incongruous grin. I felt a tug of labyrinthine love so strong I thought it might tow me along behind them like a tin can.

If you're going through hell, put your foot down. That seemed to be my motto, because two hours later I was greeting my mother at a spa hotel in Oxfordshire and wondering how to break it to her that Phoebe had checked in already. Since our last altercation they'd had the same rapport as, say, a gun-toting Islamist and a Jewish settler. I was hoping to act as a UN peace-keeping force by bringing them back together. I so desperately wanted to return to the days when we were close knit, inflicting pain occasionally, but kissing to heal it better in the same instant. Loving, laughing, fighting, defending – that had always been our way.

'That cold of mine that won't go away? Well, it led me to the clinic with a sample of something to be tested that I have never carried around in a Chanel tote before. Anyway, the clinic have put me on a ludicrous detox which means I can only sniff asparagus or drink neat vodka – am obviously opting for the latter.' My mother pulled a bottle of spirits out of the voluminous pocket of her shift, which was guacamole green. 'Eat well, stay fit, die anyway.' She winked, taking a nip.

Vodka wasn't exactly on the organic health spa

menu. I glanced around, worried we'd be taken into custody by the Colon Constabulary, but it was Phoebe who appeared armed with barbs and scowling menacingly. When my mother and sister realized that I'd invited them both for the night, I began to wonder if it was too late to email the UN to request an armoured personnel carrier.

'Will you two please kiss and make up?' I pleaded, pulling on an invisible flak jacket.

'I would apologize, but it's just not in my nature. Sorry about that,' my mother said superciliously.

'I'm sorry too,' my sister replied, adding caustically, 'that you can't say sorry, that is.'

We managed to change into our terry-towelling bathrobes and reconvene around the indoor pool with no bloodshed. But the atmosphere was as taut as an Olympic rower's thigh.

'So, darling,' my mother asked me, 'how did you get time off work?'

'Well, actually, I've decided to give up work, Mother.'

My mother's high-rise hair, turbaned in a towel, toppled forwards as she swivelled to face me. 'What?'

'Jeremy's offered to support me, so I think I might take a sabbatical.'

'Don't be insane, dear. If there's one thing my life should have shown you it's that a woman needs her own identity,' she scolded.

'She'll still have her feet on the ground, they'll just

be better shod,' Phoebe rejoindered tartly. 'Good for you, Lulu. Jesus Christ, I'd give up being a space waitress if I could. Do you know how tired I am of standing in the aisle of a plane saying, "Your exits are here, here and here"? I want to be saying to my billionaire lover, "Your entrances are *here*" ' – she pointed to her pudenda – ' "*here*" ' – she pointed to her mouth – ' "and *here*",' she concluded, vaguely gesturing towards her rear.

I looked at my sister agog. This kind of talk was just so out of character. Was she high? Had she joined a less literal kind of Frequent Flier Programme?

My mother, who was reluctantly biting into the stick of celery protruding from her organic health juice, washed it down with another gigantic gulp of vodka. 'To be honest, dears, I can understand why wives want to hook up with their ex-husbands. It saves so much time ... I mean, you already know he's a complete prat.'

'Sure there are grounds to despise Jeremy,' Phoebe consented, wearing a green moustache of vegetable purée. 'But what about finding grounds to like him again? Look how Jeremy's helped Lulu with Merlin. He's got a shrink now, and he's at a wonderful school.'

'It's true, Mum. Do you remember how I dreaded speaking to all his headteachers?' I shuddered at the thought of all those belittling meetings. 'Well, even though Merlin's having trouble adjusting, his new teachers ring me full of optimism. Jeremy has lifted a huge weight off my shoulders. I'm much less stressed. Honestly, I've cut down to only about four heart attacks a day.'

'Mark my words, lying and manipulation are the only emotional skills that man will ever master,' my mother warned. 'Jeremy Beaufort would cheat at solitaire.'

Phoebe scoffed, loudly enough for the other spa habituées to look up from their hand-reared arugula and crane around in their sun-loungers to gawk in our disruptive direction. 'Why?' my sister rebuked. 'Because he's upper class? Because he's wealthy? Because you're a stereotypical, prejudiced, *Guardian*-reading bigot? He abandoned the Tories. Doesn't that earn him any Brownie points?'

'It doesn't matter what party he belongs to. The man is drunk on power. I can see him now, dear, sitting in the Houses of Parliament, stroking a cat whilst having people killed at whim and laughing maniacally.'

Phoebe was not amused. 'Why do you always have to be a non-conformist, just like everyone else? . . . So, where are you off to next, Mother? Knitting your own orgasms in Uzbekistan? Getting a third-eye infection in Goa? . . . Can't you see that we're sick of mothering our own mother?'

I placed a hand on my sister's arm in a gesture of calming entreaty. 'Phoebe, I think it might be time for you to go to the vets and get your claws done.' My gentle sister had become so bitchy of late she needed to wear a flea collar, and perhaps a little muzzle.

'May I suggest you stop being so jealous,' my mother said curtly. 'That particular shade of green has been discontinued.'

'How many ways can I say this? Taking advice on life from you, Mother, is like' – she verbally hovered before alighting on the appropriate metaphor – 'asking a Saharan camel-herder how to build an igloo.'

My mother and I were shell-shocked by the change in Phoebe. In the past few weeks, her personality had shifted up several gears from Doris Day to Bette Davis. She used to bring happiness wherever she went. Of late, she brought happiness *when*ever she went.

My animated mother usually laughs a lot, whilst making many exaggerated, comical gestures. But she sat stock-still now, her hands folded mutely in her lap. 'I only want what's best for my girls. It's all I've ever wanted,' she finally said. 'Why do you think I stayed with your father through thick and thin? Or rather thin and thin, as it was most of the time. I stayed long after my happiness warranty expired,' she said sadly. 'For you girls.'

'Even if Lucy didn't have any feelings for Jeremy, which she obviously still does, she must go back to him because she needs the money. As do we all. Christ, we're already benefiting. Who do you think is paying for this happy little family jaunt of ours?'

My mother practically regurgitated her celery. 'I

thought you won this spa treat in a raffle, Lucy?' She cocooned herself more tightly into her terry-towelling robe. 'That's what you told me, dear. I never would have come if I'd known Jeremy was paying for us.'

'I'm not going back to him for the money. I'm going back to him because it's the best thing I can do for Merlin. And because he's kind. And because it's so lovely to be taken care of. And because he stimulates me intellectually.'

'Really? I would say all that man's read with any real interest is his father's will.' My librarian mother smiled thinly. 'Are you sure you're not just going back to him because his *Who's Who* is ten inches long?'

'Oh Mum, you honestly think I'm that shallow? Besides, Jeremy is not in politics for the power and the glory. He wants to make the world a better place. He's matured. Come and hear him talk, Mother. He's become a man of character—'

'"Character" is when you do the right thing when nobody is watching,' my mother asserted. 'I've met Jeremy's mother and, believe me, that man was raised to be enchanting, not sincere.'

'And you raised us to be irresponsible and spend-thrift . . . but that doesn't mean we've followed your example,' Phoebe said bitterly. 'I scrimp and save every last penny. In fact, next strike day, I'm crossing the picket line.'

My Labour-voting mother gasped, as if mortally wounded.

'Listen.' I quickly took both their hands in mine, before things deteriorated any further. 'The West of England Chamber of Commerce have chosen Jeremy, as the fastest-rising MP, to host their big event in the terrace pavilion in the new year. There's hundreds of MPs coming. All the ministers and lords have been invited. The Tory bigwigs say that Jeremy's headed for the top. A ministerial job beckons. The PM called him an "outstanding economic thinker". Why don't you both come along and see him in action and then decide? I'll put your names on the list.'

'Why on earth would I want to come and hear a coalition politician prattle on about himself for approximately eternity?' my mother disparaged.

'Because you'll get free champagne and a crate of cider to take home,' I encouraged.

My mother flinched. 'Surrounding oneself with neocons, dear, is only one step up on the pleasure scale from an appointment with a proctologist.'

'Will you come, Phoebe?'

'Sorry. I have my stamp-collecting class . . .' She sighed, followed by an exuberant postscript. 'Free champagne? On the river? Of *course* I'll come, you idiot! Try and stop me.'

We spent the rest of the day in tense silence. When my mother went for a swim, I asked my sister why she seemed determined to get a doctorate in Bitchery.

'I'm sick of being nice all the time. Expecting life to be kind to you because you're kind to life is like expecting a shark not to eat you because you're a vegan.'

I stroked her arm. 'But you used to be so positive. You were positively Pollyanna-esque. What happened?'

'Oh, I can still be positive. A positive attitude may not solve your problems, but it will definitely annoy enough people to make it worth your while.' Phoebe cackled alarmingly.

When my sister went for a swim, my mother blurted out that Phoebe had become so annoying, even a Buddhist would murder her right now. 'She needs to take more HRT. At the moment she could use her raging hormones to heat the whole of Hampshire.'

This had turned out to be a mini-break from which I needed a mini-break. We went to bed before they served the decaff organic coffee and checked out un-expectedly early, straight after the bowel-cleansing, bran-intensive breakfast. Driving back to London, I started to think that distant relatives might be the best – and the further away the better.

'Be careful what you wish for, because then you might get it' is one of the great lies. I wish for Johnny Depp naked, and there'd be nothing better than getting him. Except for getting my other wish as well – a chocolate-coated Hugh Jackman for dessert. I also wished for a happy family life. Which is why the contented tableau that met me when I arrived at Jeremy's house in

Mayfair that Saturday morning lifted my jaded spirits. Veronica was surprised to see me. Well, I was eight hours early. But she greeted me warmly: 'What a delightful treat!' Smiling down at me, she seemed as plump and comfortable as a cushion. She then ushered me into a cosy and welcoming sitting room for 'drinkie-poos'. She'd recently started putting the word 'poo' at the end of everything. 'Drinkie-poo? Lunchie-poo? Chrissie-poo?'

The living room was festooned in Christmas decorations, classical music was wafting and there was a smell of hot coffee and warm mince pies. Jeremy and Merlin were sitting arm in arm on the couch whilst a photographer snapped, crackled and popped around them. Jeremy looked up, laughing.

'Oh gosh, Lucy. My secret is out. Yes, I admit it. I'm a closet sentimentalist. Don't tell anyone though! I want some snaps for my office desk. I'm so proud of Merlin. And I want hundreds of photos of you both to make up for all the years I lost,' he said, coaxing me into the family portrait.

I sat between the two men in my life and felt bookended by happiness.

'Are you okay, darling?' I asked Merlin, kissing his cheek.

'I Am Having A Great Time.' Merlin said it that way too, with each word capitalized.

'Nothing but good times ahead!' Jeremy said, clasping our hands and, once more, I experienced the euphoric joy of yielding. Nothing more was needed to enhance my mood of utter contentment. I felt a tingling sense of well-being surge through my veins, almost frightening in its physicality.

My mother and sister had promised to bury the hatchet for Christmas Day, though I felt sure it was only buried in a shallow grave, right next to a shovel. But I now had another family hearth where I could warm myself.

I squeezed Jeremy's hand back. 'Nothing but good times ahead,' I chorused. 'Good-times-aheadie-poos!'

24

Testicle Carpaccio on the Disorient Express

A first-class upgrade is the third best thing that can happen to you, after going up two bra-cup sizes and falling back in love with the father of your child. Having someone to help shoulder the responsibility of Merlin felt like a bank error in my favour. Weatherwise, Christmas, New Year and January were as bleak as *Wuthering Heights*, colder than Pip's Estella, but I was cosy with contentment.

February 12th, ringed in my diary, marked the West of England Chamber of Commerce function in the terrace pavilion, which Jeremy was hosting. Happily ensconced with him, I'd hardly spoken to my feuding family over the last six weeks but hoped they would turn up to celebrate his success.

His aftershave invaded the Commons bar first. I

turned to see Jeremy striding towards me as if on invisible cross-country skis. With his sharp suit, perfectly knotted tie and well-groomed coiff, it was no wonder the press had dubbed him 'The Silver Fox'. Brainy, powerful, charismatic, he exuded that naughty-but-nice Cary Grant, Clintonesque appeal. He kissed my hand, his fingernails professionally polished to a porcelain sheen.

'Where's Merlin?' I asked, peering over his shoulder. 'He told me you were picking him up from school.'

'But he told me *you* were.' Jeremy *tsk*'ed his tongue. 'Oh, no. Don't tell me he's run away again. Not today,' he sighed in his most mellifluous tones. Taking my arm, we glided across the mint-green carpet and down the oak-panelled stairs towards the terrace. People were pumping Jeremy's hand, as usual, and slapping his back in recognition of his meteoric rise within the coalition.

My lips stretched over my teeth in what I felt resembled a smile, but my mind was clattering. What had happened to Merlin this time? One thing was clear, I had given birth to a soap opera. My heart pounded out panicked beats. Don't overreact, I told myself stoutly. But whenever my son went missing, a thick, dark, clammy dread would creep up from my innards into my throat. The function was in full flight, as though celebs had been ordered by the metric tonne. I secreted myself in the corner, trying to suppress the brutal fear taking hold of me. My voice jagged with alarm, I instinctively rang first Phoebe, who was already on her way to Jeremy's function, and then my mother, who was mid book club. Despite my aloofness of late, they both immediately set off to search Merlin's favourite haunts. I wore off my own fingerprint pressing 'redial' on my son's number, willing him to pick up. I dialled my finger to the bone. I was nervously gulping down an entire plate of hors d'oeuvres that had just passed by when my phone trilled. I pressed the answer button and an unexpected voice barked back.

'The whole world may think of me as a washed-up, arrogant, has-been bastard—'

'That's not true, Archie. The whole world hasn't had the pleasure of your company yet,' I replied mockingly.

'Hey, to know me is to love me,' he drawled.

'I can't talk now. I've lost Merlin.'

'That's what I'm tryin' to tell you, if you'd just can the third-degree sarcasm. The whole world may think of me as a washed-up, arrogant, has-been bastard . . . but not your son. He's here with me. At the pub.'

'Thank God!' I felt winded with relief. 'But why's he with you?' My mother had told me that Archie had moved into a room above one of Camden's Ye Olde Bucolic-Plague-riddled pubs.

'I reckon you'd better ask him that.'

'Archie, I know it's a big favour, especially after the

way I treated you, but can you bring him to me? I can't leave. I'm at the Houses of Parliament. It's Jeremy's big day. I'll put your name on the guest list. Bring ID – say, a passport or a driver's licence or something – okay?' I hung up quickly so I could call off the family bloodhounds. I left separate voicemails for Phoebe and my mother telling them that Merlin had been found, added Archie's name to the guest list, then dived into a glass of champagne.

When Archie sidled into the cocktail function forty minutes later, totally sartorially out of place in Stetson, cowboy boots and black jeans, my eyes raked the space behind him. When I saw my bedraggled son in tow, I practically gazelled across the room. I hugged Merlin to me hard. His hair smelled like daylight. I was so angry but love blurred my vision. Even though I was still deep in Merlin-land, for a moment my senses were enhanced by the spicy, wild, warm scent of sweat mixed in with a musky tang of petrol and cigarettes that is Archie. The dolorous tug at my heart-strings surprised me. I put it down to indigestion from hors d'oeuvre overload.

'Nice tan,' Archie drawled.

'Really?' I asked, surprised.

'Yeah. Must be from baskin' in your ex's reflected glory.'

'Oh, ha ha.' I would have bantered some more but just then Jeremy disengaged himself from the admiring throng in awed orbit around him and draped his arm across Merlin's shoulders. 'Merlin. You had us worried sick. Are you all right, old chap?'

Merlin smiled, but his eyes didn't relax. They jumped around the room. His denim jacket looked as though it were wearing him, and not the other way round.

'So, why did you go to Archie's place?' Jeremy persisted. 'Did he lure you away?' he demanded darkly.

Archie's fury was tight and monumental. Although livid with each other, because the marquee was journalist-infested the men said what they had to say in even, conversational tones.

'The kid needed some fatherly advice,' Archie sotto-voced, his voice heavy with weary exasperation.

'Are you implying that I'm not a good father?' Jeremy quietly seethed in reply. 'My son's very happy.'

'Yeah . . . you haven't done him any damage – where the self-harmin' comes from, I just can't fathom,' retaliated Archie sarcastically.

'It's totally unscrupulous to use the child as a way of wheedling your way back into Lucy's life and affections,' Jeremy fumed.

'Is that right?' Archie replied with cool thoughtfulness.

'*Is* it right?' I asked Archie suspiciously, not knowing what to think.

The watery February sunlight flickering through the riverside windows cast a mosaic of light and shadow on to Archie's face so that I couldn't read his expression. 'I think your mum might have somethin' to say about that, Lou.'

'You've been talking to my mother?' I cross-examined him, surprised.

'I rang to let her know Merlin was okay. She's on her way. In fact, there she is.'

In crimson culottes, my mother was arriving. She picked her way through the sea of grey pinstripe towards us. She had an exultant look on her face but said nothing as she thrust some kind of pamphlet at me. It took me a moment to focus. Then the photo of Jeremy, Merlin and me took shape. It was one of the photos taken in Jeremy's living room before Christmas; the photos he'd wanted for his office desk and private album.

'A friend I met through the National Trust mailed this to me from your constituency, Jeremy. I suppose you thought we'd never see it. Let me read you the caption. *"Family matters. Where would one be without them?"* Perhaps not being shoved through some stranger's letterbox for a start.' My mother yowled with derision. '*"My son has special needs, which makes him even more special,"*' she read on. '*"It's my job to look after the little people."*'

I stared at Jeremy, consumed by doubts. 'Why didn't you clear this with me?'

'Oh Lucy, I'm so sorry. I meant to, darling. I've been so frantically busy that it slipped my mind. The photos were so charming that the party spindoctor was desperately keen to use them on the pamphlet. Look how handsome Merlin is! I just wanted to show my son how proud I am of him.' He placed a protective arm around Merlin's tense shoulders.

'Very fuckin' touchin',' Archie drawled. 'So it's got nothin' to do with the fact that a politician with no children is about as popular as a Japanese whaling harpoonist.'

'Don't waste your breath,' my mother told Archie. 'You can't shame or humiliate a politician. What used to be called humiliation and shame is now called "getting a high profile".'

Jeremy's mother, champagne flute in hand, barged into our gathering with all the grace of an ocean liner colliding with an iceberg. 'Oh, it's so splendid to be back on one's old stomping ground,' she gushed. 'And I've just heard that the PM's definitely popping by!'

My mother's smile narrowed with combative disapproval. She brandished the pamphlet, shoving it into Veronica's drink-flushed face. 'Did you know about this, Veronica?'

Veronica calmed her tweed skirt with her free hand as if it were an unruly pet. 'Of course I did. It was my idea. Politicians must play the family, preferably the family sympathy card, to appeal to some middle-class demographic. It makes us look more' – she searched for the right word, a word that was obviously foreign to her tongue – 'human.'

'But surely there's nothing less human than talking about your child's problems with strangers for political gains?' My mother shot off a thin-lipped look of scorn in the Beauforts' joint direction.

Veronica's strained Queen's Christmas message accent became even more pronounced. 'Various polls have shown Jeremy to be deemed lacking in compassion. The party spindoctor suggested he do a photoshoot at a local special needs school. "We can do one better than that," I told the spindoctor. "We have a special needs *child*!!!"' She lunged at a passing waiter to nab a chicken skewer. 'Sarah Palin had her pregnant teen daughter. Cameron had his handicapped child who died . . .' The subject matter made her so animated, she began aimlessly to conduct an unseen string orchestra with her kebab, totally oblivious to the fact that we were all staring at her aghast. 'Joe Biden's wife died in a car crash, I believe . . .'

'But political sympathy wasn't my motivation,' Jeremy interrupted quickly, his expression locked on to diplomatic cruise control. 'Merlin's my son and I want to show him off to the world because I love him,' he said in a monotone which belied his apparent joy.

I glanced down at the photo again. The way Jeremy was bent over Merlin reminded me of a documentary I'd seen on 'Night Predators in the Kalahari'.

'And we discussed it first, didn't we, Merlin? You're happy to be in Daddy's pamphlet, aren't you?' Merlin's knee jacked up and down, as if working an invisible pump. 'Merlin wants to play a role in helping achieve wider understanding of special needs in the community.'

Archie was so angry he was rocking from one foot to the other, almost stamping, like a dancer or a boxer. 'You know, there are two things I've always disliked about you, Beaufort.'

'Oh yes. And what are they?'

'Your face,' Archie growled.

'Merlin, darling, did Dad clear this with you first?'

Merlin gazed reflectively at me. He had the glassy-eyed look of a teddy bear. His shoulders were now up around his ears. A mental snapshot of him the day the photos were taken popped into my mind. 'I Am Having A Great Time,' he'd said, but each word had been eerily capitalized. 'Darling, why are you so quiet?' I asked him gently. He was holding himself very still, as if he were an overful glass of wine which might spill at any moment.

'He's quiet because your bastard of an ex told Merlin that *he's* the reason you two broke up.' Archie was now using the kind of voice Moses would have used to part the Dead Sea. 'He also told the poor kid that if he wants you two to get back together then he has to do everythin' Jeremy says, includin' press interviews and photoshoots. And that he couldn't tell you about their conversation ... Which is why he came to tell me.'

I shook my head as though I had water lodged in

my ears. I couldn't believe what I was hearing. 'You told Merlin our divorce was his fault? Jeremy! How could you say that to a child suffering from anxiety and low self-esteem?'

'Of course I didn't say that. It's preposterous.' Jeremy's voice, which I had always loved, suddenly had the sound of something grinding away unoiled with no maintenance. It grated on my ears.

Merlin's expression was one of disoriented incredulity. He'd developed the charisma of a crash dummy. He covered his ears and started to rock back and forth.

'If at first you don't succeed, lie, lie again,' Archie snorted with contempt. He then looked me right in the eye. 'Merlin cannot lie. You know that.'

'No, but he can misunderstand . . .' Jeremy ran his hands through his hair in a practised, poised gesture perfected before hundreds of mirrors. He gave a calculating smile – the smile of a puppeteer, a man who knows exactly how to pull the strings. 'I was only trying to explain to Merlin the good we can do by publicizing his plight. In the beginning, yes, I was, I suppose, mourning the loss of the son I would never have. Nothing can assuage your disappointment in the universe and the gods. Then you realize that this is the hand fate has dealt you and you just have to play it.'

Merlin stared at his feet dejectedly. He looked like a bewildered nocturnal creature caught unexpectedly in the daylight.

Fury welled up in me. 'Merlin's not a "bad hand". He's inventive and original and unique.'

'Of course he is! And that's what we want the world to know!' Jeremy rocked back on his heels and smiled, a smug smile – the smile of a man who was sure that he knew exactly what was going to happen next. But one thing he hadn't predicted was Merlin's unpredictability.

'Well, Polar Bear, it will soon all be okay, because your next cub will be normal,' Merlin said in an anaemic murmur.

Jeremy's head jerked back like a snake surprised by a mirror.

Merlin looked up at his father and said in a quiet, tentative voice, 'The last time I was staying over at your polar-bear lair I overheard you and Grandma conversing. You told Grandma that your girlfriend is "knocked up", which Archie says means that she's having a baby . . . But I heard you tell my grandma that you're not going to marry Audrey until you ascertain whether or not the foetus is normal.'

Something in my stomach churned and twisted. Was it possible to be completely astonished and yet not remotely surprised at the same time? 'Is this true?' I said, through lips that didn't feel like my own.

'Of course not!' Jeremy spluttered. 'You know how Merlin misconstrues things.'

I also knew how good he was at eavesdropping,

feline-footed, then parroting whole conversations, verbatim.

'Whatever you thought you heard, Merlin, you definitely got the wrong end of the conversational stick, dear boy. Now come along everyone. Drink up! I'm speaking in ten or so minutes . . . Lucy, darling, it's all a big misunderstanding.' There was a slight sheen on Jeremy's face, the only giveaway that there was any crack in his composure. 'We'll sort it all out later.'

I felt as mystified as the first day I ever saw algebra. I told myself that there had obviously been a misunderstanding, even though Jeremy's replies sounded as straight as Elton John in a tutu . . . Yet why was I so willing to give him the benefit of the doubt? Was it because I just simply couldn't bear to hear the wheel of fortune hiss as it deflated? The faces around me became indistinct, as if we were all underwater. Which is why it took me a moment to summon cognition when the crowd unclotted to reveal Phoebe clutching Tawdry Hepburn. I blinked myopically. My mind rejected what my eyes so plainly saw. Audrey. At least four months pregnant.

'I drove everywhere looking for Merlin,' Phoebe gushed. 'Your place, Mum's place – finally, Jeremy's flat. And look who answered the door! Fresh in from Paris, having quit her job, apparently. Then I got your voicemail that Merlin was okay and coming to the party. Well, Audrey seemed very intrigued to know that Jeremy was hosting a soirée without her.'

Jeremy had the look of a poker player who has over-played his hand. Dark crescents bloomed in the armpits of his shirt. Mother and son exchanged a panicked look.

'Don't all jump for joy at once to see me,' Audrey drawled, her mouth lipsticked bright red with bravado. 'I can't believe you're having a party and didn't invite us, Jerry,' she reprimanded him, patting her big belly. 'Luckily, the security guys recognized me, so I could blag my way in. You told me you were working late.'

We all stood there facing her, silent as geometry.

Veronica was the first to find her vocal cords. 'Well, yes. As you can see' – she spoke in a monotonous bark, as if addressing an audience of deaf Eskimos – 'apparently, Audrey has fallen pregnant.'

'Fallen! Ha! I was pushed!' Audrey flared her eye-brows indignantly. 'Jerry only left me because I didn't want a family.' She made her trademark move to fluff up her breasts but then realized that pregnancy had made them so huge there was now no need so batted her eye-lashes instead. 'So sorry, sweetie,' she said to me, 'but he just used you as bait to get me back. And hey, look!' She patted her abdomen again. 'I'm hooked!'

I shuddered and shrank from her words as though they were blows. Jeremy had come back to me vowing undying love in September. It was now February. You didn't have to be Stephen Hawking to do the maths. The man I thought I loved was affecting an air of insouciance, but I'm sure if he opened his mouth wide enough for me to see his teeth they would have been ground down to stumps. 'And you . . . you're the f–father?' I stammered.

'There'll be a DNA test, of course.' My ex-mother-in-law's tone was one of pained geniality. 'And we're yet to see the results of the amnio. But, you know, the heir and the spare. One must be practical about these things.'

'The self-satisfaction,' my mother muttered, recoiling. 'The condescending largesse . . .' It had become clear to us all that Veronica was Head Honcho of the International House of Manipulative Mothers.

'What a brilliant double act,' Phoebe marvelled, attempting to shake Veronica's hand. 'It's so entertaining the way your puppet Jeremy addresses the audience while you drink a glass of water.'

'Yes,' my mother deduced. 'Derek was a little wet really, wasn't he? Didn't make it to the top. But, with Jeremy, you could go all the way to Number 10.'

I was opening and closing my mouth in pantomime astonishment. My head throbbed like a twanged tuning fork as the aftershock of the revelation reverberated through me. The pain was acute. I felt sure that if I looked at this spectacle for much longer my retinas would detach. Too dumbfounded to cry, I hung my head and just hugged myself round the waist. I felt I was in some vile reality-TV show, only there was no way of voting myself out. The slow, thick drip of betrayal sank into the pit of my stomach. I wasn't sure my legs could support me. I must have been swaying, because Jeremy took hold of my arm.

'Lucy, my love,' he purred softly, out of Audrey's earshot, 'it was only a momentary lapse. The child may not even be mine. I'll explain it all . . .'

'The PM's here!' Veronica suddenly hissed.

Jeremy immediately shook me off as though I were a moth. And then the truth clung to me like a chill. He had only been using us. I couldn't believe that I'd allowed him to wound me once more with a heart-shaped bullet. He was like the knife in the kitchen sink, slick with soap, that you don't see until it's too late.

'BBC.' A journalist insinuated her way into our tightly knit group, shoving her mike into my face. 'So what do you think of your ex-husband's meteoric rise within the coalition?' I could almost taste the microphone it was so close to my teeth. 'Some are predicting he's future prime minister material.'

'Oh, you wouldn't want to hear what I think. According to my husband, the only intelligent thing to come out of a woman's mouth is Einstein's cock.'

If Veronica had been a nuclear reactor, she'd have gone into meltdown. Her weekends at Chequers, the PM's country retreat, were suddenly in danger of slipping out of her reach. Jeremy's eyes bore into mine, his smile as sharp as a razor.

'Lucy!' He spoke harshly, like a foreigner, before

composing himself. 'You've obviously had too much to drink, dear.' Jeremy laughed lightly then beamed at the journo, platitudes pouring out of him like sweat.

I interrupted his spiel. 'My ex-husband possesses a streak of charisma and charm so disarming that you can easily mistake it for sanity,' I went on. 'Isn't that right, Jeremy? Or maybe you should ask Mr "Family Matters" why he walked out on his three-year-old child when he found out he had autism.' I shoved the brochure at her. 'And why he's now waiting to see if his girlfriend's baby is normal before he'll marry her.'

'What!?' Audrey rounded on Jeremy, her famously beautiful face suddenly distorted into a red gargoyle mask. 'You said that?!' I got the feeling Audrey was about to experience her first pregnancy craving – and it was for testicle carpaccio. 'You duplicitous fucking wanker!'

Jeremy was making the noise of a sink backing up.

'What have ya got to say for yourself now, you little shit-weasel?' Archie scoffed.

When Jeremy didn't reply, Archie punched him in the face. Officials scattered like broken glass. What Jeremy lacked in articulation he made up for by bleeding. Blood spurted all over his immaculate suit, just as he was summoned by microphone to the stage to greet the prime minister.

And then, once and for all, I finally pulled the sheet up over my marriage and declared time of death.

25

The Idiot and the Savant

When fate opens one door, he invariably jams your fingers in another. This is what I thought as I raced after Archie through the Houses of Parliament. The heavy wooden door hinges winced as Archie banged outside into a cobbled courtyard. I was only a few steps behind him.

'I'm not a stupid person, Archie. I'm not. I can hotwire a car, decrypt a sonnet and read *Beowulf* in archaic English. But I let Jeremy dupe me.' A light bulb or ten went off in my head. 'Oh God, that bastard really did plant those drugs and porn in your bag, didn't he?!'

At that moment, two things became clear to me: 1) I was depriving some poor village somewhere of its idiot and 2) It was unlikely I would ever get a job as an investigative journalist. 'And I believed him. How could I have been so gullible? I'm so, so sorry, Archie.'

'It's too late for sorrys now, mate.'

I was surprised by Archie's cold abruptness. 'Don't you have any feelings for me any more?' I asked tentatively. 'It doesn't look like you do.'

'Just because you can't see them doesn't mean they're not there. My heart was designed by the China Nanchang Aircraft Manufacturin' Corporation. It's a stealth heart. But what does it matter? You're so deeply in love with your love for Merlin you don't leave any room in your heart for anyone else.'

'What do you mean?' I demanded defensively.

'You need a twelve-step programme to break your Merlin habit. You don't want Merlin to grow into a man because havin' a handicapped child gives you diplomatic immunity from every normal human activity, like makin' friends, plannin' for the future . . . and fallin' in love.'

'That's not true! I want Merlin to be independent.' Wind gusted around the corners of the courtyard, rattling the stained-glass windows.

'Bullshit, Lou. You don't want to feel that little jab of dispensability, do you?' His sudden, fierce anger pinned me against the stone wall. 'Be honest. You get a certain grim enjoyment from bein' the victim, admit it . . . J'know what I think? I reckon you need him more than he needs you.'

He was pumping out the words like bullets from a sub-machine gun.

'You don't want him to fly the nest 'cause he's your life, your identity. You're the one holdin' him back. It's not Merlin who's handicapped. He's a crutch for *you*.'

Cue the sound of heartstrings being twanged. My insides felt like a grand piano falling down a staircase. This whole melodramatic evening had been like dot-to-dot cliché. But it wasn't a cliché, because it was my life. Archie was now pounding down the worn stone steps towards the police barricades of Parliament Square. I bolted after him and caught his arm.

'I'm the gravity which holds Merlin in place. Otherwise he could fly off into space.'

Archie wheeled round to face me. 'That's because you just won't accept him the way he is. Why do you feel you have to bloody well change everyone?'

Archie's fleshy mouth had grown taut. His tone was as harsh as the outback terrain of his homeland. 'The kid doesn't have Asperger's or autism. He just has Merlin Syndrome. You're the one who needs to change, by acceptin' him for who he is. Merlin might be a savant but *you're* the idiot.'

Archie looked at me long and hard, as though memorizing my features. And then he stomped away through the police barricades and out into the square towards Westminster Abbey. If there'd been a sunset, he would have walked into it, but instead he was enveloped by a group of Morris dancers who were doing some impromptu hanky manoeuvres on the street corner.

Merlin materialized behind me, the *tss, tss, tss* of his earphones barring all conversation. I took his hand and we walked across the flagstones through security and then into the gullet of Westminster tube. Commuters were coughing and blowing their noses in a contagious way. I held my son close, trying to keep him out of the way of infection.

When my mobile phone reconnected on the walk home, I had three requests from journalists wanting to speak to me and ten texts from Jeremy, all of which begged to know how he could make it up to me.

'Just ask yourself what would Hitler do?' I texted back.

Phoebe was the first to my door. 'How bad is it?'

'The pain is bad, but no worse than your average unanaesthetized leg amputation,' I told her, already retreating into my familiar defence mode of glibness and sarcasm.

My mother arrived by taxi. In the next half an hour she only delivered about 362,000 versions of the 'I Told You So' lecture. A domestic storm erupted, with my mother blaming Phoebe for encouraging my rapprochement with Jeremy and my sister blaming my mother for leaving us so destitute that Jeremy was even an option.

'The trouble with you, Phoebe, is that you've never met another person you couldn't blame,' my mother protested.

'So, we live in a blame culture, whose fault is that?'

my sister retaliated. It was not a conversation you'd want to put into a time capsule.

I felt exposed, like an open wound. I was also overcome with a sense of what felt like homesickness, which was odd, as I was at home. When Merlin tumbled downstairs and loped into this electrically charged atmosphere, I knew what I had to do. My vision was miraculously clear. Even though I was boiling inside, there were no tears, no ache in the chest, no all-consuming rage. I simply told them both to go. I held the door open and looked out at the sticky neon street lights reflected in the rain-slicked street. 'Now.' The shock I unleashed was hugely satisfying.

When they'd finally departed, under protest, I held Merlin to me and kissed his melted lemon drops-coloured hair. 'From now on there'll just be me and you, Merlin,' I reassured him.

But my son shoved me away. 'I'm not a mummy's boy! I don't like having to talk to you every day. It's babyish. I'm not a baby.' His eyes scalded me. 'I'm not going to be a robot and follow society and do what everyone expects me to do. You just want me to stay here to toughen me up and turn me into a top house resident,' he said with sudden savagery.

'Okay, Merlin. You want to be independent? Then let's practise. Why don't you make me a cup of tea?' I flumped back into a kitchen chair, exhausted.

'Why should I?'

'What?' I replied, dumbfounded. 'Why *shouldn't*

you? Why don't you just think back on all the millions of things I've done for you, Merlin?'

'Yes, but you haven't done anything for me *today*.'

I stared at him, flummoxed by his logic. 'But what about all the meals I've cooked for you? The schools I've driven you to? The friends I've made for you? The parties I've thrown for you? The men I've given up for you? . . .'

Merlin's faux pas chalked themselves up in my mind like a grocery list. As I thought about my ruptured life, bitterness took root again. I could feel it entering through my feet, working its way up into my heart, where it knotted and twisted so tightly that it screwed up my face into a mask of rage. The unfairness of my plight, the incomprehension of the burden, the loss of the brilliant boy who could have been, the loneliness of the years ahead, reared up like a tidal wave and tsunamied down upon my head.

'Why are you always trying to change people, Mum? Archie told me that you can't accept people the way they are. If *you* were an animal you'd be a woodpecker, or a rooster or a wasp.'

His voice burnt like acid on my ears. 'Merlin, you have to start thinking about what you're saying before you say it.'

'Thinking is overrated. I'm not a genius,' he announced with quiet lucidity 'Everyone keeps expecting me to be a genius. But I'm not.'

I was on the point of flying apart like an exploding

light bulb. I wanted to shout out, '*I don't want you to be a genius! I just want you to be normal! Why can't I just have a normal son?*' It was on the tip of my tongue. I bit it back. I promised myself I wouldn't say it. 'I just want you to be happy, Merlin,' I said instead.

'I'll never be happy!' he shouted. 'It's not my fault. *You* made me. Why did you make me like this?'

The sound of anguish detonated in my head. 'I know it's not your fault! But it's not my fault either! And yet I'm the one who has to pay. For the rest of my life!'

Unused to my temper, Merlin shrank away from me. 'I think you need to see a talking doctor. Or perhaps it's senility. Old age makes people cranky. Either way, therapy would be advisable.'

I felt my body clench and cold ripples shiver up my spine. It was the last psychological straw. 'Why? And why exactly do you think *I* might need therapy? Could it be because I'm wrung out? And lonely? And at my wits' end?' And then the words, the careless words I didn't really mean and would regret for the rest of my life, just tore themselves from my throat.

'*You've ruined my life. I wish I'd never had you. Why can't you be normal?!*'

Merlin and Me

How long have I been sitting here, aching body and soul, telling our story to whoever will listen? I pine for the miraculous comfort of my son's smile. But Merlin lies as flat as roadkill. His hand is flung across his chest.

A nurse I don't recognize nods sympathetically and pats my hand. Feel I've been talking for ever. Raw with shame and desolate from weeping, I'm shocked when the nurse tells me that only two days have elapsed since my son was run over. I'm just not myself at all, and it's quite clear I won't be again. I simply find it impossible to look ahead from one minute to the next.

Doctors come and go. They talk at me about head trauma, airway management, imaging, scans, possible damage to the brain stem, bilateral damage to the reticular formation of the hindbrain . . . I put the information into the swill I call my 'thought process'. Their medical jargon is obfuscatory, and I'm glad because I don't want to decode 'negative patient care outcome' or 'terminal episode'. My take-charge planning gene is horribly frozen.

Merlin is hooked up to a catheter, an arterial line, IV drip and heart monitor leads. I never take my eyes from his face, as I pray to gods I don't believe in for the faintest reassuring twitch of an eyebrow, the tiniest squeeze of my hand. But fuzzy hours follow; long, dim stretches of bleak desperation. All I can taste is thick, furry-tongued self-loathing and recrimination as I'm lacerated by the memories of what I said. I am flaying myself alive. How I long to breathe myself back in time, to hover invisibly there and not launch those verbal Exocet missiles which propelled Merlin from our living room out into the road.

My eyes are gritty with sleeplessness. The room pitches around me like the deck of a sinking ship. Merlin's bed seems to undulate slightly and I can't make the objects around me stop moving. But sleep is impossible. Whenever I lean my head back against the chair and close my eyes I descend into the cold damp shaft of my guilt. Savaged by nightmares, I jerk awake.

I'm watching the sun rise again in a gory display of colour as violent as a car crash. My grief has no texture now – just an ache in the throat and the chest. It is simply darkness, a cloak which shrouds me. A nurse enters. She's wearing her bright hostess look, as though presiding over a cocktail party, not a coma patient. 'How are we today?'

She's come to wash and turn my darling boy. I leave the room to give him privacy, and pace the corridors. The linoleum is bile-green. It billows under my feet like clouds. It's an effort to press it down. The hospital smells of decaying flesh. Feel I'm stumbling through a giant intestine. The clanking radiators rattle emphysemically. A death rattle. The radio on a hospital orderly's belt gives a spluttering cough, as though it's contracted some contagious ailment. People seem to be giving me a wide berth in the corridor. Can they smell the grief on me? Lose a husband, you're a widow; a parent, you're an orphan – but what am I?

In the relatives' room, I push my hot face up against the cold windowpane. Below me, London's gruesome arteries are already choked with peak-hour traffic, jostling and honking. I'm incredulous at the vivid hum and thrum of life, the happy riot of pedestrians engrossed in their own charmed lives, still with all their luck. I glimpse my own face in the window. I look at the sunken caverns of my sockets and shed silent tears.

Back in our corner of intensive care I perch on the side of Merlin's bed and hold his hand. The hot wine-dark worm of my child's blood inches through a clear tube. A nurse hands me a note which she's found crumpled in my son's jeans pocket. I stare at the familiar loopy, ungrammatical scrawl for a long time before I can bring myself to read it.

Happy Valentines Day. You are stunningly beautiful inside and out. The last 16 and a half years have been an absolute joy and you are a girl for the world. I adore u and whenever I see you, u always brighten up my day. I am your greatest admirer and I think you are a living legend, a legend of society, a genius and the world's funniest and wittiest best mother. You have style, flair and panash and I am enamoured on you, u divine love goddess. You look beautiful in every outfit you have a sublime smile and a mesmerizing figure. Make this day bring happyness and love to your life You are my favourite woman in the world and I love you from your intriguing handsom and phenomenal son Merlin the king of swing.

I check the date on my watch. February 14th. He'd intended to give it to me today. I bury my face in Merlin's hair and breathe in the familiar sherbet aroma. And then I'm sobbing. Huge heaving gulps of pain. There is much talk about calling my family. I let them take my mobile phone from my pocket. I'm told I'm in shock and need support. From a long way off I hear the nurse asking if she can contact the numbers on my speed dial. I slump back into the chair by Merlin's bed and cry myself into a state of exhaustion. Darkness topples down and pulverizes me.

A clicking sound wakes me. The brittle winter afternoon sunshine is knife bright and slices into my eyes. I see the Queen of England hairdo first. Then the number-nine needles, as if she's waiting for heads to fall into the basket by a guillotine. She manoeuvres her lips through a series of rubbery contortions which are trying to become a smile. The smile a crocodile would wear, if a crocodile could smile. 'Can I get you anything?' my ex-mother-in-law asks, in a voice meant to discourage. 'The hospital rang. We came straight away. Jeremy sat with Merlin for a good two hours but now he's had to go back to vote. So I'm holding the fort.'

Vote? The only vote he's interested in is the vote of sympathy. He was probably holding press conferences right now about his handicapped son, tragically run over and now in a coma. I can envisage the heads of female journalists nodding compassionately as they surreptitiously fluff up their breasts in their bra cups.

Reoriented, I look up with urgency to Merlin's bed. His chest is rising and falling rhythmically. No change. Numbness washes over me.

Veronica sniffs and dabs at the corner of each eye with her thumb pad. This is the sort of woman who would normally only ever shed a tear if the Ascot racetrack went underwater in a freak thunderstorm on Ladies Day.

'It's unbearable.' But I also detect in her voice a tinge of excitement. 'But you mustn't despair. It could be a blessing in disguise, have you thought of that?' Veronica shifts in her hardback chair and orchestrates her tweed skirt around her. 'Perhaps Merlin will wake up from the coma completely altered? Some people wake up from comas to find they're suddenly talking fluent French or Farsi. Or playing concert piano. The shock may rejolt his mental wiring,' she reflects, her voice both wheedling and commanding. 'Perhaps he'll be cured?' She touches my arm the way you touch the pet of an acquaintance even though you're allergic to it. 'He's such a handsome lad, isn't he? It's so unfair that such a beautiful shell should house such a disappointing occupant.'

A scallop of sunlight falls across Merlin's fine features. 'I don't want him cured! I love him just the way he is. And he's not disappointing. *You* are.' It takes an enormous effort to stop myself from yelling this at her. But my voice must be raised because she rears up in her chair. Her bouffant puffs up around her head like the hood of a cobra.

'I think it would be advisable for you to see a counsellor, Lucinda.' My addled thoughts fly back to the supercilious social worker La–ah, with her noisy dash. Oh that's *just* what the doctor ordered.

The door wheezes and my mother bursts into

intensive care. My normally chic parent is wearing odd shoes, one leopardskin and one blue suede, and is all wild hair and no make-up. Crumpled with anxiety, her flamboyantly coloured clothes hang on her frame like boat sails in dead calm. 'Darling, oh darling, why didn't you call me!?' She throws her arms around me and rocks me back and forth for a full five minutes before she notices Veronica. She regards her with slant-eyed hostility.

'I just came to offer some words of hope.'

My mother takes a leaf from Phoebe's book on bitchery. 'Well, while you're here at the hospital why don't we book you in for a scruples transplant? And maybe we can find a spine donor for that cowardly son of yours.' Her chilly monotone signals that the conversation is over.

Rising to her feet, my mealy-mouthed and small-minded former mother-in-law gives a forced smile, but her eyes glitter with indignation. 'I'll report to Jeremy and pop back at regular intervals. It's the least I can do. As a concerned grandmother,' she barks, then closes the door on us magisterially.

My mother then holds Merlin's hands and cries. 'The tear ducts have gone along with the rest of the plumbing. I'm a very leaky woman,' she tells me, trying to control herself.

Phoebe arrives next, straight from the airport, her stockings laddered in her haste. The war between them is forgotten as my mother now throws her arms around her two daughters. 'Only women's hearts can know the blind devotion of a mother for her child,' she says, and we sob together in a huddle.

Emotions spent, the best anyone can do is breathe in, breathe out and wait. The day crawls by. The next time I glance out of the window, the sky has turned into a big black bruise. The grey actually feels as if it's in the air. The air seems almost solid. Some indiscernible amount of time later, from out in the squelching world, Archie arrives, emitting a damp fungal reek from the rain. He takes off his wet outer garments and folds them on to the radiator with care that is almost like tenderness. Then he sits with us, silently. A cleaner regards us with uninterested eyes, completely unconcerned that our lives are now smudged with grief.

As the day seeps into night, there's a tentative, timorous acceptance of how long the wait might be. I'm vaguely aware of a schedule being decided amongst my family, a roster. Over the next few days, they come and go, my mother trying to tempt me to eat occasionally, Archie strumming his guitar softly – some Beatles, Pink Floyd and Bob Dylan songs which Merlin has always loved – Phoebe brushing my hair.

I just sit by my son, reading and talking and willing him to claw his way back into consciousness; urging the fibres of light to crawl into his cranium. I hold him gingerly, as if he's made of crystal. I watch over him as he lies there either bathed in starlight or awash with sun, wisps of light flitting across his beautiful face like dreams.

And then, with biblical drama, the fog just lifts. It's like something out of the World's Most Popular Plots. If this were a Dickens novel, it would now be discovered that Merlin has a secret benefactor who has left him his estate. If we were on an Oprah-type chat show, a miracle cure would be discovered called Merlin's Oil. But the truth is, he just wakes up. My son is merely one of the statistically 10 per cent of coma victims who recover.

When his eyelid flutters, I think I'm hallucinating. The room seems to tilt and start sliding slowly towards the street. An eye peels open. My son looks at me – then smiles his goofy grin. I scan his face anxiously.

'How are you?' he asks me croakily.

It is the most meaningful question I have ever been asked. I nod so hard I'm surprised my head doesn't fall off and roll out into the corridor. 'I'm good! I'm excellent!' In fact, no one has invented the adjective I need, so I have to make do with a great whoop of joy. The variety of sound effects available to me as a human seems insufficient and I wish I were a kookaburra so that I could cackle with joy at the fact that my son has woken up. Sobbing, I cling to him much like a rescued ocean swimmer miles from shore clings to the dorsal fin of a friendly dolphin.

Merlin pushes me away. 'Ugh! No cheesiness! That

smile! Do *all* mothers want their boys to be little again, or is it just you?'

As he sips from the water bottle I hold to his lips I explain to him with faltering voice what's happened – the crash, the coma . . .

'Am I a figment of my own imagination then?' Merlin asks suddenly.

After reassuring him, I try to explain more, about the hospital and the doctors, all the time scanning his face for signs of brain damage.

He interrupts once more. 'Am I an organ donor?'

'Well, yes . . .' I shrug.

'If I had died, it would have been so nice of a total stranger to give up almost all of themself to keep my organs alive, wouldn't it?'

Elation engulfs me. Merlin is his normal, abnormal self. His light has not been snuffed out. I laugh with giddy abandon and glee, my arms warm around his neck. Despite his fractured ribs, he hugs me back with debilitating enthusiasm. It's his usual hug – the kind of hug that will require weeks of intense physiotherapy, I think, euphorically, happy for once to be crushed.

I feel reborn, as though I've just discovered that the earth rotates around the sun and that the moon dictates the tides. Nurses are suddenly boiling around the bed, prodding and probing. People are on pagers summoning other people. But all I can do is kiss his golden head.

'Is there anyone you'd like me to call?' asks the same

nurse who admitted us all those long, terrifying days ago.

I'm about to say no – that there's only ever been Merlin and me. But then I pause. Because it isn't true. There's also my mum, Phoebe, Archie . . . hell, I'm so jubilant I nearly call the woman in the brothel.

My mother returns from the cafeteria with two mugs of steaming tea. Her laughter is incredulous at first and then vibrant with relief and affection. Tea spilling to the floor, she ruffles Merlin's hair. 'Thank God you're okay. I have a trip to Argentina to study tango planned,' she adds, between elated sobs, 'followed by a stint in Colombia restoring a butterfly habitat.'

'Of course you do, Mother,' I laugh.

'And I thought maybe you'd like to come, Merlin, dear? When you're all better?'

South America? Drug cartel capital of the world? My first reaction is to pull him protectively to my chest. But the umbilical cord is stretched to twanging point. 'If you'd like to, sure,' I say to my son. 'It's your life.'

'Actually, my life goals are simple,' Merlin philosophizes. 'Socially, I want to make as many friends as possible. Personally, I would love to visit Sydney, China, the Galapagos Islands, Japan, the moon and possibly Mars. But South America would be mesmerizing and has everything your heart could contend.'

My own heart expands like an accordion to hear him talk so.

Phoebe arrives next, wet mascara pandaing her eyes. 'When you're all better, Merlin, and we've got our pay rise, maybe you'd like to fly with me on a couple of my European trips. Rome? Barcelona? Moscow?' she enthuses. 'Now that I'm single, I'll have more time.'

'Single?' my mother and I say in unison.

'I didn't want to say anything . . . but Danny's having an affair. With the au pair. You know how lazy men are. They'll just use anything that's lying around the home. It started before Christmas. October actually. I've been taking so much HRT – which is mare's urine, by the way – that I'm practically steeplechasing and eating hay. But I still wasn't enough for him. He's run off with her.'

My mother's lioness focus shifts from Merlin and me on to my sister. 'The worm! The cad . . . There is one good thing, though, dear. The man's going to have to go through the menopause twice.'

We laugh as my mother cradles her oldest daughter. Life is going on, in all its messy glory.

When Archie arrives he laughs so ecstatically that he sprays my face with his happiness. His eyes also look suspiciously moist.

'Don't go soft on me now, you wicked old horn dog.'

'I never go soft in the places that count,' he swaggers. 'Now Merlin's well again, I guess I'm superfluous. You'll now have a man in the house to do your DIY. Meaning I'm not needed at all . . .'

'I don't know. I still have some needs . . . Many of them special.'

Archie twinkles at me before biffing Merlin good-naturedly on the arm. 'Let's get you back into the saddle, kiddo, then take you down to the casino and get roulette rash makin' money out of that bloody amazin' memory of yours. Or maybe you could just break into the Kremlin's computer system and we can sell the info to a foreign superpower?'

My immediate reaction is to rebuke the Aussie larrikin. But then I shrug. 'Okay. If that's what Merlin wants.'

'You have a wonderful memory too, Mum,' Merlin says, matter-of-factly. 'For forgetting things.'

I laugh, because he's right. I forgot how much I love and need my friends and family. And I forgot how much they love and need me. My mother and sister and I cling to each other once more, in an exhausted embrace, like boxers nearing the end of a final bout.

The door rasps and Jeremy and his mother sidle inside. My ex-mother-in-law's face is full of expectation. 'Any changes?' she asks, with eager hopefulness. 'Can you tell yet?' She peers expectantly at Merlin as though he's an experiment in a test tube. 'Or is it too early?'

Jeremy looks as uneasy and as evasive as a school-boy summoned to see the headmaster about how the math-teacher's bottom got glued to the chair. He kisses Merlin perfunctorily on the forehead before taking me aside.

'The papers are printing hatchet jobs. Journalists are clamouring for comments about my private life. They never understand the complexities. Life is not black or white. It's beige more than anything . . . I'm begging you not to talk to them,' he said in the flat, lifeless voice of a man who can see that the writing on the wall probably includes his name.

'You know, Jeremy, you've always been a bit of a snob. Like the way you're always saying how most people only use 10 per cent of their brains. Well, you only use 10 per cent of your heart. And that's the worst kind of heart trouble. No defibrillator can save you,' I tell him.

'We could prevent you from becoming tabloid toast though,' my sister interjects, 'for a price.'

'Personally, I'd prefer nailing your nuts to an ants' nest,' my mother lambasts. 'Wouldn't you, Lucy, dear?'

My mind is electric, filled with the present. 'I think I could be encouraged to maintain radio silence,' I say. 'But only if you write Merlin a cheque so large that when I cash it the whole bank bounces.'

Jeremy's eyes glitter with rage. 'That's blackmail.'

'Not black, more *beige*,' I taunt.

'Yes, exactly,' my mother cackles. 'Stealing money from a lying, thieving cheat isn't robbery, dear, it's irony.'

I leave my family to finalize the deal and turn back to my darling son.

'So, Veronica,' I hear Merlin say to his paternal grandma, 'is love sewing sequins on to the world for you on this dazzling day?'

My ex-mother-in-law's hopeful expression falters.

'Today are you living for tomorrow? ... When you see animals squashed on the side of the road are they really suicides?' he then asks her. 'Maybe they're just depressed? Maybe they need a talking doctor? ... Are they real animals or are there humans inside laughing at me? ... Do you have funny thoughts about Archie when you're in the shower? ... I do.'

Veronica's mouth becomes loose and her eyes unfocused. 'He's just the same,' she says, with profound disappointment.

And I nod appreciatively. Yes, my son lives in a parallel universe. But it strikes me now that it's quite a captivating place to dwell.

'So, what does the future hold for me?' Merlin asks the stethoscope-wielding doctor. 'Is the world my oyster?'

The doctor looks taken aback. But I diagnose a yes. And Merlin will grow into a pearl, grain by gritty grain.

A nurse opens the blind with a snap. The room is seared with light. I look out at the seamless winter sky. It's a frosty morning. The hospital garden is wrapped in winter, like a gift.

'It's intriguing, being me,' Merlin suddenly says.

With his sky-blue eyes, blond curls and persimmon-red mouth, my son has the bearing of a mischievous cherub. 'It really is,' I agree.

Merlin smiles at me. And I smile back. With our eyes. It's a language Jeremy will never master – the secret language of the heart.

Another doctor arrives. She asks me the name of my son. 'Merlin . . . I called him Merlin because I wanted him to be different. And he is,' I tell her, proudly. 'Mesmerizingly, intriguingly, dazzlingly.'

Acknowledgements

Writers make a living out of lying. But for injecting the fact into the fiction, I would like to thank the following people:

My beloved sisters Elizabeth and Jennifer, who always cast a perspicacious eye over my first draft.

Heartfelt thanks also to second-draftees, Max Davidson, my literary coven Amanda Craig, Jane Thynne, Veronique Minier and Kate Saunders, and especially Julius and Geoff Robertson. For vernacular veracity, thanks to Gerard Hall for medical tips, Emma Woodhouse for teaching insights, Brian O'Doherty for musical fine tuning, Dennis McShane, Alan West and Joan Smith for political verisimilitude.

My gratitude also to my publishing team, most of all Larry Finlay for all his kind encouragement and Cat Cobain for her nuanced editing. And last, but never least, to Ed Victor, the Ed-ocet missile of agents, and Maggie Phillips.

But most thanks of all to my darling son Julius and dear daughter Georgie, who inspire me every day.

To Love, Honour and Betray

Kathy Lette

Lucy's life was supposed to be idyllic once she and her family moved to sun-soaked Oz – but it couldn't be more of a mess.

NO SOONER HAVE they unpacked their Marmite, than Lucy catches her darling husband Jasper inflagrante. With her best friend Renee. In one double blow, she loses the two people she trusted most – and now has to fend for herself.

While Lucy battles her daughter (low self esteem is hereditary – you get it from your teenagers) and desperately tries to turn herself into an Aussie love goddess to win Jasper back, she meets Jack "Lockie" McLachlan. He's a rugged lifeguard with plenty of experience in rescuing damsels in distress. But Lucy can do without any further complications in her life right now. The only question is, without Lockie's kiss of life, will she sink or swim?

Nip 'n' Tuck

Kathy Lette

**Journalist Lizzie McPhee has always thought of beauty
as a case of mind over matter – if you don't mind,
it doesn't matter.**

BUT ALL THAT changes when she begins the countdown towards
the big 4-0. Suddenly, she's comparing her butt buoyancy to
that of women on billboards and worrying about wrinkles.

But the pitter-pitter-pat of tiny crow's feet is soon the least of
Lizzie's worries. In the space of twenty four hours, she is
replaced as news anchor by a young himbo who keeps fit by
doing step aerobics off his own ego. And then she catches her
surgeon husband Hugo cheating with catty soap actress
Britney Amore – a woman whose bra cup size is bigger than
her IQ.

Suddenly, Lizzie is in free fall. Can she turn back the clock, and
win back her life? Or will she discover there's a better way to
grow older gracefully?